Praise for Duff Brenna's *The Altar of the Body*

"We cannot help but read *The [Altar of the Body]* ... Western, emerging momentaril... landishly exaggerated and intima...

"Brenna succeeds in making each principal character a symbol of unusual resonance. . . . Refreshingly redemptive."

—*Milwaukee Journal Sentinel*

"Top-notch stylist Brenna returns with a fourth confederacy of grotesques, and with gusto and love reveals their big, gnarled hearts and stunted minds. . . . A monstrous beauty."

—*Kirkus Reviews* (starred review)

"Brenna has a stunning talent."   —*Elk Grove Times* (Chicago)

"Poway author Brenna, an English professor at Cal State San Marcos, is a talented writer, and Joy, George, Buck, and Livia are complex, well-drawn characters. His prose is elegant; his descriptions are subtle yet straightforward. Brenna takes the American obsession with beauty and youth and shows us how destructive it can be."   —*San Diego Magazine*

"The author's most stunning accomplishment with *Altar* is in sketching a cast of larger-than-life characters who do and say preposterous things and then, gradually, by revealing layer after layer of their souls, making them real and complex and utterly moving. . . . It's a fun read from start to finish, delightfully over-the-top in all the right places, yet full of deeply touching moments. The characters are ravaged and torn by the choices they make; those who survive intact are the ones who learn they can't choose only a part of themselves but must embrace the whole. It's a worthy lesson in a beautiful package."   —Bookreporter.com

"Literary and entertaining, his characters are unlike those we have come to expect . . . there is exuberance, a rare commodity in a literary America of minimalist Kmart realism."

—*Frank: An International Journal of Contemporary Writing & Art*

"Grounded in reality, [*The Altar of the Body*] brings George, Mikey, Joy, and Livia to life in every passionate detail."   —*Booklist*

"Brenna never allows their easily caricatured gestures to overwhelm [the characters'] considerable natural dignity."   —*Publishers Weekly*

"Duff Brenna's new novel *The Altar of the Body* is a gift of grace and wit. With elegant precision, Brenna takes us into a world that is part real, part dream, familiar yet always surprising. An unlikely group of people—each buoyed by disparate dreams—struggle to understand what is essential while balancing on the edge of joy and despair. This is a story that transcends the willful obsessions, the relentless self-absorption of contemporary life, that reinvents family and illuminates what is both painful and best at its heart."   —Claire Davis, author of *Winter Range*

"Pitting a ruthless greed for beauty against its equally inflexible and undeniable counterpart, death, Brenna's *The Altar of the Body* twists through flashes of intense and freakishly fleshy brilliance on a hell-bent drive toward destruction and chaos."
                    —Laura Hendrie, author of *Remember Me*

"From one of our best and most original novelists, Duff Brenna's astonishing new novel *The Altar of the Body* is at once hilarious and profoundly unsettling: it's a sexy, muscled-up page-turner, full of all manner of mayhem and blessed with a wild and utterly unforgettable cast of characters, each of them fiercely and unforgettably alive. It's also a wise and compassionate meditation on youth and beauty, cruelty and courage, love and death—a hymn to our wonderful doomed bodies, our frail and glorious humanity."   —Mick Cochrane, author of *Flesh Wounds* and *Sport*

"*The Altar of the Body* makes you remember what great fiction is for—an escape from reality that brings you back again wiser, spiritually enriched, a little more certain of what really matters. Told in elegantly simple prose, this is a novel as American as the Minnesota heartland where it is set, as American as the obsessions with youth, strength, and physical beauty it so brilliantly, comically, and movingly portrays. Duff Brenna has once again confirmed his place in the elite ranks of the best American novelists."
                    —Thomas E. Kennedy, author of *Drive, Dive, Dance, and Fight*

"Leavened with eccentric comedy, Duff Brenna's *The Altar of the Body* is a gritty and violent take on the human condition that transcends its surface to show us the drama each man and woman plays out in the struggle to love and be loved. This is a novel that doesn't turn aside from the hard questions and doesn't fail to come up with some viable answers. Brenna has written a richly rewarding page-turner—impossible to put down."   —Gordon Weaver, author of *Long Odds*

ALSO BY DUFF BRENNA

THE BOOK OF MAMIE

THE HOLY BOOK OF THE BEARD

TOO COOL

The Altar of the Body

a novel

DUFF BRENNA

Picador USA
NEW YORK

In Memory of
Janice E. Miles

And for
Carol Marie and Michele Renee

We only live, only suspire
Consumed by either fire or fire.

Picador® is a U.S. registered trademark and is used by St. Martin's Press under license from Pan Books Limited.

For information on Picador USA Reading Group Guides, as well as ordering, please contact the Trade Marketing department at St. Martin's Press.
Phone: 1-800-221-7945 extension 763
Fax: 212-677-7456
E-mail: trademarketing@stmartins.com

Library of Congress Cataloging-in-Publication Data

Brenna, Duff.
    The altar of the body : a novel / Duff Brenna.—1st Picador USA pbk. ed.
        p. cm.
    ISBN 0-312-26865-3 (hc)
    ISBN 0-312-26914-5 (pbk)
    1. Bodybuilders—Fiction. 2. Man-woman relationships—Fiction.
3. Mothers and daughters—Fiction. 4. Minnesota—Fiction. 5. Cousins—
Fiction. I. Title.

PS3552.R377 A78 2002
813'.54—dc21   2002067324

First Picador USA Paperback Edition: September 2002

10 9 8 7 6 5 4 3 2 1

The beautiful in
body, the used and the unused
those who had courage
and those who quit.
— PHILIP LEVINE

PART ONE

Many a Lecherous Lay

I, George

THE FIRST TIME I SEE HER she is steering a Lincoln Continental through the neighborhood. Slow as vodka logic she comes, looking left and right, searching for something. Tree leaves reflect fractal patterns off her windshield, smearing her image, bringing her in and out of focus.

I'm on the porch, sweaty from working in the Minnesota heat, my shirt clinging to my back, my toes steaming inside my shoes. I'm smoking my pipe and drinking a can of Grain Belt and watching the Lincoln, the bumper low, sniffing the asphalt. It's an old car, a four-door boater, champagne-colored, with rust patches showing through the wheel wells, roof dented in the center looking like a little birdbath or a holster for a cannonball. The tires suck at the hot pavement. The engine is idling. A valve lifter ticks beneath the hood.

When she gets closer I see platinum hair, bushy, like a dandelion gone to seed. Her hair shines in the sun for a second, then darkens as the car enters shade, then it shines again. When the car comes parallel, she spots me. The passenger window is open and she is leaning toward it, keeping one hand on the wheel. Her pale skin and pale hair make me think of Icelandic girls with hard cheekbones and translucent skin and eyes bold as glaciers.

The rest of the car eases forward and I can see a man pushing it, a big man with big shoulders, his huge hands splayed across the trunk. His head is down, his back bull-like bulges, his legs churn in slow motion. He glances at me and I see heavy-lidded eyes. Strands of hair cling to his forehead. His breath is harsh, sobbing with effort.

The woman pulls the car to the curb and the man leans his forearms on the lid for a second, then he straightens and pulls his shoulders back, rolls them and groans. I don't know if I've ever seen a chest so big, nor shoulders so wide or a neck so thick. He puts his hands on his hips and grins lopsided and says, "She's a heavy hussy, man."

I point my pipe at the old Lincoln. "Lincolns," I say.

"Freeway floaters," says the man, "but hell to push when they break down." He winks at me. There is something familiar about him, but I can't place it. Eyes big as June bugs. I've seen those eyes, I tell myself. I've seen that jutting chin, that tic of a dimple in it.

Sunlight through the trees shimmies over him. A gold stud in his earlobe sparkles. He glances back at the woman in the car. She is looking at herself in the mirror, fussing with her hair.

And then he says, "Hey, I'm looking for George McLeod. Does that bugger still live here?"

I stand up and cram the can of beer into my shirt pocket. "That's me. I'm that bugger," I tell him.

"Hey, George, that really you?"

"Yessir. What can I do for you?"

"What happened to your hair, George?" I finger the top of my head where a few hairs still mark a path down the middle. He smiles and I notice that his upper lip has a fleshy hook pushing it slightly over the front teeth. And that's when it hits me who he is—big eyes, olive skin, the hook-lip grin. "Mikey?" I say. "That you, Mikey?"

"It's me, George."

4

"No way."

"Yeah way."

I laugh and say, "How the hell you get so big, Mikey? Jesus, you look like . . . like a Sequoia."

"Pecs, abs and gluteus to the max," he sings, shifting his butt sideways and patting it. "I growed. I'm not Mikey no more, George. I'm Buck Root."

"Buck Root?"

"It's my stage name, my show name."

"Buck Root," I say, savoring the sound of it. "So where you been all these years, Buck Root?"

He says he's been everywhere—east coast, west coast, midwest, down south and up north and down Minneapolis at a competition there: Mr. Minnesota. And he says he thought he might as well come by Medicine Lake and see if I'm still kicking.

"Still kicking," I say. "Older, fat as a toad and damn near bald, but still kicking, yhah."

Above him the leaves move. The tip of a leaf brushes his hair and he swats at it. "Thought it was a bee," he says, staring at the tree as if it has done a whimsical thing. I'm thinking he's a woman's dream of what a man should be, nose heroic, velvet lips, and eyes that say bedroom-bedroom.

"So, George, you got a hug for me?" he asks.

I stick my hand out to shake. He grabs it and jerks me in and nearly crushes me. I smell beef on his breath, hamburger beef. He kisses my cheek and roughs me up, then lets go and steps back and looks around. "Hey, I'm glad to know you're still in the same place," he says. "Things haven't changed so much as I thought they would. I expected there would be some shopping mall here, you know. Or maybe some big resort and old ladies in bikinis trying to get laid. But it's still the same. Trees, houses, lawns, the lake. I remember that tree there." He points at the spruce in the front yard. "That bugger got tall. What is it now, sixty feet? Seventy?" A wistful look glides over his face. "Lot of wind gone through them needles. Lotta time," he says.

The woman kills the engine. She has kept primping in the mirror, touching her hair, painting her lips, but now she's ready. The door protests like old doors do when they're never oiled, *kaareak, ba-wham!* as she flings it closed. She moves toward us and I'm watching her hips moving in a sheath of leather skirt and I'm whispering, "Oh wow," and she catches what I say and she puts on a look like she's the homecoming queen and she says, "I'm Joy Faust."

I take her hand. She has a large hand for a woman. The touch of it makes me feel giddy. She's as tall as me, very thin, with arms pale as taproots. A gold earring drilled through a flap of skin in her navel flashes beneath a blue tanktop that has *IMAGINE* written on it in silver letters, Gothic style. Her nipples look like bullets pressing against the cloth.

"This is him," says Buck to her. "This is cousin George."

"Cousin George," she says.

I feel my ears burning. I feel my lips quivering, smiling. I make a helpless gesture toward the apartments and say hoarsely, "I live here." She lets go of my hand. My palm is moist. It feels swollen.

"This is the address all right," she says. "We almost didn't get here." She chucks her chin toward the Lincoln. She looks at me with crinkling, smiling eyes. Her eyes are blue with flecks of gray beneath lashes thick enough to float a toothpick. She has a delicate jaw, a rounded chin, a small nose with a tiny, ball-tipped end, a tempting mouth, the lower lip large and chewy, the upper lip slightly thinner.

Buck is beside her and, even though she is tall for a woman, she looks petite next to him.

"Buck and Joy," I say. Sunlight shines around them. "You guys look like moviestars," I say.

Buck's eyes glitter with pleasure. "Quite a change, hey, George? What's it been, twenty years since you last saw me?"

I think on it for a second and say, "It was not long after Dad died when you left. So what's that? I was fifteen. Now I'm forty-four. Twenty-nine years, can it be that long? Twenty-nine years?"

Buck says to Joy, "We all lived right here in these apartments. Both our families. Us upstairs, them downstairs."

"I know," says Joy.

"Buck was so skinny back then he had to stand up twice to make a shadow," I say to her. "But look at him now."

"I growed and growed," he says. And he raises his arm, shows a massive biceps. "I'm Buck Root: Mr. Los Angeles, Mr. Philadelphia, Mr. Chicago, Mr. Mount Olympus."

"And Mr. Baja Peninsula and Mr. Minneapolis Thighs," adds Joy.

"That name Buck Root," I tell him. "It rings a bell. I feel like I heard it somewhere."

"Where?"

"Don't know." I concentrate on his name, trying to remember.

"Talkin about me," says the weightlifter, glancing at Joy. "Everywhere I go, people have heard of the Root. It's a catchy name, once you hear it, you don't forget it. Hey, a word to the wise. Fame is in the *name*. If you know what I mean. Hey, Marion Morrison a.k.a. John Wayne; Archibald Leach a.k.a. Cary Grant; Bernard Schwartz a.k.a. Tony Curtis. Get the picture, George?"

"Norma Jean Baker a.k.a. Marilyn Monroe," I answer.

Buck looks at Joy. "Told you my cousin was cool."

"I think I saw you doing some kind of advertisement," I tell him. "Some kind of thing on TV?"

"The Tube-Flex!" he says. "Hey, you saw my Tube-Flex commercial: *Maximum Buff!*"

"I didn't know it was you. How about that! That was you?"

"That was a while ago. Hey, you got a good memory there, George." He looks at Joy. "George always had a good memory."

"Buck's was better," I say. "He memorized *Alice Through the Looking Glass*. You remember that, Buck?"

"Sort of do, yeah."

"My mother. She got you into it. You two seeing who could memorize most. Mom loved you, you know. She said you had the mind of an artist."

"Hear that, Joy? Mind of an artist."

I turn to Joy and say, "But mostly he was shy as a mouse, hardly said a word. Mikey Mouse, we called him."

"Not my Bucky, no way," says Joy, looking at him as if seeing him new.

"That was then and this is now," says Buck. He puts his fists into his waist, sticks out his chest and in an announcer's voice he says, *"Be buff! Get Maximum Buff!"*

"Buck's posed in magazines," says Joy.

"Pumping Iron, I was in that about two years ago. Hey, I've been in *Bodybuilders*, and *Steel Body*. In *Body Sculptors*, I was a big article in there. They called me the dean of bodybuilders."

"Little Mike, the dean of bodybuilders," I say.

"That's right."

"We won Mr. Minneapolis Thighs this morning," says Joy. We all pause to look at Buck's thighs. He is wearing faded jeans and his thighs put a strain on the fabric.

"In Minneapolis . . . Mr. Thighs," adds Joy, her words drifting. Then she points at the lake and says, "You get to live on a lake. Lucky you."

"That's Medicine Lake," says Buck. We all look toward the curve at the end of the street, where the lake shows silver threads visible through some trees. "Used to swim right off there, me and George, hey, George?"

"Kids still do," I tell him. "It's kid-paradise."

A car goes by on the road. A bearded figure waves. It is our cousin Ronnie.

"George!" he shouts.

"Ronnie!" I shout.

He honks and keeps going.

"Is that cousin Ronnie?" says Buck.

"That's him," I say.

"Another one of my cousins," says Buck. "How about cousin Larry? Is he still around?"

"Larry's a Golden Valley cop."

"A cop! Holy shit, a cop."

"And Ronnie owns a bar over at Foggy Meadow Lake. He's got topless dancers."

"Ronnie owns a topless bar." Buck shakes his head. He looks at me as if I'm sprinkling wonders all over the place.

"I've heard all about you crazy kids," Joy tells me. She touches my arm. "Crazy kids," she says again.

I wonder what Buck could have told her that was crazy about us. I recall summer days swimming with my cousins and friends, Mikey hanging at the edges sometimes, but mostly staying indoors, reading, watching TV, eating pretzels and drinking Cokes. Sometimes he would sit for my mother and she would paint him and he would tell her jokes. Buck was a joke collector, kept them on three-by-five cards in a shoebox. He clung to my mother, took her over for a while and made me jealous. His mother, my aunt, was a depressive, stupefied on pills. She couldn't cope with him. I'd hear her yelling at him, calling him a little bastard, telling him to get out of her sight. My uncle had given up on her, had taken off, disappeared and she cut her wrists then and Mikey stayed with us for months, until my aunt got out of the hospital and took him away, she and Buck going west with some pipefitter she met.

"Hey, our car won't go when you put it in gear," Buck says. "Tromp on the gas and the engine roars and nothing happens. What you think is wrong with her?" He is looking at me the same way he did when we were boys and he'd bring his math over. Smart as he was, he never caught on to math. Said it made his head hurt.

I chew my pipe and study the car. "Transmission be my guess. The bands."

"The bands," he repeats.

"Or maybe the fluid's low."

"The fluid."

"Something like that."

"How much to fix it?"

"Hard to say. Something like that can be tricky, it'd be a wad. You remember Joe Cuff? He can tell you. He's got a garage over at Crystal Lake."

"Joe Cuff? He still around? I hated that sonofabitch. He was always kicking my ass. One time he told me I couldn't go past that telephone pole—that one right there. He said on the other side of that pole was *his* territory and if I wanted to go through his territory I had to pay a quarter." Buck starts chuckling, and he tells us how he would sprint past the telephone pole and buy his mother her cigarettes at the store and sprint back, but sometimes Joe Cuff would catch him and beat on him and take his change.

"He's the same," I say. "Still likes to fight. He was in Vietnam. Couldn't wait to get there, afraid the war would be over before he got old enough. Only seventeen and he went over there and won medals—a Bronze Star and a Purple Heart. Shot in the kidney. He's only got one now. A big scar where the other one was. That's Joe Cuff for you. No fear."

"Hated that sonofabitch big-time," grumbles Buck. He cocks a serious eyebrow at me. "You see these fists?" he says. His fists look hard as stones, the knuckles volcanic. "Next time we meet, I'll be taking *his* quarters, you watch."

~

I LOOK AT THE CAR and feel pity for it. Old and decrepit and starting to cause trouble, the Lincoln is a candidate for the bone yard, get rid of it. Everything about it is sagging. Tires are curb-chewed, bits of body rusting away, showing a dozen rusty red holes, like steel termites are living in it. I run my hand over the dent in the roof and think about taking a bathroom plunger and sucking the dent out. "How'd this happen?" I ask. "Somebody shoot a cannonball at you?"

"That's his fist," says Joy. "Hammered it that way. Just one blow. Bam! The day we lost Mr. Reno. Buck was mad. Boom!" She makes a fist and brings it down on the roof to show how he made the dent. "Boom! like that," she says and the roof reverberates.

"Hey!" yells a voice inside the car. "Quit poundin on my head, goddammit!"

I hadn't noticed anyone in the backseat, but then I see her and she is hardly bigger than a monkey, a hoop of a lady bent over, her head hiding between her shoulders. I nod at her and say, "I didn't see you there."

"I seen you," she says, her tone crabby. She has violent red hair and a face seamed like a walnut. She has a yellow-and-black-striped afghan across her shoulders. On her lap is a paperback book and next to her is a pug-faced, black-and-white dog. The dog raises its head, looks at me with foggy eyes, opens its mouth to bark, thinks better of it, lowers its chin on its paws again.

I glance at the title of the book: *West of the Pecos*. A narrow-eyed, dark-skinned cowboy is looking at me and drawing a gun from a holster.

"That's my mom," says Joy. "And that's Ho Tep."

"Ho Tep," I say.

"Chinese god of happiness," says Joy. "Or maybe it was Egypt. I can't remember. Mom, is Ho Tep Chinese or Egyptian god of happiness?"

"What you askin me for? You named him, didn't you?"

"I wouldn't be asking if I had." Joy whispers, "She's getting forgetful."

"Ho Tep," I repeat. The name makes me smile. "The god of happiness, huh?"

"He's seventy-seven in dog years." Joy leans her head in the window and shouts, "Mom, this is him, this is Buck's cousin, this is George McLeod!"

The old lady puts her hands over her ears. "Am I deeef?" she says.

"You are when you wanna be," mutters Joy.

The old lady snorts. Then she looks at me and works up a bloodless smile and she says, "Pleased to meet you. I'm Livia Miles."

"Pleased to meet you, ma'am."

"He says ma'am," says the old lady. She has slightly crossed eyes and I don't know which one to look at. "I'm thirsty," she says, pointing to the top of the can sticking out of my shirt pocket. I slip the beer out and offer it to her and she snatches it, finishes it off in a few swallows.

"Good beer," she says, and burps politely behind her fingers.

Stepping over to the trash bucket at the curb, I drop the can inside and a mess of flies fly out and swizzle around my head. One flicks off my chin and I swat at it and watch it zip over to the Lincoln and land on the back window and feel its way around a nickel-sized hole in the glass. The hole has a web of fine lines circling it. I go over and wiggle my pinky through the hole, feel the edges tugging at me. Joy and Buck are watching.

"Big hole," I say.

"Big gun," says Buck.

"It went off," says Joy.

She and Buck look at one another. I am wondering if the bullet came from inside or outside, wondering who was shooting at whom. I wait a second for the story, but no one says anything. Joy takes hold of the hem of her skirt, gives it a shake, then waves at a mosquito.

"Minnesota's sticky," she says, shaking her skirt again.

I'm downwind. A not unpleasant scent of female drifts my way and I think how long it's been since I smelled Connie Hawkins.

Joy pinches her nostrils and says, "I'm ripe. I need a shower."

I check inside the car and see the bent lady holding the book, turning a page, her lips forming words. The dog sleeps with the tip of his tongue sticking out. His lower canines thrusting up on each side full of tartar. A cross-breeze runs through the open windows and pecks at the old lady's hair and I see patches of scalp. She doesn't seem to feel the heat. The afghan over her shoulders hangs like furled butterfly wings.

I tell Buck and Joy that they might as well come in and use the phone. Joe Cuff has a tow truck that can haul the car down to his garage.

"That's a plan," says Buck, looking at Joy.

"Them too?" I ask, pointing at Livia and the dog.

"Let them stay," says Joy. "They won't even know we're gone."

I lead the way up the walk to the porch and stand to the side, motioning Joy and Buck to go first. The wooden stairs, dimpled with age, sag under Buck. His body fills the entrance, his head dipping as he goes through into the hall.

"Same place. You know where it is," I tell him.

Livia Miles

Cody Larsen's spurs jingled and whistled in the western wind as he rode Old Paint out of the arroyo and onto the sage-laden prairie.

"JEFF CHAW'S A WRITER that's a real writer—*spurs jingled and whistled in the western wind.* Only a real writer can write like that," she said, "a writer real as rain. You pay tention now." She scratched behind the dog's ear and he looked at her, his glossy eyes making her think of Buck Root and how his eyes made her dissolve when Joy brought him home that time. But the years had gone by and Buck-type men in Livia's life were fading coals of memory.

"My wild oats has turned to prunes," she grumbled sourly. "I'm the shits."

Having loved him, now she hated him and wished she was young and the fox she used be, the one who broke men's hearts just by walking into a room and then, by god wouldn't she just break Buck's heart to smithereens. Make him cry her a river. Make all men cry rivers. Except Cody Larsen, not him.

She went back to the book, reading it aloud to her dog, whom she loved more than white-faced daisies and butterflies:

Cody Larsen's spurs jingled and whistled in the western wind as he rode Old Paint out of the arroyo and onto the sage-laden prairie. The endless prairie stretched in front of wolf-eyed Cody like a great quilt sewn together by the Great Quilt-Maker in the sky. Cody Larsen reined Old Paint in and scanned the distant horizon, the rolling hills and cutbanks of dry rivers, gnarled scrub oak, wild grasses, all of it going on forever over the flatiron earth. His study of the land missed nothing. He had high, hard cheekbones and knife-edge eyes, half-breed wolf eyes black as coal. He turned in the saddle and looked back at the mysterious arroyo out of which he had come to the edge of the Platte River valley. He was heading south as fast as he could go, hoping to make it west of the Pecos River in the Sangre de Cristo Range, where he would find his people and they would hide him. Cody knew the posse was behind him somewhere, tracking him, coming on relentlessly, never giving up until they had their man, or until enough of them died to make the rest of the posse back off. That seemed to be the plan forcing itself into Cody's equations. More men would have to die. More notches would have to be carved on the ivory heel of Cody's forty-four—

"The heel of my forty-four," breathed Livia. She reached to the side and lifted the big gun, hefted it in her hand. She sniffed the barrel, smelled traces of gunpowder. "Hav'ta clean this here thang," she said, giving the gun a twirl into her holster.

Ahead of her was Indian territory, Pawnee and Arapaho, ruthless tribes that liked to skin you alive, pour honey over you and stake you to an anthill, watch you squirm and scream as the ants ate you. Farther south were the Pecos Pueblo Indians, the last dozen of them living near the river—Livia's mother and half brothers and half sisters and the rest of the tribe, and that was where she wanted to go. But she would have to run the Indian gauntlet first and probably have to do something about the posse behind her.

"That's no posse that thar's a lynch mob," growled Livia. "A lynch mob filled with hell's horrors!" The phrase echoed in her mind, *hell's horrors, hell's horrors*. She saw the sagebrush quivering in the wind and herself riding under the hot sun, her white hat sweat-rimmed, her spurs jingling and whistling. She felt the rhythm of the horse between her legs, her knees and inner thighs chafing. She smelled sage and leather and horse sweat. She licked her finger and turned the page.

Old Paint was picking through the sage, his anvil head bobbing lazily, the branches brushing against his sides and Cody's chaps. Out of nowhere flashed a rattlesnake, its body curled and ready to strike, its rattles shaking furiously. Cody's instinct-driven hand whipped the silver Colt out of its oiled holster and a bullet blew through the rattler's vicious, triangular head, hitting it like an ax dead center and splitting its brain in half. The snake shuddered and rolled, then lay in the dust bleeding and squirming, leaking bits of glistening brain and rich red blood.

Livia blew the smoke from the barrel and twirled the gun in a fancy way before holstering it again. "It's a deadly gauntlet from here till we get to the Pecos River, Old Paint. Our people and little White Dove, she and Mama, will be saying prayers to the Great Quilt-Maker, asking him to help us get back to them. I hated to leave them, but what was I going to do when those low-down skanks kilt Palabra that way? I had to avenge my brother, didn't I? Nothin I could do but run them down and make em pay. That's right. Live like a man, die like a man. You lissen, my kid? Open them eyes and look at me, lazy bum. I'm sayin, when we go we're going like men. We're not afraid. Me and Cody and you. Pay tention now. Be tough."

The dog was smiling, his tongue panting, saying, *Uh-huh, uh-huh, uh-huh*—

She thought about how the McMurtrys had killed Palabra, bound him and cut his throat and scalped him and cut his privates off and stuck them in his mouth. Meanness for meanness sake. The sight had made Livia go crazy. She put everything else aside and rode after the McMurtry brothers, tracking them to Casper, Wyoming and shooting all three dead in the Silver Dollar Saloon—had let them go for their guns, then got them dead center through the forehead, splattering their brains against the wall, which was always Livia's signature. She always went for the head, and she seldom missed.

"Right through the intuition dead center and splattered their brains over the wall," she said with satisfaction. "That's some real shootin. That's how we do it, you and me, huh, Cody?"

"Yes, ma'am," said Cody. He tipped his hat and escorted her into the saloon. Music was playing. Couples were dancing.

She flung the thick red hair off her eye and gave him her patented smile—a smile, she had been told, that could raise the pecker of a dead hombre.

"Have this dance, ma'am?" Cody asked.

"Don't mind if I do," she said, and took hold of his arm. It felt like a band of steel, but kinder than steel. He embraced her and told her she was a fine armful. She felt safe with his big hands around her waist, her nose pressed against his neck, smelling his manly smell as he whirled her round the floor, the piano playing "Clementine." Him singing it to her in a voice like shy thunder:

Oh, mah dar-lin . . . oh, mah dar-lin . . .

I, George

BUCK OPENS THE APARTMENT DOOR, looks in and says, "Geez, George, nothing's changed. Even got the same paintings on the walls, geez. See those, Joy?" He points at my mother's landscapes hanging above the couch. "My aunt did those. Our family has talent. My aunt was the painter and my mom was the writer. She sold a story to *Redbook*."

"I know," says Joy.

Buck and Joy inspect the two paintings of Medicine Lake caught in separate seasons—*Summer on the Lake*: rumpled water sparkling in August light, distant trees touched with varying shades of green; *Winter on the Lake*: swirling snow, windswept ice, black-forked trees on shore, a whitewashed, ghostly sky.

"They're good," says Joy. "Buck told me your mother had talent."

Buck says, "Joy knows art when she sees it. She studied it in college." He poses for her, throws one arm forward and the other one back, like an athlete about to launch a spear.

"Yes, Bucky, I know art when I see it." She winks at me and whispers, "He's such a kid."

Buck flops on the couch, grabs the remote and turns on the TV. "So, you into sports there, cousin? What are you into?" He channel surfs. *General Hospital* comes on. "Hey, George," he says, "do you know how you can tell who the Irish guy is in the hospital?"

"Nope."

"He's the one blowing foam off his bedpan."

There is a pause, then Buck throws his head back and guffaws. Joy rolls her eyes.

Buck keeps playing with the remote and he says, "I got a million of em. I did a standup gig at The Improv in Vegas. I had them cracking up, didn't I, Joy, rolling in the aisles. I got great comic-timing. Hey, George, how many cops does it take to push a black man down the stairs?"

"How many?"

"None! He fell." Again Buck laughs loud enough to rattle the windows, and then he says, "Yeah, none, he fell, there you go. So, George, what have you been doing all these years?"

I tell him about working as a blocklayer and cement finisher until I had enough to pay down on the apartments.

"You own these places now, George?"

"Yhah."

"A landlord, huh?"

"Yhah."

"Geez, my cousin the capitalist. That's good. Work the system, George. Work the goddamn system, you know." He looks around, clears his throat and says, "So, do you live alone? No wife, no kids?"

"Who would want a fat fool like me?" I say.

"You're not fat," he says. "Just got a tummy."

"Like a tumor."

"Naw, you look solid, cuz. You look strong. Got muscle definition in your forearms there."

Joy points at the Medicine Lake paintings. "Your mom was for real," she says. "Those could hang in a gallery."

I think about my mother and how she would call me to come

see what she had done and how her eyes would shine with tri-umph. I remember her taking my hand in hers and having me move a brush over the canvas, the feel of the wooden handle massaging my palm, and she'd say, "Feel that, Georgie? It's talk-ing to you."

I tried sketching bees on flowers and redbreasted robins and such. In winter I'd draw skaters swooping over Medicine Lake. But try as I might, I never painted anything worthy of a frame. My mother would always insist I had talent, but I never believed her.

Buck stretches and yawns and tells me his mother commit-ted suicide. He says she took forty Seconal.

"I'm sorry," I say.

He shrugs and says that it was for the best. "She was always miserable, you know, a suicide waiting to happen."

For a few moments he is quiet, his eyes brooding, then he says, "Maybe if she had made it as a writer, huh? She'd try to write, you know, but then she'd say, 'What's the use? What's it matter? We'll all be dead and forgotten in no time.' Her type-writer would gather dust and she'd stare at her drink and talk about my dad leaving her and how she didn't blame him because she was such a mess, who could love a mess."

"Yhah . . . your poor mom," I say.

He gazes at me, his eyelids lowering. It's hard to tell what he's feeling, if he's angry or sad. His voice has an edge: "Your mom was the artist, not mine. What about you, George? You paint or write or anything?"

"Not me."

Buck says, "Nothing to say, huh? Me, I got plenty to say. Hey, talking about art—what did that reporter call me in *Body Sculptors*, Joy? What did he say about me? You remember?"

"Said you were a work of art."

"By Michelangelo."

"Yeah, Michelangelo."

He looks at me as if daring me to deny it.

"Hey, this guy is one of the top writers in the country on bodybuilders, George. He called me a work of art by Michelangelo. Predicted I would go places. Said I'd be big."

"He was close to breaking through then," says Joy. "We got a lot of calls when that article came out. There was talk about making a movie." She pauses a second, then adds, "That was five years ago."

Buck makes his biceps jump again. "You like that, George?"

"Look like baseballs," I tell him. "Ever bust a vein doing that?"

"I'll tell you what, I knew a guy, he had so much muscle the bone couldn't support it. He pumped it up harder and harder and the bone cracked from the pressure."

"That's hard to believe."

"I wouldn't lie to you."

I carry some beer cans to the trash, then sweep the newspapers off the sofa's armrest and drop them on a recycle pile near the front door. I bring the Minneapolis directory to Buck and tell him to look up Joe Cuff under Automotive Repair.

I bring cans of beer from the fridge and pass them around, then ease into the recliner and pull out my pipe, clean the bowl, scraping it with my penknife. Opening the humidor, I refill the pipe, thumbing the tobacco down. Then I light the pipe and blow out clouds of cedar-smelling smoke.

Joy indicates the bookcases crammed with books. "You read all those?"

"Quite a few."

"I gave up reading," Buck says. "Writers don't know shit. Hey, you know what Ezra Pound said at his last interview? 'Words no good.' That's all he said. No joke. That was the whole goddamn interview. 'Words no good.'"

The box fan hums in the window, working hard at rustling

the curtains and sweeping the pipe smoke side to side. There is a black-and-white ad for Dean Witter on TV. I get up and turn it off.

Buck yawns, stretches, says, "Wore my mind out pushing that car."

He sits with spread knees on the couch, crowding Joy. He puts the beer on the coffee table and burps soft behind his fingers, like the old lady did. "Hits the spot," he says, holding the can up.

"Another?" I ask.

"I hate to put you out."

I go into the kitchen to get more beer. The telephone book stays on the armrest. I'm wondering if I should make the call to Joe Cuff. I'm wondering if my cousin and his girl are planning on staying for long.

By sundown the apartment is cooler. I've spent the time listening to Buck telling me how great he is, how he grew to six-foot-four and started lifting weights by the time he was eighteen and got on a steroid called Dynamo and bulked up to two hundred thirty-five pounds. He has tons of trophies, he tells me. He believes the body is an altar on which certain gifted people can erect true art. He says bodybuilding is his religion.

He takes his shirt off, showing me a washboard stomach and lats that look like rolled tenderloins and pectorals that I'm thinking will need a bra when Buck is sixty and sagging. He turns this way and that, showing how he poses in the competitions.

"How pretty am I?" he keeps saying.

Joy has been watching him. She is a little drunk, her mouth askew, lower lip wet from the constant flicking of her tongue.

"He's got it, whatever *it* is," she says to me.

I think about her. Does it ever get old to her, the big body so swollen, the dark skin looking like blind moles are burrowing through it?

22

"Anybody hungry?" I ask.

They both nod.

"I got beans and bratwurst," I say.

"Hey, beans and brats, that's good," says Buck.

"I'll fix it if you want," says Joy. She rises unsteadily and makes her way to the kitchen. I show her where everything is, and she goes to work, her back to me, the leather skirt shining under the light, vertebrae showing between the skirt and the tanktop. A mole on her waist winks in and out of view as she moves.

I lean on the doorjamb, taking in the black border of her skirt and how it contrasts with her legs, how her legs look like dust wouldn't dare settle on them. She reaches in the cupboard, grabbing dishes, and I watch her hips and the mole beneath the tanktop's trim and I hear myself breathing.

When I return to the living room, I find Buck with his head to the side and his eyes closed, his mouth open. He is sleeping.

"Make yerself ta'home," I whisper.

I go to the window and look at the Lincoln. The shadows are deep inside the car. I can't see the old lady, but I can see the bullet hole where twilight rays catch the edges just right. Maybe it was a getaway, I tell myself. They robbed some store or something and the owner came out and got off a round.

"Should I get your mom and the dog?" I ask Joy.

There is a lapse and then she comes to the entry and says, "I spose."

"She'll be hungry, I bet."

"Not her, she doesn't eat."

"I'm always hungry," I say.

"Me too, I eat like a man," says Joy. "It's a wonder I don't weigh three hundred pounds. I burn it off. I'm very active, physically speaking. I do five hundred situps a day. Dancers have to keep in shape." She pats her abdomen.

23

I pat my paunch. "I need to do some situps," I say. "Too many beers and brats."

She smiles knowingly and goes back to the stove. I hear her stirring the beans, knocking the wooden spoon on the edge of the pan. I find myself not wanting to eat in front of her, not wanting her to see what a pig I am.

Livia Miles

"ARE YOU AWAKE, ma'am? Would you like to come in and have a bite? It's just beans and brats and salad."

She opened her eyes and saw a face poking in the window, intruding on her and she wanted to slap it, wanted it to go away, but it kept talking. She could smell beer breath. A beer would taste pretty good. She remembered drinking a warm beer and wanting more. That was . . . when?

"I'm thirsty," she said. "Ho Tep's thirsty." The man had reached in and was rubbing the dog's ear.

"Whyn't you come on in?" he said.

She squinted at him to get a better look. He had kindly eyes and a double chin. He had silver sideburns. She liked silver sideburns. She liked his voice. A soft lonely sound to it, like prairie wind. He was saying how the evening breeze was picking up coolness as it crossed Medicine Lake. "It always does that," he told her. "Gives us sleeping weather." He kept rubbing Ho Tep's ear.

"Watch out," she told him, "that dog bites quick as a rattler. If I say the word, he'll go for your throat."

The man smiled. She saw that one of his front teeth was chipped at an angle and she wondered what happened to it. "What happened to that tooth?" she said. "Somebody poke you?"

"Tooth?" He touched his mouth. "Oh, that's ages ago when I

25

was a kid. I was drinking at a fountain and Joe Cuff pushed my head down and my mouth hit the fountain head and broke my tooth."

"Hoped it was a fistfight," said Livia, putting up her fists and pawing the air.

"No, just kids horsing around."

"Do I know you?" she asked.

"We met earlier. I'm George."

"I don't know no George."

"George McLeod. Buck's cousin. Your daughter sent me to get you, ma'am. To bring you to supper."

"Where is she?" said Livia.

"Cooking dinner," said the man. "She's inside cooking it. Won't you come in? Have something to eat."

"Where are we? What town is this?"

"You're in Medicine Lake."

"Wyoming?"

"Minnesota, ma'am."

"Minnesota? What we doing in Minnesota? How'd we get there?"

"Drove," he said. "Won't you come in and have a bite?"

"Bite what?"

"Beans and bratwurst, ma'am. Some salad."

"I like salad. I like those hard centers. Those are crunchy. Those are gooood."

"We can pick you out some of those."

"You got coffee?"

"Yes, ma'am, fresh brewed just now."

"My husband calls me Tarpot. I like my coffee strong and black. No sugar, no cream. Yeah, I'll have coffee," she told him. "You got beer?"

"Yes ma'am," he said.

"Get us a beer, Cody."

"George, I'm George."

He opened the door for her and reached in to help her out, but she shoved his hand away and told him she weren't no baby. Her bones ached. She had arthritis in her back and hips and knees, but she slid across the seat and forced herself to stand at the curb. She felt dizzy and had to lean on the car. She felt Cody straightening the afghan over her shoulders.

Finally, the world quit whirling and she let go of the car. She reached back and got her dog and her book and told the man she was ready. She held the dog in the crook of her arm as the man led the way, looking at her, his eyes checking her out. Men never changed. Always got a look. She decided to be nice to him. She reached out, curled her fingers around his elbow. She heard music, a piano tinkling. There were voices, laughter, someone shouting. The air was heavy with booze and cigarettes.

"The Silver Dollar Saloon," she said, stepping on the boardwalk and breathing deep. The swinging doors were in front of them, the lights, the music. "Sure, I'll drink with you, cowboy," she told him.

"Yes, ma'am," he said, giving her hand a pat as he led her through the doors into the bustling saloon.

~

"Was she sleeping?" asked Joy.

"Napping some," said the man.

"Booboo, what you doin?" Livia asked her.

"Sit down, Mom, food's ready."

"I wanna beer."

The table was set. There was a steaming pot of beans, bratwurst floating among the beans and juice, and a big salad in a plastic bowl, and there were biscuits and butter. Ho Tep perked up when he smelled food. He started squirming in her arms. "Keep still," she ordered him. "Not taking nothin from you today. Not from nobody. Especially not from you, Booboo!"

"Sit down, Mother."

The big galoot was sitting at the table, stuffing his face, not waiting for nobody. He shot a look at her. She stuck her tongue out at him and said, "That's you, Mr. Selfish, there won't be nothing left for nobody."

"Why don't you just shut up," he said.

"Try and make me," said Livia, sticking her tongue out again.

He sighed and bent over his plate and shoveled food noisily. It was sickening. She smacked him on top of the head. "Eat quiet, goddammit, close your mouth. Were you born in a barn?"

"Better sit your mother down or I'm going to knock her down," he said to Joy.

"Mother, please."

She snorted her contempt, then sat down with the dog in her lap and she put the book beside her plate, where she could look at the picture of Cody on the cover, and then she went for the salad, picking through it, going for the hard centers. The dog sniffed and wriggled. She told him he better watch it or else she'd make bratwurst of him and have him with mustard on a bun.

The man with the silver sideburns brought her a can of beer. He walked to the sink and washed his hands. He was civilized. He was not like the galoot sitting there stuffing his galoot face with his galoot hands. Moving his muscles. She hated his muscles. If she had her forty-four she would shoot him and then he would see how hard those muscles were.

Cody looked at her and gave a wink. He dried his hands on a kitchen towel and walked back, his gait bowlegged and his spurs jingling and whistling in the western wind. Joy spooned up beans and meat, putting them on Livia's plate.

"Booboo, you hear that?" she said. "Who's that sound like jingling and whistling in the western wind?"

"Eat, Mom. Pick up your fork and eat."

Her neck hurt, but she eased it back and tilted her head to the side and stared at the man, giving him the come-on as he took off his gun and hung it on a peg. She was smiling sexy, till her upper plate slipped and a piece of lettuce fell from her mouth. Got eaten by the dog. She turned away and thumbed her teeth back in. Then she nodded at cowboy Cody. He winked at her and she winked back. The piano played "Clementine" again. She smelled whiskey, she smelled beer, she smelled something cedar. Heard Cody singing. Singing to her—

Oh, mah dar-lin, oh, mah dar-lin, Cle-men-tine . . .

"Sit down, Cody," she told him, "right near to me."

"Aim to," he said, grinning at her, pulling the chair out and

. . . lowering himself stiffly from the saddle, he walked to the river and lay down on his chest, sipping water off the top, letting the cool water slide down his parched throat. Fresh, fast water full of mineral taste and the memory of snow. Old Paint dipped his muzzle in and drank. Cody thought perhaps he would stay awhile, rest up, bathe his feet . . .

Livia looked north and west toward the mountains, and she saw no dust rising, no signs of the posse, and so she started taking her boots off to bathe her feet in the river. She didn't get the first boot half off when the arrows started flying, *zing-zing!* missing Livia by a whisker's width. Then an arrow caught her through the chaps and pinned her to the ground. Another arrow got her in the left arm and a third hit her in the left shoulder.

She drew her gun and fired. In front of her, charging across the river on splashing horses, were four Arapaho painted for war. The Indians were screaming and whooping, waving tomahawks and spears.

"Quit that, Mom! Quit that."

"Quit what? What am I doing? Don't be tellin me what to quit, you floozy."

Livia looked at the floozy waiting to take her order. Her mouth was crooked, but cute. Her hair made Livia think of a palomino with a cropped mane.

"How you been?" she asked her.

"Okay," she said. "How're you?"

"Tip-top, never better," said she. She reached out and took the floozy's hand, patted it and said, "Gimmee *whuskey*, baby, and don't be stingy."

"Don't wave your arms like that anymore, okay?" she said. "George here is going to think you're crazy."

"I ain't crazy, you're crazy."

Cody cleared his throat and said, "Let's make it two whuskeys."

"Juss bring the bottle," Livia ordered. She made her eyes look the way men liked them to look, faraway elf eyes, not quite with it, a little cross-eyed dreamer.

"I got elf eyes," she told Cody. "This one turns in a tad. Everybody says it wanders when I drink. It wants to look at my nose. You think I got a nice nose? Cute as a button I'm told." She took the tip of her nose between her thumb and forefinger, wiggled it. Tittered.

"I noticed that wandering eye," he said.

Her ankle caught Cody's ankle underneath the table.

"George is the landlord here, Mom. He owns this whole building."

THE ALTAR OF THE BODY

Livia was chasing the bubble of Cody's calf with her instep. "Who is?" she said. "What landlord?"

"Him . . . George there. *Mom*, the dog is eating off your plate. Ho Tep, no!"

"Some days you're the dog, some days you're the hydrant," Livia said, breaking into a cackling wet cough that went on and on until it was choking her.

Joy reached over and patted Livia on the back.

"Sounds like cancer to me," said Buck, his voice prickly.

Livia said to him, "Don't you talk at me, you skunk."

The floozy reached across with her fork and stabbed some meat and held it to Livia's mouth and told her to eat it, told her she needed protein in her brain, her brain was getting erratic. "Eat it, Mom," she said.

"I'm a vegetarian," said Livia.

"You are not."

Livia pushed the hand away and said, "If I say I'm a vegetarian, then goddammit I'm a vegetarian!" She went back to the hard centers of the lettuce leaves, popping one after another into her mouth. The floozy ate the piece of meat on the fork.

"Yeah, you eat it," Livia told her. Livia picked out another bite. "Eat this," she ordered.

"Eat it yourself," she said. "Look at that dog. Juice running off his chin, the slob. God, I give up."

"You're too goddamn skinny," said Livia.

"You're worse than skinny. You're like something from a concentration camp."

~

WHEN SUPPER WAS OVER, Livia decided to be helpful. So she cleared the table. Her daughter got up and helped too, and they piled all the dishes in the sink and filled it with soap and water. Behind them somebody turned on the music. It was country. It

31

reminded Livia of honky-tonks and cowboys and beer. It reminded her of being in the backseat of some car with a heavy-breathing man on top of her. The music made her twitch her hips as she washed dishes. Accidents in the backseat cause . . . she looked sideways at Joy drying a pot. No, Joy came late. It was Harold Jr. who was early, he was the accident.

Out the window, she saw stars over the trees, one faint star, then another: *Star light, star bright*, she prayed. *Gimmee Cody.* She inhaled the lake's wet-mud smell and could see strips of light reflecting off it far away. And there were houses bordering the water, lights in the windows, lights burning on the porches, everything peaceful. A postcard picture. She heard the sound of a motor. A boat moved across the water, its lamp in front leading the way like a firefly. *Gimmee Cody, to make my toes tingle*, she prayed.

~

SHE AND WHITE DOVE went into the saloon and sat at the bar, listening to music, Frank Sinatra singing he did it his way.

"It's a good life, I don't care," Livia said, patting White Dove's knee. White Dove didn't answer, and Livia thought that maybe she hadn't really said anything and so she tried it again, but when she opened her mouth she felt something searing the inside of her skull and the words wouldn't come. It had happened before a couple of times. She closed her eyes, then opened them when the searing was gone.

Someone switched the station and Sinatra got replaced by country music.

"That's more like it," said Livia.

Cody Larsen was at the long bar talking to the bartender and the floozy with the bleached hair. Cody's Stetson was pushed back on his head and his six-shooter hung low on his hip. He had a bottle of whiskey and kept passing it back and forth, filling the floozy's glass, then the bartender's glass, then his own, and he was drawling like a Texan. He slugged back a shot and looked at Livia and offered her a drink.

She took it and White Dove got one and Cody lifted his. The three of them clicked shot glasses and Livia toasted Cody's horse, "To Old Paint!" and drank it all in a gulp, feeling the warm whiskey sending feelers through her chest and gut. "Waters of life," she said. She clutched the bottle and poured another and the floozy said, "That's enough of that, Mom. You're gonna be sick."

"I gotta iron gut," said she.

A new song filled the room, one of those Janine Sherry songs she had heard lots of times—

> I'll keep my jeans and wear his shirt
> and drive his Chevy truck . . .
> cus I'm just a country girl. . . .
> and I don't need that muuuuch.

"I'll keep my jeans and wear his shirt and drive his Chevy truck," Livia echoed. "Ooo-la-la! Let's dance, cowboy! It's Friday!"

She pulled on Cody's arm. "Not me, ma'am," he said.

"No, not me neither," said White Dove.

"Party poops," said Livia. She moved her knees in and out and jigged around the dance floor, while everybody in the bar stopped and watched. They started clapping in time to the music.

"Born to dance! Born to dance!" she shouted. She put her fists on her hips and did a heel-toe hop across the floor and back again, and then twirled and stumbled a bit, but caught herself and pretended the stumble was part of her act, stumbling on purpose and laughing and throwing her black-and-yellow afghan around, a bullfighter swirling her cape, teasing the bull.

"C'mon, Cody, charge!" she shouted, but he didn't charge. He watched her, a chipped-tooth grin on his face. His silver side-burns glistening in the light.

"When I get to heaven, I'm gonna do a jig for Jesus!" she told Cody.

"Okay," he said.

"She probably will," said the floozy.

"No doubt about it," said the barkeep.

Everybody grinned at her. All those teeth hanging out. She was a born entertainer. She line-danced for them, kicking her feet and moving her hips. "See me? See me?" she said.

It was fun, more fun than ever and she wished it would last till she dropped flat dead, that's how she wanted to go. "I wanna die on the dance floor!" she bellowed.

"She means it," said the floozy.

The barkeep came out and grabbed her and jittered her back and forth. "This is how I love you, this way!" he yelled. "This is the Livia we know and love. Hey baby, go baby go! Look at her, Joy! Yo mama!"

"Yo mama yo ass!" shouted Livia.

They zipped here and there. He threw her on one hip, then the other. He lifted her up and her head tapped the ceiling. He turned her in circles, the room whirling and him shouting at her, calling her "Partytime Liv!"

"Careful with her, Buck!" cried the floozy. "Don't hurt her, she's fragile! You'll break her bones tossing her that way!"

"I ain't fragile!" Livia yelled. "To hell with that!"

She loved him again as she had loved him before when they used to go out and drink and dance and he had teased her and flirted with her and she with him and he was the best boyfriend her daughter ever had, and he had said many times to her when she talked about getting old, "Never you worry, I'll always take care of you! You got a home with us."

He lifted her and dropped her into his arms, cradling her like a baby, whirling in circles and grinning at her, his eyes warm, wanting her to be the Livia her heart told her she still was. "I'm still eighteen in my head," she told him. She was gasping for air a little. Her throat was dry, was hot, was hurting. There was a sharp pain in her back between her shoulder blades. Both knees sore, thighs trembling with weakness. She panted for breath and hung on his neck. "Gimmee sugar," she commanded him. "Gimmee sugar, buckaroo!"

He smooched her face, tickling her with his day-old beard, the music pounding in her blood and the world zipping faster round in a blur that became a smear, then a fog. Seconds later her tummy went funny.

"Uh-oh. Oh no!" she said, and out came whiskey and shreds of lettuce and the room turning and Buck shouting, "Shit, she's sick!"

There was nothing to hang on to.

The next thing she knew she was waking up on the floor and Booboo was saying, "You wanna kill yourself, Mom? That's enough now!"

Livia couldn't answer. A little voice told her she was dying and the whole business scared her so bad she wet her pants.

~

AFTERWARD, bathed and her hair brushed flat and her pajamas on (cowboys and Indians printed on flannel), she lay in a bed in a strange room, a lamp beside her, her teeth grinning in a glass of blue water. Her dog and book were there, the dog curling by her side, like a heat pad for her sore hip. The book was on the nightstand, the sprung cover at an angle, so she could see the outlaw Cody Larsen staring at her, his hand on his gun, ready.

She heard noises on the other side of the door. A man cater-wauling. Down-and-dirty drunk like a real man should be once in a while. Smell of whiskey and cedar when Cody carried her to the bath and she had hoped he would bathe her too, soap her up with those workerman hands. His eyes, so sympathetic and worried, had hypnotized her. Those hard cheekbones, she had wanted to bite them like apples. Wanted to lick his silver sideburns.

"I need some," she breathed, and the book cover stirred. "I need some."

Against the wall was a blond dresser with a large round mirror and a chair tucked under and a gold comb-and-brush set and a clock and a picture of a woman, a sober woman with pressed mouth and white hair and sad eyes and a brittle jaw. Lots of pain in those eyes. Lots of weakness in that jaw. Livia knew she wouldn't have gotten along with that woman, wouldn't have liked her, wouldn't have tolerated her whining.

The noise increased on the other side of the door. It sounded like a fight, thumping and yelling going on. It sounded like someone getting killed. Was Cody killing them guys? Who was Cody killing?

George! that was the fella's name. Yes, that's what he told her was his name. George . . . George with the silver sideburns.

She concentrated on the name and she remembered a husband named George Lee Miles. Tall fellow in cowboy boots and a bollo tie made of leather strings, a silver dollar on its cinch. Black hair and brown eyes and a square jaw and sideburns and he was—George Lee Miles, a mile high and handsome as sin and a great kisser.

"Whatever happened to you, George Lee Miles?" she said. "Did you die?" And soon as she said it she knew he was dead. All that drinking in honky-tonks, all that booze before breakfast. It got him when he was forty-nine and going silver in the sideburns. Yes, he turned yellow as urine and his belly bloated and he vomited what looked like coffee grounds—liver bits spilling out his mouth. She saw it—bloated belly, those coffee grounds coming up smelling fecal. All his beauty turned to horror.

"Why have I got to remember you that way?" she said. "That wasn't George Lee Miles."

Old memories came in better than new ones. The childhood ones were clearest of all, the ones on the farm with Uncle Jim and Auntie Ann were never any trouble. She remembered milking cows and walking to school with brother Billy and sneaking rides on a Shetland pony and one day the pony bucked Billy off and he cracked his head and died.

And she recalled standing on a porch somewhere watching her father leave with a suitcase. He got into his car and drove away and never came back and she went out on the porch every afternoon to wait for him and say, *When is my daddy coming home?* And her mother would tell her, *Hush, child, don't pester me.* And then her mother started cradling the booze, and started chasing her and Billy with the belt, beating them, cursing them, calling them her ball and chain. Then Uncle Jim and Auntie Ann came and took them away and Billy died falling off the Shetland pony. And Livia's mother was seen keeping company with notorious men and drinking gin and whiskey and it lasted until years later there came a call from somebody saying Livia better come if she wanted to see her mother alive once more.

"Mama died . . . throat cancer." The words made Livia cough. "Couldn't talk when I came to say goodbye. Just looked at me with that look."

That was the second death and it wore on Livia and made her nervous. Uncle Jim followed. Or was it Auntie Ann?

"Where are you?" she said. "I ain't scared of you. Hell, soon enough I'll be dead as a doornail, dead as dirt, dead as—" She couldn't think of what else to be dead as. "You can just wait till I'm goddamn good and ready, mister!"

She snatched the book off the bedside table and ran her eyes over the picture of Cody Larsen. He was the same as George Lee Miles, tall, dark, handsome and strong. In life she had been married lots of times, couldn't remember how many exactly, but it was always to real men, not those namby-pambys tied to their mothers' apron strings, but John Wayne and Rock Hudson types, who knew what to do with a woman in bed.

She opened the dog-eared page and found that Cody

. . . dropped the first Indian, then got the second. The third got closer and threw his tomahawk, which grazed Cody's cheek and sliced off a piece of his ear, but Cody aimed and dropped the third Indian with a bullet between the eyes. The fourth Indian was already in retreat. He made it back to the far side of the river and looked at Cody and made threatening gestures, screaming savagely before he rode off to get another war party to chase Cody down and scalp him.

After the lone Indian rode away and the other three warriors had floated downriver on their bellies, leaving blood on the surface of the water, Cody pulled the arrow out that had pinned his chaps to the ground, and he stood up and whistled for Old Paint, who came running, bobbing his head, snorting and anxious for Cody to get back in the saddle. He broke the arrow off in his shoulder and the one in his arm, but he left the tips in. He knew that if he tried to pull them out, they would tear his veins to pieces and bleed him to death, so he let them be as he mounted the horse and rode across the river, continuing south.

"We're wounded real bad," Livia whispered to the horse. Blood streamed down her left arm and trickled from her notched ear, the wind blowing it back, leaving spots of it on the pale earth for her enemies to follow. "I'm in trouble now," she said. "These wounds is gonna do me in."

She and the horse kept moving toward the snow-scruffed Sangre de Cristo range. Behind them Livia knew a bigger war party was gathering and on the northern horizon she could see the posse's dust closing in on the Arkansas River. Westward was the high sun and drifting over the white mountains, getting ready to pinch off the sun, were storm clouds boiling, their centers greenish. In a few minutes, spears of lightning were hurling at the high plains, one after another like jagged pitchforks. And then hail started falling, pea-sized balls of it sweeping toward her in fractured sheets.

"If arrows or bullets don't get us, the weather will," said Livia. "Giddyap, boy."

Old Paint didn't need any urging to cut and run. All Livia had to do was hunker down and hang on.

She put the book on the nightstand and turned out the light. In a moment moonlight bleached the open window. Cool air licked lightly over her face and she smelled the muddy lake. She heard the shade tapping time. Crickets telling the temperature. She yawned, closed her eyes. Glad to be home. Glad for her bed.

The dog's snoring stopped. His head flew up. He stared at the door, sudden violence slamming against it. Booboo screaming at Buck. Cusswords flying. Glass breaking. The thud of fists on flesh. Livia clung as hard as she could to the horse's sides. Wind tore tears from her eyes. Wounds weakened her and she felt it coming, the final breath, the lonely fall.

I, George

CHURCH BELLS WAKE ME. I flip to my other side, cover my ear with my arm and try to sleep, but the bells keep calling to the faithful and my head is pounding and my bladder aches and I am thirsty and my throat is sore and probably I'm coming down with something.

I wish I could take back the night. It had started out fine, cousin Larry and Joe Cuff dropping by with two cases of beer and sitting down with Buck, talking with him about old times. But the drinking led to fighting, Joe Cuff and Buck slugging each other because Buck told the joke about the Irish guy blowing foam off his bedpan.

The more Joe Cuff drank the more he kept giving Buck the offended eye and waiting for an excuse to start trouble. "You insulting me? You insulting my people?" Joe Cuff had asked him.

"Shoorah dunt tyke it parsunal, boyo," Buck had replied, trying an Irish accent, trying to make another joke of it, make Joe Cuff lighten up.

But then Joe Cuff had asked him if he knew why Italians never got acne: "Because it slides off."

"You insulting me, boyo?"

"Are you a wop?"

"I'm a wop who shits on shamrocks," was what Buck said.

"Wop greaser cunt!" Joe Cuff fired back.

A look came into Buck's eyes, deranged, wild, vicious. He had a bottle of beer in his hand and he swung it at Joe Cuff, but Joe Cuff did a little feint with his head, just enough that the bottle missed and shattered on his collarbone and cut him and there was blood covering his shoulder. Joy was screaming at Buck, screaming his name and telling him *No! Don't!* and he was staring at the jagged neck in his hand like it might explain what had happened. And then Joe Cuff's fists were working from all angles.

They punched each other, hurt each other. They were both dazed, both backing off, rubbing their jaws. "Let's call it a draw," I had said. "C'mon fellas, let the past bury the past, what do you say? We're not kids anymore."

"You never get over it," Buck had said. I think he meant you never get over having your ass kicked when you're a kid, never get over the humiliation. The two of them sat there looking away from each other, then Joe Cuff muttered something that I didn't catch and Buck said, "Kiss my tan Italian ass, Joe Cuff!"

"Kick your ass, did you say?" And he came out of the chair and Buck punched him so hard it lifted Joe Cuff off his feet, Buck clubbing him, swearing to God he was going to break his neck. But Joe Cuff got out of it and they slugged piss out of each other some more.

Larry and Joy and I broke it up, grabbing arms and waists, pushing the men away from each other, Larry putting on his cop-command voice, ordering Joe Cuff to leave, and then escorting him out the door. Joe Cuff warning Buck that it wasn't over, and Buck saying to come on anytime. "I'll kill you next time," Joe Cuff had told him.

"Not you, boyo, you're nothin!" Buck had answered.

Joy had kept in front of her man, hands on his chest. He could have walked right through her if he had wanted to, but he had had enough of Joe Cuff.

After the door closed, I said to Buck, "Welcome home, Mikey Routelli."

"Jesus Christ, nothin's changed," he said.

~

I CRACK MY EYELIDS and see Mama's paintings hanging peaceful on the wall and I say, "Why can't I do something like that? Why didn't I get some talent like that?" I imagine painting Joy, how great it would be. I see her lifting the tanktop over her head. Shimmying out of her skirt. The gold ring glistening in her navel. I drape her over the couch, knee cocked, left arm hanging, the wrist bent over the edge of the cushion. My brush is swift. She falls in love with me because I am so gifted and have immortalized her beauty. *Genius*, she calls me.

You inspire me, I tell her. *Your beauty makes me a genius.*

That would work. If I could do it. But I can't do it and even if I could she would never love an old putz like me. I look down my length and see the blanket swelling around my belly and my toenails rising like pale moons. On the armrest my work shirt looks like a tabby cat curled asleep. Next to me on the coffee table is Emerson's *Essays*. Last night, Buck had read a passage I had underlined years ago when I was picking Emerson's brain, trying to find a philosophy to live by.

A foolish consistency is the hobgoblin of little minds, Buck had cited. And then added, "That's why I keep an open mind. No foolish consistency about me, is there, Joy? I guess I'm an Emerson man."

"I don't know about that," she had said. "You're pretty predictable, Buck."

Beer bottles lie next to the book and the empty bottle of

White Horse Whisky. Sun glares through the windows. The church bells go off again. The curtains stir. When I carried the old lady to bed, I felt her breath on my cheek as she whispered, "You're fambly, so I don't have to wear my teef." It made me chuckle and I kissed her forehead and hugged her to me harder and she said, "Cody fweety, watch out, I'm horny."

When she got sick from the dancing, when she was vomiting and wetting her pants, I had thought she was dying. She had looked so *bloodless*, so done for. But Joy had known what to do. "Take more than a tummy ache to kill this one," she had told me.

～

MY EYES BURN, my stomach is doubtful. My mouth feels coated in glue. I've got a hard day ahead of me. Have to get into the main line running alongside the pine tree and get the roots cleaned out. Everybody complaining about how slow the water drains and how the toilets don't flush good. Lots of grunt work to do. Lots of pick and shovel and the new plastic line to adapt to the old tile line, and who knows what else I'll find down there? And I don't want to do it anyway.

Maybe put it off a week or two? A couple weeks couldn't hurt. At least wait until the heat lets up. I have to be careful about heat. My father died at forty-two from heatstroke. Same power plant I see on the way to Elk River, the same cement floor behind walls where people are making electrical power and walking back and forth over the very spot where he collapsed on a ninety-degree day. Minnesota summers: hot-sticky-suck-you-dry. Salt tablets? Forget it. He fell into the cement he had just finished smoothing with a trowel.

A day later at the funeral home my mother threw herself on the body, crying, "I'm coming soon, Papa!" Which upset me so bad I got dizzy and had to lean against a wall. I've never been good at handling my feelings. Too much emotion is unbearable for me. My nerves go all to hell. So I do my best to stay low-key and not get too involved with people. My remedy for trying situations has always been to go home and read a book and have a few drinks and go to bed early. When my mother threw herself on my father's body, Mikey's mother hustled me out of the room, she cursing, saying, "Goddamn Sissy and her goddamn histrionics." But I don't think it was histrionics. My mother was no actress the way some women are who make themselves the center of attention at funerals. Her grief was large and uncontrollable.

The landscapes on the wall are conservative compared to the ones she did after my father died and she started painting portraits of what some might call *bizarre* women. She hung up a framed print of Marcel Duchamp's *Nude Descending a Staircase* and started painting expressionistic figures falling on thorns or hanging from crosses upside down, legs wide apart, or floating on air, stretched out like stratospheric clouds, or rooted to the earth, looking half human, half tree. Their mouths were always thick and luscious. They never had eyes. They never had noses. They had mouths and they had hands in the form of scooped hooves and their heads were always hairless and fissured like a brain or a pair of buttocks. They always had breasts hovering like little balloons about to float away.

Who can say what she was after? I've never really understood. But I know that the paintings were good. And they were smart. And I knew that somehow they reflected my mother's insights about herself and her life and her grief. And her love.

I had not known how much she loved my father. So much that it would break something in her when he died. I've never come close to loving that intensely, but I've seen it's real and I've seen what it can do and I'd rather not go there. It's a fearsome love that creates ogres in the mind. *Love moderately*, the

Friar tells Romeo. But Romeo wouldn't listen and look what happened to him.

She painted me once: painted a baseball cap cocked back on my head, its caption saying HARMON KILLEBREW—MINNESOTA TWINS. A blunt-nosed kid with polished cheekbones, a chipped-tooth smile and eyes like a sociable coon.

Papa still lives, my mother had said, tapping the portrait. *You're your father to the life. His eyes are your eyes, Georgie.* And she had stroked my chin with her turpentine-scented finger and told me he was the kindest man in the world, a tender man. She never saw him mad, not once. In sixteen years of marriage he had never raised his voice. She would yell at him or go whacko about something and he would call it artistic temperament, and say, *Now, Mother, calm down. Let's talk this over.* She told me that he understood her like nobody ever had. *How I miss him, Georgie,* she had said. *God oh God, how I miss that man.*

He was a mild fellow, true enough, but maybe he was holding it in—anger, frustration, the stress of his job, the stress of home—and maybe that's what killed him so young.

She kept working and the years flew and it was as if she had a mission. She told me once that she felt a river of creativity flowing through her veins. Brushstroke following brushstroke, dots and strokes together, all of them carefully aimed by her tireless hand as she sat in her chair, the easel and canvas in front of her, table beside her, turpentine and rags and colors and brushes. And the paintings piled up. I put them in the closet, a hundred of them or more.

Then one day she started passing blood and was diagnosed with bladder cancer, the galloping kind. It had spread spots over her lower spine and hips. It was in her lungs and in her brain. Nothing to be done. She took to bed. The doctor ordered morphine and it eased her pain. A nurse came in twice a day and cleaned up and gave her the shot, but I stayed with her most of the time, feeding her, reading Emerson's *Nature* to her—*In the woods we return to reason and faith*—giving her sips of water, petting what was left of her cobweb hair. I would tell her everything was going to be all right. "Never fear, Georgie's here," I would say, she nodding at me, her eyes lost in hollow pools of violet flesh, her breath piddling.

She died in the winter, in January, a foot of snow on the ground. On an icy, windy day we buried her. Cousins Larry and Ronnie serving as pallbearers, along with Clarence Duff and Big Dewey Barnes, Joe Cuff and me.

The wind swept over my mother's coffin that day and snow beads danced in front of us, looking like ghosts rising up to watch. The preacher told us the Lord was our shepherd, we shall not want. We stood around hunched in our coats, kicking our feet to keep warm.

I stayed on when the others made for the cars, and I watched chrysanthemum tongues quivering and then becoming still as the coffin was lowered into the ground, touching bottom with a soft bump. Down in shadow, I could barely see its surface shimmering. I got self-conscious about standing there. The men pulled the straps up and took the brass frame away and were waiting for me, so they could finish. I had no choice but to leave my mother in her frozen world.

After she was buried, a depression settled in that has never really gone away. Even after all these years, I brood about her, wondering if I could have done more to help her, could I have been a better son? I'm sure I could have. I keep wondering where she is. Is she with the others in some kind of heaven, or is she a cool, unfeeling vapor? Are her atoms taking up space— Mama as the grass or flakes of snow or drops of the Mississippi flowing to the sea? ". . . look for me under your boot-soles," Whitman had said. We recycle, go round and round and come up yellow-eyed daisies or the wing of a crow, who can say. Has Mama stopped somewhere, waiting for me?

~

A DOOR OPENS down the hall. Seconds later the sound of tin-kling in the toilet. I think about my cousin and Joy and the old lady and her dog. There are people living in my home. Filled with drunken generosity I told Buck he was family and could stay as long as he wanted. I had helped haul the suitcases in. I had insisted that Joy and Buck take the bedroom at the front of the apartment overlooking the street. Joy had hung clothes in the closet. She had changed the sheets on the bed. On the nightstand she had placed a pint-sized book called *Mother & Me* and a framed picture of her little girl.

"She looks like one of those kid models," I had told her, "on the cover of a magazine."

"She lives with her dad. They're Jim and Joyce," she had answered. "Actually, it's an old picture, she's big now, a big girl." She had held her hand heart high to show where her daughter's head would reach. I had looked inside the *Mother & Me* and it was full of poems (*Baby, baby I love you so/ Mommie wants you to never grow/ Stay young and cute and full of love/ And always be my turtledove.*) and watercolors of a mother with her child, each drawing and poem a scene of adoration inspired by Disney.

I hear the toilet flushing. Then Livia comes down the hall, her slippers scuffing. She is thumbing her teeth, pressing hard on the upper plate. The dog is behind her, smelling the base-board. I watch to see if he is going to lift his leg.

The old lady stops when she sees me and her brows furrow. An exclamation point sits between her eyes. "Who're you?" she says. Her voice crackles around obstructions in her throat.

"George," I mumble. It is an effort to speak.

Her lips press together and she looks offended and she says,

"What a mess." She waves her hand at the coffee table piled with last night's leftovers. She coughs and clears her throat and looks around as if searching for a place to spit. The dog sniffs at me. I toe him away.

"Go home," she orders. "You go home now, it's morning."

"Yhah, this *is* my home," I say.

And she says, "Your home!" And she looks around and it dawns on her that she is in a strange place. "Oh," she says. She digs inside her ear, her pinky working. Then she says, "Ringing. It drives me nuts. So what's your name?"

"George."

She smiles politely. "Pleased to meet you, George."

"Pleased to meet you, ma'am."

"Dust mites," she says.

"Who?"

She points at balls of dust resting in the corner near the TV. "They live in your ears. Nasty things. Give you . . . allergies . . . allergies and ringing ears. So where's your vacuum? Where's your dustcloth?" She stamps her foot. "Them bums can sleep, but not Livia Miles, she pays her way."

From down the block the bells bong again. Church is over. The old lady freezes in place, her ear cocked, listening. When the bells finish, she crosses herself and says, "Where's your vacuum, son?"

I try to reason with her, but she is having none of it, and finally I show her where the cleaning closet is and she snatches the Dirt Devil, plugs it in. The bug-eyed dog bolts for the bedroom, his tail tucked. She flips the switch and the vacuum storms. She takes off with it, the curtains ballooning as she passes the window, her hair flickering like points of flame.

I retreat to the bathroom and take a shower, lathering soap in my palms, while I think of Joy with the washcloth and cotton balls and Neosporin and Band-Aids, her fingers moving tenderly over Buck's wounds. Slender, tapered fingers so unlike my own. Any man would be glad to give himself to her frothy hands.

~

THE ELM TREE SHADES portions of the garden and the yard. Some half-dead branches reach toward the house—Dutch elm disease creeping along. Beyond the yard, where a pathway through the trees and houses reveal it, are flashes of Medicine Lake, golden scarves stretching out in the morning sun, the rough wind making them sparkle. The air has gotten heavier, moist. Mosquitoes probe the screen. I hear Joy entering behind me.

"Mornin," I say.

"Mornin. Boy, I'm hungry," she says. Her eyes are bloodshot but wide-awake. The irises blue as pilot lights. She wears a man's black bathrobe. Around its collar, frills of blue nightie can be seen. She opens the fridge and fills her hands, then closes the door with her hip. She sets eggs and bacon and butter on the cupboard next to the stove. I've got the coffee on and she grabs herself a cup.

"Coffee always smells great in the morning," she says. "How's eggs and bacon sound?"

"Good."

She lights one of the burners on the stove. It makes a whooshing sound. She adjusts the pan so it is centered over the fire. She turns and stands beside me and together we look out the window and she asks if it is my garden and when I nod she says, "You've got a green thumb, George. I love gardens. Gardens say, *This is home.*" She yells at the dog, "Ho Tep! Get out of there!" The dog is meandering and sniffing and lifting his leg. "He's nearly deaf," she tells me, her eyes pitying the dog.

Pug-nosed and pink-tongued, Ho Tep looks at us as if he's saying, *Wuz-up? Watcha-want?*

She goes back to the stove. "How many?"

I hold up two fingers. She throws strips of bacon on the pan. The bacon sizzles and does a little jig. After the bacon is nearly done, she scrapes some of the grease to one side and taps two eggs with the spatula and lays them neatly in the pan. The eggs bubble next to the bacon.

"Short-order cook, that's what Mom did years ago when we were kids. She hated cooking at home, so she taught me and I made most the dinners. I was cooking when I was ten years old. And then she went to night school and got a dietitian certificate and became a dietitian at a hospital."

"Dietitian?"

"She used to know how to eat healthy. She made us eat lots of fish for our brains. To this day, I can't stand fish. Even a can of tuna puts me off."

"Hard to see her as a dietitian," I say.

"She was nothing like you see now. She wore a white lab coat and her hair in a net, you know. She was professional. Walked around like a doctor giving orders, telling the cooks what to make for this patient and that patient. That used to be one sharp lady, George. Don't let her looks fool you."

I think about it. Livia bustling around, snapping orders, checking the food trays for her patients, making sure everything was as it should be.

Absentmindedly, I give voice to a thought Joy doesn't need to hear, "She likes the hard centers of lettuce now."

A shiver runs through Joy. She closes her eyes. "The hard centers, yes. And Western paperbacks. And that stinky little dog. And beer."

After I eat, my throat isn't sore anymore and I know I have escaped again, gotten stupid drunk and no harm done except some brain cells dead and some more fat on my fat-coated liver.

Joy is shoving a piece of toast at Livia, coaxing her to nibble.

"You ever seen anything cute as Booboo?" says Livia to me. She takes a long look at Joy and adds, "I was her age once."

"She's a fox," I say.

"I was a fox," says Livia. "Men used to fall over each other tryin to get to me. Wasn't for kids I would've been a moviestar. But I had kids to take care of." She glares at Joy, who is nodding like a person bored with hearing the same old story.

"The older I get the better I was," Joy mutters.

"I was!" says Livia.

She pushes Joy's arm and gets up, goes to the screendoor, looks out. She has an ossified hump at the base of her neck. Her elbows hang like crinkly leaves beneath the sleeves of her shirt.

"Look at those ta*may*ters," she says. She goes outside, the screen slamming.

"Mom always kept a garden wherever we lived, even if she had to plant it in pots," says Joy, watching out the window. "We lived all over this country, hardly more than two years in one place at a time, but Mom always had her garden. Mom's a wanderer. She can't sit still. Mom! Don't pick those tomatoes! Those aren't ready! Pick the red ones!" Joy shakes her head, smiles tiredly. "I've aged twenty years on this trip," she says. "Her and that dog. Some days I feel like Job, like the wrath of God has got me—" She presses her palms to her eyelids. There is a tic in the corner of her jaw. For the first time I notice how rounded her shoulders are, how they look as if she is carrying weights.

"She's definitely not the brightest crayon in the box anymore," Joys says. "Easing into senility and taking me with her." A bitter burst of laughter and a shake of her head and she comes over and sits down again. "It's hot," she says. She slips off the robe, emerging from it like an iris. The robe drapes over the back of the chair. "That's what happens sometimes, you know, the patient goes on and on and the caregiver has a heartattack and dies."

"It's the stress. Stress kills you."

She nods. Her blue nightgown is sloppy at the neck. When she moves, her nipples shift. She leans forward, elbows on the table, coffee cup between her hands.

I stare and look away and stare again. I think about Connie Hawkins, farm girl, dancer, and part-time prostitute, shaking her assets at The Body Shop. Midnight in her van, the mattress huffing beneath us and I'm hurrying so she can get back inside.

"I hope we're not putting you out," says Joy. "We don't want to be a bother."

"No bother. Heck, I'm glad for the company. Living alone gets . . . gets lonely sometimes."

"We'll buy groceries."

"Don't need to."

"We want to."

"We got a little drunk last night," I say.

"Sure did," she says. "I'm sorry about the fight. Buck just hates that Joe Cuff. I'd heard about him before and how he used to bully Buck when they were kids."

"I thought maybe they had grown out of it."

"Buck fights at the drop of a hat," she says. "Just between you and me, I think he's got too much steroids in him. He just suddenly goes crazy. Smash you with a beer bottle like he did Joe Cuff. Just boom and he doesn't know he's done it till he's done it."

I shake my head. "Last time I saw him all he wanted was to read books and watch TV and collect jokes in a shoebox. He'd come sit with my mother and read her one joke after another and they would laugh. Anytime we'd get bored we'd say, *Mikey, tell us some jokes*, and he'd go on till you stopped him. It'd be an hour or more and never the same joke twice."

"He's still the same. Loves a joke, loves to laugh. But I'll tell you what. Comedians are actually depressives. The joke thing is a cover-up, did you know that?"

"Buck's a depressive?"

She lowers her voice. "Actually, yes he is. He's on mood elevators, you know."

"Mood elevators?"

"It's all my stupid fault."

"Why?"

"Because of her," she says, jerking her thumb toward the backyard, where Livia roams through the garden. "He's scared of her. Scared of what's happening to her. His mother went nuts, you know."

"Yhah, I know. Yhah, she was a pretty lady and all, but she sure had problems."

"She still haunts him, let me tell you. The things she did to him, he'll never get over. But he always excuses her, you know. He says she was mental, she couldn't help it. Boys always want to love their mothers, don't they."

I nod.

"He writes poetry, did you know that? Some of it's pretty good. I bet he could publish it if he tried. But his body is his art now. He's a poet of the body, that's how he puts it."

She leans forward like she has a secret to tell. Things shift to a better angle and I find myself eyeing a pinkish corona big as a Ritz cracker.

"He pumps iron like it's life and death," she says. "Dedicated like you can't believe, working so hard to make something of himself. And you should see him on the platform when he's oiled and doing his routine, it's a sight to make you think of Mount Olympus, know what I mean?" A contented smile creases her lips.

"I'd never have guessed he'd become a weightlifter," I say.

"Bodybuilder," she corrects.

"Never would've guessed that in a million years."

"You want to see something?" she says.

"What?"

"I'll be right back."

She leaves the kitchen and I'm thinking she's going to get some of his trophies, but when she returns she has a cigar box in her hands, and she pulls out a picture of herself looking like some exotic bird. I see white feathers fanning up behind her shoulders and back and hips. She wears a glittery G-string and glitter on her nipples. Her legs are smooth-muscled the way ice-skaters' legs are. "That's when I was at The Sands in Vegas," she says. "What a body, huh?"

"Voom, voom," I say.

She shows me another picture, a woman that looks like her but isn't her. The face is full of mischief. The hairdo is forties or fifties, brushed high with soft curls in front and thick waves drifting down the back of her neck. She has a broad, smooth forehead, arched eyebrows and smiling crescent eyes, one eye turning inward slightly. A tipped nose, small curved nostrils. Lips voluptuous. Teeth are perfect. A slender neck.

"I bet that's Livia," I say.

Joy nods. "That's Mom. She's eighteen there. Isn't she gorgeous? I'll tell you something about my mother. One of her husbands told me one time that she was so gorgeous it practically petrified him. She'd walk in a dancehall and all the heads would turn and all the men would be wanting to buy her drinks and dance with her. I think that's why he finally took off. He couldn't compete. He said the first time he met her she touched his arm and he felt electricity running through him and the hair stand up on the nape of his neck. That's the kind of impact my mother had on men." Joy stares at the picture. "A long time ago."

"You look a lot like her," I say.

"So I've heard," she says.

She puts the pictures away and brings out some letters tied with frayed ribbon. "From my daughter," she says. "You want to read one?" She slides one over and I read:

Dear Mommy,

I saw a little leprechan he had a funny beerd. He had such funny clothes that I laugh intell I turn red. And than he saw me and he jump and ran under his toadstool. And than he went to sleep. And than his too brothers came in and saw him than they said what are you doing sleeping under that dum toadstool. Happy Birthday to you. I love you.

your loveing daughter me

The paper looks old, yellowish and like it has been fingered a lot. I look at more of the daughter's letters. Most of them are about leprechauns or elves or a hairy dog who licks her face. One says, Love is eating popcorn together. Love is kissing some body. Another one calls itself a poem: My poem to MOMMY.

The wind blows wooo
and says booo
and when I am scared
I want to snug in bed with you.

your loveing daughter me.

"Sweet kid," I say.

"She loves her mother," Joy replies. She is fingering a white-beaded Rosary that she has lifted from the box. "My First Communion," she says, holding it up. "I went through a very religious period when I was little. I still say my prayers at night, three Hail Marys and An Act of Contrition, just in case I die."

She crosses herself and gives Jesus a kiss. She puts the letters and the Rosary back in the cigar box and closes the lid. "I miss that little girl with all my heart," she says.

A long silence follows. Then as if to break a spell she points to her breasts and says saucily, "What do you think of these?"

"Very nice," I say.

"Fake," she says. She pokes each one and says, "Fake, fake. I had a big butt and nubbies." Then she pokes her hip. "This is liposuctioned. Wanna see the scars?" She stands up, shoving her nightie aside and showing me full-cut cotton underwear encasing her like a chastity belt. She rolls the elastic rim down an inch and points. "There and there," she says.

I see tiny white scars and dimples just above her tailbone.

She turns round and lifts one breast and then the other, looking at each in turn and jiggling it and eyeing me critically as I suck my pipe. I don't know if I'm supposed to do something or not. Is she inviting me?

"What law says we should go through life hating how we look? It was Buck who made me take a hard look at myself and say to nature, 'No way!' George, tell the truth, do you think I'm sexy?"

"Most sexy thing I've ever seen. You should be in the movies," I tell her.

"Not too old? Skin not sagging?" She pats the area beneath her chin.

"You look perfect."

"I love you," she says, adding a breathy laugh.

She slips onto the chair and picks up her spoon and starts cartwheeling it on the table and she tells me that one true thing she has come to know is that life is filled with fakes. Fakes rule. "It's who you *know* and who you *blow* and how good can you lie. I'm sick of all that. I want to always tell the truth. No more lies, no more fakery."

"I don't think you're fake," I tell her. "You're a genuine dish."

"A genuine dish?" she says, chuckling. "You're showing your age, George."

"Too damn old," I say. "But my heart's still willing."

I'm about to tell her more, but just then the weightlifter shuffles in, yawning and scratching.

~

HE WEARS a sleeveless T-shirt and polka-dot pajama bottoms. His beard is prickly, the chin hairs peppered with white. His eyes are suspicious. There is a violet lump under his left eye and a flesh-colored Band-Aid on his brow. His nose is swollen, his bottom lip raw. "That coffee?" he says in a phlegmy voice. "Get me some, would you, sweetness?" He sits down at the table and says, "How're you this mornin, cousin?"

"Fine," I say. "How're you? You lookin kind of crumpled."

"Yeah, my mouth is sore, my nose hurts like the devil. But I'll be all right. Hey, I gave that bugger blow for blow, didn't I? I bet he was shocked. Lil ole Mikey comes back and whups ass."

"You drew blood."

Buck winks. "Felt good," he says. "Hey, you can sure put it away. You drank most of that bottle yourself, straight, no chaser. You must have cast-iron guts, George."

"Not really. Actually the doc told me I got a fatty liver and I should quit drinkin."

"Fatty liver? If you've got a fatty liver I've got just the stuff for you."

"What's that?"

"Hey?"

"Hay's for horses."

His heavy eyelids lower. "Oats is cheaper, grass is free. I ain't heard that one in about twenty-nine years."

Joy gives him a cup of coffee and kisses him on top of the head and starts massaging his neck.

"Hay's for horses, I'm sore," he says.

"Ohh," she whines in sympathy.

"That bugger. One of these days I'm gonna drive his nuts up into his nose."

"Mama make it better," she says, her hands kneading him.

"My deltoids," says the weightlifter. "Yeah, that feels good, sweetness." His hair sticks up on top, scalp showing through. I look at the clock behind him on the wall and watch the minute hand scribe a circle.

~

AFTER THE MASSAGE, Joy fixes him breakfast and while he eats he talks to me and asks if it will be all right to workout in the backyard. He has three hundred pounds of iron in the trunk of the Lincoln. "I'm getting older. I have to work twice as hard to compete. I'll tell you what my secret is, though. Should I tell him, sweetness, what do you think?"

"Tell me what?" I ask.

"He's family. He deserves to know," says Joy.

"Tell me what?"

"You're right, sweetness, you're always right. Hey, he's got a fatty liver, for Christ's sake. Go get the goodies, sweetness. Let's save his liver, he's my cousin."

"What goodies?" I ask.

"Patience, George, patience."

Joy leaves the room. Buck continues to eat, chewing thoughtfully, trying to keep his tattered lips uninvolved. I study my pipe. I take out my penknife and start scraping the residue inside the bowl. It powders the edge of my thumb and I remember Ash Wednesday and the worshippers coming out of church with their foreheads smudged. I think about Joy praying every night and how she doesn't look like someone who says hail marys and acts of contrition, she who shows her breasts and liposucked butt, the tiny white scars and dimples. I feel myself getting stirred up and part of me wants it and part of me wants to stay with what's familiar—crowded garden, old books, White Horse Whisky and beer. Quiet nights.

Joy returns and she has a box in her hand. Buck wipes his fingers on his undershirt and takes the box, holds it up. "It's Nova Life, see?"

The box is white. It has a picture of a green pill on the front. The pill is shaped like a blimp. There are arched letters above it saying, NOVA LIFE, then below in smaller print: NEW WAY TO NEW LIFE.

"The fountain of youth, cousin. Just one-a-day gives you all the hormones, vitamins, minerals and herbs you need to stay young and supple and handsome and strong." He raises both arms, curling both biceps. "Look at me," he says. "You'd never believe we're the same age, would you? How old do I really look? What do you think? Be honest."

I'm going to say forty-four, but I know what he wants to hear, and so I say, "I don't know. Thirty-two, thirty-three?"

Buck beams. He looks at Joy and she is beaming too.

"How old is Joy?"

"Twenty-five?"

They both laugh. Buck reaches inside the box and brings out a dark green gelatin pill. "The fountain of youth," he repeats. "We've been taking these six years now. Not many people know about these buggers, George. Actually, the hormones make them slightly illegal, don't you know. A trace of growth hormone and steroids in there. A drop of testosterone." He snickers slyly and taps the pill and tells me that he has a source in San Diego ships him as much as he wants. He has lots of sales*persons* around the country working for him, selling new life to people who don't want to go gentle into that good night. *Do not go gentle into that good night*, George.

"Where there is no hope there is underwear," I tell him.

A delighted laugh bursts from Joy. Her hand passes over her hip and she snaps her panty waistband—*snap!* "He's silly. George is silly like you," she says.

"Underwear?" says Buck.

I shrug. "I think it was Allen Ginsberg who said it."

Buck nods tolerantly, but I can tell he wants me to be serious. I put on a sober face, but inside I'm feeling giddy, I don't know why. *Snap!* I hear it. *Snap!*

"I get a percentage of every Nova Life sold," he tells me. "This is how you make money, you see what I'm sayin?"

I lower my eyelids thoughtfully and place my finger upside my nose.

"That's right," he says, touching his own nose carefully, then pointing at me. "You get persons working for you. They send money orders. No checks. Cash or money orders only. It adds up over time. You mainly get someone to handle the mailings, and you sit back and collect." He looks at Joy. She is nodding her head, confirming everything.

"We're thinking of branching out, right, sweetness? Maybe settle down in one place and get a bigger operation. Rent a warehouse with offices and phones, you know what I'm sayin? Get into other things: women's care, health creams and such. This alpha hydration stuff is big. Wipe it on your face and it eats dead skin and eats your wrinkles and plumps your cells."

"Alpha hydroxy," says Joy.

"Same thing," says Buck. "They got acids out there can give you baby skin. Retin A, and even better concoctions. Hey, I've got access to all of it, whatever you want."

"People want to look young," I admit.

Buck stabs his finger at me. "You got it! And they'll pay *anything*. You know what these little pills cost me? It doesn't matter, because people will pay whatever I say if they think they're buying youth. And they are! I'm a testament to that. Am I not? You see what I'm sayin what I'm tellin you?" Buck holds a pill, crackling its cellophane wrapper. "You want one? Here take one." He hands me the pill. He takes one himself, and so does Joy.

"Go on," he says, "don't be afraid. It's cool."

I unwrap mine and roll it in my palm.

"Hay's for horses, listen up. You know what I'm about to do? I'm grateful for your hospitality, George, and to show you how grateful I am, I'm cutting you a deal. No, I want to. I want to make you my Medicine Lake distributor. What do you think of that?"

"I dunno."

"You don't know? He doesn't know, sweetness."

Sweetness smiles at me, her eyes promising things.

"Look, I'm letting you in on youth. *Youth*, cousin George, think of it. Baby boomers turning fifty. Think of all those wrinkles, all those saggy faces and unhappy people, millions and millions. God, do we hate to get old! Invest in youth products and you can't lose. Am I right, sweetness?"

She says he is right.

Even I know he is right. Youth is a booming business. It will outsell cars and groceries and everything else in the future. People rather be young, no matter what. Desperate people taking pills by the handful, spreading on creams, washing with special soaps, getting lasers to wipe away age spots, having operations to tighten skin and create pecs and abs and plump breasts, steel buns.

I hold the pill between my thumb and forefinger. Hold it up high so it catches the morning light and glows like an emerald, an icon, a modern eucharist. I see millions bowing down to receive it from Preacher Buck, their grateful mouths open, eager tongues out. And him chanting. *The body of youth. The body of youth.*

"Here's what I'm doing for you. Here's something I only do for family. Are we family, George? Hay's for horses, you bet we are, and I'm giving you this box at cost. *Cost*. No, don't thank me. Hey, you take it and you try it, and then we'll see. It's a month's supply. And if you don't look better and feel better in a month, then we'll just forget it. I'll never mention it again. But I won't have to. You'll be begging me to let you in on the Nova Life way." He leans forward, his eyes crafty. "You know one of the best things that's gonna happen to you, George? Little side effect you'll notice the next time you get laid." He winks at me. "You'll be a new man with a slow hand, you understand what I'm saying?" He takes a quick look at Joy and tells me that she appreciates the power the pills have given him. "What say, *compadre*?"

"How much?"

"How much. He says how much, sweetness. Should I tell him? How much for youth? How much for well-being?"

"Tell him, Buck."

"Only thirty-nine ninety-five for the fountain of youth. Hey, I know it's ridiculous. I know you thought I'd say at least a hundred bucks for the fountain of youth. But it's hardly more than a dollar and change a day. Hey, I must be crazy giving it away like that, but what the hell, you're my long-lost cousin, I've got to be good to you. Is it a deal?"

I scratch my chin and look at the little Nova Life in my hand. Maybe it's for real. Maybe Buck is on to something, the ground floor of what will sweep the nation like other pills have done— the sleeping herb, whatever its name is, and the pill that's supposed to make a man potent. Things on TV and in magazines and people flocking to the health stores, buying bottles of youth, all of it jacked up triple the price because it is in demand.

"It eats up fatty deposits on the liver, guaranteed," says Buck, pushing the box across the table.

"What the hell, sure, why not," I say.

"I knew you would," says Buck.

"Take a check?"

Buck gets a pained expression on his face. "Cash or money orders, I told you, George."

I reach for my wallet and Buck laughs. "No, no," he says, "I'm only kidding, just kidding. Your check is good, George."

~

MIDMORNING we get the weights out of the car and carry them into the backyard. Buck wears leather gloves and gym shorts and high-top tennis shoes and a wide belt to support his lower back. I have on my gray sweats.

"Best part of my day," says Buck as he slaps disks on the bar. "Get the kinks out, get the blood pumping, the heart working, get my body feeling like it's made to last forever, like I'm Superman. You understand what I'm sayin? Pumping iron makes you *feel* like iron." He scrutinizes me. "Need to work on you," he says.

I feel sloppy, my sweat suit hanging in folds off my shoulders and legs and tight over my belly. The sun is overheating me, making me perspire. I know my face is shiny and too pink. The last thing I feel like doing is lifting weights. "I do have a job this mornin," I say. "Got to dig a trench out front and replace some root-bound pipe. That pine tree—"

"All muscle. Don't tread on me," interrupts the weightlifter, flexing his arms, his muscles rippling from wrist to shoulder. "But look here, let me show you a few things, a couple easy ones. It'll warm you for your digging."

I would prefer for him to volunteer to help dig the trench, but there is no mention of it. He does some pushups and situps and deepknee bends, coaxing me to join in. Which I do. We do a few jumping jacks together. He puts his heart into it. I make motions with my arms, bend my knees a little and say, "Hup, hup."

"Hey," says Buck, "I got another deal for you, George. Look here, how about you buy that Lincoln?"

"Buy what?"

"The car. Fix it up! It's got air-conditioning. It's got a fine radio. Quad sound, baby. Let me tell you something, that old thing rides like a magic carpet, smooooth. A freeway flyer. A thousand bucks, she's yours. What do you say?"

"I got a car, Buck."

"Five hundred, she's yours. Hey, it's a *Lincoln Continental*, man."

I think about the car, how used up it is, a throwaway sitting forlorn and ailing, waiting for fate to take a hand, waiting for someone to end its misery. Some tender loving care and it might be a fine-looking machine again.

"Hey, c'mon, take her off my hands, whaddya say?"

"Give you two-fifty," I tell him.

"Hay's for horses, that's robbery!" Hands on hips, he turns in a circle, scowling. Finally, he scratches behind his ear, clears his throat. "Make it three."

"All right, three," I say, not knowing why I'm offering anything.

His upper lip hooks in the middle and he's smiling Mikey again. He goes back to the weights, while I stand to the side and watch his muscles bloat, veins swelling perilously, eyes detonating.

Sleek-feathered starlings sit in the elm, twisting their necks and fixing yellow eyes on him. They are excited, their heads darting back and forth. When he grunts and snorts and the bar goes up, they freeze in place, like divers ready to leap off a cliff. A bird pivots on one wing and lands facing the others.

Nature holding its breath in awe, they tell him.

Joy comes out wearing a yellow outfit, a scrap of skirt, a scrap of halter. The dog has followed behind her and taken a wrong turn on the steps and disappeared.

"That dog," she says, "he's blind as a bat."

"Ought to put him to sleep," says Buck. "Do him a favor."

The dog gives a hoarse bark.

"C'mon, Ho Tep!" says Joy. "Get out of there!"

The dog barks again. "Well, what's he doing?" she says.

I go over to the steps and look over the side and there is Ho Tep jammed in the juniper bush, his tail in the air, his legs thrashing. "Stuck," I say, and I pluck him out, brush him off. He trots with me to the blanket Joy has spread in the shade.

She is sitting with her legs tucked to the side, her body curvaceous and slim and big-breasted, belonging on the cover of *Cosmopolitan*. I see myself bowing down, licking her toes if she would allow me to.

I'm sick, I'm a sick man, I tell myself.

"What's that smile for?" says Joy.

I tell her it's because she looks like a sunflower.

"Lemon cake and banana cream pie!" Buck says. "Somebody oughta take a bite of her."

She and I watch the weights rising and falling.

"Gotta admit, he's incredible," she says.

"Belongs in a Roman colosseum," I reply.

"Look at his forehead. Wouldn't you call that an intelligent forehead? And his eyes"—Joy fans her face with her hand—"the first time he laid those eyes on me, my knees buckled and my heart stopped and I said, 'Oh my God, that's Victor Mature!' Do you remember Victor Mature, George? He was Samson in *Samson and Delilah*. I saw it ages ago on television when I was a kid and I fell wildly in love with Victor Mature. I was going through the *TV Guide* all the time trying to find movies he was in. Those bedroom eyes, those shoulders out to here. And when I saw Buck at the gym the first time, it was like the son of Samson come alive. I even asked him if he might be Victor Mature's son. He liked my asking that."

Buck bends to the weights.

Pumps and pumps.

"Ooo-la-la," croons Joy. "Yumm, yummm, Bucky." Her mouth is lively. I can see her teeth and her tongue, her moist, mobile lips. I'd give a month's rent to kiss her. What if I slipped my hand up her thigh to that narrow yellow band, what would she do? Or if I leaned over and kissed a nipple? Would she respond in kind or would she slap me? Call me a dirty old thing. Or maybe Buck would beat me up. *Don't beat me, Buck, I'm love-struck*, I'd tell him.

"You sure got eyes," I hear her saying. "Rather look at me than Bucky?"

"I don't mean to stare. Don't take offense."

"Offense? Worst day of my life will be when men no longer stare. I don't mind how you look at me. It's not like some creep leering so you can see his filthy thoughts. Your eyes aren't ugly, George. You got nice eyes, very peaceful." She takes me in a moment, then adds, "But kind of sad too. Do you have sad memories?"

I think of my mother and father and others I've known who have suffered and gone, but I don't say anything and she keeps talking.

"I don't see you getting psychotic on me. Too many men are psycho these days. This guy in a bar one time, he says, 'Baby, I'd eat a mile of your shit just to see where it came from.' Now that's nauseating, don't you think? Turns me *off*. Where the hell's a guy come up with that? It's disgusting. I like it when men just watch me. Appreciate me."

"I'd never say anything nauseating to you," I tell her.

"You're sweet as pie," she says. She pats my leg.

"Nyaah!" shouts Buck. The weights flip to his shoulders. The veins gorge. *People die that way*, I'm thinking. *Papa popped a vein. Died facedown in the cement.* I imagine the weightlifter keeling over on the lawn. Shock and sorrow following. The funeral and a weeping Joy. She needing comfort. *You're so kind to me*, she would say, leaning on me for strength. And I would be good to her. I would treat her so good.

I reach out and pat her knee, rest my tingling hand just a second, then take it away. She doesn't seem to notice. Her eyes are filled with Buck Root. The weights drop again and another set of grooves appear in the grass.

"Good for my soul!" says Buck. "I need it like born-agains need Jesus and Catholics need Confession. I get awful when I don't workout, George. My brain gets depressed and sluggish and stupid and—"

He doesn't finish his thought. His eyes are caught on his image in the window. He comes closer and stands at the edge of the blanket, turning his torso, flexing his arms.

"A tucked and rolled epitome of manhood, sweat covering him like a sugar glaze," he declares loudly.

Joy ogles him. Her mouth is open, her eyes expectant. She rises to her knees and runs her hands over his chest, and down his washboard abs, her fingers jumping. She pinches skin at the side of his waist and tells him he will have to work on it.

"Five hundred situps, my boy," she says.

"I'll do a thousand," he says.

He watches her fingers move back and forth, up and down.

Her eyes are full of veneration.

~

I GO INTO THE KITCHEN to the sink and splash my face with water and let it run down my neck. The dog is scratching at the screendoor. I fill the sink with water and dish soap and bring the dog in to give him a bath.

Oh no! he says, his four legs stiffening.

"You smell like a mildewed rug," I tell him. The dog turns his face to me and I inhale the odor of rotten teeth. "Jesus, you could mortify the dead with that breath," I say.

I lather him, scrub him, then rinse him off and take him to the back porch, so he can shake. He sits on the porch in the sun, his tongue out, his eyes blinking lazily. A pair of flies is on the screen inside, stuck together, one riding the other. The one on top has a green vest. I sneak over with the swatter and slap the flies so hard their fragments mingle. Ho Tep scurries off the porch.

"Come on," I say. "I don't mean you." I cluck to him. He comes up the stairs and I let him in. His tail is tucked. "Little god of happiness," I say. "C'mere." I massage his ears and he is reassured.

Then I get my pipe and stand at the window, puffing smoke and watching Buck play with Joy. She is horizontal and he is using her like a barbell. Her body is stiff. Her hands are crossed on her chest, ankles crossed, too, and he is lifting her up and down. It looks fun. He sets her on her feet and she tells him she wants more. It's as if she is a little girl bouncing around, trying to get attention from her daddy.

He grabs her by the waist. Her hands go on his wrists as she rises, and he flings her into the air and catches her, and he flings her again, does it several times, trying to get her higher and higher, while she squeals. Like a sunbeam she shoots up, her little skirt flapping, then curling at her waist as she comes down, showing yellow underpants flashing, the effortless rising and falling, cheerleader style at the apex—arms out, legs split— and *Weeee!* down, and *Weee!* up. Watching her sends pulse after pulse of longing through me. I see how small I am, how worthless, weak. And I have a chipped tooth and gray side-burns. Not at all the man my cousin is. Buck is what the women want.

In a faint voice, I hear Livia reading her book in the living room, her voice slow, each syllable carefully pronounced:

> . . . his keen vision seeing the movement at the bottom of the pass, where the posse raised dust that rippled in rays of yellow sun washing over the searchers, their long rifles erect, rifle butts fixed to lean thighs, barrels glittering like polished swords.
>
> There was nothing for Cody to do but climb higher and try to slip into obscurity on the other side of the mountain. He clucked his tongue at Old Paint, urging him on. The bloody arrow wounds ached fiercely and forced little moans from Cody's mouth as the jolting horse plunged up and . . .

The words drift away and there's a long pause and then I hear Livia talking angrily as if someone is with her. "I'll tell you this," she says, "if all is not lost, where the hell is it?"

I want to hear more about Cody and the posse, but Livia doesn't continue and in a few minutes I know by the way her breath is rattling that she is asleep. Under the table the dog is sleeping too. Outside I see Joy and Buck making love beneath the dying elm.

Joy Faust

DELICIOUS WHEN HE THREW HER, wisp of yellow, her skirt opening like a daffodil, the slender stems of her legs growing from his hands. There had been few such moments with him since the old lady had parked herself in the back of the Lincoln, a spoiled baby squatting there saying *gimmee, gimmee.*

Buck had wanted her happy-go-lucky, dancing, drinking, laughing at his jokes. Her collapse, plus doctor bills and Buck's lack of income from his body had created a bad environment— had made Buck edgy and bitter and snappish. If George hadn't been there, Joy couldn't imagine what would have happened. What would they have done? She would have had to turn tricks somewhere. Go to a bar and sell herself. Or Buck would have had to rob somebody.

Lately, she had been having premonitions of something evil coming her way. Something frightening. Bad dreams haunted her nights, dreams of herself tapped out and homeless on the streets, living out of the Lincoln, going to soup kitchens and hustling drunks in bars, getting diseases that would make her teeth fall out. In one dream she had seen herself dying in an alley, coughing up bits of bloody lung. And she told herself it was what she deserved for the treacherous bitch she was.

Tart, tart, you got no heart, Buck had sung to her the last time he was drunk and blaming her for all that had gone wrong in his life. She was constantly wondering if he loved her anymore. She would say *I love you* and he would always say it back, but most of the time mumbling it automatically, wearily.

She reran images in her mind of when their love was new: Buck jumping out of bed and doing a funky butt grind to "Mother's Bad Luck Child." Curiously graceful for a man so large, grinding his hips like a whore, his shoulders shifting, his penis flopping, his hands beckoning. Two bodies in the moonlight, whirling like pagans, the rites of spring. And then Buck rising over her, swollen and saying, *Let's see how many times we can make Joy come.*

Six years ago. Six years and they grew used to each other, no surprises left. Six years and she could tell he was tired of her. She was not his muse anymore. His lust came in self-indulgent bursts, usually when he was drunk and off his Elavil. He flirted with other women, made love to some of them, mocked Joy's tears, told her she had asked for it, she should have stayed with Jim Faust, poor, dumb bastard.

Too often he would nurse the bottle, turn on the TV and sit there lumpish and sullen; or worse yet, his eyebrow would arch and the booze would make him mean and he would tell her how stupid she was, what a faithless woman she was. "My love for you is aging me," he would say. "I'm getting old because of you. Before Joy Faust, I was a *man*—a man who was winning, who was on his way to the top. Then you made me leave Patsy. You give me these lines in my face. When's the last time they gave me first-place money?" And there would be murder in his tone, his lips twisting as if he were getting ready to spit her out.

Mean.

Scary.

Men.

Nikos Pape, her mother's third husband, had been the first scary man. Just his booming voice or the sound of his feet pounding the floor had made her mouth go dry, her bowels turn to water. He had been unpredictable and she had never known what would set him off. He had regularly beaten her brother and once blackened her eye and called her a little slut because she threw herself on the couch one evening to watch TV, wearing only her nightie, a thin cotton thing that clung to her body. And when she was barely twelve, not even wearing a training bra yet (but having a big, capable ass), he came into her room one warm summer night and showed her what he meant by *little slut*.

Many years later when she took off with Buck, it hadn't occurred to her how much like Nikos he was (the same Mediterranean fever), but as the years passed she saw that he and Nikos were too similar for it to be coincidence. And so she decided it had something to do with *her*, something that made her go for rapacious men, something needing to be hurt, needing punishment.

~

HE HURLED HER. She fell into his arms and he tossed her away, caught her, held her belly against his chest, his massive hands squeezing her liposuctioned butt, pressing pubic bone to breastbone, the pleasant pressure of it. He reamed her navel with his tongue, flipping the gold earring up and down, she giggling moronically as he called her, "Banana cream pie."

His hand from behind went between her legs, the fingers probing, a knuckle slipping past the rim. Sliding in a thick forefinger.

"You can't do me here," she told him.

"Wanna bet?" he said.

He carried her to the trunk of the elm, held her up with one hand spread across her rump, pubis pushing just beneath his throat, his chin rubbing her humid hairs, while he fumbled with his shorts, and then brought her down, sliding the crotch of her panties aside, opening her, his arms pumping her up and down as if she were his barbell again. She reached above and caught a branch. Clung to it. Flakes of bark fell on them, light as moths brushing her skin.

"I love you, I need you," she said. "Do you know how much I need you?"

"I love you," he murmured.

He pushed her halter out of the way and his battered mouth tugged at her, but she barely felt what he was doing. There was no longer the pleasant pull at her abdomen that used to come from a man at her nipples. The implants had numbed them, turned them into ornaments. A tiny leaf fell into her hair, tumbled and stuck to Buck's wet neck, glistening like a jewel, an arrowhead of jade, and she wanted to say, *How lovely a leaf is, how delicate the veins are*. But she remembered she should be moaning, he wanted her moaning. She moaned and looked around to see if anyone were watching and she caught George staring out the kitchen window. He backed away, but she could feel him in the shadows, his eyes stroking her.

She stood in his shoes and saw what he saw—saw it as a movie called *Daughter of Sin*, about a girl gone wrong, the kind of girl talked about in women's magazines and on TV shows, a body made for bad men and bad luck and sex too soon. She moaned some more and Buck redoubled his efforts, his big hands crushing her as he slid her slickly up-down up-down. She was starting to feel it. It was gathering it was happening. What was George feeling watching her? What were his thoughts? Where were his hands? What was in his mouth? What was he doing? "Oh mah gawd," she murmured. "Oh mah gawd, . . . umm-uhh-*uhnnnn!*"

I, George

YEARS AGO I watched a couple having sex at Big Thunder Lake up north. It was in a cove called Blue's Beach. It was a nude hangout, cut off by mile-wide water and two small peninsulas that were filled with spruce, forming a secluded crescent where nudists lounged in the sun. I was walking across the cove with my fishing pole and a string of fish, and I saw two bodies under a blanket writhing. I could hear the girl moaning. A small crowd had gathered as the couple wormed around and made sloshy, desperate noises. Then the girl threw the blanket off and straddled the boy and impaled herself.

Waves slapped the sand behind me. Foam surged around my feet, bubbles bursting, the rising vaginal odor of the water, the girl riding her clit on his pubic bone fast. Lemon hair trembling as she cried out, "Ahh-ahhh-ahhnn!" And the voyeurs cheered and someone shouted, "Touchdown!" Moments of soft breathing following, then she slipping off the boy, curling beside him, flipping the blanket over them, their eyes closing, their noses touching, lips smiling.

I remember wondering about the act itself, those bodies unconscious of anything but their need. Was it beautiful? Holy? Avant-garde? Was it disgusting? Shameless? Evil? Stupid? Dogs humping in public? Should someone have doused the couple with a bucket of water? Or did it matter what anyone thought? Were shame and modesty irrelevant?

A passion on the sand.

And so what?

Would I even recognize them if I saw them again? I don't remember their faces, only their bodies, his as slim and smooth as hers, weasel bodies, delicate arms, clenched fingers on each other's shoulders and the spot where their dampish hairs melded, forming an hourglass of fur. So many people in the world, on TV, at the beaches, in the cities, an overkill of flesh.

~

I CAN SEE Joy's arms are tired. She's hanging on to a branch and I can hear it cracking and she lets go. She grabs onto Buck's head, kissing his ear, sucking the lobe and murmuring, "Come, baby, come." And at last he shudders and growls and lunges a few times and stops. He holds her a moment, caressing her fanny and saying, "Oh, sweetness, sweetness." Then he sets her down. "Is you is or is you ain't my baby?" he says.

"I is," she says.

He holds her head against his chest and rocks her. "Whoever fucked you good as me?"

"Nobody. You're my man."

"And you're my lady," he croons.

"Never getting rid of me," she says.

"Never want to," he says.

And they stay like that, cooing in the backwash of love. Tree leaves tremble in the wind, and the garden, stretching out in half shade, half sun, is swaying, tomatoes wobbling, bean bushes shuddering, carrot tops lacily reaching for each other.

Joy glances over her shoulder in my direction again, then she looks at the weights. And I look at the weights, beetle-back disks grazing the lawn. I am alone in the shadows with a cold pipe in my mouth. Behind me the old lady snoozes. The dog sleeping on his side pants for air.

Buck Root

BEFORE GOING TO THE BODY SHOP with George, Buck checked himself in the mirror and noted how he was losing ground, and he asked himself if it was time to face his age and get out of lifting. He considered writing an article for one of the muscle mags, giving the inside dope on pumping iron, how a smart bodybuilder could psych out opponents. It would make a good article, what he had done to his competitors, how easy it had been to mess with their minds. *Look at how unbalanced your calf muscles are*, he might say to a young, strutting stud, and then watch him nervously lick his lips and gaze at his calves.

He would also write about how bodybuilders put sheaths over their cocks to pad themselves. *Is that a nose cone you have in your shorts or a tumor?* had been one of Buck's favorite lines for those guys. Simply telling a man that he looked pasty, or asking him if he was losing weight, could throw him off and make him perform poorly.

Buck told himself that his knowledge of human frailty would teach the young bodybuilders how to get an edge, how to give no quarter, how to destroy the competition and win.

"You'd be good at that," he said aloud. "You got the mind for it."

"You have a gift for phrases, yes, always been able to write.

Got that from your mother," he told himself. "A gifted person. Gifted."

"Yes I am," he agreed.

He saw himself in the writing role and decided he would wear a bow tie and some wire-rim glasses and blue jeans and a leather vest. Smoke a pipe and lay a trail of cedar in the air like George. Some kind of hat. A beret. No, a Greek fisherman's hat, something eccentric like that.

"Poems would add an alluring touch," he said. "Show how deep I is."

He wondered how many poems he had written. Thirty-three came to mind, yes thirty-three stolen from here and there, but having a certain voice that became his own when he added a phrase, a word, a break in the line that was pure Root rhythm, or a special couplet that often fell on the page in just the right place. He went to the nightstand and pulled them out, a tidy stack, hand-printed. The top one he had plagiarized from Anonymous in *The Oxford Dictionary of Quotations*. It was called "The Rogue's Delight." He read the first two lines:

> *My honey love by God I swear*
> *Your eyes outshine the fire more clear*

The first line had said, *My honey chuck*, but he had changed it to *love*, giving it a modern sound. He pictured a volume of Buck Root poems—poems so beautiful that women wept over them. He saw his name prominent on the jacket. He would write about love and bodybuilding and the world of taverns and bars and all the tarts he had known, all the hearts he had won and broken.

He put the poems away and went back to the bathroom, back to the mirror to appraise his looks more closely. The image was misty, but what he could make out was one hundred percent hard-rock man. He leaned closer, squinting. The pores covering his nostrils were getting large. Grease got in them and made blackheads and little pimples and that was bad. There should be no flaws in a man like Buck Root. People getting close to the Root wanted to see human perfection on the hoof. People wanted to know that perfection was possible. He posed, bending his arms, his volcanic biceps erupting. From a few feet away he was as phenomenal as ever. Should have been winning in the overall category as he had in his twenties and thirties. Nothing about his muscle definition had changed as far as he could tell. It was just his face, the signs of gravity at work, the receding hairline, the thinning widow's peak. He looked down at his legs and saw how beautiful they were, how they looked carved from oak.

Mr. Minneapolis Thighs.

He had smiled and said thank you but had wanted to take the little trophy with its gold-painted pair of thighs and beat them over the head with it, those judges. Once they knew a man's age, that was all they saw.

He swiped deodorant over his armpits and slapped Old Spice on his cheeks. Combed his hair until it lay flat wet shiny, the scalp showing trails of pink on top. Time for a transplant? A dye job? Gray hairs coming in on the sides near the temples. More gray at the roots where the hair wedged. There had been gray hairs on his chest the other day, but he had plucked them out. There were even some gray hairs on his balls. He had taken scissors and cut them close and his balls had been itching ever since.

He closed one eye, squinted the other, and the lines in his forehead, temples and cheeks deepened. He had to remember not to smile too hard, because that's when the lines came. He practiced smiling with his mouth, keeping his facial muscles relaxed, but it was hard to do. He stared and stared, wishing the lines and the ugly pores away. Then he thought of Livia Miles and he didn't feel so bad. Her face hung on her like moss, her lips sinking inward like an imploding asshole. Everything deteriorating. She would be dead before long. Leaving this for where? Rot and worms.

Sometimes the old girl remembered the promises he had made when they were boozing buddies. He could tell she was remembering he promised to take care of her, promised she would always have a home with him and Joy. But those promises were made when she was well, when she had "faculties." How in the world could anyone deal with such an old nitwit, a brain-shrunk dope? Hopeless, hopeless. There was nothing you could say or do. She was a drunk, a drooler, a bedwetter, a bag of skin and permeable bones and not the person the Root had promised to care for in her old age when it seemed like she would be a feisty-fun broad. He had made promises to that one, the fun one, not the nitwit one.

He wished she would do the decent thing and die. That was what he would do if it were him going downhill like that. Yes, he would spare everyone the disgusting process of it, the memory of who you were versus the thing you became. She had no decency, self-obsessed old tart. Never seen what she put her kids through neither. Blind to what she had done. Her son Hal goes off and drowns himself in the ocean, was that an accident? Or was that from too many blows to the head from Nikos Pape? Joy's breakdowns were because of her, all those men she brought into the house, and that perverted motherfucker diddling Joy, and Livia oblivious to it all? How could a mother not know? What the hell, wasn't she paying attention? What kind of mother was that?

Musing on Livia, he predicted that the old lady would give Joy another breakdown soon, same as when Joy put her in the home and she had carried on about it, bawling like a two-year-old and accusing Joy of abandonment. No more wandering, no more roaming, Livia had phoned six times a day to give her daughter hell. *Come get me, Booboo, come get me, goddammit. Don't abandon me. There's nothing but* old ladies *here.*

He saw Joy curled on the bed, unable to eat, unable to take care of herself, saying to him, *What have I done to my mom?*

He shook his head, Livia's image pattering around him like drops of sweat. People had to go on, that's what they had to do, and not dwell on all the shitten excrement life threw at you. He saw himself over the hole again, his three-year-old legs treading air, his mother's face full of hatred and madness, her hands shaking him, rattling his brain, trying to make him let go of her. Trying to bury him.

Buck cleared his throat and spit in the toilet bowl. "Shitten excrement of life," he grumbled. He made a muscle in the mirror to comfort himself. "No bitch drop this bad boy in no fuckin hole," he said. "Got to go on! Get it behind you, man." His ex-wife Patsy had gone on in the end, gotten on with her life without him. Sad-lipped little thing. He had thought she might die after he left her. She *had* gotten sick and had said, *What am I living for now?* and said she was going to kill herself, but she didn't. He had felt bad about her during those first months. But she recovered. She moved on. And she found that he wasn't vital to her after all. In fact, it seemed that she had gotten over the Root awfully fast, once she decided to. It had sort of hurt his feelings, her going out with boyfriends, going on trips to San Francisco and Branson, getting out and really doing things. And she told people she had never been so relaxed and happy in her life and she wondered how she had put up with him for so long. She hadn't realized what a bad habit he was or how much anxiety there was in having him around.

"The nature of a woman's love," he told the mirror. "It's never forever like they say it is. Better off without them. Love them and leave them, Bucky-boy." And he sang:

Oh, Bucky-boy, the girls, the girls are ca-all-ing
But let them go, before they break your balls.

But then some days he did miss her. Yes. Missed her a lot. And he would tell himself: *I still love that girl.* He would have been safe with her. He hadn't felt safe since he left her. Had kept his body a sheath of steel, but didn't feel safe inside it. She wasn't as glamorous and sexy as Joy, but she was steady and a fine, gentle human being and more and more often he wondered if he had done the right thing in leaving her. He wondered if leaving her had started the beginning of the end for him. Things hadn't gone well. All his dreams and Joy's dreams had come to nothing in the middle of Nowhere, Minnesota, stuck with Mr. Boring To The Bone. How did cousin George stand it? What was he living for?

Panic stirred in Buck's belly. He had a sense that this was it, that he would never go farther, that the glory days were over and he would end up like his cousin, just putting one foot in front of the other, no future plans, no sense of destiny. Sit and smoke a pipe and read a book. Watch some TV. Have a beer. Take a shower. Go to bed alone and lonely. Get up and start all over again. Lonesome George had that look about him, no kind of promise, no prospects, no expectations for tomorrow. Buck knew he could never stand it.

"Brrr, I couldn't live the way he does. It'd kill me."

He got his Elavil from the medicine cabinet, swallowed two with water and put the bottle back. He stroked his arm, caressed it, squeezed it and thought of Joy's breasts, how fun they were to play with since she'd put the implants in.

"I still got it, baby," he had told her. "And when I don't, I'll be a writer. I'll write about my adventures. They'll say of me, *Buck Root wrote from his heart and his vast experiences and he told the damndess truth anybody ever told.* That will be a blurb on the back of my book, and they'll say I flashed like lightning across the sky, a brilliant blaze who came and went. Buck Root was wondered at, pointed out. One of the immortals. Centuries will pass and the world will still be in awe and they'll be saying, *Remember Buck Root? Buck Root, oh yeah, wasn't he something, wasn't he incredible?*

If only they would remember him, say his name once in a while, that's all he was asking.

~

HE LAID OUT black slacks, a black cashmere pullover that would mold itself to his torso, a pair of black Italian loafers, down at the heel but shiny on top and tasseled. He dressed himself from the bottom up. He pulled black socks over his feet and up around his muscular calves snug. The slacks were next. They were tight the way girls liked them. He turned sideways and could see in the mirror how hard and rounded his ass was. He tightened one cheek, then the other and went back and forth jiggling each cheek, watching his back pockets keeping time with a tune he made up on the spot:

> *Bucky, Bucky, I've been thinking*
> *what a fine world this would be*
> *if the girls were all deflowered*
> *by ole rootin-tootin me.*

Women liked a hard ass on a man, small-curved-chewable. He pushed the sleeves up on his sweater, then reached down and scooted his balls into place. Looking at his groin, he could see the lump on the inside leg of his trousers. Women's eyes straying to that lump, unconsciously licking their lips.

I, George

HOVERING SMOKE SHIFTS as a waitress walks by, the smoke following her like an urge in motion. The jukebox plays "Suzie Q," and it makes me think of *Apocalypse Now* and how the cowgirl in robin-egg blue danced for the soldiers and they all went crazy and chased her into a helicopter, her with a tiny ass that would fit in the palm of your hand. Old movie now, but it had something about it, something bitter and ironic and unbearably true. She probably has Hottentot hips now and grownup kids and breasts as flat as fry pans. Maybe she weeps at the reruns, when she sees her petite-sweet-self twitching to the beat of "Suzie Q."

The music stops and starts again and I see Connie making her moves. I see Buck watching her, his heavy eyes at half-mast. If I had Joy sitting at home waiting for me, I wouldn't be looking at Connie.

When her dance ends, she comes over and slides into the booth with us and I introduce her to Buck and they start talking and he tells her that he's been in movies, lived in Hollywood.

"You know Bruce Willis?" she asks. "He is so cool."

"Bruce Willis, yeah, him and me go way back, and Hulk Hogan and Arnold Schwarzenegger and the Italian Stallion. Let me tell you the truth, I gave him that name. Yeah, he got it from me."

"What name? Who?"

"The Italian Stallion, it was my name, that's what they all called me around The Wood, 'Here comes the Italian Stallion,' they'd say." Buck nonchalantly pokes a finger at his chest. "And then one day Sly says to me, he says, 'I wish I had thought of that first.' 'Thought of what?' I say. 'That Italian Stallion they call you.' 'You like it, you can have it,' I say. He didn't believe me, but I told him I never bullshit a friend. 'You really mean I can have it?' he says. 'It's yours,' I tell him. And that's why you and everybody knows him as the Italian Stallion."

"Is that really true?" says Connie.

"Does a bear shit in the woods?" says Buck. "Will a duck float? Does a skunk s*tunk?*"

She chortles like a scatterbrained girl and says, "Yhah."

"I wouldn't shit you, Connie. There are a million Hollywood tales in here." He taps his temple. "Christ, I've been everywhere, done everything. My life would fill a book the size of . . ." Buck pauses, his brows furrowing.

"*War and Peace?*" I offer.

"*War and Peace*, that's right."

He says that he is famous in Las Vegas and most metropolitan centers, and, ticking his titles off on his fingers, he says that he won Mr. Los Angeles, Mr. Philadelphia, Mr. Chicago, Mr. Mount Olympus, Mr. Baja Peninsula.

"Geeez," breathes Connie.

"And he won Mr. Thighs in Minneapolis," I add.

Connie says, "I bet he did." She has a throaty voice, every word ending in a sigh. I'm sure her voice and her smile and the look in her eyes are familiar to Buck. He gives her the same look back. Buck told me earlier that he had had Body Shop types a million times, married or unmarried, old or young, Christian, Jew, heathen, whore—

I wonder why he never fears it, the look women give him, the way it gets his blood going, the hopes they must have of him in bed. I could never take that kind of pressure. I'd never be able to live up to a body like his, the way it advertises itself, the way it raises expectations. He told me that women were all the same brains—but different elsewhere: no two were exactly alike in bed, no two tits, no cunts, no kisses. Hundreds of women he's had, and each one unique in *some peculiar way*. He wondered what it would be with the next one, what *speciality* would she have, what lovely where, what place in her clinging to him like a rubber band? And he sang—

> *I'm the man for sat-tis-fac-tion,*
> *The one who owns the main attraction*
> *Oh, it always gets reaction*
> *From the girls with giddy hair.*

"You know that one, 'Giddy Hair'?" he asked.

"It's a familiar tune," I told him.

"The good ones never go away," he said.

~

WHEN HER TURN COMES AGAIN, she goes onstage and her eyes keep slipping toward Buck as she make her moves. She smiles for him and he leans over to tell me that she has been playing with his leg under the table, "The tart." He grins and smells his finger and says, "I know where this is going later tonight."

Topless, Connie wears a black thong. She moves her hips to the music. Her breasts swing. Her hair sweeps back and forth over her shoulders. Her hair is different tonight, not black, but light brown, streaked with blond.

"What makes us do what we do? You ever figure that out?" says Buck. "How come I've got no control when it comes to tarts like that?"

I shrug.

He is quiet, his eyes following Connie. Then he says, "I always catch myself thinking like that. What makes me need a pussy? Can't be me, can it? You know what I'm saying, George? George, you're not listening."

"It's your nature, Buck," I tell him.

"My nature, that's right."

"You are what you are."

"I yam what I yam and that's all that I yam. Maybe I've got a split personality," he says. "Sometimes I think so. I always thought it would be great to be two people, be Mike Routelli and Buck Root both. Hey, be the guy everybody wanted you to be and there he is all tucked up nice and neat and predictable for his wife and kids; and then be this other guy too, the one that went off and lived whatever he felt like living. Wild motherfucker to the max."

"I've never wanted to be two," I tell him. "I can't hardly handle being one." I lift the pitcher and pour more beer. We shift our attention back to the stage.

"So what's the story with that little gap-tooth tart?" Buck asks.

"Connie? She's a farm girl. She owns a farm near Elk River."

"Owns a farm?"

"Her parents left it to her. They died in a car accident about two years ago." I watch Connie work. "All those chores, you can see it in her body. Look how strong she is." I sip beer and feel woozy and I say, "Damn if I ain't getting drunk again."

"I'm a bad influence," says Buck. "People always follow my lead. She will. She'll end up doing anything I say." He points at Connie.

"Con's okay," I say. I start digging at a callus on my palm, peeling off a layer. Buck has no calluses. He has large, soft, woman-caressing palms. "She's got a heart big as a barn. You need twenty bucks or somethin, Connie will give it to you. You need a place to sleep, she'll fix you up in her van. She's a good gal."

"A good gal," Buck says. "I know all about good gals."

"But you don't want to get her mad," I continue. "Man, she laid a guy out one night, you should'a seen it. She flattened him." I uppercut the air with my fist and explain how Connie put her knee right in the guy's face, how he was trying to drill her with his finger up the backside, and she whirled around and gave him one. "Pow! on the button and he went over in the chair, bleeding out his nose. They threw his ass outta here, Joe Cuff and Ronnie threw him out."

"She's tough, huh?" Buck says. "I wouldn't mind a macho woman. She'd be wanting me to take charge and conquer her. Lots of boom boom in bed to see who's boss." He looks at Connie moving and grooving. "What a body. Those are natural tits, you can tell. Look at that pussy pooch on her, begging for someone to nibble. 'I'm so sexy,' it says. Jesus, she's makin me—"

"Joy sure is fine," I interrupt. "So graceful the way she walks. Her feet prance like a pony. Like a dainty pony."

"I tell you what, she could dance circles around these tarts," says Buck. "These are nothin to her. Joy's a hell of a dancer, George. She's a pro."

"She want a job?" I ask. "Ronnie's hiring. He'd give her a job, I'm sure."

Buck says she might and I tell him to bring her by, let Ronnie take a look. "There are never enough girls with real talent, Ronnie says. Bump, bump, that's all most of them know, that's what Ronnie says, bump, bump. And they're always running off with some guy."

Buck winks at me as he reaches over and gives me a nudge and tells me that he knows women as well as he knows his own sweet cock. "Cock and load," he says, smiling sloppy. "Buck Root's never met a woman he couldn't have. No brag, just fact. Women go off around me. Doesn't matter if they're married or

old or young or what, they go off. They lose all sense of proportion, you understand what I'm sayin?"

I suppress a yawn and look away, hoping he'll talk about
something else, but then he gets my attention by telling me he
made love to a nun.

"A nun, no way," I answer.

He raises his palm vertical. "I swear it's true, a *boner-fidee*
nun. No virgin, mind you, but a nun nonetheless. Had the habit
on, the hood and the whole bit. I ain't lyin. If I'm lying, may my
cock lose its cunning."

"How the hell? Where'd you meet her?"

"Easy as pie. I met her on an airplane going home to visit her
family for Christmas and she missed her connection in Denver
and had to *lay* over till the next day. I got her to have dinner with
me and after wine and oysters, she went docile as a puppy and I
take her to a motel and she's putty in my hands. I'm over her, see,
and the hammer is heavy, man, heavy in her face, and you know
what she says? She says, 'The Lord has risen.' I'm telling you the
God's truth here, George. May my cock lose its cunning."

I explode with laughter.

"The Lord has risen, the Lord has risen," Buck reiterates.

"I gotta tell Ronnie," I say.

I go to the bar and repeat Buck's story and Ronnie wheezes
with laughter, his beard trembling. He makes a wicked face and
does a Spooner on the last line, "The *R*ord has *L*isen!" He gives
Buck a thumbs-up.

I talk to him about Joy and he says to have her come by. He
sends me back with a free pitcher of beer.

"Ronnie says to bring Joy in and have her dance for him," I
tell Buck.

"That'll be fine," says Buck. He runs a finger over his knuckles. "I have an itch to slug somebody," he says. His eyes are nar-

row. His jaw muscles flex. "You ever heard of ultimate fighting, where men are put in a cage and there are no rules except you can't bite? Did I tell you I'm heavyweight champ of California?" Buck shows me his fist. His left eyebrow arches like a tiny boomerang. I search his face for battle scars and consider if he has really done any ultimate fighting in a cage.

Maybe he has, who knows?

"I know when someone is overwhelmed by my exploits," he says, staring at me. "I'm larger than life in your eyes. But that's not true, really. I'm not larger than life, George, but one more layer of skin and I would be. No brag, just fact."

Then he asks if Ronnie needs a bouncer. "I've been a bouncer in lots of joints, dealt with lots of bums and broads. Does that sound like Mickey Spillane? She was a dame with the kind of curves that could stop traffic. Ever read any of his books, George?"

"One or two."

"Pulp fiction. I could do as well as him. I could crank out stories and publish them. I bet I could."

"Joy said you were a poet."

"I can do anything I set my mind to."

"I believe you."

The conversation lags. We watch a girl grinding it out. Men are pushing bills at her.

"How's your hammer hangin?" says Buck. "Been gettin any lately?"

I try to look crafty.

"Good for you," Buck says. "Hey, lissen, you want a woman? Learn some poetry. You memorize poetry, I guarantee you'll get laid."

"I know a poem," I say. I clear my throat, waiting for the words. "Wait a minute, wait a second. Shit, give me a few drinks and my mind turns to curdled milk. *Though we cannot make our sun stand still, we can make him run.* Something like that. 'To His Coy Mistress,' that's the name of it."

Buck pokes me. "You're a funny little bugger," he says. "But listen, I'm serious. Verse is an aphrodisiac. We get home, I'll write you some."

I shake my head. "I do fine without verse," I tell him.

Joy Faust

IN THE EVENING, Livia woke from a nap and said, "You like them, Booboo?"

"They're wonderful," Joy told her. She had been pulling them from the closet, lining them up along the bedroom wall.

"Look at this, Mom." She pointed at a woman leaping (legs doing splits) off a giant tongue. Below her was a round-headed monolith.

"Ooo-la-la," said Livia. She pulled out her Western, plumped her pillow and got comfortable. "I'll read to you, Booboo, if you want. Cody Larsen. Member him?"

"I remember," answered Joy. She eyed Cody on the cover, the gun half out of its holster. The image made her think of the time that Livia tried to kill Nikos Pape. Livia furious, the gun jumping each time she pulled the trigger, filling the air with *pop! pop! pop!*, while *he,* Nikos, ran for his life, pounding the earth like an ostrich, his feet creating dirt puffs one after the other hanging over the road.

Joy had confessed to a priest, *Bless me, Father, for I have been impure with my stepfather.* The priest had ordered her to say a Rosary and go home and tell her mother.

When Livia heard what Nikos had done, she cried, *He's touched you? He's touched you? He's touched you?*

When he came home, she was waiting for him with the gun,

the little twenty-five automatic that he himself had put in the nightstand. Joy saw the grin of terror on his face and how his eyes bulged and his upper lip quivered. It made her feel strangely sorry for him, that he couldn't keep his cool—Mr. Bad Nikos Pape, looking like anyone would who was about to die. His face had turned the color of Muenster cheese, and he had run out the door, Livia chasing him, firing as she ran. The gun popping, the bullets vanishing.

He got away.

And Livia had come back and pointed the gun at Joy standing in the road, and the two of them had stayed several heartbeats staring at each other. And then Livia had grumbled, "Goddamn you, kid. Don't tell me you didn't know better. Don't tell me you didn't know what you were doing."

Joy had tried to speak, had tried to explain the fear that had frozen her. *I should've told you*, she had wanted to say. *But he said it would kill you, so I didn't.* In light of what she had seen her mother do, Joy's excuse had felt contemptible to her. She had opened her mouth but the words wouldn't come and she never then, or ever, tried to explain herself.

"It's the good part," Livia said, flipping the pages of the book. "You wanna hear?"

"Yes, I wanna hear, Mom."

Her mouth moved meticulously, the words coming one by one forced into sound, telling how Old Paint was leaking lather and how the harsh wind blew the lather over Cody's face. Cody hunching down, his head beside Old Paint's neck, urging the horse over Pecos Pass, while the posse stormed behind them, the bullets flying past Cody, missing him by inches.

"Ain't it somepin, Booboo? Don't it give you shivers?"

"Yes it does, Mom." Joy put another painting in the row against the wall. She marked it in the steno pad as:

Painting 44: Woman Womb-Ballooned.

"Jeff Chaw's the best," said Livia. "Nobody gets me like Chaw."

Joy went to her, leaned over and kissed her on top of the head, and said, "I'm so glad you're having a good night, Mom."

"I always have good nights!" she answered. She continued reading, her lips smacking:

. . . was losing blood steadily from the arrow wounds in his left shoulder and arm, and the vicious wounds jolting him with pain with every galloping thrust of the exhausted horse over the snow-covered ground. There was nothing to do but run. Cody couldn't fire back. He was weak and dizzy and needed all the strength of his right arm just to keep astride Old Paint.

The Pecos River came into view, three times its usual size, swollen and running wild with melted snow. Cody figured he would plunge into the icy river and he and Old Paint would ride it downstream and maybe elude the posse that way.

But Old Paint wasn't meant to reach the swollen Pecos. A bullet meant for Cody caught Old Paint in the rump and he stumbled and slowed and shifted sideways. He tried to keep going, but another bullet blew a hole in his belly. He turned, stumbling and screaming. Then the coup de grace hit him in the head and dropped him instantly. Old Paint tumbled once, like grain in a gunnysack, and Cody went flying off, somersaulting through snow-dusted brush and earth.

The old lady had her good days and her bad days. It had been a good day all along, nothing outrageous and painful to witness, no wearing of layered clothes with afghan shawl in ninety-degree heat, no eating the hard cores of lettuce, no stripes with checks, her bra on backwards, her sweater inside out, one blue shoe, one black shoe, no pretending to know places she had never been, no forgetting Buck's name or her own age and what year it was, who was president, and—

Sometimes Joy couldn't bear it. It made her sick with fear and filled her with anger too, that she was in charge of her mother's life. Joy recalled one of her mother's posters, framed behind glass and hanging on various walls in various houses where they had lived in the early years of Livia's restless wandering:

GOD WON'T GIVE
ME ANYTHING
I CAN'T HANDLE

"I don't know," said Joy, feeling the tic in her jaw. Sometimes she thought about giving the old lady chocolate-covered cherries and Pepsi mixed with whiskey, keep her deliriously drunk and fed on Xanax one by one until her heart got too sleepy to beat. Letting her ease out of this life, go with a shred of dignity left. Instead of what it was bound to be: tied to a bed, babbling, soiling herself and guess-who cleaning up after her. Something she would not have wanted. She had told Joy years ago when they were discussing old age and senility and diseased bodies gone past the point of no return, she had said, "Just shoot me, hon. Let me go if I ever get that bad. You promise?" And Joy had promised to shoot her. But it was not so easy to shoot your mother. Easy to say you would, but immensely difficult to do— make the body obey what the mind reasonably approved. The responsibility was wearing her out, making her heart dither. She had awakened nights gasping for air and in tears. She had had similar symptoms as a teenager concealing her sins. "Panic attacks," a doctor had told her. He had given her drugs and they had made her not give a damn about anything.

"You listening, Booboo?"

"Yes, Mummy."

She saw gallant Cody leap in the river and tumble over the waterfall and plummet through space, then smacking the water hard, driven under so far he touched boulders on the bottom, bending his legs and thrusting upward with all his might and rising gasping to the surface as the current carried him toward a sharp bend and a pile of driftwood, where he hid himself, his arm draped over a log, sustaining his battered head out of water, his lungs heaving.

Joy took a Kleenex to the spit gathered in the corner of her mother's mouth, pushed brittle hairs out of her eye. The roots were white again. Would she notice if her hair were allowed to go white? Would she notice if she wasn't a redhead anymore? She had been proud of being a redhead, proud that men called her Red and called her Irish and said she had an Irish temper. Livia could outwork, outplay any woman half her age. Invincible. A woman who seemed destined never to die. Joy couldn't imagine it, her mother's death. She had left six husbands in her wake. Six, and never looked back. Would no doubt find a seventh if she could.

Joy assessed the Sissy McLeod paintings she had labeled. All the women in the paintings had what looked to be hooves instead of hands or feet. Scooped hooves like sick cows have, or maybe they were warped frog feet or duck feet, Joy didn't know for sure. She looked at her hands. They were large and smooth, the nails scarlet, nothing hoofy about them. Then she looked at Livia's hands, withered and mapped with veins. Her mother's hands sickened Joy. The years would turn over and there was no escaping what the hands would say.

Livia's mouth kept moving, the words still potent coming from her mouth even though her tongue often stumbled. Joy reached over, wiped again the glistening tucks of her mother's lips telling of time passing in the dark, where Cody floats inside the logjam, delirious and imagining that White Dove is waving to him, telling him to come to her, come to her waiting arms and motherly bosom and her soft ebony hair. Come, Cody, come.

"I gotta stop. My voice hurts."

"You rest," Joy told her.

"Ain't Cody somepin?" Her eyes stayed on Joy, watching as she shuffled the paintings and wrote numbers and words on the steno pad. "Cody's my man," Livia said.

Joy went to her and took her chin and said, "You just watch now, Mom. I've got a feeling about these paintings. These paintings are why we're here. So I could discover them, a thrilling artist. A woman ahead of her time brought out of the closet into the public eye because of me. Think of the painstaking work, the thousands of tiny dots and paint strokes she put down day after day to make these images. Every dot a heartbeat. Every stroke a pinch of her soul. Wait till the right people see these, just wait!" Joy felt a whisper of cool air pass over her brow. She closed her eyes and waited to feel more. "I feel her spirit in the room, don't you, Mom? Can you feel her here? I think I feel her, I really do."

Livia's eyes flickered like film on a screen. Her mouth was open, waiting to receive.

I, George

PAST MIDNIGHT, I am finally able to get the weightlifter out of the booth. At the time Connie is dancing close to a guy who is feeding her bills, and that pisses the weightlifter off, and he says, "Puttin her mangos right in that motherfucker's face!" And I tell him he's got better stuff waiting at home and he agrees and we leave.

In the car, he drapes his arm over my shoulders and calls me a real pal. And he says, "I can't resist nothin but temptation, you know who said that, George?"

"Nope."

"The only way to resist temptation is to give in to it."

"That's true too," I tell him.

"I really like you," he says, and kisses my cheek.

"I like you too, Buck." I'm wishing he'd move over a bit, he's crowding my driving.

"You understand what I'm sayin, George?"

"I'm with you, man."

"You like me?"

"Hey, what's not to like?"

"You humorin me? You don't hate me? Some people hate me, you know. Yeah, it's hard to believe, but some people do."

"I like you, Buck. I really do."

"That's right, by gawd, what's not to like!"

"Everybody should love the Root," I say and he laughs.

I make my way carefully up 55 past Golden Valley to Medicine Lake and turn down Evergreen Lane and the safety of the trees and the slow road. In a minute I see the apartments lit up and I pull in behind the Lincoln. As we get out of the car, we hear music coming from inside the building. On the window shade is a swaying silhouette, a woman's slender body.

"Rites of spring," says the weightlifter.

"A bit loud," I say.

When we get inside we see Joy dancing and Livia is coaxing her, saying, "Shake that thing, naughty bish!"

Joy is swaying. She wears pink matching panties and a bra.

I watch her, comparing her to Connie, her body, her dancing. Joy is the better dancer: loose arms, hips fluid, more graceful than Connie, more synchronized to the beat: more professional somehow.

I hate to turn the music down and stop her, but I have to think of the tenants. I go to the stereo and ease the volume. Joy stops dancing. Her body is shiny, her stomach heaving, showing ribs and smooth-toned muscle.

"We've been having the best time!" she says.

"I see," I say.

"My boomer can dance!" says Livia. "I taught her. It's a mother thing, mothers are special. I told her, 'Listen to your heart,' that's what I told her. Right, Booboo?"

"About a million times."

Joy throws herself on the couch, her knee up, her wrist over her forehead. "I wanted to be a dancer so bad when I was little," she says. "Mom got me ballet lessons, but after a couple years we ran out of money and I had to quit. But I kept practicing and Mom showed me all she knew. We love dancing more than anything, don't we, Mom."

"Born to dance!" shouts Livia.

"Joy danced in Vegas," says the weightlifter.

"I danced at a place called *Les Girls* first. It was good money, full of high-rollers, the tips phenomenal. I rode a mechanical bull in my act. And then I danced at The Sands. That was the best."

The weightlifter is sitting in the recliner, staring at Joy. He has her skirt. He is twisting it. He smells it. He tells Joy he has worked it out with cousin Ronnie and she is going to start dancing for him if he likes what he sees.

"I've had enough of dancing in dives," she says.

"It's what you do!"

"But I don't want to," she says. "I'm better than that."

The weightlifter has an exasperated brow. "She wants fetters . . . scuse me, feathers and frills. She wants to pretend she's still Las Vegas at The Sands. Hay's for horses, I can't get it through her thick skull." He glares at Joy. "You forty, dumbshit."

"Thirty-nine!" she says.

"You were never good enough noway anyhow," he says. "Hay's for horses, she never got out the chorus line. Anybody can do the cancan."

"Gee, thanks a lot," says Joy.

I stay silent. I want them to go to bed. I can hardly keep my head up. I look at the dog sleeping curled under the coffee table. *Only one with sense,* I tell myself.

"Hay's for . . . tell her about The Body Shop," says Buck.

"Good joint," I tell her.

"Tell her about it."

"First-class joint."

"There. Cousin George don't lie."

Joy's face is skeptical, but she doesn't say anything.

"We gotta have income, sweetness, till my enterprises take off. Until Nova Life gets going. Until I get my bisness ventures solvent. Hey, c'mon, you know that."

"I know," she says.

"The Body Shop is upscale. Uh-huh, I'll tell you what, you've danced in way worse. *Les Girls* for one."

"*Les Girls* got me started. Made me a pro. I'm never gonna put it down."

"You've danced in shitholes, sweetness, and this is no shithole, and look here, you just said how you love dancin."

"Yeah," she says.

"I'll take you there and look it over. You don't like it, you don't hafta. Next weekend is amateur song night. George, tell her." The weightlifter burps into his fist. Pushes forward in the chair and burps again.

"That's right," I say.

"Ugh . . . get me them Rolaids, sweetness."

Joy gets up, goes to her purse, tosses him a roll.

I explain about amateur song night: "Ronnie does a karaoke thing. You make up lyrics to karaoke music and the best X-rated song gets a hundred dollars and all the beer you can drink. It brings them from all over to compete."

"X-rated songs?" asks Joy.

"Yhah."

"Sexy songs?"

"Sexy songs, sure."

"I'll enter it," says the weightlifter. " 'Lil Of The Golden West.' I'm not kiddin."

Joy brightens up. "You gonna do Lil?" she says. "Oh gawd, honey, not Lil."

"It'll kill em." The weightlifter laughs and pounds his knee and a fine Rolaid dust drifts from his mouth.

"He can sing Hank Williams to the life," says Joy. "You remember Hank Williams way back when, what? the fifties? sixties?"

"*Your cheatin heart . . . will tell on you . . .*" Buck croons. And he does sound like Hank Williams, all nasal twang and whine, but at a somewhat lower register.

I'm glad to have everybody happy again. I have noticed that Buck sets the tone for Joy. If he is in a good mood, Joy is in a good mood. If he is depressed, Joy is depressed. Whatever vibes he throws off, Joy absorbs them.

I say to her, "You want me to turn the music up? I don't care. You wanna dance, Joy? C'mon . . . dance." I turn the volume up, but not as loud as it was.

"He don't like my Hank Williams," says Buck.

She dances. I get the White Horse and pour everybody a drink, then sit with the bottle on my lap, keeping my eyes glued to Joy. She loses herself in the music. The beat of the drums is the beat of her feet on the floor. The rhythm of guitars is the rhythm of her legs strumming, her backside swaying. Her pink panties turn translucent with sweat.

We drink the bottle gone and Joy never stops dancing. An hour later as she still undulates in the center of the room, the weightlifter rises from the chair, picks her up and carries her off.

I'm eyeing Livia. She is glum. Her head unsteady.

She mumbles something, gets up, weaves toward the door, then stops and says, "Used to be me makin bisness. Used to be me. Use it while you can, Cody. Get on that pony and ride. When the fire goes out, it don't get lit no more."

I follow her into the bedroom to get my blanket and pillow and it startles me to see my mother's paintings out of the closet, lined up in rows under the *Nude Descending*.

In my mind's eye I see Mama hunched in the chair dabbing at the canvas, her wrist scarcely wider than the brush itself. A scooped hoof appears. She dabs it into life with a thousand perfect dots.

I flip through the paintings, then raise my eyes to the

jagged nude on the wall. She did not paint like Duchamp. She painted like nobody else. Beside me on the dresser is a steno pad filled with numbers and titles. One says, 36: Woman as Geometric Star. Another says, 37: Woman as Pinwheel Fire.

Livia is already asleep, a soft whistle coming from her nose. I stand over her a moment, listening to her and listening to the noise of Buck and Joy thrashing in the other room.

I wish I could wave a wand and bring Livia back to what she was. I picture Connie Hawkins in her black thong, that space of pale flesh, her galloping ass poking out bare, her shoulders wriggling. I picture Joy Faust in pink underpants, the dark pubic patch shadow, the graceful moves. I think of Livia all sexy in youth and men fighting over her like angry gophers.

"Livia," I whisper. "Elf," I say, stroking her hair. "Tired old elf."

I pick up the paperback book on the nightstand and read a scene:

. . . had to push the arrow through his shoulder, while Cody bit on the knotted rag and almost fainted. The point broke the skin and Lily pulled it out, and she said, "There, that's the worst of it. It's over. I'll bandage you up now and you can get some rest."

"I'm obliged to you," said Cody. He groaned, his eyes shutting tightly as he felt every inch of his arm on fire. Through chattering teeth he told Lily that he couldn't thank her enough, "Can't thank you enough for being kind to a stranger falling on your doorstep with arrows sticking out of him like a porcupine. I know I'm a sight. Must've scared the bejesus outta you."

"You live out here, you gotta be ready for anything," Lily said.

Getting the blanket and pillow from the chest, I go back to the couch and undress and lie down and pull the blanket over me and listen to the sounds of night—a cricket in the wall, wind purring through the pine out front, the curtain billowing softly in front of the window—and I see Livia and a time when her bed is empty. The vanishing takes just a moment and the little chorus goes on, the nightlife in its multitudes chirping and buzzing and whirring as if nothing is happening. Across Medicine Lake I hear a plaintive loon.

"It'll be over before you know it," I whisper. I hear the sex starting up again, the wall thrumming, Joy's chirps and bleats in rhythm—faint, muffled, needy: affliction cloaked in bliss.

There is a scratching at my elbow and I see the dog on his hind legs, looking at me, lamplight reflecting in his glossy round eyes. The dog's tail is wagging with hope. He scratches at me again and says, *Can I? Huh, can I?*

"All right," I say, lifting him, placing him between my knees, "but keep your breath south."

The dog yawns and it makes me yawn. I put out the light and lie there thinking about something Buck told me just before we left The Body Shop.

"She smothered her baby," is what he said. "Shhh, don't tell," and he made a gesture like smashing something on his chest and said, "Shh, don't let her know you know. She shows that picture. You seen that picture, George."

"Yhah, and the letters too," is what I answered.

And he said, "*What* letters?"

"She showed me some letters."

"She's never showed *me* any letters."

"In a cigar box. I read some. They were definitely written by a kid."

Buck had been puzzled by the letters and he said he had

never seen any and he wondered what was going on. And then he said maybe she was writing letters to herself.

"Added a new twist," he decided.

I asked him if he really meant it, that she had smothered her kid, and he replied that *maybe* it was so, but nothing about it is known for sure. And he explained that her story was that she nursed the baby early one morning and fell asleep and when she woke up it was dead under her boob.

A nervous breakdown followed.

"She thinks God is after her," he told me. And he said, "I didn't even know it at the time, but she had already fallen in love with me when she was pregnant. She was already scheming how to get us together. After she gave birth she started working out where I worked out and I noticed her and how she was always there when I was there. She timed it that way that we would be together like that. This went on for a while and she's looking good. And one day she asks me to spot her on the bench, so I spot her and she does some reps and then she asks me if I'd like to celebrate her birthday with her. I was still married then, but she was married too, so what the hell, I took her out on her birthday and the rest is history. Baby's death is a sacrifice to our love. I didn't ask for it. I was minding my own business and I shouldn't be blamed, but sometimes I feel to blame. I feel like I'm shackled to her. Like I couldn't get away if I wanted to. I don't like how that works. Sometimes I say, 'Man, just get the hell away from her before she smothers you too, Buck Root.' That's what I tell myself. It's a temptation every day to just fuckin leave before it's too late, before she buries me in her hole of Calcutta. Women got holes of Calcutta, George."

And he said that Joy wasn't mother material. Not motherly mother in the way of the mother who makes Thanksgiving a holiday. He said some are and some *ain't* and definitely his own mother should never have had him. "Motherhood isn't just because you're female. Motherhood is an art," he told me.

"An instinct," I offered.

"That's right, an instinct. A mother with instincts is not going to roll over and smother her baby is she? Or drop him in a hole is she? Take my word for it. Things I know you don't want to know." Left eyebrow frozen in its omniscient arch, he had glared at Connie doing pelvic thrusts at the edge of the stage. "Hey, I guarantee you that that young *thang* is not mother material. She's the kind. She's when you know somethin's *gunna* happen."

Then he embellished the story about Joy. And he said that she told her husband it was crib death killed the baby. She put the kid back in the crib and called her husband at work and said their daughter was dead in the crib.

"I'm the only one who knows the truth," he added. And he said that Joy was given to telling tall tales, exaggerating for effect, and a man never knew when he was hearing the truth from her, so maybe it was crib death, maybe not.

I didn't understand the point of her saying she smothered her own baby if it had really died a crib death, but he said that smothering was more dramatic. Joy was a self-dramatizing woman and she knew how to manipulate a man, how to play with his heart, how to get the maximum sympathy from him. Smothering your infant was far more traumatic than crib death. Buck said he had cried when she told him about the smothering. They had both cried about it and she said she loved him all the more because of his tears.

"I'm more sensitive than anybody understands or gives me credit," he had added. "I'm not just a big old stupid jerk like some people think."

I had wanted to know who the girl on the dresser was, the cute thing in curls that looked like a model. "Who's she?"

Buck's answer had been that Joy bought her picture at a garage sale. Had said her daughter would have looked like that, little Joyce at that age would've looked the same.

"But who is she really, that kid? Who the hell knows, George? Nobody knows. Not Joy for sure. Not me."

Joy Faust

SHE SAT AT THE BAR wearing a tight red skirt and a silky red blouse with billowing sleeves. She had a cigarette in her hand and a vodka-rocks in front of her. She was looking at herself in the mirror behind the bar, seeing ambiguity there, hair teased into platinum spikiness, false eyelashes making shadows over her cheeks. An uncertain mouth, half pout half pucker.

She shifted her gaze to an aluminum oven for readymade sandwiches and a list of what was available—pastrami, salami, hot dogs, polish dogs, pepper beef, meatball with melted mozzarella. There were stacks of potato chips, pretzels, Fritos on a rack, mixed nuts in a can. Over the polished surface of the bar, she saw ashtrays cradling cigarettes, saw dented packs of Camels, Salems, Marlboros, saw coins and bills and amber drinks, clear-eyed vodkas, beer in mugs. Climbing the back wall were shelves loaded with bottles and glasses of various sizes forming crystal pyramids. A cash register anchored itself in the center. Over the cash register hung a blue neon sign advertising Old Milwaukee.

Behind the bar Ronnie and another bartender hustled back and forth mixing drinks and pouring beer. Buck had gone out to the car to get the Nova Life pills to show Ronnie. George was at a table talking with friends. Livia was leaning her elbows on the bar. She had a vague smile on her face and she nodded now and then, her lips moving, talking to Cody.

Nearly everyone was smoking. Clouds of smoke bumped the ceiling and spread across the room and settled, making the air look vaguely unreal. The place was filling up, getting noisy. Waitresses scooted between the tables, trays full of drinks. Country music whined from speakers high in the corners—

I've got a tan-gled mind and a bro-ken heaaart . . .

Blue-velvet walls were trimmed in gold and covered with framed portraits of nude women, their flagrant curves abstractly connecting in Joy's mind with the *Nude Descending* in Sissy's room, its geometric lines and copper-oxidizing hues. Joy eyed the poses, the breasts, the soft-curving bottoms, and knew that she (with proper lighting) could look as good. Lighted steps ran the length of a stage in front. The ceiling above was one vast mirror. At the back was a karaoke machine made of black metal and chrome. It sat on a stainless-steel table, looking like a huge, impossible jewel. Everything was designed to work as a looking glass in which the girls could be seen from every angle.

Ronnie had told Joy that he wanted artistic dancing. He wanted the girls to try new things. It didn't have to be bump and grind and putting your pussy in some sweaty bastard's face all the time.

Experiment. Express your inner beauty.

If art and inner beauty were what he wanted, that's what Joy would give him. She was an artist of the beautiful. It was what a man had called her one night in a nightclub in New York. Joy naked and losing herself in a sentimental piece called "The Swedish Rhapsody," swaying and dipping, bending and exposing, all melancholy love-yearning wrapped in breathy violins.

When the dance was over, a man had grabbed her ankle and said, "Do you know how good you are? You are an artist of the beautiful, lady." No one had ever called her such a thing before or made her think of herself as artistic. *Artist of the beautiful, artist of the beautiful.* The words had echoed in Joy's head and made her wonder if, in her own way, she was a female equivalent of Buck.

~

THE FRONT DOOR OPENED and Buck came back, a box of Nova Life in his hand. He slid onto the stool next to her and plucked a pill from the box and held it in front of Ronnie, who was leaning forward, his eyes focusing on the pill as if it were going to levitate.

"Cousin Ron, this is the Nova Life miracle," Buck began in a seductive voice. "Everything is in this pill that scientific research tells us we need to stay young and healthy. One-a-day cures old age, stops cancer in its tracks and renews the hormonal balances of the inner organs." Buck leaned close and whispered, "Testosterone's in there, Ron. Tes-tos-*terone*, I'm saying." He rotated the pill in Ronnie's face, then glanced at Joy. She nodded gravely to emphasize what Buck was saying.

"Old age is just a disease," Buck continued, "like ulcers or strokes, it can be prevented. A daily inoculation of Nova Life and the aging process is put on hold. I've been taking them six years. So has Joy. Look at us. I mean, *look* at us. We are walking advertisements for youth and health and the Nova Life way. It's this pill that keeps us so goddamn pretty." Buck paused for effect, his eyes oozing sincerity.

Hanging from the ceiling at the far end of the bar was a television. On-screen an injured football player was being carried off the field strapped to a stretcher, the fans applauding him.

"Larsen's made of tissue paper," said a man sitting on the other side of Livia.

"Time to hang it up, Larsen," said another man. "He's a goddamn detriment to the team."

"Larsen!" cried Livia.

"Not *Cody* Larsen, Mom," said Joy, touching her mother's arm.

"Better watch your mouth, cowboy," said Livia. She downed her beer and banged the heel of the mug on the bar to get Ronnie's attention. The two men smirked at Livia, then put their heads together and whispered.

"Oh, shut up!" Joy told them. Their eyes darted over her and away, back to the TV.

The old lady kept muttering. Joy winced and turned her head, so she couldn't see her. She leaned against Buck and stroked his leg. He was the prettiest thing in the room all right, the most interesting, the most manly. Just touching his leg made her heart quicken.

Though Ronnie voiced his doubts about Minnesota barflies taking to Nova Life, he agreed to stock the pills and sell them in thirty-day packages. Buck said he was taking a beating on the deal, but after the customers got hooked, he would make up for his losses.

"I'll rush it then," said Buck. "I've got some pamphlets I'll leave that explain the Nova Life way. And you can have this box to get started." He propped the box where the bar curved flush against the wall, then he spun toward Joy and gave her thumbs-up. Another sale. Another distributor. Joy looked at the numbers on the order pad.

"I've got cool cousins," said Buck.

"Great guys," she agreed.

Livia raised her mug high and finally Ronnie noticed her.

"Comin up," he said.

George was saying something that made his friends laugh. One of them slugged him on the shoulder and George slugged him back. Friendly punches. That's the way Minnesotans were, the men scruffy and rough and sort of distant and shy until they had a few beers; the women vaguely Nordic, lots of dishwater blondes, casual dressers, very little makeup, good feeders and beer drinkers, inclined to plumpness and low laughter.

"He knows everyone in town," said Joy, nodding toward George.

Buck looked at George. "You would too if you'd lived here all your life." Buck leaned close. "Think of that, Joy. Cousin George has never been anywhere, never done anything but scratch his balls and drink in this bar and see the same god-damn moldy faces night after night. What kind of life is that? It could have happened to me if my mother had stayed put. I'd be a Medicine Lake boy, sporting a beer belly and a baseball cap and a beard and you'd never have met me."

She thought about Buck as a Medicine Lake boy. Probably she would still be with Jim Faust, growing old in front of the TV with him. She had met him in junior college in San Diego when she was only twenty. On their first date he won her by saying she should be in the movies, she had the right stuff. They made love in his Chevy pickup that same night and in two months she was pregnant and they ran off to Las Vegas for a quicky marriage at a drive-up window—*Donna's Driveup Wedding*—sitting on the tailgate and holding hands, while organ music played and Preacher Donna pronounced them man and wife. At their motel, after a night of debauchery, Joy had a miscarriage, a tiny clot of something she shamefully flushed down the toilet.

She and Jim dropped out of college and stayed in Vegas and Joy started dancing in nightclubs to support them, while Jim went to a school for heavy-equipment operators. It was while

THE ALTAR OF THE BODY

Jim was in school that Joy got six months of work at The Sands. She felt she had found the pathway to stardom. She danced in a chorus line and waited to be discovered. But she got pregnant again, had another miscarriage, went back to work in go-go bars and over the years went from G-strings and pasties to topless to totally nude, draping herself around poles onstage while men eyed her hungrily.

A decade went by and Jim ran backhoes and dozers and cranes and finally bought his own backhoe and got a contract to dig foundations and pipelines for houses. He had a reputation for good work and he was making enough money so that Joy could quit dancing if she wanted to. She told herself that she had had enough and she quit and stayed home but soon wearied of it. Found out she wasn't housewife material. The lights of Vegas beckoned. But before she could return to the Strip, she got pregnant for the third time. Took her doctor's advice, kept calm, stayed in bed a lot and brought the baby to term. But it was stillborn and Joy went through weeks of suicidal depression and she knew then for sure she was cursed and that hers was a womb of death and she told herself she didn't want to do it anymore. No more *babies*.

It wasn't only Buck's charms that made her leave Jim in her thirty-third year. It was also the way her life had become so frighteningly hollow and how she was aging and how the hope in her womb always managed to die. It was Jim too, the lint in his navel, his padded jaws, his oxlike attitude toward work, toward building his business. The milky blandness of him day after day, coming home smelling of diesel and sweat, throwing himself on the couch, a lump in front of the tube, those mind-numbing football games, the stale odors issuing from him in bed. Buck was a catalyst. But the movement away from Jim Faust had begun long before.

She glanced at her mother sipping beer, a foam mustache on

her upper lip, her tongue licking it off. The old lady would snore loudly tonight. Joy pictured her dead to the world, her toothless mouth open like a baby bird waiting to be fed. She had been complaining of headaches and pacing a lot and she (always so careful about her toilet) would stink unless Joy gave her baths. She couldn't handle buttons or zippers very well or dress herself in clothes that matched. But she could still get out and hoof it at a bar and read her book and put herself in Cody's world. One night Joy had caught her trying to read the book upside down, mouthing contortions:

> . . . *lifting, haze drifting slow to turned, lightened darkness the . . .*

and when Joy turned the book right-side up and told her she was making no sense, Livia had said, "I was seeing if I could."

"Make sense?"

"Message hidden the get!" Livia had said, looking at her as if she were dumb as a toad.

Joy wondered if reading backward was symptomatic of a disease. What could it mean? Each day it seemed Livia was evolving into someone else, certain brain cells turning off, winking out. She scarcely remembered a thing about the past anymore. A little of this or that about her childhood, but very little after: *What six husbands? Not never have no six husbands!* Memory was an odd thing, a matter of chemistry and the will to remember. If the chemistry or the will changed in a certain way, the memory vanished. It seemed to Joy that her mother was a case of chemistry and will declining in one area and increasing in another. She literally knew *West of the Pecos* forward and backwards, but she had no memory whatsoever (or claimed she had no memory) of the men in her life.

"Nikos who? Never know no Nikos," she had said when Joy

mentioned him. She even had a hard time remembering Harold, Joy's own father, who had died when she was seven. Died when an electrical short ignited fumes at a Clark Oil depot, where he was loading his tanker with gasoline. Joy remembered the casket covered in flowers, the petals looking like crowded tongues, protesting the whole awful business. She remembered everything about it. But for Livia it was a void. "Harold?" she had said. "Harold who?" He had been Harold, his father had been Harold and Joy's drowned brother had been the last of the Harolds.

Her mother turned toward her, leaning in, saying, "How do I look, kid? Do I look okay? Are my eyes on straight?"

"You look great," Joy told her, though her penciled brows were arched a little high, giving her eyes a startled look.

"I do?"

"Yeah."

She wondered if it were true that the daughter became the mother. She saw herself at seventy-three, with thinning hair and glassy eyes, her body a foul rag-and-bone shop, jutting bones wrapped in shapeless, buttless pajamas and an afghan over her shoulders shivering with cold in the summer air.

She closed her eyes. "Jesus spare me," she said, and downed her drink. She held the empty glass up, rattling the ice.

"*Todka vonic*?" Ronnie said.

"*Rodka-vocks*," she answered.

Ronnie laughed. "A Spooner lover?" he asked.

She nodded, though she wasn't quite sure what he meant.

~

GEORGE CAME BACK. He stood on the other side of Livia, his elbows to the bar. He was wearing a tan work shirt and pants and boots. Joy liked his weathered face and his rugged hands. His silver sideburns and wispy dome looked good on him, she thought. If he would just lose some weight, get rid of that gut, firm up those shoulders, he'd be a fine-looking man.

"Sure, I'll have a drink with you, Cody," said Livia, offering her mug.

"Give my gal another," said George over his shoulder to Ronnie. "You my gal, Livia?"

"You know it, bub," she said, grinning at him. Her eyes were nearly lost in rings of blue-green shadow and false lashes. She was dressed in black, wearing Joy's leather skirt and a blouse open at the neck and a gold choker.

Joy looked at her watch. It was a tick after ten. Ronnie slid a vodka in front of her and a fresh beer in front of Livia. He stood for a moment, looking at Joy and stroking his white-flecked beard, petting it catlike, then squeezing its ends together. "You guys ready for the show?" he asked. His eyes made her think of a frisky colt.

"I'm ready if you are," she told him.

~

HE WENT ONSTAGE and held his arms up, asking for quiet. From his pocket he took out a list of people who were going to sing and he said, "Now let me *F*arn *w*olks here, there ain't nothing p.c. about what we're doin. Yhah, if you're prone to take offense at obscenities, you best go and leave this place to the perverts." He grinned wickedly.

"Shut up and bring on the smut, Ronnie!" someone shouted.

"Yuck *f*ou, Clarence Duff." Ronnie pointed at Clarence Duff and Clarence Duff pointed back. He was a heavyset, round-shouldered man with a white mustache and eyes magnified behind thick lenses.

"Bring on the smut!" he hollered. He held up an arthritic finger that curved toward his head.

"Okay, don't say I didn't warn you," said Ronnie. "First up is . . . first up is Big Dewey. C'mon, Dewey!"

A horse-faced fellow wearing jeans and a checkered shirt and an Old Man River baseball cap resting on his ears went onstage and plugged a number into the karaoke machine. A tune started playing. It was something soft, with fiddles and Spanish guitars, but Joy didn't recognize it. Dewey took the microphone, stepped forward and crooned in a deep bass voice—

> *Oh sparrow, oh sparrow*
> *where did you get that arrow,*
> *oh sparrow, that arrow*
> *plugging up your butt?*

His sound was country, his face a study in sorrow as he told the story of the sparrow with the arrow.

"Sing it, Big Dewey," Clarence shouted. "Sing that sparrow."

Big Dewey sang about the sparrow flying over Foggy Meadow Lake with an arrow sticking out its behind. Who dared do such a thing? Who dared shoot a sparrow?

> *Was it a boy with a toy?*
> *Was it a putz with swollen nuts?*
> *Was it a girl with a curl?*
> *Or a miracle, my word?*

He asked if a sparrow with an arrow was a signal of the Second Coming? Was it a sign from a dove, were its wings from above?

> *So the next time you kneel and pray*
> *You remember what Big Dewey say*

> *it's not a nerd, not a turd,*
> *but a miracle, my word—*
> *is a sparrow with an arrow up its butt!*

The crowd applauded and stomped and whistled as he made his way back to his table.

Joy saw her mother rubbing at a spot behind her ear, her eyes squinting.

"What's wrong, Mom?" Joy asked her.

"Unh?" grunted Livia.

"What's wrong?"

"Head hurts here. Let's go home."

Joy lit a cigarette and puffed hard. "Wait till Buck's done. He's going to sing too," she said.

Livia stopped rubbing her head. "Me too," she said. "I'm a born entertainer."

Ronnie introduced Connie Hawkins and told the audience she always sang sizzlers and toe ticklers. "We call her Triple-X," he said.

"You can always count on Con," said Clarence Duff. "Go for it, purty thang!"

There were more claps and whistles. One of the guys close to Joy whistled so loud it hurt her ears and made her want to slap him. She wondered if her sensitivity to shrill noises meant that she was getting old. She looked at Buck. He was leaning forward on his stool, his eyes fixed on Connie Hawkins. Joy watched her mother light a cigarette and take it from her mouth. It was trembling in her hand, the smoke shuddering. Her eyes were squinting toward the stage, straining to see what was going on.

Connie programmed the machine and a tune livelier than Big Dewey's came on. In a nasal twang she belted out some lyrics about a man she couldn't love because he didn't have enough to satisfy her. She found—

> . . . it weren't a handful
> it hung just like an anvil
> wouldn't rise for all entreat'n
> head hung down like it was beaten,
> twas a pitiful little twig,
> hiding half inside a wig.

She did a high kick, whirled, bent over and mugged the audience from between her legs. They roared at her.

"Yhah! You're taulkin booot Clarence here!" cried a little woman sitting next to him. He denied it. He held his hands out, measuring off a foot or more.

"Yhah! Like hell!" said the woman. She rose to her feet, stumbling a bit as she hung on to her chair. Clarence tried to get her to sit down. He was smiling, but he didn't look happy and finally he took hold of her arm and jerked her into the seat. He leaned over and said something to her and she quieted down.

Connie was a natural onstage, posturing, making the audience part of her act.

> But now I've found a man of iron,
> who don't leave me nights a cry'n
> for a bucket in my well,
> for a clapper to ring my bell!

She was pointing at Buck and everyone was turning to look at him. She wiggled her finger at him, but he waved her off. When she finished, she hurried through the tables to him, threw her arms around his neck and kissed him on the mouth. People hooted. Joy moved toward George until she was practically in his lap, her fingernails digging into his leg.

"Take it easy," George told her, pushing at her hand.

Joy plastered a smile on her face, but she was burning inside, wanting to rip the nose off Connie.

Buck said to her, "You got talent, Con. You sure know how to hold an audience. It was good, baby."

Connie whispered something to him.

"That wouldn't have gone over in Vegas," snipped Joy.

"We ain't in Vegas," snipped Connie right back.

More X-rated singers got up and entertained the crowd. Song after song came and went. Some of them funny. Some of them just filthy, but people laughed and applauded no matter what.

~

WHEN RONNIE CALLED FOR HIM as last on the list, Buck slipped his black polo shirt over his head, handed it to Joy and smoothed his hair back with both hands. Torso naked, he strutted to the stage and the crowd quieted. The women stared at him, their eyes greedy, but sort of angry too, as if mad at him for being so sexy, or maybe mad at themselves for wanting something they would never have. His tanned body was shiny with sweat. Heels clicked a rhythm as he walked. He had a gold chain around his neck and a gold stud in his left ear. He did a little flex and show for the crowd and bands of muscles rippled from his shoulders to his waist. Some people snickered.

Joy heard comments:

"Will you look at that."

"Who's he think he is?"

"Look at that show-off."

"What is this, Chippendale's?"

He set the machine to play "Your Cheating Heart," then came forward and sang and his voice was authentic imitation

Hank Williams down a decibel. Just the sound of it seemed to win the audience over. A few bars into it and they forgot to be envious or irritated or to hate him because he was beautiful.

> *Oh, here's to Lil . . . of the gol-den west,*
> *her tits hung down . . . like two wasp-nests,*
> *the skin on her tum . . . was tight as a drum,*
> *old Lil could make . . . a dead man cum . . .*

"Just downhome," Joy heard a woman say.
"Just folks," said her companion.
"He's Hank Williams to the life," said another.

> *The rumor spread . . . from town to towwwnnn*
> *that Lil could bur-rrn . . . any cowpoke dowwnnn—*

On it went, Buck listing the prowess of Lil, who screwed a thousand men into early graves. He sang long nasal notes, he flexed his lats and pecs, turned his stomach into a six-pack. He flashed his Hollywood teeth. And Joy had to admit as always that Buck Root was a phenomenon extraordinaire.

Connie beside her said, "What a hunk of man, Jesus."
And Joy said, "Hands off him, honey, he's mine."
"I'm allowed to admire him, ain't I?" said Connie.

They looked each other in the eye, and Joy could see that they were enemies and she felt hatred for Connie, and she was glad they had not yet become friends and had never opened up their private lives or anything else to each other.

> *Then across the ri-ver . . . called shag-ass creek*
> *came a gig-o-lo . . . named Pecos Pete*
> *with jizz on his toes . . . and cum on his feet*
> *and sixteen inches . . . of swinging meat.*

A man in the crowd yelled out, "He stole my measurements!"
"Mine too!" cried another.

Men and women guffawed from one end of the bar to the
other.

> *He laid his pecker . . . across the bar,*
> *was sixteen inches . . . from thar to thar,*
> *sixteen inch-ches . . . from stem to stern,*
> *and in between . . . was a stud-mannn's cuuurve.*

"He's funny," said George.
"Wait'll you hear the rest," said Joy. "It'll kill you."

The audience got very still as they listened to Buck sing the
last stanzas of the song.

> *The date was set . . . by Windy Bill*
> *that they would fuuck . . . on asscrack hill*
> *e-ven the boys . . . from the county seat*
> *came up to waaatch . . . Pete sink his meat.*
> *They fucked for days . . . they fucked for hours*
> *They tore up trees . . . and shrubs and flowers.*
> *Lil, she tried . . . the Gilligan twist,*
> *but Pete had learned it . . . from his sis,*
> *So she tried . . . the African smoth-er*
> *But he'd learned that . . . from his dear moth-er.*

Buck crooned the last lines in a funereal voice. He took out a
handkerchief, dabbed at his eyes, dabbed at his nose and finished off with a whiny couplet.

> *She was done . . . her tail was through,*
> *that chea-tin taaart . . . had turned to goo.*

He tossed the microphone to Ronnie and bowed to thunderous applause. Joy heard someone shout, "He's a renaissance man, that is!" Some in the crowd went up and patted his sweaty back and gave him high fives. Some yelled, "Encore! Encore!"

Buck grinned, hung his head, acted humble and shy. He talked with this person and that. He laughed, he pumped hands. He made muscles for women to gawk at and poke. He told jokes. People howled at practically everything he said.

"What an act," said George.

Livia, her headache forgotten, was on her feet doing a little dance, a shimmy-shimmy shake-shake. "Ain't he fun!" she said. "Cody!" she called and dived into the crowd. Ronnie was talking into the mike, saying, "I think we know who's won." More cheers and whistles followed. Ronnie called Buck back onstage and said. "This Franklin's for my cousin Mike Routelli. Now known as *Ruck Boot!*" Ronnie handed him a hundred-dollar bill. "And all the booze you can drink, *Fig bella!*" he added.

Buck waved the bill. "Round of drinks on *Ruck Boot!*"

"Is that really my cousin?" George asked Joy. "It flabbergasts me, God's truth, he ain't nothing like he used to be. I mean, where did Mikey Routelli go?"

"You change your outside, you change your inside too. People do it all the time," Joy said. "He'll have them all sold on Nova Life before the night is over, just watch Mr. Flim-Flam go to work."

Livia was in the crowd gathered in front of Buck onstage. She was nudging people and saying, "That's my man! That's Cody!"

The audience made him sing the song again.

> *Oh, here's to Lil . . . of the gol-den west—*
> *Her tits hung dowwwn . . .*

"Yhah," Clarence hollered, "Bucky goddammit, you gotta turn pro!"

~

JOY WAITED AN HOUR for Buck to come to the bar, but he didn't come. People pulled him to their tables. He had to drink with them. Hands kept reaching out, touching him, fingers prodding his muscles while he flexed. Livia was moving from table to table too, laughing, singing, sitting on laps, drinking drinks, mussing this and that man's hair, dancing in between the tables when the music came on. People in the crowd were pointing at her, getting a kick out of her.

"She's gonna make herself sick," Joy told George.

Girls were shuffling around onstage. The music had switched from western to blues, "Boogie Chillun." Men were offering the dancers rolled bills, trying to coax them nearer. Joy watched the girls work on the men. Livia was getting money too, hip-hopping from table to table, shaking her toot-toot and getting dollars, waving the money around before stuffing it into her bra. Her smile was youthful. Wrapped in smoky light she almost looked young again.

Joy turned her eyes from Livia and searched for Buck, but he had disappeared. Connie Hawkins was gone too. Joy still had his polo shirt in her hands. She put it on the stool and started searching the bar, walking past the booths into a hall into the men's room, where some man yelled for her to come give a hand. Big Dewey and Clarence were standing at urinals.

"Buck in here?" she said.

"Wish my name was Buck," said Big Dewey.

Clarence cast his magnified eyes lasciviously over her and said, "Boy, I'd sure like to get in your pants, and not because I just shit in mine."

Joy rolled her eyes. She went back to the bar. "Where is he?" she asked George.

"Dunno," he replied. "Seen Buck, Ronnie?"

Ronnie looked around. "Where'd he go? Where's Connie?"

The music died, then started up again, a metallic rhythm, hard bass slapping the walls, a voice joining in, singing, *Boom, boom, boom, boom . . . gonna shoot you right down . . .*

She went outside. Her heart was doing its arrhythmic thing, making her cough. She folded her arms and walked through the parking lot, looking in car windows, expecting any second to see him and Connie Hawkins. Fear made her stomach burn. She saw life without him, the emptiness—how losing him would make her a futile, contemptible creature, another in the list of millions who had given everything for a man and ended up lost and loveless and bitter, a hater of everything male. She thought of her husband and felt sorry for how she had broken his heart. Nothing mattered but Buck back then. But she didn't have the stomach for it anymore. If he was with Connie . . . if he and Connie were together . . .

"Fool, idiot, jackass," she muttered, biting her lip. "God, Joy, how can you be such a dumb dumbshit?"

She walked to the edge of the parking lot and stared down the road, the overhead halogen lamps tinting it pinkish. Car lights appeared, the beams closing in on her. The driver stuck his head out the window and said, "How you doin, sweet mama?"

"Get lost, jerk!" she told him.

And he yelled, "Fuck you, bitch!" and sped away.

She sighed. Shuddered. Looked into the night. Saw a double ring around the moon, sooty clouds inching toward it. The air was warm, humid. Crickets chirping and the smell of lilacs. The sizzle of mosquito wings. An annoying puff of wind fiddled with her hair. She wandered back toward The Body Shop.

I, George

I SAY TO JOY, "Your mother's gone wild onstage, taking her clothes off. The crowd's egging her on."

We can hear the clapping and whistling inside. The music throbs.

"Where is he? Where is that bastard?" she says.

"I don't know. I haven't seen him."

"Nor that goddamn Connie, I bet," she says.

My eyes scan the lot, coming to rest for a moment on Connie's van. "Maybe he went to get more Nova Life to sell," I say. "Did you check the car?"

She looks at the van and then at me. Her eyes say that she doesn't want to go see, but she can't help herself. "God, how I hate him," she tells me.

"He'll turn up," I say. "Where you going? Your mother's taking her clothes off. Don't you think we ought to—"

She goes to the van, grabs the handle on the side and the door slides back and there they are. Connie is on top, her hair hanging. I flash back to the couple at Blue's Beach, the girl climaxing, the crowd clapping, the man shouting, "Touchdown!"

"You animals!" Joy screams. "You faithless fucking animals!"

Connie grimaces, pissed off.

"Cow," says Joy.

"Hey, if you can't keep your man—" says Connie.

"Close the door," says Buck.

Joy shakes her fists, paces back and forth, kicking the gravel and shouting at Buck, calling him a no-good fucking bastard. "After all we've been through together! After all I've stuck by you and everything! Everything I've done for you! Supported you! Worked my ass off for you! Give up home for you. Give up any kind of normal life! Let you drag me all over hell! Doing what I could to make your dreams come true and every time I turn my back this is what you do! And you come home with diseases and I still take you back and I give and give, and you take and take!"

"I told you to close the door," says Buck.

"I'll close the door. I'll close the door for good, you bastard!" Her finger shakes at Connie. "You, you goddamn cow, don't think he'll be yours either, don't flatter yourself. You don't know what you're in for! I pity such a stupid cunt as you!"

Joy grabs the door and slams it shut. She turns around and sees me standing there. "Take me home," she says. "Will you take me home, George?"

"Your mother—"

"Fuck her!"

"Come on, let's get her, then we'll go."

I go back into the bar and Joy follows and there is her mother down to pantyhose and nothing, her breasts looking like figs about to fall. She is dancing back and forth, multiple images of her all over the wall and ceiling mirrors as she sings, *"I'm a silver dollar lady in a two-bit bar . . ."*

Paper money and shiny coins are scattered beneath her feet. The crowd is urging her on. Feet are stomping. Tables are being pounded. Whistles and shouts and laughter fill the air.

Joy marches to the stage and takes Livia's hand, but she pulls back and says, "Hey, you!" Then tries to get Joy to dance too, but Joy clamps the old lady's wrist and takes off with her, Livia stumbling and hurrying and yelling, "Hey! Hey!"

I go behind, gathering Livia's clothes from people in the audience. There is continuous applause, beaming, sweaty faces.

"Life in the old girl yet!"

"God love her!"

~

Joy DRAGS HER MOTHER to the car, then pulls up and waits for me. I feel her nails raking my hand as she snatches my keys.

"I'll drive," she says.

We all climb in and she gets behind the wheel, starts the engine, rips out of the parking space and backs up. She slams the bumper into the side of the van, then she guns the motor, pops the lever in gear and peppers the van with gravel. The rear of the car fans back and forth. The tires shriek when they hit the pavement. She keeps gunning the engine as the car fishtails. She takes out some bushes at a corner, skims bark off a tree, drives over someone's lawn, bangs a row of trash cans, sending them flying.

"Ooo-la-la!" shouts Livia.

I hang on to the dash and holler, "Whoa, whoa."

"Where am I going!" yells Joy. "Tell me where to turn!"

I direct her away from Foggy Meadow Lake and onto 55. She goes seventy, then slows down a bit. The back of her hand wipes at her eyes.

~

By THE TIME WE GET TO THE APARTMENTS, the engine is chattering and there is a rattle coming from underneath. Joy jumps out and hurries inside, while Livia and I follow. Joy goes into the bedroom and starts pulling Buck's clothes from the closet and piling them on the bed. She opens the window and throws the clothes out piece by piece. After she is done, she heads for the kitchen, flipping on the light and heading for the cupboards. "Where's the White Horse?" she asks, banging the cupboard doors, shoving boxes and cans aside.

"We drank it," I tell her.

"You got vodka?"

"No. How about a beer?"

She doesn't answer. She opens the refrigerator and grabs a beer and pops the tab and drinks fast, the beer spilling from the sides of her mouth, running over her chin, staining her red blouse. When it is empty, she crushes the can and tosses it on the table, it tinks and tumbles.

Livia is standing beside me in her pantyhose, her skeletal body like something torn from a grave.

"Mother, you get in bed!" orders Joy.

Livia doesn't move.

"Now!" says Joy.

"Saddle up," says Livia. "We're not welcome here." She looks at me, or at least in my direction. I've noticed that she was certainly right about the more she drinks the more her left eye wanders.

"C'mon," I tell her. I take her by the hand and lead her into the bedroom. I help her into her pajamas. She looks forlorn. Her mouth turns way down, the upper lip vanishing in an arc of wrinkles.

"Gotta headache," she says, rubbing her temples. "No fun. No life in fun."

"Where there is no hope, there is underwear," I say.

"Huhnn?" she says.

"I think it was in *Howl*."

"Whazzit?"

"I don't know. Never mind."

She crawls into bed and I put the dog beside her and tuck her in and turn out the light.

~

WHEN I GET BACK TO THE KITCHEN, Joy says, "Let's get blasted! You wanna get blasted, George? Let's get blasted! You wanna? Goddammit, you better wanna! Here's your chance," she says. "You've been wanting it, here it is." She starts unbuttoning her blouse, but her fingers shake so badly she can't work the buttons.

"Hell with it!" she says. She shifts her skirt, drops it and drops her underpants. Steps out of them.

I haven't moved. I am observing her, wondering what I should do. A good guy wouldn't take advantage of the situation. A good guy wouldn't want her this way.

"It'll pass, Joy. Everything passes."

"That's what *you* think."

The tips of her blouse dangle over her abdomen. Her bush is blondish, carefully trimmed. She advances on me, puts her hands behind my neck and kisses me. My mouth stays stiff and I am shivering a little.

"Jesus, what kind of man is this?" she says. She pulls back and scrutinizes me. "What is it, honey?" she says. "Don't you want me?"

"I do, Joy. But—"

In her eyes I can see a touch of scorn for a man who won't take advantage of what she is offering. A real man would put her on the counter or bend her over the table and screw her. Then she could know him and despise him like she despises Buck Root.

"Jesus, lemme go," she says, though I'm not touching her. She picks up her skirt and her underpants and goes into the bedroom and flings them at the wall. They bump softly and fall to the floor.

She stands by the window, looking out, and I stand close behind her, pale light filtering through the trees, Buck's clothes on the lawn, lumps of him in the dark, like she has slaughtered him and strewn his parts around. The street and the parked cars glisten. A cloud passes in front of the moon and the dark room gets darker. The wind rustles the leaves. I smell rain. She closes the window, her bottom bending toward me. I touch the shadowed cleft. My fingers curl, cupping her tentatively. She straightens up. We stand a few seconds like that, my breath stirring the hairs at the base of her neck.

"I think I'm cursed," she says.

"Who isn't?" I say.

"I wish . . . I wish I knew who I was and what I believed. I feel like a bee going mad from flower to flower, trying to find the perfect one." She hesitates. Sighs. Says, "I should've stayed home, stayed married to Jim and tried for another baby and lived a regular, boring old life. What is this shit I'm doing? What makes me do it?"

Then she says, "I believed in love, that's how stupid I am. I believed that if my love was big enough—"

And I say, "I've loved you the second I saw you. I know I'm a homely mutt, but I'd be good to you, Joy."

"Whiskey talking," she says bitterly.

"I'm not drunk," I say.

She's quiet, then she says she knows I would be good to her, that I would no doubt spoil her. And then she says, "I bet you don't understand why I take Buck's shit?"

"I guess you love him."

"You don't know him," she says. "Buck is more than anybody knows. He's not just a hunk, you know."

She switches on the lamp, opens a drawer on the nightstand and fusses through some papers, pulling a couple of them out. "You should read these," she says. "They're not smutty 'Lil Of

The Golden West' stuff. This is the side of him people don't see." She reads one aloud:

> I've got Joy and I'm her boy
> And we'll never dance alone.
> Oh, love me lots, love me long
> Is the burden of my song.

Her voice breaks on the last line and she puts her hand over her mouth. "You see?" she says.

"Is it good?" I ask.

Joy looks at the page, but doesn't answer.

"It's nice," I tell her.

She pulls more poems from the drawer and shows them to me. "When we were falling in love, those first months when you're out of your mind, that's when he wrote them. Listen to this."

> White thy hands, red thy mouth
> And thy body dainty is.
> Lie down and sleep with me
> In the night, quick me kiss.

"That's not bad," I say.

"Soulful," she says, and goes over the lines again. "He hasn't written me one like that in I don't know how long. These are it to sustain me." She shakes the pages, sniffs, brushes her palm across both eyes, and then she says, "Why can't it last? Why does everything burn out?"

She leans into me. "Boy, am I down," she whispers.

She puts the poetry in the drawer, then turns to the window again. I come close. She reaches back and touches my hip. I cup her bottom again, my fingers working slowly. My other hand runs under her blouse, over her breasts. My lips nuzzle her. She eases her legs a little and I hear a liquid sound. She smells of beer and cigarettes mixed with something musky, which is herself, I realize, her odor stirred by my fingers. Resting her head in the hollow of my shoulder, she twists her neck so our mouths can meet and we kiss. Her lips are wet, soft, gluey.

She pulls back and says, "You're a good kisser, George."

"Am I?"

"Yeah."

"I want to please you."

"Tell me," she whispers. "Tell me something good. Tell me what I need to know."

I open my mouth. Her mouth reaches. "Joy," I breathe.

She takes hold of me and pulls me toward the bed.

~

I CATNAP through the night. My mind is filled with her and I wake in the dark and find my hands on her again, my body over her, my knee pushing her legs apart. *It isn't real*, I tell myself. There is no way she has let old George McLeod have her.

When I finally wake up and know I'm awake, it is not yet daylight and she is sitting at the edge of the bed, her milky back shaped like a tombstone.

"What is it?" I whisper.

"Shh," she says. "He's out there."

She leans over me, her breast brushing my stomach, making me want her again. "He's prowling around and he's dangerous. He's nuts when he's like this, George. I want you to go down to the Lincoln and get the gun."

"Gun?"

"It's under the seat, the passenger side, wrapped in a towel. Get it. Watch out for him. Be careful. You know how he can be."

No, I don't know how he can be, but I get up and slip on my pants and go outside, down to the curb where the Lincoln sits bulky as a bulldozer under a tree. The weightlifter's clothes have disappeared from the lawn. There is a loafer lying boatover on the sidewalk. The air is heavy. The trees drip.

I am about to open the car door when the weightlifter comes out of the shadows and asks me what I'm doing. I say, "Hey, Jesus, man!"

"Hay's for horses," he says.

"You scared shit outta me."

He puts on an injured expression. "Would I hurt my own cousin?" he asks. He is wearing a hooded sweatshirt, the hood framing his face. His hands are balled in the pockets, stretching the material. I think of gangbangers all alike in their sloppy clothes hunched against the cold. The tie strings hang over his groin, tiny knots at the ends bobbing around as he comes close and stares down at me.

I force myself to look into his eyes. A drop of rain hits my back. Then another and another.

"So what you up to, George?"

Without thinking, I tell him the truth. "Joy wants her gun."

"What for?"

I don't answer.

"I wouldn't give it to her. I would not do that," he says.

"Why not?"

"She might shoot you. She's a perilous piece, haven't you noticed?" He glances toward the bedroom window. The curtain moves. "You need to watch yourself with her. Nothing's what it seems with Joy Faust. She's got a hidden agenda."

"Hidden agenda?"

The weightlifter's odor, a little rancid, offends me and I step back. Despite the coolness and the breeze, the man is sweating. A bead of sweat rolls between his eyes, another one trickles over his cheek, tickles his lip. He licks it, then he goes to the rear of the car and pokes his finger through the bullet hole.

"You know this?" He wiggles his finger. "Joy put it there. I ever tell you how that happened? She was pointing the gun at her mother's head. She was an inch away from blowing her head off. I ain't lying. Scout's honor. This is the kind of woman you're dealing with. If I hadn't nudged her arm, it would have been soup for brains and we would have been burying the old tart in Wyoming, on the lone prairie. She was driving Joy crazy. She wanted to go back to California. She wanted us to buy a house with a room for her with a rocking chair. She wanted a fireplace and a garden, all those stupid *clichés*, Jesus Christ. Yeah, they all want to be taken care of when they break down like that. The thing is, have they earned it? You reap what you sow. Understand what I'm saying?"

The weightlifter keeps fiddling with the bullet hole, chipping at the edges. "Boom," he says. "Bullets travel fast as the finger of God. You believe in God, cousin?"

I shrug.

"Me neither." His voice drones on, tells me how they pulled off on some lonely stretch of road, mountains west, prairie east, and got out of the car and Joy got the gun and she said she couldn't take it and it would be a favor to her mother to do it quick, instead of letting her go inch by inch tortured by her own flesh. And she aimed, but he hit her arm as she pulled the trigger. He tells me that's what Joy can do, she can kill you if she thinks she should.

And he says, "I stopped her from murdering, that's the kind of sonofabitch I am. I suppose you've heard all kinds of bad things about me now?"

I shake my head. "She didn't say anything about you. Nothing except you're a poet. She showed me your poems."

"Torn from my lacerated heart, George. Now you know how complex I am. The Root is a sensitive man, a tender soul." His eyes look damp and I wonder if he's crying. He turns away from me, clears his throat, sucks in a breath. Then he says, "But do you understand what I'm saying about her? I'm saying, be careful with her. Don't trust her. She's a liar and she's got a hidden agenda."

I have my fingers on the door handle, watching Buck to see if he is going to stop me.

"Let your cousin give you one big truth about women," he continues. "There's one truth that applies to all of them, George. Every man knows it, but he doesn't want to admit it. All women are destructive, they will destroy you. Women want to eat men alive, you understand what I'm saying?" His voice rises a little and he says, "Full of treachery. Cannibals at heart. Man-eaters, I'm saying. They hate us, George. In their lonely, lying, cold little hearts, women truly hate men. Be careful. Promise me you'll be careful, cousin."

"I'll be careful," I say.

"I don't really like them at all, George. I hate it that I need them. I really, really hate the hold they got on me. It's all physical, that's all it is."

I have the door open and I'm rummaging under the seat. I pull the towel out and unwrap it and there is the gun. It is a big chrome thing, a serious piece with revolving chambers big enough to put the tip of my pinky in. It is loaded and I think, *Buck makes a move, you can shoot him.*

"Hey, better give me that." He reaches out and I pull back. "It's my gun," he says. "I bought it."

I square my shoulders and say, "Buck, don't hurt her anymore, you understand?"

"Or what, will you shoot me?"

"Maybe . . . I don't know. All I know is I want you to leave her alone."

"I intend to," he says.

I hand him the gun.

A light flickers across the street. The interior van light is on. Connie opens the door and steps out. "George," she says.

"Connie," I say.

The weightlifter bends down and picks up the loafer. Then he goes to Connie, the gun in one fist, the shoe in the other. "Get in," he tells her.

She holds my eyes a moment. "Don't think too bad of me, George," she says.

"It's none of my business, Connie."

"Well . . . but I hope you won't think bad of me. I'll see you around, honey," she says. She gets in the van, the doors chunking, the engine starting. Rain is falling steadily now.

~

IN THE HALLWAY is Joy, an inkblot in the uncertain light. "He took it, didn't he," she says.

"Yhah," I say. "I wasn't going to fight him for it. I guess it's his gun? He said he bought it."

"Yeah," she says.

It is almost dawn, but the clouds and the rain keep the hall in shadows. "Who knows what'll happen?" she says. "He might come back and blow us all away."

"He said you—"

Her voice cuts me off—"I'd rather he died! I'd rather he was *deader than dead* than to leave me for another woman! I can't stand it, the thought of him out there with her, leaving me for her! Abandoning me! I feel like such a worthless slut. I see them, George. I see what they're doing. If death took him I could stand it, but I can't stand this. I left my husband for him. Now he leaves me for that whore. Because she's young. He wants it young." She puts a hand over her eyes. "I'm such a fool." And then she says, "Who can love a fool?"

She brushes by me and goes into the bedroom and slams the

door. I stand outside, not knowing what to do. I want to go in and take her in my arms and reassure her. I'm thinking maybe I could tell her something simple, that I will take care of her and her mother and she isn't to worry about a thing. I put my ear to the door. I picture her holding a pillow to her face, wetting it with tears.

I leave and go to the window and look at the rain coming down harder, making a broom-sweeping noise. Leaves dip and shake and break loose, go plummeting. I see the hole in the Lincoln's window, the rain dripping in. Three-hundred-dollar hunk of junk, but it's mine and Joe Cuff has promised to help me restore it. With a new transmission, the engine humming, the body smoothed and painted its original champagne color, how rich and important it will look. I could take Joy up to Grand Portage, take her canoeing on the Pigeon River, take her fishing and camping. I tell myself that's what I'll do. And then I pray to a god unknown, I say: *Oh wild god, let her love me a little and keep cousin Buck away. Don't let him want her again.*

I get a can of putty from my toolbox. Just temporary, but it will work all right.

Plug it in, plug it in, my mind sings as I walk out to the car and start working the putty in my hands. The Lincoln is going to cost a small fortune to fix, but it will be worth it. A woman like Joy has to go in style. It pleases me, but it scares me too, not knowing if I can do right by her.

Slapping the putty over the hole and thumbing it at the edges, smoothing it, I tell myself that I don't give a rat's ass what it costs, I will spend every dollar I've got. Mortgage my apartments if I have to. Wind drives the rain hard into my face, pecking at my eyes, blinding me as I work to fill the hole.

PART TWO

Do Not Go Gentle

Livia Miles

Oh, Livia Marie most anybody can see
that you're the girl I idolize
and I pray for the day
when I hear you say
you're mine, all mi-i-ine . . .

LIVIA PACED with a slipper on one foot, a muddy sock on the other, through the garden to the fence and back again, but she couldn't get away from the song in her head—

Oh, Livia Marie most anybody can see . . .

"Shid up, shid up," she told it, squeezing her ears. The song had kept her awake all night, kept her tossing and turning and getting up and pacing and trying to sing something else—

Oh, here's to Lil with her golden nest—

But it didn't work. The words came from all angles, sometimes straight forward, sometimes jumbled:

anybody most Livia Marie—

She had gone outside in robe, slipper and sock and had pulled the last tomatoes off the dead tomato plants and piled them on the porch. Work was the antidote for everything, always had been. Work, work, work, her whole life work. Harvesting the garden was a big job. All the other veggies were harvested too, cucumbers-cauliflower-broccoli-zucchini-beans-peas ready or not. It was all on the porch or scattered over the grass where the last rumors of green were disappearing and the dog sniffed, lifting his leg. Sniff. Lift. Pacing after her but couldn't keep up, his stubby legs going from one side of the yard to the other back and forth, back and forth, till it wore him out.

She was going in circles, going and blowing. It was working on her this thing. It had been coming on stronger and stronger, ever since the light scalded her brain. That was when the song started playing. The need to pace had grabbed her and she couldn't stop, couldn't be Cody, couldn't sit watching TV or eat dinner or talk straight. Got to pace and sing! Body tells her so and away she goes.

Two figures came out the door, man and woman, their breaths mingling in the cold air. She knew him. She knew her. The two of them talked but she didn't stop.

"Mom, please stop pacing and come inside, it's freezing out here, you're going to kill yourself!"

"No mom me. Lemmee lone!"

"You're driving us crazy. Come inside. Come in where it's warm, Mom."

"Can't! Won't!"

"Ho Tep! Quit peeing on everything! I'm sorry, George."

"It's okay, Joy. Most of it's overripe anyway."

Done for, done for. Livia paused to look at the garden and it looked like it was done for. Which meant she had done her job

just in time. She combed the lawn and gathered up stray tomatoes clinging to vines and a bush worth of crackling beans in
purple jackets. She added chrysanthemums and some brittle
leaves from the brittle elm, and she had herself a bouquet. She
held the bouquet to her nose and sniffed.

And sneezed.

The dog barked.

Who was that dog? What was he doing?

"C'mere you! . . . Why's he runnin?"

"You're scaring him, Mom."

"I wun hurt it!" She handed the bouquet to her daughter and
took off pacing.

What people didn't understand was that she had to walk to
stay ahead of what was waiting to snatch her if she stopped. In
dark corner hallway, in closet under bed, down cellar she saw it
in unlit air waiting for her to weaken, so it could suck her in, the
singer of the song, singing to her, unnerving her. Had to keep a
step ahead of the singer, then turn when forced to and do battle
on the plains, the red buttes at her back, she alone against the
song. The sky above. The dust below. Look at her fight, look at
her go. Hero of our time is Livia Miles. And then to die the worthy death and have your boots turned back in the stirrups,
turned back as they led Old Paint behind your coffin, the whole
nation mourning their hero.

Oh, Livia Marie . . . most anybody can see . . .

The world has lost a great soul. She won the West. She was a
dead shot with a forty-four and the best rider west of the Pecos.
Give her a twenty-one-gun salute. We are not to see her like
again in this bleeding bitch of a world. God help us all Livia
Miles is gone!

And that's how it should be—a grand legacy, speeches, a parade, a band, a sorrowing horse clip-clopping along.

That you're the girl I idolize . . .

She felt it pricking her and she heard the voice teasing her, saying, "Here it comes, it's happening! Not to someone else but to you! It's *your* turn—it's your turn!"

And I pray for the day when I hear you say—

"Bloody hell away me!"

For years she had watched all the ones taking their turn working their way to the edge and she had taken consolation each time that she was far behind. Young yet. Fifty years yet. Forty years, thirty years, twenty years, ten, five—and the line in front got smaller-smaller and finally she could see where it ended, the very place where the bluff broke.

As long as you're walking you can't die. Dead people don't move. Movement is life.

. . . mine, all mi-i-ine . . .

"Outta my way! Dun me touch!"

"Take these pills, Mom."

"Whazzit?"

"Something to make you better."

She stopped and swallowed pills with water and found she was thirsty and she drank the whole glass of water, forcing it past an Adam's apple that hurt.

"Throat," she said, gasping.

"I know, Mom, I know."

She wanted to say something but words slipped sideways or

came backwards out her mouth. Her mouth moving as she pointed at the words floating above her head. "Name? Name?" she asked. Then slowly: "Name . . . yours?"

The girl smiled, her eyes glistening. And she said, "Booboo. My name is Booboo."

"Yop." Livia grabbed her head and squeezed and wondered where the names were stored.

"Booboo."

"Mom."

"Names hide."

"This is George. I'm Booboo. That's Ho Tep, your dog."

"My dog! My dog that ain't. My dog brown my—"

"Mom."

"My dog E Ching. Come here, boy! Where E Ching? Where takin me you?"

"A hot bath. It'll warm you up. It's getting too cold out here."

Livia pushed her face forward, her nose almost touching her daughter's nose, and she sang angrily—

> *Oh, Livia Marie . . . most anybody can see*
> *that you're the girl I idolize . . .*

Booboo put her hand over her mouth. "That's Daddy's song. Daddy wrote that song for you," said she. "For your birthday, Daddy on the banjo and me and Hal round the cake and the candles lit and we all sang 'Oh, Livia Marie.' So you remember that. You remember when we were the four of us."

She joined Livia and they both sang "Oh, Livia Marie" and Livia didn't mind it anymore.

> *I pray for the day*
> *when I hear you say*
> *you're mine, all mi-i-ine . . .*

"Harold Burden," Livia said when the song was over, "I member Harold Burden. Harold was one hell of a dancer."

"And banjo player."

"And fun and a singer."

"Yes . . . yes . . . yes," said Booboo. "Yes, he was."

THEY COAXED LIVIA into the house, stripped her and put her in a tub of hot water that turned gray with scum.

"Eeek!" she cried.

"It was all that messing in the garden, getting yourself so muddy, Mama."

"Dun unplug . . . the drain." She remembered about drains, how some fella was sitting on the pot and a snake came up and bit his ass. Snakes lived down there. And rats. And—

"I won't pull the plug, Mom."

Tears fell on Livia's forehead, shoulders. "You keep cryin, Booboo?"

"Can't help it. This life of ours."

"Ever-thing . . . be okay."

"You used to bathe me, Mom. And now I'm bathing you."

"Yop."

"Everything's backasswards."

"It is?"

She stood up and grabbed the good daughter—always can count on her but that boy forget it! What was his name?

"Name. Brother," she said.

"Hal," Booboo told her. "Harold Burden Jr."

"Hal . . . Harold Burden Jr. Call him up."

"Hal's dead, Mom. Surfing drowned. Remember?"

She got out of the tub, watched her daughter pull the plug and the water started down the drain. Booboo dried her off. Fresh pajamas. Hair brushed. Afghan over shoulders. And—

Safe.

Cody sprawled, smoking a pipe, watching TV.

"Milk and cookies, Mom. Chocolate chip, just for you. Still warm. George made them."

"Coffee," demanded Livia.

The coffee came and she put two spoons of sugar in it. Still not sweet enough, so put two more.

"You used to drink it black," Booboo told her. "Remember when they called you Tarpot?"

"Tarpot? Tarpot?"

Booboo shook her head, fed Livia a cookie. She could swallow a cookie if she ate it with coffee and the coffee melted it down her throat. Booboo tried to get her to eat more but she *couldn't* she *wouldn't.*

"Well, at least she ate one."

"What happened to me?" Livia asked.

"You had a little stroke the other day," said Booboo. "Doctor thinks maybe you've had some ministrokes, a few of them over the past year or so. That's what's been going on."

The word *stroke* scared Livia. She jumped up, spilled the coffee. The song started in her head again. She tried to outrun it. Back and forth. Back and forth, like a train going *chug-chug!*

"I can't stand that pacing!" cried Booboo. She got a towel. Soaked up the coffee, wiped the floor, the table.

Cody got up from the chair. Went out. Came back. He had the *Book* in his hand.

"Here you go. Read to her, Joy," said Cody.

"You read, George, I can't."

White Dove took Livia's hand and led her to the sofa. She sat down and White Dove put an arm around her shoulders, pulling her tight and patting her head. She was a good girl. That boy Hal you couldn't count on him for nothin! She remembered him in swimming trunks baggy to the knee, loping off with a surfboard under his arm. He never wrote, never called. Blamed her for all the pain in his life, those bruised eyes, punctured eardrums, split lips. She called to the dog but he hurried over to Cody and pawed to come up, scratch-scratch. Cody lifted the dog into his lap, pet the ears, pet the head. Dog tongue panting happy.

"Read, George," said White Dove. "Let's hear about Cody."

~

THE PAGES TURNED and the story filled Livia's mind. She could hear the bloodcurdling howls and screams, while fire shot from the cabin, engulfed the little barn and the shed. The men had Lily on the ground in front of the cabin and her clothes were torn and they were taking turns on her, whipping each other into a fury of lust. Galloping to the rescue, Livia dug her spurs into Old Paint Two and rode hard. She had her rifle out and as soon as she got in range she started shooting. A man fell across Lily's naked bosom, back of his head blown off. The others turned to face Livia and another one fell with a bullet between his eyes and another and a fourth. To see four of their pals fall so quickly and accurately shot through the head like that, spooked the rest and they ran for their horses and cut across the meadow.

 . . . was nothing more Cody could do. She was nearly gone, her eyes already glassy. He pulled the dead man off her chest and knelt beside her and took her hand and he told her he wouldn't rest until he got them all and she was revenged. Her eyes found his eyes and she blinked once to show she understood, but then the light faded and he could see the last sparks flickering and her mouth moving but no words came. She squeezed his hand once and then the glimmer that was the earthly Lily went out of her and she was no longer looking up at Cody but looking down on him, watching him kiss her hand, his lips smeared with blood.

Cody buried her on a hill overlooking the Pecos River, and he put up a cross, carving on it:

HERE LIES A HERO OF THE WEST LILY MILES 1886.

"IS SHE ASLEEP?" asked White Dove.

"No," answered Livia. She opened her eyes. She had perked up when she heard the last name of the heroic dead. She raised her hand and tried to say something but nothing came out, so she pointed at the book and pointed at herself.

"What's that?" said White Dove.

"*Miles,*" squeaked Livia.

"Yes, Mom, that's your name."

She put her head on White Dove's breast. She heard him ask if he should keep reading and heard her saying, "Let's let her sleep." The dog was laid by her side. The dog licked her chin. "E Ching," she mumbled, "is my dog."

She took a peek inside her mind and saw herself tracking those who murdered Lily Miles.

She didn't need to hear it from the book. The book lived in her head untouched, like the song husband Harold was singing:

Oh Livia Marie . . . most anybody can see—

Free of fear and full of anger, she rose from the grave of Lily Miles. Spun the chambers and reloaded her forty-four. She mounted Old Paint Two. She saluted Lily, spurred the horse toward the west and began tracking the posse that had been tracking her.

Buck Root

"Hey, Buck!" Mac greeted him, and the others at the bar waved and he heard somebody say, "There's Buck. Buck is here."

"You gonna do your standup again?" said Mac. He was wiping the bar down, running the little towel in circles and smiling at Buck, glad to see him.

"If you get me drunk enough, I will," Buck told him.

He took a table in the middle of the room and ordered a double whiskey neat. His hands were trembling as he felt the dent in his forehead where Con had driven her high-heel shoe. The dent sucked up the tip of his finger. She was the kind of woman who would kill you if you slapped her. He knew he would have to watch it from now on. He didn't like a woman who fought dirty that way. Joy never had, nor had Patsy. Patsy had never even raised her voice.

A waitress set down his drink. She smiled provocatively. "I caught your act," she said. "You're funny, Buck."

"Funny-looking," he said.

"Naw," she said. "I laughed at your jokes. The one about the girl who asks the cop what disco she's at, that sort of happened to me one night when I got pulled over. All those flashing lights. I was like, 'Where am I?' "

"Were you drunk?"

"Hell-yeah. They put me in jail."

150

"You're too cute to be in jail," said Buck.

"Tell me about it," she said. "Those cops got hands like you wouldn't believe."

"Let me clue you in about cops," said Buck. "If cops weren't cops, they'd be criminals."

"Tell me about it."

Buck watched her walk away, her tray hanging lazily, her backside moving in a lovely, fluid motion. He glanced at a table close by and saw Con with her pussy in some old pervert's face. He was smiling. His hands were gripping the bottom of his chair. Con slipped over him, inches above his lap, and moved around in a swishing motion. Everywhere Buck turned, women were lap-dancing chair-gripping men.

The drink trembled as he lifted it. He set it down and whispered, "Stupid hands." Leaning over, he put his lips on the rim of the glass and sucked in a mouthful of whiskey. Waited for the warm, calming glow.

He looked at Con squirming faster and faster and the old pervert's face getting darker and darker. And then his hands cutting loose, taking hold of Con's hips. She was instantly off him.

"Don't touch!"

He put his hands on the chair again, but she wasn't coming back. She had his money and was moving on.

"Hey, sweetpea, come on," he said, but it was no use. He got up and followed her. He caught up to her and said something in her ear.

Buck took another sip of whiskey and looked at his hands. A little bit of shaking in the fingertips still. He picked up the glass and finished the drink quickly. He was warm all over. His cheeks felt feverish. He took out his pen and grabbed a napkin and wrote on it in a crabby hand: *She's a boy toy, a Con-coy for perverts to play*.

He worried the pen over the napkin, but couldn't think of

what more to write about her. She didn't inspire him the way Joy had. Joy had nurtured his dreams, went along with his way of seeing things. But Con, she—

He turned the napkin over and on it he tried to sketch forms that were supposed to be him lifting Joy like a barbell.

"Joy, what happened?" he said.

He put the pen down and stared at the drawing.

"Why do these tarts have to own you body and soul? Why can't a man have a bit of this and that and then come home and not have to pay for it for the rest of his life? What's the big deal? Can you tell me what the big deal is?"

The man at the next table gave him a quizzical look.

"Can you tell me?" said Buck.

"Tell you what?" said the man.

"Hey, can I get another round here, honey?" Buck asked a passing waitress. "And a beer chaser," he added.

"Gotcha, Bucky," she said, waving her fingers.

The girls moved between tables gracefully with their trays held high. Lap-dancers writhed to the music, it sounding like, *whap, whap, unnnh, unnnh, umm, umm*. He fingered the stud in his left ear. The lobe was sore. Glancing at the little stage, he watched a naked woman wiggle. He wondered if he should get up and do his thing—sing "Lil of the Golden West" or maybe do the bit he had done the other night. Mac would like that. The girls would like that. Everybody would.

How can you tell the Irish guy in the hospital?

"Got a big laugh from that," he murmured, remembering shouts of laughter, intoxicated smiles.

And the one where the blonde turns to her husband and says, *Let's send the kids out to P-L-A-Y so we can fuck.*

The Nazi tampon one was good too. *A twatstika.*

The same girl brought his order again. "I'm going on lap duty in a while," she said. "Would you like me to come back, Buck?"

"How much?"

"You know."

"Check with me," he told her. She was a cute little thing, no bigger than a minute. Her name was? Was?

"Gettin bad with names," he told himself.

He lifted the whiskey. Chased it with beer and cackled at nothing and the guy at the next table gave him a look again. Smarmy eyes.

"What you lookin at?"

The guy looked away.

"I oughta kick his ass," Buck muttered to himself. He thought he might get to it pretty soon if his mood didn't change. He searched the place for Con but couldn't find her. The old pervert was gone too.

A century note, a sweaty moment in the van.

She was the only one who could make any money. Nobody in Chicago gave a damn about a has-been bodybuilder, once semi-famous but now forgotten Buck Root. He sold a few vitamin pills, but that was it. The body was failing. It was time to get writing, time to write that bio. Time to wow the world with his fascinating life. Instead of sitting drinking, he should be in the motel with pen and paper writing up a storm.

"Yeah right," he grumbled.

The band took a break and the place got quieter. People's voices went down a few notches, enough so a fellow could hear himself think. Buck took in the clink of glasses, a woman laughing, a man saying, "Now look what you done!" Buck closed his eyes and remembered a poem he had copied one time and tried to pass off as his own, until someone made the point that he was ripping off Auden:

> *God may reduce you*
> *on judgment day*

to tears of shame,
reciting by heart
the poems you would
have written, had
your life been good.

"Had my life been good," he said as he looked around the bar at the nearly naked bodies passing by, smelling of cigarettes and booze and fading perfume. Dark-eyed men and women leaning over toadstool tables, fists wrapped around tall drinks, raised to eager lips, then to the tabletop, back and forth, up and down all night long, bodybuilders pumping glass. He didn't have to think about how good his life had been and who he should blame and he wondered if anything had ever truly gone well for him in his forty-plus years and had there ever been anyone, man or woman, who had cared about him as a person and how hard he had worked and how so little had come of it and how it seemed that no one gave a shit that his life was nothing but lost dreams and broken hearts and no one ever loving him just for himself alone, but loving his face, loving his body, that's all; but not the real him, the complex visonary that he would have been, given half a chance.

His lips felt rubbery. "I'm gettin pissed," he told himself. He took an ice cube from his glass and rubbed it over his forehead, his hot cheeks, let it melt a little, let the droplets trickle along the edges of his nose and mouth. He started feeling cooler within. Life wasn't so bad. He had done some things. George had seen him on TV doing the Tube-Flex commercial. Thousands more must have seen him too. Admired his physique. And the magazines he had been in, the articles about him, the titles he had won. All those accomplishments were nothing to sneeze at.

He took a pen from his pocket and pulled napkins from the holder, opened them and smoothed them flat and wrote on the top one in jittery letters:

I am born.

My proud parents christen me Michelangelo Buonarotti Routelli, but as soon as I realize what they've done to me, I change my name to Buck Root.

As you can see by my christian name, my mother and father had big plans for me. They wanted me to be an artist like Michelangelo, but my art turned out different than his. I became a Michelangelo of the body.

When I was three my father left my mother and she lost her mind. One day she dug a hole in the backyard. She took my hand and marched me outside and she gave me a hug, which made me delirious with joy. It was the kind of Mama-loves-me joy that kids need. When she picked me up and held me over the hole she had dug, I could see hatred in her eyes. I shrieked and kicked and clawed and grabbed at her, my hands digging at her neck and hair and I promised her I would be good. That is why she was burying me, because I was bad. What else could it be? So I was shrieking that I would be a good boy and she was trying to peel me like you would peel a cat that had his claws in you. And then the neighbor came out on his porch and yelled over the fence, 'Hey! What's going on with you? You fixin to make a chalk body of that boy?' And Mama ran with me back to the house.

I was terrified of her ever since, until I grew big and she got small. I'm very big now, full of muscles that any man would be proud to have. I'm Mr. Los Angeles, Mr. Philadelphia, Mr. Chicago, Mr. Mount Olympus, Mr. Baja Peninsula, Mr. Minneapolis Thighs. No woman can throw me in a hole now. No man neither. No one can hurt the Root, unless the Root lets it happen.

~

BUCK SQUINTED HARD, pressuring his eyeballs, shaping the corneas so he could read what he had said. He thought about needing glasses and it made him angry. The words came into focus and he pondered them and wondered why he was compelled to repeat the same story about his mother and the hole over and over. He must have told it a thousand times and thought of it every single day since it happened. It was like yesterday to him, the image of it.

He read his words carefully and told himself that maybe they made a good opening. Did the thing sound like a real-live book? He thought it did. It occurred to him that he had a natural gift for storytelling, that his life was a stormy adventure, which fit right into what storytelling was about. First you get experiences and then you write them down. He remembered Ernest Hemingway saying something like that, something about needing to live before you can write anything worth a good goddamn. Buck had read lots of Hemingway's stories and knew that the two of them would have had some drinks together and some man-to-man talk and understood each other like soul brothers.

The band came back from its break and the music started up and the voices all around got louder and soon it was all a din of noise in Buck's ears and he realized he would not be able to hear the story of his life, and so he gave up for the moment and promised himself that he would do it another time, a time when things were just memories and silence. He saw Joy's eyes on him as he pumped iron. He was certain that Joy had loved him to some degree a tiny bit.

Was she still dancing for Ronnie? Had she done anything with Sissy's paintings? Was she balling George? Sure she was. Joy couldn't go a week without it. She said she needed sex because it was the only thing that relieved the tension of her overwhelming life. Without sex she would explode. It was why he had never really trusted her, because she would play with herself, even when he was regularly doing his best to do her, giving her orgasms if he could. He had awakened beside her some nights and she would be masturbating and it would piss him off that she hadn't invited him to participate and so he would stay away from her, and he would flirt with other women and every time he was unfaithful he was getting back at Joy for her finger nights, the orgasms she had had without him, count-less many he was sure, and all of them reminding him of how inadequate he was, how unnecessary to her and to all women cuddled up with their fingers and their vibrators, knowing in the depths of their souls how disposable men were. So she had to take some blame for how he acted, wasn't all just him being rotten-no-good.

~

THE MUSIC FADED. Then the beat began again. The sweet thing no bigger than a minute came back. She wore a diaphanous teddy, gauzy white. She smiled at him and he nodded and she started swaying and rocking and giving him bendovers so he could peek at the strip of cloth sheathing her hole. He slid his chair away from the table, so she could get at him, her legs spreading as she moved toward him backwards. He wasn't sup-posed to kiss her ass, but he did it anyway and she swooped down and did a slick squirm over his lap and stood up and turned, high-kicking her leg over his head, giving him a whiff of perfumed pussy, then adjusting herself so she was facing him, her impossibly large and rigid tits in his face and her bottom grinding on him, her groin touching his tumescenting self, coaxing it along.

He let her work and his thoughts drifted to Joy again and how exciting it had been after they first met, how they would make love in her big Lincoln with its lay-back seats and she would get over him and work him inside her and move and grind and get herself off and get him off and how exciting it was in the dark in the car in parking lots where people might walk by any second and see.

The first months were the best. She was at her best in the beginning and he was at his best too, but that was then and this was now: twenty dollars minimum for a woman to bounce over his lap. And Con in the van with a dirty old pervert.

When the music was over the girl's shadow lifted. She turned to the table and fingered the money he had left there. She took a twenty and a five. "Tip?" she said, her voice breathy. "Did I earn it?" she said.

"What's your name?" he said. "Slip my mind."

"Bree Walker."

"Bree Walker, that's it. Bree, I love to eat Brie . . . Brie cheese." He chuckled, smiled. She smiled back.

"You've heard that a million times, I bet."

She nodded. "Another drink?" she said.

"Hell yeah, sure," he said.

He kept watching the door to see if Con was coming back. She was taking a long time. He wondered if she was really out there or had she taken off? He kept waiting for that, for her to hop in her van and boogie. He had no idea what he would do without her. Who would put a roof over his head? Who would feed him and give him money? She had been talking about going back to her inheritance in Minnesota, the family farm near Elk River. She was renting it out, but the tenants had said they were moving and she had said, "Let's go back there, Buck. Let's go run my old man's farm. Get some cows and chickens and plant some corn and—"

"Can you see me as a farmer?" he had asked her.

He sipped his drink, his hand rock steady now, his mind

mellow. "I'm okay," he told himself. "I still got it," he added, tightening his thighs, secure in their bulk.

He drank to Mr. Minneapolis Thighs.

The door opened and the Lake Michigan wind blew premonitions of winter and there was Con. She gave him a look. Acid. She wouldn't want any of him tonight and he wouldn't want any of her. She went over to the bar and said something and motioned toward him, then she went into the back hall. In a minute Bree brought him another drink. "Con paid for it," said she.

"I always do what I'm told," he answered.

The whiskey went down with the slight bite of the cheaper brand. He was feeling very fine now, his mind a humming dynamo. He thought about the time in San Diego when he was eighteen and still had an innocent heart and he and Patsy went to a coffeehouse on University Avenue in North Park and poet after poet stood on a little platform, reciting poetry to the crowd, and Patsy coaxed him into performing and he had felt very Kerouac-on-the-road-cool as he stood there chanting:

> *Fingering Patsy's places*
> *shuts other lives in dormant rooms*
> *restoring the beat of an unknown heart*
> *with the cadence of bodies pacing*
> *like the measure of cymbals mimicked*
> *or horns haunting the moon*
> *or drums chasing tambourines*
> *these are the primitive tunes.*

A poem he had written himself before he lost confidence and started borrowing from others, letting their work fill the place that was drying up, folding inward, making room for body art, for the art of the body. He owed to Patsy the need he had once had to write poetry. Her lean look, her sweet hazel eyes and her love of literature had inspired him. At least for a while. There was poetry and there were the weights and it seemed finally he couldn't handle both. Had to focus. Had to concentrate on one.

But he missed Patsy. Would always miss her. He missed Joy. Missed both. How could that be? Missed Patsy. Missed Joy. Loved them and now missed them. He wondered if he loved Connie. Maybe so. Probably he wouldn't know until after she was gone.

~

"What's that there?" said Con.

Buck looked up and saw her eyeing the pile of napkins.

"My autobiography," he told her.

"Good," she said, "it's time you got to work."

He could see how disappointed she was in him. He had seen the same look in Joy's eyes and sometimes in his wife's eyes, how he hadn't lived up to their anticipations. Like Patsy and then Joy, Connie had expected exciting times, rubbing elbows with celebrated people and having money and fame. But she hadn't known how tired he was and how his belief in himself was fading with every gray hair, every wrinkle that appeared.

"I'm still best-seller material," he said, grinning boldly at Connie, hoping that he looked good to her. "Are you still my baby?"

She bent down and kissed him, her lips going sloppily round and round, tasting of smoke. Promises percolated through his groin. He wanted her to sit on him and wriggle like Bree Walker had done, make something happen. "Yes, I'm your baby," she replied.

The music jumped in deafening. "Dance on me, lap-dance

me," he said, his voice husky. But she was already gone, already scrutinizing other men.

~

BUCK PASSED MORE HOURS doodling some of this, some of that—a line, a phrase, a word, a drawing. He saw himself on talk shows, people hanging on his every word. Probably he would win an award, the Nobel prize. He saw himself giving speeches. He was famous all over the world, his works translated as often as Shakespeare's.

"I used to be a thinker. I used to use the words," he said. "Must be in there somewhere still. Got to dig down and find them is all. Fan the flame. You can do it, Buck. No one ever called you stupid."

When closing time came, he read over what he had written and knew it was powerful, wonderful, maybe even brilliant, and his heart sang and he believed in his destiny. He laid the ink-stained napkins one by one in a pile on the table, smoothing each sheet with his palm, and sat back satisfied.

"Good night's work," he announced to nobody.

A drunken old man lurched by and hit the table and the napkins fluttered into the air, twirled like severed wings. Whiskey went too, the ashtray, the little pole lamp with its red shade. Everything shattering.

"Goddamn what you done!" Buck shouted.

He jumped up and stood over the drunk, who had fallen and was retching. Buck cursed him, called him a motherfucker and a piss-poor excuse of a human being. He drove each point home with a kick in the old man's bony ass. The old man whined and slapped at Buck's foot. He lay on his side curled up, his hand reflexively waving as if ridding himself of a bad smell.

"Iss sor-ry," he said. "Ass-i-dent, ass-i-dent."

He was a gaunt old bastard, pitiful. The anger drained out of Buck and he went to the bar, grabbed a stool and ordered a shot of White Horse and waterback. "You got an old fart there can't hold his liquor," he told Mac.

"I seen," said Mac. He signaled the bouncer and the bouncer picked the old man up and maneuvered him to the door.

Connie came out from the back with her street clothes on. She saw the ruined napkins. "Is that your biography?" she asked. "Who puked on it?"

"A putz with swollen nuts," Buck told her. He waved her to come sit and have a drink with him. He wanted her close, their knees touching, a length of warm thigh in his hand. She had made a promise with her sweet-smoky mouth, the wet kiss she had given him. He needed more of that to put some heart in him, make him feel that life was still worth living.

Maybe they would make love tonight. Maybe they would be okay.

Joy Faust

AT THE BODY SHOP she wore a schoolgirl's uniform—navy blue jacket with pleated plaid skirt. Beneath the jacket was a white blouse, the open collar spotlighting her throat and a heart-shaped locket. She wore white Nikes with white stockings rolled on her ankles. She had dyed her hair Irish red. It was slicked back, curling behind her ears, boyish.

As she danced, the pleated skirt swayed and clutched at her hips. She moved the hem back and forth, stirring it in such a way that the skirt climbed her thighs, flashing white V's at the men in front. She affected the gullible schoolgirl, the amoral woman/child, helpless, hormone-driven and dumb. Enthralled by perversion. Tie her down. Tickle and diddle and tongue.

Indolently she stripped, working her way to a translucent thong and nothing else. She rolled her hips, shimmied her breasts, pooched her pubis and struck statuesque poses— cameo roles for nymphet fountains.

Ronnie had told her she was worth any number of Connies. He said he didn't miss Connie, not with an artist like Joy on stage. Joy had increased his business. Most of the men who came in were there to see her. If she wasn't there, they'd say, "Where's Joy Faust? What time is she on?"

Cigarettes glowed in the velvet air. Smoke created a flimsy curtain, separating her from the crowd. What were they thinking? she wondered. What had they already done to her in their minds? How many laps was she sitting on? Who was kissing her where? She thought of her mother, the men, the muffled noises in the night, giggles, cries, groans. Who had she hauled home, taken down the hall, past the pathetic signs hanging on the walls, one telling her to *Listen to Your Heart*, another saying *Her Children Shall Rise Up and Call Her Blessed?* The boozy smells. Banging bed. Livia's squeals. The moaning, the creepy whimpering. And in the morning that hungover look that said I-hate-you-and-all-the-world.

"Fun night, Mummy?"

"Gimmee coffee and shut up, Booboo."

Livia was well into her fifties before her looks collapsed and she started slowing down. The tug of gravity, its cruelty working on her, would not let the good times roll. An unremarkable moment came when men's eyes no longer praised but slid away. She fought back with a face-lift, breast implants, B12 shots, estrogen and aerobics, and gave herself a few more years of parties and bars and steamy interludes, but eventually everything worth living for came to an end in her late sixties. From then on, she avoided mirrors telling her she was now the nightmare she had always feared.

A spasm ran through Joy, a nauseating premonition, and she knew she had seen her mother's last dance, the moment two months back when Livia performed on the same stage where her own feet now moved in silence. The remembrance of Livia's corroded body made Joy's legs lose their cunning and she quit dancing before the music died. She stood listening to scattered applause, feeling sick, her eyes fixed on the future, the lights washing over her red to blue to white. Dollar bills, looking like legless caterpillars, were curled at her feet.

~

AFTERWARD she showered and dressed, then sat at the bar. She saw Joe Cuff coming back from the men's room, going up to Clarence on a stool and mussing his hair. "Goddammit!" Clarence yelled, while Joe Cuff spread his hands in mock innocence, and said, "What? What'd I do?"

When he sat next to Joy, he said, "Clarence Duff loves his hair. It's about all he's got left, look at him."

She looked over Joe Cuff's shoulder at Clarence, paunchy, slope-shouldered, red-faced, but with thick, wavy, Hollywood hair.

"Did um mess um up him pwetty hair? *You're so vain,*" Joe Cuff sang.

"Shut up. You should talk," said Clarence.

"Vanity," said Joy. The word made her think of Buck, the gold stud in his left ear and how he never met a mirror he didn't love. But then again, she was the same way. Buck had had a joke about that, *You want to know how to drown Joy Faust and make it look like an accident? Put a mirror at the bottom of a swimming pool.*

"Men are getting more vain," she said. "I read that more men are getting their hair colored than women these days."

Joe Cuff was shaking his head. "Candy asses," he said. After a second, he asked if George and Livia were coming in.

"Mom is getting bad," Joy told him. "I'm afraid her bar-hopping nights are over. George is baby-sitting her."

She appreciated George all the more because he made it possible for her to be away from home. If it hadn't been for him, she thought she might have gone crazy with all that had happened. Turmoil didn't get to George the way it got to most people. She wondered where he got his easygoing ways. She wondered why she couldn't be like him. She knew that her nerves were harming her, probably stress was giving her cancer or setting her up for a stroke, but she had no control. The pressures eating at her made her think of suicide. She had decided the best way was what she had imagined for her mother, to take all the Xanax and drink as much booze as she could hold without getting sick. And just go to sleep and never have to deal with anything again.

She glanced at Joe Cuff's thick blond hair, ice-chip eyes. Purple capillaries clutched the border of his battered nose. He looked like a ruggedly handsome, blue-eyed, red-cheeked psychopath. Brutal hands, the fingers thick as rolled quarters.

He noticed her stare and leaned toward her and said, "You know what I'd like to do for you, sugar? I'd like to bring in a camcorder and tape your act, get you on film for future generations to gawk at."

"Me?"

He touched her leg with his knee and kept it there. "I'd like to preserve you. A piece like you deserves preserving."

"That's right," said Ronnie. He was wiping glasses and restructuring pyramids on the backbar shelf.

"Before I lose it," said Joy.

"We're all losin it," said Ronnie.

And Joy said, "That's what film is for, isn't it? To freeze time. Let you see what you were. Except when I get old I don't want to see what I was. I'm depressed enough without that."

Ronnie said, "Everybody gets old. It's *h*ound to *b*appen if you don't die young."

"You say that because you're a man. Men age better than women. Women turn into crones. Men become distinguished."

"Men turn into crones too. Look around, you'll see." He patted his gut. "I used to be flat as a board and have shoulders like a bricklayer. Age has got me like it gets everyone. I'll be turkey wattles everywhere one of these days." He chuckled and repeated the word *wattles* as if it gave him pleasure.

Joy ran a finger under her chin. Firm, no wattle there or any-where yet. *These breasts will never sag,* she told herself. *And if they do, I'll pump them up again.*

"Too many six-packs," said Joe Cuff. "You got to get out like me and work it off."

"Who cares?" said Ronnie. "Best thing about getting old is that you get comfortable with yourself."

"Not everybody is like that," said Joy. "I think getting old drives some people crazy. Some people go nuts, I mean literally."

Ronnie's fingers combed his beard thoughtfully. "Maybe so," he said.

She looked at Joe Cuff's fingers and imagined them on her body. They were eager for her now, but how much longer? In ten years she would be on the cusp of fifty. What then? Who then?

She gazed at the wall at the clipping taped there: *One-Woman Show: Sissy McLeod.* Beneath it was the box of unsold Nova Life. She opened the box, picked up one of the gelatin capsules and squeezed it. Soft in the middle, filled with elixir.

"Youth," she said, offering the pill.

"Minnesotans are skeptical," said Ronnie.

Joy had seen the customers come in for a drink and gaze blankly at the pills, while Ronnie talked about the fountain of youth and how aging was a disease like polio, which Nova Life could cure. The customers would chuckle and wink and say, "Oh yhah, Ron, you betcha." Joy had heard one woman ask how much, and when Ronnie said the price, the woman said, "Jesus, I can buy twenty shots of gin for that."

The men were worse. Most wouldn't let him finish his pitch. They might ask him if he was on the pill and when he admitted he was, they would laugh and shout out, "Ronnie's on the pill!" And it would always get a big reaction and somebody would point at Ronnie's belly and say, "It ain't workin!"

The music stopped. The pretty girl on stage gathered her tips and walked wearily away. Some people at a booth got up, waved and went out the door. "Good night!" yelled Ronnie. "Drive careful!" Turning to Joy, he said, "In thirty minutes we can all go home and go to bed." He yawned into his fist.

"I suppose I should go," said Joy. "Tomorrow is a big day. You coming to Sissy's show, Ronnie?"

He shook his head. "Can't. Gotta be here, gotta work. But it's great what you did, Joy."

Joy said she didn't do anything, just took some paintings to the dealer and he liked them and called in a critic from the *Minneapolis Star-Tribune*, who wrote the article. She gazed again at the article hanging next to her.

"George and his mama," said Joe Cuff. "Her in that room paintin, you know, and him takin care of her so she could. It just about killed him when she died, you know. Never knew anyone grieve so hard. We had to haul him out now and then and get him drunk or he'd never have left his apartment."

"He was always Mama's boy," said Ronnie.

Joy thought about how she used to be Mama's girl, how when she was little everything about her mother had seemed wonderful and glamorous and how she had seemed the voice of wisdom, a woman who understood everything there was to know about the human heart. Joy drained her glass, then shook the ice.

Ronnie poured her another drink. "Yhah, it's good what you've done for George," he told her. He set the bottle down and tapped his finger on the article and said, "'One Woman's Vision.' That's a neat title."

Joe Cuff said he didn't understand half of it. "Greek to me," he said.

"It's just showing off," said Joy. Squinting her eyes in the muted light, she read the words aloud, while Ronnie and Joe Cuff and the others at the bar listened:

ONE WOMAN'S VISION

Remember the name Sissy McLeod. McLeod's work will be on display at Picasso Blue in Minneapolis next Thursday, 18 November. McLeod has been dead for fourteen years, but her work was recently exhumed from a closet in her son's apartment at Medicine Lake. In this critic's estimation McLeod was immensely talented and a gifted visionary, a poet of the palette. She wrapped primitive artistic instincts in geometric abstractions that rivet the attention of both brain and heart. Her work is loaded with epiphanic explosions of form as idea, wherein one experiences what is commonly called aesthetic arrest. In each composition one sees WOMAN as a set of geometric segments: cone-breasts floating away from the body, leaving behind erotically swollen derrieres and sticks for arms, open legs, and hooves that pass for impotent hands and feet, each image a separate segment of body, held together oftentimes in a bath of pointillism, a technique that went out with neoimpressionism and Georges Seurat; but in McLeod it is the old made new as dot after dot in their thousands are united with perfect lines that curve around an entire universe expressive of the female condition.

I was invited to a preliminary viewing of some two dozen paintings by McLeod, and I must say I've not been so intrigued or enraptured by an artist's work since I first saw Georgia O'Keeffe reveal the libido of flowers. Not that McLeod is at all like O'Keeffe. McLeod's influences can be traced to Seurat and Picasso and Duchamp, with liberal helpings of Georges Braque and Hans Bellmer, but the product created is entirely her own.

The following questions were overheard at the private viewing: "Why are all the figures eyeless?" "And why the geometric flowers and vines coming out of (or are they entering) orifices?" "What does she mean by women having hooves instead of hands and feet?" "Why are her figures mostly done in black on white or white on black? Do the gold gilt trimmings mean anything?" There were many more questions, but no definitive answers. McLeod's purposes will remain obscure and no doubt generate numerous critical appraisals. McLeod's one-woman show is long overdue. I am reminded of what a depressing cliché it is that our best artists have to die before we can appreciate them. Do yourself a favor. Come appreciate Sissy McLeod at Picasso Blue.

When Joy finished reading the review, the patrons at the bar nodded and smiled as if it all made perfect sense to them: They had known all along that Sissy McLeod was a genius. They started talking amongst themselves, Clarence saying loudly to Big Dewey, "I was a painter with potential once." He held up an arthritic hand, the knuckles swollen, the little finger and forefinger curving at the tips. "I painted some goddamn good landscapes in my day."

"Bullshit," said Joe Cuff.

Clarence swung toward him. "I've got proof hangin on my goddamn walls, pal."

"I seen your proof. Those are paint by the numbers."

Cheeks coloring, milky blue eyes swelling behind thick lenses, Clarence shouted, "Bring your magnifying glass, baby, and you tell me, you prove to me I paint by the numbers and by gawd I'll fucking give you the deed to my fucking house! I got a blue ribbon for my painting of Lake Superior on the curve of Duluth. You seen my blue ribbon."

"He put it in a frame," said Big Dewey. "I seen it."

"Bought it at a garage sale, that's what I heard," said Joe Cuff. He grinned wickedly. He and Ronnie winked at each other. Clarence's forehead flushed like a wild pink rose. His jaw trembled.

"Okay, okay, cool it," said Ronnie. "You always make it too easy, Clarence. Teasing you is almost cheatin."

Whirling on his stool, Clarence stood up. "I ain't gotta take this," he said.

"Clarence Duff in a huff," said a man at the end of the bar.

"Clarence Duff in a huff," they all repeated in unison.

"Duff in a huff, Duff in a huff," kept echoing around the bar.

By the last huff, Clarence was out the door and the red light beside the cash register was winking on and off. Joy saw it over Ronnie's shoulder. "You got a phone call," she told him. He went to his office. She grinned to herself. Giggled quietly. She had enjoyed the men heckling Clarence. She liked it when men did that to each other. The bar could be fun when they did that. She wondered if Clarence Duff (he who had told her he wanted in her pants, "and not because I just shit in mine,") really could paint. No couth, but she supposed he could. One thing she had learned was how much talent was around—men like Buck who wrote poetry and could sing Hank Williams's songs, and a hidden treasure like Sissy who painted masterpieces in a back bedroom.

Joy could see Ronnie through the open door, standing by his desk. Phone in hand. He looked at her and motioned her over and told her that Livia was missing.

"Missing?"

Ronnie handed her the phone. It was George. Livia had wandered off. He had been outside searching but couldn't find her.

"I thought she was in her room sleeping," he told Joy. "I don't know how she got past me, unless it was when I went to the bathroom. I've been sitting in the recliner reading a book is all. I don't know how she got past me."

Joy's heart was racing. She saw her mother in the cold night stumbling around, falling in the lake, drowning. Or maybe wandering into the path of a car.

"Oh dear God," she said, and crossed herself, "we got to find her, George! Poor Mom!"

She hung up the phone and looked at Ronnie.

"We'll find her," said Ronnie. "She can't be far."

Ronnie closed the bar and he and George and Joe Cuff searched together, dropping Joy at the apartment first, just in case the old lady came back.

Slow minutes passed, while Joy wandered restlessly from room to room, stopping now and then to look out the front window. In her mind, she heard Buck's voice telling her to leave Livia in San Diego in the home, where things were familiar and there were professionals to take care of her. But Joy had refused to listen. She had known best what her mother needed.

"I'm such an idiot," she told herself.

She remembered the day her mother had wandered off in the shopping mall. She had taken her window-shopping and when they came to a candy store, Joy had asked her if she wanted chocolate-covered cherries. Yes, she wanted some. Joy had left her sitting on a bench and when she returned Livia was gone.

Joy stopped people and asked them, "Have you seen a little red-haired lady? Have you seen a *skinny* little red-haired lady?"

And then there she was, shuffling along, an old man in a black beret leading her back. He had told Joy that Livia had followed him down to Sears and had taken his hand and had called him Harold.

That was the day Joy asked her if she remembered saying she wanted to be shot if she ever got senile and didn't know her ass from her elbow. "You wanna shoot me, kid?" Livia had replied.

"No, I definitely did not want to shoot her. I wanted her to shoot herself. She had told me that if she wasn't too far gone, all I had to do was tell her it was time. And that's what I said. I said, 'Mom, I think it's time.' And she said to me, she said, 'Time for what?' Fuck! What am I gonna say? Time to shoot yourself, Mom!"

Joy laughed angrily and Ho Tep behind her backed up, scooting partially under the coffee table. He had been twisting his head from side to side, watching her, trying to make sense of things.

"Never mind, is what I told her. Never mind."

A mist was falling outside, pattering the window. The trees were blurred and bare. Leaves covering the dead lawn looked like clammy starfish. A halo surrounded the lone streetlight. Joy went to her purse and pulled out a pamphlet and read the heading: TENDER LOVING CARE. She had been checking into nursing homes and had found one that seemed right. It advertised WOMEN ONLY. It was a family dwelling, with four bedrooms and a fenced-in yard and a registered nurse on duty twenty-four hours. Joy had dropped by to look things over. The pamphlet told how successful they were in dealing with senility and Alzheimer's. In business eight years. They had only three women at the moment, so there was plenty of room. The caregiver had urged her to do the right thing. It would only cost fourteen hundred a month for a shared room. And that included meals. With her mother's Social Security check and Joy chipping in, the price was doable.

"It's what I should have done," she whispered. "I'm such a dope."

She went out on the porch, hugging herself and looking up and down the street. The mist had turned into rain. An irritating trickle ran off the eave and made tapping noises on the wooden steps. Tree limbs looked like desperate arms reaching toward heaven.

Bless me, Father, for I have . . .

"Watch over her," Joy begged. "Watch over my mom."

She saw her mother getting drenched, getting pneumonia, coughing, gasping, dying. It would be over then. No more worry. No more guilt at having moved her and lost Buck because of her, because she made him remember his mother's madness. He had told Joy a hundred times that Livia would be better off dead, that no one in her right mind would want to walk around demented like that and be a burden to her daughter. Do her a favor. Do it out of love, mercy. Have some *compassion*.

Joy thought of the morning in Wyoming when they had been driving and drinking all night and by daybreak he had talked her into it, all three of them so drunk they could hardly stand. They had helped the old lady out of the car, leaned her over the trunk, where she flopped facedown, then slid off. Curled up in the dirt. Joy had raised the gun, but couldn't shoot. Buck had taken over then, but on the instant of firing, Joy had nudged his arm and the bullet went through the window and the front seat and the firewall and put a hole in the exhaust and blew out a tire. The dog had scurried up the old lady's skirt and made a bump, a quivering ball of terror that wouldn't come out. The whole thing had seemed hysterical at the time, especially all the damage one bullet had done. One bullet and all that and what might it have done to Livia's head? It wasn't funny, but they had laughed insanely. And afterward Buck told Joy she would curse the day she had pushed his arm. She would think back and wish she had let him do it. They could have buried the old girl on the lone prairie where she wanted to be with cowboy Cody Larsen. Now they would have to watch her crumble.

Joy went to the kitchen and found the bottle of White Horse in the cupboard and poured herself a large whiskey, sipped it, then gulped it down and coughed and felt nauseated. She stood over the sink, ready to vomit. She looked at her reflection in the glass and hated it.

"I'm not doing this anymore!" she said. "I'm putting her away. I can't live like this. My life would have to stop just for her and I'm not going to let it. She didn't stop for me, she lived for herself. And me and Hal were shoved to the side to fend for ourselves. I'm not doing this anymore, no sir. I've got my own life to live. She's lived hers. She's had her day!"

Her outburst tired her. She leaned on the counter panting, staring at the drain, remembering the fear her mother had of pulling the plug in the bathtub.

The dog was peeking around the doorway. Joy turned from the sink, saw puzzled eyes and a busy nose. "Why me?" she said. "Why did I get stuck with you?" She stamped her foot and the dog disappeared. She could hear his nails clicking as he headed for the bedroom, the space beneath the bed.

~

SHE WAS SLEEPING on the couch when George shook her awake. She opened her eyes and George said, "Look what I got here."

Livia, shivering, soaked to the skin, her hair flattened like scraps of straw, stood next to him.

"Where have you been?" said Joy.

"What's this," said Livia, her voice belligerent, "the incommission?"

Joy stood up, towering over her gnome of a mother. "That's it, old lady. No more. I'm finding you a place where you can be safe, where you can get the care you need."

"Don't you call me a old lady!"

Joy sighed. Then she said, "I can't live this way, worrying about you wandering out and turning into roadkill."

"Who asked you?" said Livia. She clutched at George's arm. They looked like an improbable pair of stairsteps.

"Tomorrow," said Joy. And then she squeezed her head and said, "No, I can't tomorrow. Sissy's show is tomorrow and I have *got* to be there. George, will you take her for me, *please*? We can't risk another night like this. We can't keep up with her. She'll wander off when we're sleeping. She's going to end up dead in the lake."

"Take her where?" said George.

Joy rummaged in her purse and pulled out the pamphlet for Tender Loving Care. "It's perfect," she said. "It's a home for ladies like her. A home like any home. I've been there, I've talked to them, it's really nice. It's got a twenty-four-hour nurse and everything."

George took the pamphlet. "I don't know," he said.

"Please," she said. "Oh please, George, you've got to help me. Won't you, please? Won't you?"

She could tell that he hated the whole idea, but she didn't care. She told herself to get tough. Only those survive who make themselves tough. "I'll make it up to you," she promised.

I'm not a bad person, a voice told her, inhaling, exhaling, her heart beating raggedly, catching in her throat. "You'll do it, won't you? I really need you to come through on this. We can't let Sissy down now. It's her big moment, her moment to shine. I *have* to be there. I'm her agent."

"I guess," said George, staring at the pamphlet with stricken eyes. Livia still clung to his arm, her head trembling, her thin lips moving, detonating words before they could be heard.

I, George

THE OLD LADY'S FINGER is making motions in the air as if she is conducting an orchestra. I switch the car's heater to high. Warm air rushes through the vents.

"Mmmm," she murmurs.

She is wearing pumpkin-colored pants, with a dark brown turtleneck sweater and a navy blue jacket. Joy has dressed her as if she were going for a job interview. Her eyes are glassy and her cheeks are overrouged, making her look mildly feverish. She has new henna hair, piled and stiffened and rounded on top like an eraser. Her legs are crossed casually, her elbow on the armrest. She keeps pointing at things and saying, "There. Ummm. Been there."

Seeing her hobbling down the street last night and staring dot-eyed into the headlights, rain-soaked hair sticking to her scalp, clothes clinging like cellophane, filled me with a gloom that won't let go. Ronnie and Joe Cuff and I got out of the car and surrounded her and she had a fit, swinging at us and saying, *I'm no coward! I'll show you!* She pounded on my chest until I took her in my arms and held her, hugging her as she trembled and moaned and finally slumped against me and let me carry her to the car.

"Memm-ba," she says, her finger stroking apostrophes in the air. "Been . . . there." She leans toward me, tapping my leg. "Hate cold, don't you?"

"I hate cold," I say.

"Me too," she says.

We drive past Bass Lake and in a few minutes turn north-northwest toward Saint Michael. The wipers are on. They swish intermittently over the glass, from clear to obscure to clear.

"Rain," says Livia.

"Rain, rain, rain," I echo, muttering it, feeling mean about it. *Could at least be a sunny day,* I tell myself. Sun might soften what I'm about to do.

A billboard advertisement appears suddenly in red, white and blue. The words shout COME TO KANSAS!

"Kansas, what the hell's in Kansas?" I grumble.

"Kansas," Livia says. "I'm born there."

"Joy said you were born there."

"Where?"

"Minnesota."

Livia thinks a moment then she says, "Yop!" And she points out the window and says, "The *porch*."

"What porch?" I say.

"Daddy," she says.

Then I remember Joy telling the story of Livia's father leaving her standing on a porch somewhere saying, *Where's my daddy? When's he coming?*

Looking at her, watching her finger flirt with buildings going by, I know she has seen it all, not missed a minute. I see her young and shapely again, like she was in the picture Joy showed me—her eyes magnetic, her lips looking sweet as maraschino cherries. Irresistible woman the length of her. An inch of plaster, powder and rouge can't bring her glory back now. Thirty-five years ago she looked like Joy, her smile heating men's hearts. But now she is off to the home for throwaways.

We drive past a Kentucky Fried Chicken, the Colonel smiling benignly from a tilted bucket that turns round and round on a thirty-foot pole. "Did you know that two hundred yards from the Sphinx's nose is a Kentucky Fried Chicken?" I ask her. "I read that the other day. It's like blasphemy, don't you think? Colonel Sanders's chicken shack and the Sphinx competing with each other for tourist dollars. Understand what I mean, Livia?"

"I . . . don't . . . know . . . no . . . *pinx*," she says.

"Sphinx," I correct, and she gives me a suspicious look.

I open my mouth to explain better. Then decide not to.

~

WE MARK TIME at a red light. The rain has stopped for the moment and I can see low clouds churning. I look at Livia's violet-veined hand resting on her thigh, and it hits me how nature's cruelest trick is combining old age with a fierce survival instinct, and I wonder if it will happen to me, that I'll lose awareness and not know that I don't belong here anymore. I can't imagine that Livia knows the difference between what she was and what she is. If she knew—

"Babby," says Livia. She is looking at a billboard—a barefoot child in a tattered dress, her face and hair filthy. Tears trailing down her cheeks. A caption below says: *WON'T YOU HELP THIS BABY?* And then there's an 800 number to call.

"That's my Booboo," says Livia.

"Joy?" I say.

Livia nods. "Boohoo hoo, boohoo hoo. Cried all the time, when she was a kid. Boohoo hoo, boohoo hoo."

For some reason I think of that little book, *Mother & Me,* the sentimental poems inside it, the illustrations of the mother playing with her child, smothering her with love. Joy and Livia? Ever?

Behind us a horn honks. The light is green.

Livia's finger is conducting the invisible orchestra again. The clouds are thin in places and I can see salmon-belly seams where the afternoon sun wants to break through. The car's defrosters are working hard. I pat my jacket pocket to make sure *West of the Pecos* is there. It is falling apart, the pages coming out.

~

WE GO A FEW MILES, then come to the street I'm looking for and I turn down a winding hill, past houses, yards, cars in driveways, all numbingly alike. I remember when the same land was covered in alfalfa and corn. Forests and fields, silos and barns and old houses with peaked roofs and lightning rods sitting in isolation. Island farms. Gravel yards and tractors and machinery.

The street rises, goes down, back up and then a long hill down and another one up-down, up-down, lazy moraines left by the ice age, creating a slow roller-coaster effect, until finally I find the right address. There is a waist-high white stone fence in front. In the middle is a driveway, its entrance overarched with stone. The driveway is shaped like a drop of water about to fall. At its base is a long, low, ranch-style home made of white brick. A sign on the archway promises TENDER LOVING CARE.

~

AS WE PULL UP to the front door, Livia stiffens and becomes alert. "What?" she says.

"This is where the interview is," I say.

"View?"

"For the job for you."

"No job. No job."

I tell myself to be patient, smile, be her pal. "C'mon now, Livia, let's go talk to them, see what they say. You don't have to take it if you don't want it."

She stares at the house. Then she says, "I don't?"

181

"Hell no, not if you don't want to. We'll just go back home if you don't like it here."

"Home?"

"That's right."

"Promise?"

"Absolutely."

I get out of the car, go around to the other side and help her out. She grabs my hand and hangs on. Her hand is big, like Joy's hand. On shriveled-up Livia, such a hand feels odd, nothing frail about it. I push the button and hear bells chiming "Lara's Theme."

Somewhere, my love, there will be songs to sing. . .

Livia looks at me. She is smiling brightly and she hums the tune and she says, "Our song. Him and me."

"Who?"

"Him and me."

A moment later, the peep-gate opens and I see a blur of pale cheek and freshly painted lips. The peep-gate closes and the door opens and a woman in white appears. "Are you George? You look like a George. I'm Gwendolyn Welsh, this must be Livia, come in, sweetheart, we've been expecting you, I'm Gwendolyn. Call me Gwen."

Livia's mouth puckers dubiously.

Gwen says, "I talked to Joy this afternoon and she told me you were coming. So nice to have you here." Her smile looks etched on, the teeth very large to match her face. Her body fills the foyer, making everything around her look small.

Livia stares at Gwen, then at me. There is fear in Livia's eyes, as if some intuition is warning her, telling her that something is wrong. I try to reassure her. "It's okay, Mom," I say, pulling her over the threshold. "C'mon, Mom."

The smell: antiseptic. Something like Lysol, with an under-tang of urine. There are cooking smells too, burned toast, fried eggs, coffee drifting from the kitchen a few feet away.

"We've got coffee on," Gwen says. "Let's sit out back on the patio and talk. This way, sweetheart, let me show you."

Gwen tries to take Livia's hand, but she pulls back and clings to me. "It's okay," I tell her. "C'mon, let's have some coffee. That sounds good, don't it, Mom?"

We pass through a kitchen filled with white-tile counters and blond-oak cabinets and an oak table. There is a sliding glass door leading to a closed-in patio. All the furniture is white wicker with cushions covered in cherry blossom prints.

"This is where we sit and have coffee and read the morning paper," says Gwen. "As you can see, it's all enclosed and we have electric heaters in the ceiling. Toasty, isn't it? It's nice out here summer or winter. In winter it's nice to sit and look at the snow. So serene, you know. It's a big backyard, don't you think? Plenty of room for exercise. Those are apple trees there. And we've got blackberry vines that grow up and over the fence. In the summer you can pluck blackberries and pop them right in your mouth, Livia. Yum, yum, huh?"

She gets the coffeepot and the cups and pours the coffee. There is sugar in tiny brown packages that say ORGANIC SUGAR RAW. Livia rips four packages open and pours them into her coffee, stirs it and sips.

"Well, let's get to know something about you, Livia. I under-stand you've had housekeeping experience," says Gwen.

Livia stares through the window at the backyard. Rain run-nels off the roof, filling in the silence.

"I've heard you like to keep things clean," says Gwen loudly.

Livia's head jerks toward her. "I like ta clean."

"Perfect," says Gwen. "You're just the sort of employee we're looking for. We crave cleanliness here and your daughter said you're a cleaning fanatic." Gwen laughs cordially. She reaches across the coffee table and pats Livia's knee.

Livia nods. "I like ta clean. I always pay my way."

Gwen winks at me. "She's a dear thing, isn't she?"

"Oh yhah, she is," I say. "I hate to lose her. She keeps my place spick-and-span." I can feel the tips of my ears burning. I look down at the coffee in my cup. I'm playing a get-rid-of-Livia game, talking out of fourteen sides of my mouth at once. I have an impulse to stand up and say, *We're all full of shit! We know what's going to happen to her in this place.*

"Well, we've got plenty of work for you here, Livia," says Gwen. "We'll keep you busy. Do you want the job?"

Livia is taking in the patio. She shakes her head no. She touches my wrist. "Home," she says.

A hint of hardness appears in Gwen's eyes, but her voice stays cheerful. She talks about how long they've been in business and how rewarding it is to help people who can't help themselves. She gets up everyday feeling like she has a purpose in life. Her speech ends and she sips her coffee, her eyes over the cup tunneling into Livia.

Then she puts the cup down and says, "Let's look around." She tries again to take Livia's hand, but the old woman insists on clinging to me. Together we follow Gwen back through the kitchen and down a long hallway, off of which are doors leading to various bedrooms. One is a master bedroom, with a big bed and walnut furniture and its own bathroom, with a giant bathtub.

"This is our most expensive room," says Gwen. "Really, it's cheap for what you get. It's only eighteen hundred. Isn't it cozy?"

The place is nice. Lots better than I expected. I expected to see old people in hospital gowns roaming the halls with their backsides and age spots showing and here and there a creature mummified in bed. I expected to hear moans, wrecked voices crying out unintelligibly. But there is none of that. Everything is clean and bright and white. In the background I can hear soft music, something classical.

~

WE GO INTO A DEN. Against the wall are a big-screen TV and a CD system. Three old ladies with mop white hair and wearing terrycloth robes are sitting on a huge sofa. They are watching a cartoon. The TV is loud. It overwhelms the music trickling from the ceiling. The sofa is at least twelve feet long, curving at the ends, forming an interrupted circle. The old ladies are tiny. They look like little lumps of mold sinking into the cushions.

Gwen says, "They're resting from lunch right now. We had a big lunch, didn't we, girls? Later on, Eddie, our hairdresser, is coming and we'll have fun doing our hair. Don't we have fun, girls?"

Two of the old ladies glance at her. The third keeps watching TV.

"And we dance," says Gwen, pointing at the CD. "You should see how my girls can hoof it once they get going. Do you like to dance, Livia?"

"I'm a born dancer," say's Livia, her voice firm, her chin pugnacious.

The three old ladies look at her. I feel that Livia is better off than they are. Brighter-looking, better-looking. Maybe it's the orange pumpkin and brown-blue outfit and her makeup giving color to her cheeks, but compared to the waxy old ladies, Livia looks young and vital. She doesn't belong with them. She isn't ready for Tender Loving Care, not yet.

As if sensing my thoughts, Gwen sidles up next to me and says in my ear, "We'll take good care of her. She's a dear old thing. You're doing what's best, Mr. McLeod. In these matters you have to follow your head, not your heart."

"Yhah." But I'm not convinced. I see her sitting there with the others, her brain switched off, her body shrinking until she is no more than fluff.

Gwen shows us the other bedrooms. They all have two beds in them. "Most of our ladies don't like to sleep alone," she says. "Most want company." She reaches for Livia's hand again and finally succeeds in extracting her from my side. "Let me show you the laundry room, sweetheart. What do you think, can you keep this clean? We really could use someone as experienced as you. Let me show you how to work the washer."

As she leads Livia away Gwen looks at me, motioning with her eyes for me to go. Livia looks like a child holding Gwen's hand, a thin, helpless, red-haired child.

Come on now, it's a good home. I tell myself. *They'll take good care of her. She needs to be watched. Gwen's an expert. She knows how to handle her.*

The two of them disappear into another room. Music flows from a ceiling speaker, something Mozart. The smell of urine is strong. I see a wide stain on a mattress. I walk back down the hall, through the kitchen and the foyer again, to the front door. When I open the door, "Lara's Theme" plays and it makes me nervous that it might be calling Livia and I rush to the trunk of the car and take the suitcase out. Set it on the porch and leave.

~

I GO SOUTHEAST down 55 and over to The Body Shop to have a drink. I drive around back and stop at the edge of Foggy Meadow Lake and sit awhile listening to the water lapping, and I think about when I was a boy with a new driver's license and I used to bring girls to the lake and park beneath the trees. Girls were magic then. The smell of them, like burying your face in a nest of flowers. Gum-smelling kisses. The daring moment of cupping an unspoiled breast. I hadn't known at the time how fine it all was and how quickly it would pass and how I would get old and miss it. Miss the yearning music and the body of a Marilyn or a Donna or a Joann, their warm vibrations making you feel that something stupendous might happen if you touched just the right spot.

Ronnie raises a hand as I open the door. "George!" he says. "Where you been?"

"Bangin beaver," I say.

I grab a stool and we talk about my mother getting famous at Picasso Blue. I look at the article about her tacked on the wall. "Can't believe it," I say.

"That's something, ain't it, George?" Ronnie says.

There's no one in the place but us. No music. Everything tranquil.

I order White Horse neat. And then I say, "She never tried to sell her stuff, you know. Just sat and painted is all."

"She was quiet," says Ronnie.

"Painted and read. Made dinner and we would talk. And then I'd do the dishes and we'd watch some TV and go to bed. Everyday predictable like that."

"Yhah."

As I'm fishing for my pipe, my arm brushes my jacket pocket and I feel Livia's book. "Oh shit," I say. "I was supposed to give this to that gal." I pull it out and show it to Ronnie. "This thing works like magic," I tell him.

I tell him how the book calms Livia.

"I've just come from dumping her off. Gave her to an *expert,*" I say, feeling bitter all of a sudden. "That's what you come to in this country, Ronnie. I bet they don't do that to old people in China. I bet they damn well don't. Pour me another, will you?"

Ronnie tips the bottle again. He puts a shot glass on the counter and pours himself one. We click glasses.

He tells me his mother is starting to get on his nerves and he doesn't know what to do with her either. He wishes his sister would take her for a while, but she's got a crabby husband and a houseful of kids. "It's discouraging," he adds. "Kathy wants me to find the old girl a retirement home where she can be with her kind, but, Jesus, I feel guilty about it. She's my mother, for Christ's sake, I can't go puttin her in a home. But then, I understand Kathy's point of view too. It's hard to know what's the right thing to do."

"Eskimos dump old ones on the ice and walk away when they can't keep up. I wouldn't do that, but—" My voice trails off.

A customer comes in and takes a stool. Ronnie takes his order, Heineken lager. I light my pipe, work up some smoke.

As I head toward the men's room, I pass by the window that looks out on the lake. The pay phone hangs next to the window. I pause and then go back and grab the phone book and look up the number for Tender Loving Care. I put thirty-five cents in the slot. The phone rings and rings and I say, "What kind of business is it that lets the phone ring like that?" And then I wonder if something is wrong. Maybe Livia has run off and they are out looking for her. Maybe it gave her a stroke or a heart attack when she found I was gone. Maybe she's killed herself.

And then I know for sure something's happened to her.

"I got to get over there," I tell myself.

"Hello, Tender Loving Care, this is Karen."

"Karen, Gwendolyn there?"

"She's gone home, sir. Can I help you, sir?"

I look out the window at the lake. The sun is going down. The clouds are gunmetal gray. There are spots of light patterned over the water here and there where the wind curls a wave. On the other side I can see a serrated edge of trees. "How'd it get so dark?" I say.

"It's past four, sir," says Karen.

My thoughts are coming slow. "I . . . I just wanted to know about Livia Miles," I say. "How's she doing?"

"Oh, are you Hal?"

"No, no, I'm just a friend. I wanted to know if she's okay."

Karen's voice is unworried. "Livia's fine. The usual tantrums. She wants her lawyer, she says she's going to sue us. They all act up at first. Who wouldn't? But in a week or two she'll settle down and be part of the family. We stress the family here. She wants me to call her daughter to come get her," continues Karen. "She said her son put her here. If you see him, tell him to stay away for a while. She'll forget. That's a blessing for these people, they forget things fast. Think if they had to remember everything."

"It would be awful," I say.

"Listen, don't worry, she'll be fine."

"Okay, Karen, I guess if anybody knows, you do."

"Call Gwen in the morning if you want."

"I will. Thanks."

Karen hangs up and I stand a moment holding the phone and looking out the window. Music comes from the bar, an old Webb Pierce tune called, "Fool, Fool, Fool." And I find myself wondering if Webb Pierce is still alive. He was big once. Country music seemed purer then somehow.

I go to the Gents, then go back to my stool and throw another whiskey down my throat.

Ronnie comes back with the bottle, holding it up. "You done, George?"

"One more," I tell him, "and I'll be pickled perfect." I watch the shot glass fill. Light shines through the whiskey. It makes me think of Joy's dyed hair. "Irish auburn," she had called it.

For the art show she had put on a form-fitting suit, shamrock green with gold buttons down the front. She wore earrings that dangled tiny gold hearts from thin gold chains. The little hearts bounced off her neck when she walked. The auburn hair, the green suit, the earrings and all, made her look Las Vegas, not streetwalker but certainly showgirl.

"Ronnie," I say, "a woman can fuck you up if you let her."

"That's true," says Ronnie.

"Don't let her get a ring in your nose."

The guy at the end of the bar says, "Amen and I'll drink to that." He lifts his green bottle and takes a long pull.

"A woman can get a man to do her dirty work and make him thank her for the favor," I say.

"Yhah," says Ronnie.

"What's wrong with us?" I ask.

The other guy answers me, "Who knows? Every man is a fool where broads are concerned."

It ticks me off that some stranger is butting in on my and Ronnie's conversation. "Who asked you?" I say.

He looks puzzled. "What's that?" he says.

"Mind your own bidness, buddy."

"Hey, man, what the fuck's wrong with you?"

I jump off my stool and can't get my balance and go backwards into a table. My fists are up. The man is looking at me with a bewildered smile on his face. Ronnie is coming round the end of the bar. "What's got into you, George?" he says. "This ain't you. I never seen you act like this."

"It's a dirty fuggin tick . . . *trick*," I tell him. "I tricked her and then I snuck off. I'm a low-down sumbitch, Ronnie!"

"Now, now, no you're not. You did what you thought was best. C'mon, sit down. Take it easy now." He leads me back to the stool. The man finishes his beer, gets up and walks toward the door.

"Take it easy, fella," says Ronnie. "No harm done?"

"It's okay," says the man. "He's got troubles. Everybody

knows what trouble is." He opens the door and goes out and cold air squeezes in behind him.

"I hate fuggin winter," I say. I lean on my elbows, holding my head. "Poor old thing," I say.

Ronnie pets his beard and says, "No way out. I try to tell my wife that. That someday she's going to be like Mom and need someone to take care of her. But it scares her, you know. She doesn't want to be around it. But I don't know. I'm going to insist, I think. I'm going to build a room on back and put Mom there and get her a day-nurse. Kathy won't like it, but what the hell, you gotta be able to live with yourself, you know."

"I guess I better leave," I tell him.

"Have some coffee first, George. Have you eaten? I'll make you a sandwich."

~

I HAVE SOME COFFEE. Ronnie heats me a Reuben sandwich, its pungent sauerkraut smell filling the air. Outside, darkness takes over. The trees across the road are an inky chaos, occasionally eased by the beams of a passing car. All the houses have little warm spots of light in the windows. I lean my cheek on my fist and sit quiet, willing myself to be sober. I think of the book in my pocket and how Livia will need it. I decide to take it to her, but before I can get up, the door opens and I hear footsteps behind me. The stools move back on either side and it flashes through my mind that the man I insulted has gotten a buddy and they are going to beat me up. I glance to my left and see Connie Hawkins. On the other side is cousin Buck.

"Well, what's the cat dragged in?" I say.

Ronnie says, "Well, I'll be goddamn."

"Hey, how you been, George? Hi, Ronnie," says Buck.

Connie leans over the bar and kisses Ronnie and they shake their heads at each other and say, "long-time-no-see and what

191

the hell's going on and where you been?" And she says they've been in Chicago, but they're back now to stay. And Ronnie asks when she's coming back to work.

"I'll have to talk to you about that," she says.

"Jesus, I can't believe that I'm looking at you two," I say.

"In the flesh," says Buck. "C'mere, George, lemme give you a hug, goddammit. I missed hell outta you." Buck hugs my neck in the crook of his arm. I pat his back. He says they were passing by and saw my Impala and pulled in to see what I'm up to.

I'm thinking to myself that I want to be happy now. No more sad, gloomy bullshit. I got no enemies in the whole world. Everybody, even Buck, is my friend. "I'm glad to see you two are still alive. Let me buy you a drink," I tell them.

I order a round of boilermakers.

We move over to a table and sit down and they tell me they left Chicago and they're living on the Elk River farm.

"It's home to me," says Connie. "Me and Buck are raising cattle."

"We already got a half dozen steers and three milk cows," says Buck. "One of those cows is going to have a baby pretty soon, she's going to freshen, that's what we call it—freshen."

"Farmer talk," I say. "Good for you, Buck."

"Farmer talk, that's right. But look here, I'm diversifying. I'm building shelves in the machine shed for Nova Life and I'm setting up mail distribution from there. I'll put an office in there and phones and amenities. I got other fish frying too." He taps his head and looks shrewd. "I bought a mail-order preacher's license and put in a 900 number and I'm advertising on the radio as a phone-in confessional. I'm using the name Father Michael—confessions, penance, absolution. You'd be surprised how much business I do already, George."

Connie puts her hand on my forearm and she says, "I'm gonna come back and work for Ronnie, I think. I liked it here."

"Joy's working here, you know."

Connie closes her eyes a second. Then she says that she doesn't want trouble with Joy, she just wants to dance and earn a living.

"I'm going to run the farm," says Buck.

"Run the farm," I say. "I'll come out and give you a hand."

"Attaboy."

"This is great," I say. "Just great."

Buck pulls out a pamphlet and shows me the caption: SISSY MCLEOD MEDICINE LAKE'S ENIGMATIC ARTIST.

"Ain't she something?" I say. "Joy got Picasso Blue to give a show."

"We went and saw it," says Buck. "She's a hit. Her paintings are selling like fruitcakes."

"People are buying?" I ask.

"Am I lyin, Con?"

"He ain't lyin."

I imagine my mother's paintings hanging in houses all over Minnesota and it makes me even more grateful to Joy; but a little flabbergasted too, that such a thing is possible. People owning Sissy McLeod originals. "It's amazing," I say.

"An art critic was there from Los Angeles and I'll tell you, he was drooling over her paintings and he was begging Joy for an interview. I think Joy is onto something, isn't she, Con?"

"She is."

"Joy told everybody she was your agent," says Buck.

"I guess so."

"You could end up rich. Tell him, Con."

"She was sellin those paintings left and right, George. The gallery guy said your mother was a genius."

"Mama was a genius."

"This could be big," says Buck. "Real big. Hey, how many paintings did they hang? I should have counted them."

I shake my head. I've been keeping out of it. Unable to believe in it and trying not to get my hopes up. "A couple dozen, I think."

"Joy's found her niche," says Buck. He looks moody for a second and then he says, "Yes she has. Good for her."

"My head's spinning," I say. I try to focus, but my mind feels hollow. "I bet Joy's happy," I say. "She talked to you, huh?"

They look at each other. "Joy's got a chip on her shoulder," says Buck. "She wouldn't talk to me."

And Connie says, "Buck's got connections. He could be a big help setting things up. He called a guy in Chicago this afternoon and Joy might get to go down there with some paintings and give another show."

"I could be her agent if she'd let me," says Buck.

"Thought you were going to run the farm and mail out Nova Life and give absolution to sinners," I say.

"I am," he says. "You know me, George, I'm an entrepreneur. Got my fingers in all the pies."

Looking at Buck and Connie, I can see neither one of them is what they were. Connie doesn't look so young anymore. Her hair is stringy. There are dark scallops beneath her eyes and a sort of disjoined look to her whole face. Little pockets of skin beside her lips are sagging. Buck still looks bulky and powerful in a turtleneck sweater, but his complexion isn't healthy. He's got pimples on his chin and his skin has a yellowy tint to it. Creases have deepened along the sides of his nose and the wrinkles around his eyes are deeper too. His forehead seems higher, his widow's peak thinner and sporting long threads of gray.

"Run out to the van and get him one of my videos, Con," he says, shoving on her arm. "You'll see, George, this interviewer at the Mr. Chicago competition found out I was in the audience and he came over and said he knew me from way back when and had followed my career from the time I won Mr. Los Angeles. He spent twenty minutes on me. I was on TV. People listening to what I had to say about bodybuilding. I was in fine form. I talked about how it was not so much a sport but a calling, something holy. A religious calling, I told him. That interview was a personal vindication for me, George. What you might call a defining moment. I realized that I am a priest of the body, a priest of The Bodybuilding Church of God."

~

CONNIE COMES BACK. She hands me a videotape. "We made a ton of these. It's Buck's interview," she says. "We're sending them out."

"I'll get on the talk shows," says Buck. "I'll preach the word of the body." He raises a finger high and goes into preacherlike speech. "The body is a temple, a means of expressing beauty and love, which is all that God is—beauty and love. The more perfect your body the more you show your worship of God." He pauses a moment, taps a knuckle lightly on the table. "It's a surefire angle, George. I've never been so certain of anything in my life. With that and my confession phone I'll make a killing."

"Father Michael," I say, and he grins mischievously.

I notice a dent in his forehead, just above the left arching eyebrow, like a pellet has pocked him. "Where'd you get that?" I say, pointing.

He touches it carefully. "That's ole Con trying to drive a nail in me," says Buck. "She thinks my head's made of wood." He barks out a laugh.

"You tried to drive a nail in him?" I say, turning to Connie, whose mouth is flickering with a need to smirk but can't quite make it.

"It was an accident. We were playin and I hit him with my high-heel shoe."

I slap the table and laugh. It is too long a laugh and too loud, but I can't help it.

Connie says, "Don't get hysterical, honey."

~

MORE PEOPLE ENTER and take seats. Ronnie gets busy on them. A couple of dance girls come through and go into the changing room in back. The jukebox plays song after song, everything country—cheating hearts, love leaving, love rising out of a look, a sweet pair of eyes, a kiss—it's the maudlin voice of Minnesota. I've heard it all my life, but never quite the way I am hearing it now. I'm thinking that the three of us could be made into a song. Call it: *Foggy Mountain Breakdown.*

Buck gets up and goes to the Gents. After he disappears, Connie catches my hand and says, "I've missed you, George. You were always so nice to me."

"Missed you too, Con."

"I wish it didn't happen the way it did. I should have never done it."

"Done what?"

"Buck is . . ." She looks around to see if he is coming back, and then rapidly she says, "Buck's goin downhill faster than a runaway train. That man is not what I expected, George. He's got problems in the belfry, I'll tell you what." She nods in a somber way. "I mean, if things don't go just right, he goes *ballistic*. He scares me shitless sometimes. He beat me, that's why I hit him with my shoe. I was aiming for his eye. He's lucky I missed. You ever hear what his mother did to him when he was little? Do you know that she tried to bury him alive? In a grave she dug? His own mother? Jesus, it's no wonder he's so fucked up."

"Yhah, I remember. She was on antidepressant drugs and going to psychiatrists for years and years. Drank like a fish too. Mom kept Mikey from her. He lived with us a lot. She was in and out of hospitals and then she meets some guy, I don't know who, some pipefitter, and they take off to California with Mikey in tow and that's the last we know of them." Connie is nodding as I'm talking, and I'm starting to feel gloomy again. "Yhah, shit," I say, "he's got plenty of stuff to deal with, ole Mikey has. But fuck it, you know. You can't go round making your mother your excuse for every rotten thing you do, can you?"

We're quiet, sipping our drinks, listening to the music, Janine Sherry singing about having a part-time heart.

"So what's he really up to now?" I ask. "What's his angle?"

"Everything," she says. "He wants to be a novelist now. And a priest of the body and a phone-in confessor and a farmer and a vitamin-pusher and God knows what else. But everything he does he fucks up . . . everything!" She chews her lip. "Sometimes he cries like a goddamn baby. You should see it. Man, a big guy like him, it's unnerving, and then he'll go off and pound holes in the walls with his fists and I'm scared he's going to pound holes in me. Swear to God, I think he's having a nervous collapse, George. I know what Joy was trying to tell me now." She glances toward the men's room and a haunted look flickers over her face.

~

I DON'T WANT TO KNOW what Buck has done to her. I don't want to know anything more on this particular day. I down another whiskey fast, chase it with the last of my beer. My peripheral vision starts smudging again, creating a tunnel down which I see something murky moving toward me, leaning in. Connie has her mouth to my ear, whispering. Her hand is on my leg, the fingers sliding up. She touches my genitals, but I barely feel it. "Do you have any money, honey?"

"Nup much," I say.

"You wanna go out in the van? I've got grass and some painkillers. I've missed you. You were always good to me, honey." She pulls my hand between her legs and I feel the humidity.

I do *not* want to go out in the van. My stomach is churning and if I'm not real careful, I might throw up. "Buck wouldn like us in the van," I tell her.

"He don't care," she says.

I open my wallet and take some twenties out and shove them at her.

She puts the money in her purse. "Thanks, honey," she says. She tries to kiss me, but I turn away. "Don't worry about him," she says. "I've been makin money for him, that's all he wants." She coughs hard, clears her throat. "Pimping me, selling me like he owns me. Seven guys he brought to our room one night. Seven. Like I'm some kind of machine or somethin. Used to be I'd get it all. Now he gets it."

Connie sits a moment, her eyes reflecting the blue neon lights in the window advertising THE BODY SHOP.

I think about my own turns with her. I was quick. Shy. Ashamed that I had to pay for it.

She looks toward the window and her lips twitch again like they're trying to smirk but can't. "I'm a miserable bitch," she says, her voice hoarse. "Maybe he'll get rid of me now that I'm not as valuable as Joy. It would be a blessing. He'd like to use us both, but she won't put up with it. Give her credit, she turned away from him. He tried to joke with her, but she just blew him off."

Connie's eyes rake over the image of herself in the window. "I'm so sick of me," she says. "You can't believe how sick I am of me. How come I fell for that nutcase cousin of yours?"

"You wanna sell your van?" I ask. "Joy wants a van to haul the paintings in. We had to rent one."

"You can have that piece of shit for all I care." Then she says, "How much you give me for it?"

Before we can agree on a price, we see Buck coming back.

"Don't tell," says Connie.

As Buck sits down, I stand up. "Gotta go," I say. "Gotta take Cody Larsen to Livia."

They beg me not to go. Buck grabs my wrist.

"I put her away today," I tell him.

"Put who away?" says Buck.

"The old *tart* you hate. I put Livia Miles in an old lady's home." I snigger and clamp my hand over my mouth. Then I say, "Joy asked me to do it and I did it. I'll do anything she wants and she knows it. I'm Joy's clown."

Buck says, "Look here, George, it should have been done long ago. You did a good thing. Livia's fucked and it's time she went along with what nature's telling her. Don't feel bad about it. You did the right thing. It's for the best."

"Like the Eskimos."

"Eskimos?"

The room is spinning, my stomach is boiling and I'm mad. I twist my wrist out of Buck's hand and catch on to the table to keep from falling. I'm not afraid of Buck. I'm not afraid of anyone. I lean into his face and say, "Anybody ever tell you how full of shit you are, Mikey Routelli?"

Pulling back I whirl around and take flurried stork steps toward the door.

Ronnie yells at me, tells me to hold up, he's called cousin Larry and he's coming to give me a ride home, but I wave and go.

Drizzle hits my face and I'm grateful for the coolness. I get in my car and start the engine. I see Ronnie hurrying out the door to stop me, but I don't wait. Buck and Connie have come out. The lights pass over Ronnie and them as I turn out of the lot.

Buck holds the videotape up. Connie looks wretched, defeated. Pulling out fast, the car swerves and I almost hit Connie's van. I can see the dent in the side that Joy put there. Ronnie shouts, "Wait, George, please!"

I stomp the gas and roar off the gravel and onto the pavement and I hear honking and I see lights sweeping by and somebody calls me a dumb sonofabitch.

~

NEXT THING I KNOW I am at Tender Loving Care, banging on the door. A woman answers through the peep-gate, her eyes turning into iron bars.

"Get her, I'm taking her home!" I shout.

"Who're you? Get out of here before I call the cops!" says the woman.

I kick the door. I yell, "Livia! Livia! Livia!"

"Livia's sleeping!" says the woman. "Now you git, you damn fool! Don't you be disturbing that poor old lady after I finally got her settled down. Why would you be so cruel?"

I try to think of why I would be so cruel. It registers that she is asleep and I shouldn't be bothering her. I pull out Cody Larsen and shove him at the peep-gate, cramming the whole book through the bars.

"You read this to her," I say. "When she fusses, you read this to her and she'll be all right. Tell her, George sent it. George McLeod. I love her. Tell her I love her."

I stand there a second, the woman glaring at me.

"Tell her George sent Cody to her. I'm not abandoning her, I'll be visiting every day to read to her!"

The woman slams the little gate shut, and I am cut off, my thoughts coming slow, consisting of Livia in her pumpkin suit and blue sweater and her hair domed, hiding her bald spot.

Finally, I go back to the car and drive away and try to form a coherent view of what is going to happen. I feel a tide of bad luck coming. Up-down, up-down the road goes and halfway down some hill I pull over and vomit out the door, then I go on, my eyes swimming, watching the white line in front of me, trying to keep the middle of the car on it.

I get to the other side of Foggy Meadow Lake before the police pull me over.

"I'm a skank," I tell the cops.

A sympathetic voice says to me, "Come on, George, I've got you." It is my cop cousin Larry and I grab on to him like he is my daddy. He puts me in the police car.

On the way home I sing my heart out to Larry and his partner. *Here's to Lil of the golden west . . . her tits hung down . . .* They follow along, singing parts of it and laughing wickedly. Larry tells me that the song is famous all over town.

Livia Miles

LIVIA WANTED Gwen to ignore the *somewhere my love* and keep reading about the men who ambushed Cody and hanged him upside down from a tripod and cut him with knives and kicked his teeth in. But Gwen rose from the chair and left the room.

Livia picked up the book. Tried to pin the words down, but they wouldn't sit still.

"Co," she fingered his name. "Co-dy."

But though she couldn't read so well, her mind remembered what came next:

And he hung there and took it like a man and never a whimper or nothing. And the posse got drunk on whiskey and were falling down and one even shot another. And when they were all laid out snoring, Cody used the last of his strength to swing himself back and forth like a pendulum and he knocked against the tripod he was hanging from. And one of the legs kicked out and the tripod collapsed.

"Get em," Livia told him. "Cut their throats!"

And that's what he did. Cody got loose and cut throats, saying every throat was for what was done to Lily. And while those throats were being cut, two of the men woke up and shot Cody and he fell down and only two men were left standing and they were going to scalp him, but Livia tossed him a gun and he shot both those two and everything evil was dead at the bottom of Pecos Pass. And he climbed on Old Paint Two and pulled Livia into the saddle and said to her, "Let's go home." And she hung on to him as he put the jingling spurs to the horse and flew in the whistling wind.

"Look who's here!" said Gwen.

Gwen and the skinny one entered the room.

Said Livia, "Whistling wind."

"The whistling wind," said the skinny one. "If I had a dollar for every time I—"

"Me too," interrupted Gwen. And they laughed together.

Livia pressed her temples hard, trying to remember the skinny one's name.

"Hi, Mom!" she said, her wide smile saying nothing was wrong. "How you doing today? I've been worried about you. Look, I brought you Pepsi and chocolates. See? Chocolate-covered cherries." She broke a Pepsi from the pack and gave it to Livia and said, "You love Pepsi, Mom."

"Booby," whispered Livia, pressing her temples harder, the spot where the names hid. "Booby?"

"Booboo, I'm Booboo."

"Take me home."

"Now, don't start that again, Mom. Please don't. I'm very, very tired. Can we just have a peaceful visit?"

"Hommm."

"She moans like a . . . like a—"

"Hommm," said Livia.

"This *is* your home, Mom."

"No—"

"This is where you live. This is your home. You don't want to leave your home, do you, Mom?"

"Home, Boo—"

"Be still," said Gwen. "Calm down."

"Youbestill," ordered Livia. She looked at the can of Pepsi and could not figure it out, the thing on top that opened.

Chocolate-covered cherry melting on her fingers. Why was that?

Boo cried into a Kleenex and Gwen talked to her, patting her on the shoulder saying, "I know, I know."

Livia heard words like crickets saying *creek, creek, creek.*

"Gwen!" said Livia. "Gwen!"

"I'm here, sweetheart. Now take it easy. Here's your daughter. Don't you want to talk to her?"

"Nop, nop." She pointed at the book.

"We'll finish that later. You be nice to your daughter, sweetheart."

"Cody, Gwen!"

"A one-note brain," said Boo.

"We go backwards," said Gwen. "Back to the womb. That's where she's going. Don't fret, sweetheart. Most of the time she isn't aware of what's happening to her."

"If you had known how alive she was, Gwen. What a pistol. Laughing all the time. Singing. Dancing up a storm. She was a life-force, a life-force."

"Just keep talking to her, that's all you can do to keep her in this world awhile. Talk to her like she's your child, your baby. They respond to babying at this stage."

Boo sat in the chair, blowing her nose and talking. She said, "Mom, guess what? Buck Root came back with his tramp in tow, did I tell you that, Mom? Buck Root. You know him. The bodybuilder. Like this." Her hands moved out and out, outlining big-bigger-biggest. "Mr. God's-gift."

"Buck," said Livia.

"I'm free of him at last. George McLeod and I are partners, did I tell you that? George is wonderful. He wants to marry me.

By God, I just might do it. He loves me. It's obvious he does. He's not the greatest-looking guy in the world, but who cares? Pretty boys like Buck have only made me miserable."

"Me too," said Livia.

"I'm handling artwork now, Sissy McLeod's stuff. I'm an art agent and making money too. Won't be long and I'll be able to quit working at The Body Shop and be an agent full-time. Successful agents make lots of money, Mom."

"Money."

"Yeah, you understand the word *money*, don't you?" She smiled, patted her hair in place. Pulled a wrinkle out of her skirt. "A critic quoted me in an article, Mom. An article in a newspaper. I'm famous now, sort of. At least in Minneapolis and St. Paul. I could read it to you. You want me to read it to you, Mom? Mama, do you?" She coughed into her fist. Her legs were crossed, her foot swinging nervously.

"It calls Sissy McLeod an amalgamation of . . . well, some pretty famous artists you won't know, Mom, but let's just say she's in good company. They say her paintings are panmorphic abstractionisms. Now there's a million-dollar word. And another critic called them geometrical pannier paintings—because the women's hips are like Hottentot triangles, he said. Know what he means? Don't you just love how critics come up with catchy phrases? I coined the phrase *bovinity paintings* because almost all the paintings are Holstein-patterned blacks and whites. So that's what I called them: *bovinity paintings*. And that went into the article, and my name right here: *Joy Faust*, it says, see?" She pointed.

Livia's brain was cotton candy. She couldn't make out what her daughter was saying. It was all spun sugar! Livia's palm went to her mouth and she licked the chocolate and the cherry goop, licked it, seeing each lick, then licked again and sang some lines from a song she knew:

"*Had . . . turned to goo, had turned . . . to goo, had turned to . . . goo . . . cheatin heart had—*"

Boo stared at her. "Well, the strangest things come out of your mouth, Mom."

She went on reading. Holding the paper, reading big words. Fancy yammer.

Livia popped her teeth out, slid them into her palm the chocolate spit, flung them at her daughter, knocking the paper from her hand, the teeth dice-clicking, rolling together, stopping. Livia felt cool air on her wet gums. She pointed at her daughter and shouted, "Booboo!"

"I can't take this anymore," Booboo cried, looking at the floor, the grinning teeth.

Joy Faust

Joy DROVE AWAY from Tender Loving Care. At the bottom of the grade, she turned east, driving fast, using all three lanes to get around other cars. "Damn her, damn her," she said, hatred corroding her heart. Hatred for what the old lady had become. Hatred for the way she was dragging Joy through it. Joy didn't know how she could go on. "So damn depressing," she said. "A nightmare, an endless nightmare." The teeth clicked again across the floor. Livia's brown spitty mouth hung open. "Will I end up like that?"

It occurred to Joy that her mother's generation and the generations before hers, back to the beginning of civilization, were not afflicted in such massive numbers with the aged and their diseases, their mental breakdowns. People used to get old at sixty and die. They didn't have the medicines enabling them to go on, barely alive, not even knowing they were alive, their minds eroding faster than their bodies. She saw her mother's face, her opaque eyes, empty, soulless, inhuman.

What was it Gwen had told her?

Talk to your mother like she's a child, like she's your baby.

She remembered her mother's eyes years ago. Narrow crescents half-closed in laughter, mouth wide, showing lovely white teeth, the lush red hair bouncing on her shoulders. A beautiful woman bubbling with *a life-force big as a mountain*. That's the way husband four had put it, saying it one night while they both watched Livia dancing with friends, doing some shit-kicking steps in a hillbilly bar. George Miles was his name. A cowboy cop from Prescott, Arizona, he was her mother's favorite husband of the six.

"Mom might have been a mountain back then, but I'm thankful you can't see what she is now, George Miles. Wish to God I couldn't." *Wish in one hand and shit in the other and see which gets full the fastest*, that's what Livia used to tell her. Joy laughed and the car swerved. She slowed down.

"No hurry, what's your hurry?"

She turned off on a two-lane that curved around a lake and would connect her with Highway 55 on the other side.

"I'm not going to phone her anymore," she told herself. The last phone call had been painful and comical at the same time, the two of them groping for words, and then Livia saying at last that the phone wasn't working.

"It isn't working?" Joy had asked.

"It's gone, they took it."

"What do you mean gone?"

"Took the phone."

"There's no phone there?" Joy had asked.

"They took it."

"But then, how are you talking to me, Mom? What's that thing in your hand?"

There had been a pause, then Joy had heard her mother say, "Well, what the . . . I must be gettin goofy."

~

THE ROAD CURLED along the shore. Barren trees and brush on both sides. Daylight fading. Clouds darkening.

"Hallucinations become reality to them," Gwendolyn had told her. "They don't know the difference."

Joy saw the old lady's fingers fussing. Chocolate drool running down her chin. It was not her mother she was seeing, but rather some distorted version of her mother. "That's not my mother," she said firmly.

She didn't see the deer at the edge of the road until it was too late. She slammed the brakes on and the car slid into the deer, knocking it down. The deer jumped up, ran a few feet and tumbled down an embankment.

"Oh, dear God!" cried Joy.

She pulled over and got out of the car and ran to help the deer. She slid down to where it lay. The deer raised its head and looked at her with startled eyes.

"Poor thing!" cried Joy. "I'm so sorry! Oh geez, ohhh." She stood over it, not knowing what to do. She bent down cautiously and ran her hand over the deer's neck. "I'm sor-ry," she said, her voice catching. She looked around to see if anyone else had stopped, but the cars kept going by. Some slowed and she could see faces in the windows.

"Help!" she called up to them. "Help us!"

The deer's tongue hung like a rag from the side of its mouth. Blood dripped from its tongue. Blood seeped from its nostrils.

Joy kept stroking the deer's neck. The head settled on the brittle leaves, the dead grass. The startled eye glazed over, grew dull. Joy looked at the gaunt trees in front of her, the dark-piled clouds coming in with cold air. Her hand rested on the silken neck. The wind picked at the deer's hair and at Joy's hair. She jerked her hand away and brushed her fingers on her coat. She hurried up the slope and got into the car. Behind her a horn honked. She stomped the accelerator and the tires sizzled.

She got off the lake road and onto the highway. She stayed in the far right lane.

BUY AMERICAN! commanded a billboard.

LEXUS LOVES YOU cooed another.

WONT YOU COME TO JESUS? begged a sign in front of a small, white church.

She laughed insanely, then told herself to stop it. "You are not allowed to go nuts," she said.

The wheel clattered in her hands. She slowed down and the clattering diminished but didn't stop. The right-side fender was pushed in, the headlight broken. *Poor George,* she thought. He tried so hard to keep the car nice and she kept beating it up. He was too good, George was. How come she couldn't appreciate the good ones? How come she had a weakness for the Buck Roots?

"Because I'm stupid," she said.

She looked at the digital clock. It was four-forty. She switched on the lights. The left headlight threw a thin, comfortless glow in front of her. There was just enough time to get dressed and over to The Body Shop before her first show. Ronnie had put in a mechanical bull and she was going to ride it as part of her act, like she had done at *Les Girls* in Vegas.

She looked at her hand. She could feel the deer's soft hair tickling her palm. She saw the car going into the deer, saw the life leaving its eyes, saw too that the deer was an omen, a warning that the horrible thing she had been expecting was coming at last. Something bad. Something wicked. All over the world, wicked things were happening. What sort of cosmic plan planned for so much suffering?

"What kind of god are you?" she asked.

WONT YOU COME TO JESUS? the sign had asked. Suffering Jesus.

I can't take any more, she told herself.

She wanted to run away, but there was nowhere to go. Jim Faust was married again and for sure he wouldn't want her back. There was nobody else, no old friends, no family, nothing to turn to. She had abandoned everything, everybody, for Buck.

"I wish to God we'd never come to Minnesota," she said. "Wish to God I'd never left Jim."

Wish in one hand and—

"Wish to God I hadn't minded living with him. What was wrong with him? Nothing. Better than this. Everything up in the air. Everything so scary and uncertain and crazy. Buck gone. Mom senile. Wish to God I'd—"

Should've stayed with Jim.

She heard a *tish-tish* sound, like brushes moving rhythmically underneath the car. The steering wheel shook in her hands. Her left foot kept shaking; her knees trembled; her knuckles were white. A spatter of rain hit the windshield. The last light showed a thin, helpless line in the west. A voice kept time with the rhythmic *tish-tish* singing in her head:

> *JESUS LOVES YOU. THIS YOU KNOW*
> *FOR THE BIBLE TELLS YOU SO—*
> *WONT YOU COME TO JESUS?*
> *WONT YOU? WON'T YOU?*

Buck Root

SITTING ON THE CHOPPING BLOCK, he held her ankle for a long time. Then he dropped her ankle and nudged her leg with his boot and said, "C'mon, Con . . ." He felt his heart going like a time bomb.

She lay propped on the wood, the ax making a Mohawk ridge down the center of her head. Dim wonder in her eyes. A trickle of blood ran from her forehead along her nose and upper lip, curving round her mouth, over the side of her chin. Blood ran backwards from her head, oozing warmly over the cold wood.

"C'mon," he said, and nudged her again with his boot.

He got up and went to the barn and turned the tap on the outside and washed his face and the back of his neck and felt the freezing air take hold, waking him up. He heard a cow inside moaning. He looked around. The world hadn't changed. The fields were still the color of cured tobacco. Wet earth showing through in patches. The dark forest beyond the fields murky as ever. Everything ugly except the pointed fir in front of the house, its lush green branches flowing downward like a cape. He longed for the West, for Southern California and palm trees and the seaweed smell of the ocean. Minnesota had always been unlucky for him.

"You can't go home again," he told himself.

The phone rang in the milkhouse. He closed his eyes and listened to it ringing.

"Answer the phone, Con," he said. "Wish to God you could." He opened his eyes and she was still there, her right leg folded back at the knee, where it had wedged under when she fell. He wondered if he should straighten her leg. The phone quit ringing.

He went to the house, to the kitchen, and got a beer from the fridge, popped the tab and drank the beer without stopping. When it was empty he crushed the can and burped hard enough to rattle the window. He dropped the can in the sink and grabbed another beer. He took a slice of salami from a package, folded it and stuck it in his mouth. Too salty, but he ate it. The fridge motor clicked on and started humming. He closed the door. He popped the tab on the second beer and looked out the window. A light drizzle was beginning to fall. Night was near. He was pretty sure the drizzle would turn to slush and then to snow. He burped salami and wished he had some Rolaids. His stomach had been a mess for months, heartburn and gut pressure. Lots of gas he couldn't get rid of. It was Con's fault. It was Joy's fault too. But mostly it was Con's fault for hauling him to her smelly farm and then trying to order him around, telling him if he would just listen she could turn him into a farmer. Whatever gave her the idea he wanted to be a farmer?

"You can't do nothin!" she had told him. "What are you but a body! And not much of one either. Look at you."

Joy would never have said something like that. She knew when to shut up and let him alone. Con was stupid. Whenever she got drunk she copped an attitude. He stroked the inside of his thigh, where she had kicked him before he put the ax in her head.

"Ought not mess with a man when he's chopping wood," he said. "Ought to have more sense than that. It just happened, Your Honor. Hey, she was giving me a hard time about that calf in the gutter drowned in piss and shit because I forgot to put the grate behind her and left the cow in the stanchion to have the calf on her own. Hey, how many millions of cows have had calves on their own? Hey okay, I forgot to put the grate there so the calf fell in, but there was a million things to do and how am I supposed to remember every little detail? I'm *not* a goddamn farmer, goddammit! She said I'd never make a farmer or a writer or any goddamn thing, and she called me a loser, *Born loser!* she said. *Hay's for horses,* I told her. I said I would kick her ass if she didn't get away from me, and I turned back and was splitting more wood, hoping she would go away, but when she's drunk there's no talking to her. *Fuck you!* she says, and no one says *fuck you* to me. She gives me one of her chickenshit kicks from behind. Nearly got my balls and the ax came around in my hand like it was alive and buried itself in her stupid head, *thunk!* Just like that. *Thunk!* That's what. Tit for tat. Hey, she's who put this dent in my forehead here, goddammit!"

The phone rang again. He answered it. A man said, "Connie there?"

"Who's this?" said Buck.

"This is Ronnie. Is she comin to work?"

"Con took off. She's gone to Chicago."

"Chicago? No way."

"Yeah, took off with some guy."

"When?"

"Last night. In a red Corvette. Her and him."

There was a long pause and then Ronnie said, "I don't know, man, I talked to her today, we had lunch. She said she'd be back at three."

"She did?"

214

"Yhah."

"I thought it was that guy."

"What guy?"

Buck hung up the phone.

After a few seconds it rang again. He didn't know what to do. He paced while the phone rang. He kept glancing out the window at Con, her head a stump holding the ax. How could he explain to Ronnie what had happened? Who would believe it was an accident? Who knew the ax had a temper like that?

"Look at the trouble," he told Connie. She seemed to be smiling at him from across the yard, mocking him with a grin, slack lips, some teeth showing, looking like Elvis flashing a tooth. "You stupid tart," he said. "Look what you done."

The phone would not quit ringing, so he answered it.

"What!"

"So where is she? Don't gimme no Chicago shit, Buck. What's goin on?"

"Hey, you know what, Ron? She ran off with this guy in a red Corvette. I ain't lying. About ten minutes ago. He showed up and she took off with him and good riddance to bad rubbish, that's what I say. She was drunk, she's been drinking all afternoon and bitching and moaning at me because I ain't a god-damn farmer. I get away from her and go chop wood for the furnace . . . and *he* came in a red Corvette and took her. She must have called him while I was cutting wood. I watched them go and good riddance, I say. She was a cross around my neck. An albatross. Think I care if she's gone? I've been going south ever since she came into my life. I can't get my act together. My act has folded. It's her. She's killing me. I had talent until she got hold of me." He stopped for breath and Ronnie's reply, but Ronnie didn't reply, so Buck said, "Hey, is Joy there? Let me talk to Joy."

"She's visiting her mother."

"She's never around when I need her. What the hell she let Con win for? Why don't Joy ever put up a fight? Hey, tell her I'm sorry. Tell her I've never been so goddamn sorry."

"So Connie went off with a guy in a red Corvette?" said Ronnie.

"That's right."

"Don't sound right."

"You say I'm a liar?"

"I'm sayin nothin, cousin. I'm just sayin it don't sound right, that's all I'm sayin."

"Con don't know her own mind. One minute she's one way, next minute she's another. She's schizo. Nobody told me about her. If I had known . . ."

"Known what?"

Buck stopped to think. Then he said, "Con's a whore. She banged seventy guys in our room one night, one after another. I had to wait in the bar downstairs. I come back and she's got a thousand dollars and she throws it in my face, like it's my fault. Hey, I didn't ask her to. I'm saying to myself, what am I doing with this whore? Joy would never bang seven fuckin guys in one night."

"You said seventy."

"Seven, Ron, I said seven. I never had to worry about that with her. Joy is clean pussy. She's always bathing." He could hear Ronnie breathing. "Joy loves me," Buck added.

The other phone started ringing, the 900 number.

"I got another call, gotta go," said Buck. He hung up and answered the other phone. "What is it? What? What?"

There was a second of silence, and then a timid voice said, "Is this Father Michael?"

"Who? Yes, this is Father Michael speaking."

"Bless me, Father, for I have sinned. My last confession was—"

"Not *now*, my son, goddammit, not *now!*" Buck banged the receiver down.

He went over to the table and finished his beer. "Nutcases everywhere," he told himself, his voice mocking the caller, "*Bless me, Father, for I have sinned.* Sin-sucking prick." The kitchen was dissolving in darkness. The window was a rectangle of muted light. It was time to feed the cattle. He thought about it and wondered if he should turn them loose or shoot them.

"My gun," he said, remembering the forty-four in the van's glove box.

He got up and went down to the barn and opened the stanchions and shooed the cattle out. "You're free!" he told them, waving his arms. The cows trotted out to the barnyard, sloshed around in the mud, then stood still, looking at him. The dead pasture was behind them, the dark trees beyond. Their eyes were curious, their ears twitchy, their breath smoky. Sparse flakes of snow were falling. He went to the loft and threw down bale after bale of hay into the yard, until he had made a considerable pile. The cows were already tearing at the hay, holding big tufts in their mouths and chewing. The water tank beside the door was full. "That'll hold you," he said, "till you get the nerve to go. Get the fuck outta here and save yourselves." He went back to the house, back to the kitchen, and got another beer and sat again at the table. The salami gave him heartburn when he burped.

"Need Rolaids," he said, wishing he could tell Joy to bring him some. The yardlight over the machine shed was on. Folded backwards over the woodpile lay the body of Connie Hawkins, an impossible weight.

Joy Faust

W{\small HEN SHE WALKED} into The Body Shop, she saw the guys with their heads together at the bar. She took a deep breath. She had practiced her speech, *George, honey, something happened to the car. This big deer—*

As she got closer, she heard Joe Cuff saying, "I tell you, he canceled her." Joe Cuff was smiling. White teeth lethal.

"Here's Joy," said Ronnie, beckoning to her.

"Joy, what do you think?" asked George.

"About what?"

The three men looked at each other. Joe Cuff told her that Connie was missing.

"Connie is missing?" said Joy. "What does that mean?"

"Your boyfriend canceled her," said Joe Cuff.

"Come again?" she said.

"I'm bettin Con is among the *un*living dead," said Joe Cuff.

"She's missing," said George. "She's supposed to be here, but she's disappeared."

"She's disappeared," echoed Ronnie. "I called Buck and he said she had run off with some guy. But I saw her earlier today and she wasn't in no running-off mood. That's nonsense. Buck was lying through his teeth, I could tell. Joe Cuff just saw him driving her van and looking pretty wild."

"Waving his arms and beating himself on the head with his

fist and swerving all over the road," said Joe Cuff. "By the time I got my car turned round he was out of sight. I don't know which way he went."

"I called Larry and he went over to Elk River to Connie's farm and it was empty," said Ronnie. "I told Larry what Connie told me, how scared she was of Buck, how he abused her, beat her. The cops want to talk to him now."

"Canceled," said Joe Cuff bluntly.

"Buck Root would not kill Connie," said Joy.

"How do you know?" said Joe Cuff.

"I know him," she said.

Joe Cuff's lips twisted cruelly. "Nobody knows nobody," he said. "You don't know him and he don't know you and none of us knows a damn thing. I seen pipsqueak soldiers, mama boys, turn into stone killers cutting ears off dead gooks, making ear necklaces and wearing them stinking round their necks. Smelly meat rot. You think their mamas knew them? Don't tell me you know Buck Root. My bet is he had her body in the back of the van when I saw him. I'm gonna kill that bastard." Joe Cuff's breath was full of beer. Joy backed away and sat on a stool.

"Don't get ahead of yourself," said George. "Connie's missing, that's all we know."

"You don't know nothin," growled Joe Cuff.

"She was anxious to get started again," said Ronnie. "She was happy. She was her old self."

"Dead self now," insisted Joe Cuff. "I developed an instinct for death. I always knew when death had marked someone. You can see it. They get an aura. She had it last time I saw her."

Joy chewed her lip. She knew Joe Cuff was right, nobody knew nothing when it came to what people were capable of.

There was silence at the bar, murmuring voices at the tables. Joy's heart was dithering, she coughed to straighten it out. She ordered vodka-rocks. She lit a cigarette. Everybody lit up with her. Smoke rose like a powwow. The people at the tables were mentioning Buck's name and Connie's name. Their names bounced off Joy's ears like racquetballs. She puffed on her cigarette, sucked and blew. Her hand was shaking, smoke rose wavering. She saw her mother's hand, the tremors. She stabbed the cigarette out in an ashtray.

"Maybe Con will show up," she said.

George said, "She's run off, mark my words."

"He canceled her," said Joe Cuff. "I've got instincts about that shit. Nam give me instincts. Gimme nuther beer, Ron."

Joy remembered the gun. He had taken it with him.

"She was useful to him," said George. "He was pimping for her, you know. That's what they were doing in Chicago. She told me about it."

"He's no pimp," said Joy halfheartedly.

"I don't think he's capable of killing her," said George. "I don't want to believe that, but she did tell me he got violent now and then."

"He's capable," said Joe Cuff. "Mark my words. I know killers."

Joy closed her eyes a moment, took a breath, then said, "Truth is, he almost killed my mother. He would have shot her if I hadn't hit his arm. The bullet missed her by inches and went through the car and blew out a front tire. He said he was being kind. He said he was doing her a favor."

"He told me you're the one tried to shoot her . . . and he hit your arm," said George.

"He's a liar," said Joy.

"Is he?" said George.

She looked at him puzzled. "Are you mad at me?" she asked.

He opened his mouth to say something, then stopped and shook his head. "No, not mad. Just can't figure things out.

Things used to be in control. Nothing's in control anymore. Half the time I don't know if we're coming or going."

"You'd like your old life back," she said, her voice soft, sympathetic. "Your apartment to yourself again. Who can blame you? We came along and turned things upside down pretty bad, didn't we, George? Kind of just took you over."

"Yhah, upside down and inside out and every which way, but hell, Joy, that don't mean I want—"

"Bah! You needed shaking up," interrupted Joe Cuff. "Dull as an old man's dick." He made some moves, threw punches at George, who sighed and told him to knock it off.

Joy felt Joe Cuff come up behind her, breathing on her. She had seen him in a brawl in the parking lot one night, the guy way bigger than him, but Joe Cuff had beaten him senseless, gotten the first punch in, then wrapped an arm around the guy's neck and pounded his ear, disoriented him, then pounded his face, while the guy flailed around unbalanced.

"I'd sure like to give your boyfriend another round or two," Joe Cuff told her.

"He's strong as an ox," said Ronnie. "Those muscles."

Joe Cuff yelled, "Fuck his muscles! I kicked his ass at George's and I can do it again."

"I don't know," said Ronnie.

"I'd call that one a draw," said George.

Joy whirled off the stool. "Gotta get ready," she said.

~

WHEN HER TURN CAME, she flipped the switch and the bull churned slowly in time with blues guitar and a gravel-voiced singer saying he was—

—*in the mood, baby.*

She danced out of her shoes, wiggled out of her jacket and her blouse, cupped her breasts and swayed in front of the bull before she mounted it and felt it lifting her up and down, like soft ocean waves. She lay back and slid out of her skirt. She pressed her groin into the bull and moved her shoulders to the beat and glanced at the audience.

When she came eye to eye with Buck standing by the door, she lost the rhythm and the bull tossed her off, right on her can. She heard sniggers and guffaws. And then Joe Cuff and Ronnie saw where she was looking and she saw them moving, Joe Cuff in the lead and Ronnie vaulting over the bar with a bat in his hand. The music kept playing.

Buck turned to face the men.

I'm in the mooood . . .

He grabbed a chair and raised it. Then he seemed to change his mind and he set the chair down and stood with his hands by his side, waiting for something to happen.

. . . in the moooood . . .

Joe Cuff came on, his fists already working, though they hadn't touched Buck yet. Then the fists connected and Buck wasn't fighting back. He was staggering and letting Joe Cuff pound on him. People were shouting. Chairs were turning over. Sounds of fists thumping flesh and bone.

. . . I'm in the mooood for love . . .

Joy stood frozen on stage. She heard George yelling, "No, fellas, no!"

Joe Cuff was screaming, "Where's Con, you motherfucker!"

Buck grabbed him in a bear hug, bending him over back-wards, dropping him on the floor. Ronnie held the bat, but he wouldn't (or couldn't) swing it. Buck looked at him and said, "*Et tu*, cousin?"

Ronnie stepped back. "Jesus Christ, Mikey, I don't want to hurt you, but what the fuck you done with her, man?"

"Where is she?" said Joe Cuff, rising. He snatched a bottle off a table and threw it at Buck, popped it off his head, making his knees buckle. Blood poured into Buck's eyes. Joe Cuff dived in and got Buck in a headlock and started pounding his ear. George and Ronnie stood to either side, looking unsure of themselves. The crowd was all for Joe Cuff.

When Buck was bleeding out his ear and dizzy and unable to defend himself, Joe Cuff let him go and started pounding on his face. Buck went to his hands and knees and Joe Cuff knocked him over with a kick, and then went after his face again.

. . . baby, I'm in the . . .

"Kill him, Joe Cuff! Kill him!" the people shrieked.

"George!" Joy wailed. "Do something!"

George glanced at her, then he moved. He grabbed Joe Cuff and ordered him to stop. "Goddammit, you'll kill him! Now stop it!" George positioned himself in front, his hands pushing on Joe Cuff's chest.

"I'll kill him!" said Joe Cuff, his eyes homicidal.

"Knock it off!" said George.

"Leave him alone, you bastard!" Joy cried. "Leave him alone!" She threw herself over Buck crying, "Oh Bucky, oh Bucky!"

Around her she saw people blinking as if waking up.

The music stopped.

She could hear Buck gasping for air.

"Look at her," said someone.

Joe Cuff was shaking his head and blowing like a winded horse. "Crazy . . . goofy . . . broad," he said.

"You don't know him!" she said. "It's not his fault, he's not to blame!" She knew it was true. She knew that she was to blame as much as Buck. "It's not *all* his fault," she said.

His head was rolling against Joy's breasts. His nose was crushed and bleeding. Blood ran from his mouth and from his left ear and the bottle cut on his forehead. He got to his hands and knees and Joy and George helped him stand. Blood spattered over Joy's face. She and George held Buck, while he wobbled on unsure legs.

"C'mon, we're taking you home," said George.

Between the two of them they got him out of the bar. They maneuvered him toward Connie's van. Joy fished the keys from Buck's pocket and they got the side door open and rolled him onto the mattress.

Ronnie came out with her clothes and she got dressed. The air was freezing but her face felt hot. Behind her, in the glow of the yardlight, snow spiraled. Flakes were sticking as they hit the gravel and the car roofs. The people from the bar crowded outside, watching her as she adjusted her skirt and slipped into her jacket. The snow fell heavier and heavier, creating a curtain separating her from the people and Joe Cuff.

She looked at Ronnie. "Don't call the cops," she said.

Ronnie thought about it. "Okay, I guess. For now anyway. But find out where Connie is, will you? Then call me?"

"I promise," she said.

Joe Cuff was standing near the entrance, cooling down. "Why didn't he fight back?" he said, looking from Joy to George to Ronnie. "Why didn't he fight? I don't get it. I kept waitin for it. What's wrong with him? Last time we got into it, he—" Joe

Cuff paused, looked at his knuckles as if they might give him answers.

No one else said anything and finally Joe Cuff turned on his heel and went back inside. The people stayed and stared. George was using his handkerchief to dab at the blood on Joy's face. "You're all bloody," he said.

"Let's go, I don't care," she said.

He went to the Impala and stopped in front of the crushed fender, looking at it.

"I was going to tell you," she said. "A deer—"

He waved her off and got into the car.

She jumped in the van. She turned the key and the engine started at a touch.

"You're a fugitive," she told Buck. "The cops want to talk to you about Connie Hawkins."

"I'm fugged-up, baby," he said. He was on his knees, one hand holding the seat, the other holding a rag to his nose.

She wiped at her eyes. "Between you and my goddamn mother," she said, her words fading. "Shittin-ass world," she added. She turned the wipers on and they slammed back and forth as if panicked by the snow.

"My nose, I think is broke," said Buck. "This ear is deaf." He was quiet for a few seconds, then added, "Joe Cuff got me pretty good."

The Impala's red lights led the way toward home. Joy studied the flakes coming down harder and thicker, piling in ditches and clinging to trees, houses, roads, fields everywhere.

"A mercy," she murmured.

"What?"

"Snow," she said. "Covering all the ugly warts out there."

She could hear him breathing hard, his breath brushing her cheek and smelling raw as he whispered, "All the ugly warts."

Livia Miles

FEET SLIDING over the rug. Hand fingering the wall. The kitchen ahead. Smell of coffee. The gabble of bowls and spoons and people.

Whiteones at the table.

Prune mouths toothless.

"Work like a dog all my life."

She went behind one of the Whiteones and bussed her on top of the head and said to her, "How do, dear?"

"Uhnnn."

"You eat," ordered Livia.

"Yhah."

Down the line she went doing her job until she had circled the table and was standing in front of an empty chair. The cook pulled the chair back and guided her into it, scooted her.

"Eat," said the cook, putting a bowl of oatmeal in front of her. There was toast and orange juice too.

She nibbled the toast.

She sipped orange juice.

It was difficult to swallow.

She had to wait and think about how the juice and toast should go down.

When she did swallow, it made a lumpy noise in her ears. The juice burned her insides. She nibbled the center of the toast and then she got queasy and her throat hurt awful and she quit.

"You are wasting away to nothing," said Gwen. "You're not eighty pounds. What am I going to do with you? You don't want me to put you in the hospital, do you, with a stomach tube and an IV, huh, you wouldn't like that, would you? You need to eat, sweetheart!"

"Uhnk!"

"You won't eat?"

"Who cares? My . . . they . . . want me . . . dead. My—"

"Stop that, nobody wants you dead," said Gwen. "Now, you just stop that."

Livia got up, started clearing the table, carrying dishes to the sink.

Gwen and the cook sat and drank coffee and watched Livia work.

Two of the Whiteones got up and helped.

Together they cleared the table. Livia washed the dishes in soap and water and handed them to the Whiteone next to her, who rinsed them. Dried them. Handed them on to the next Whiteone, who put the clean dried dishes in the dishwasher and closed the door.

Behind her Livia could hear the cook chuckling and saying, "I don't mean to laugh, but some of the things they do is funny, you know. For me at least it's laugh or go crazy."

And Gwen said, "At least they're occupied."

The cook turned a switch and the dishwasher could be heard filling with water and the cook said, "Thank you, ladies."

Livia got the broom and started sweeping. "Work like dog all my life."

A Whiteone repeated it. "Work like a dog all my life." She tried to take the broom away but Livia wouldn't let her.

"You rest, dear," Livia told her, and pointed toward the den where the TV was on, its noise insisting.

She watched the Whiteone pacing the hall back and forth, her slippers shuffling over the carpet and her fingers throwing blue sparks every time she touched the wall. "Oh," she said each time she got sparked. "Oh . . . oh . . ."

Livia went back to moving the broom.

When she was done she went out on the patio, sat in a wicker chair under the heater warming her head and she looked at the snow hushing the trees and she thought of white chickens. It was a clever thought and she wanted to tell someone about it.

"White chickens." She pointed.

Some apples still hung on the trees, white caps on red apples.

"White caps," she said, pointing at the apples.

Chickens and caps vanished in a fog. She saw the newspaper on the wicker chair. She took the paper in hand, looked it up and down but couldn't make sense of the words spackled over the page. Still she stayed with it and made out a word here and there and it occurred to her that she could learn new languages—if she wanted to.

Cody's spurs jingled. He looked at her in a hangdog way, his Stetson off his forehead looking like a halo. Droopy eyes hanging on her.

"Oh, Cody, how?" she said. "How?"

She rose from the chair. She took his arm. Dug her nails into it. So he wouldn't be able to leave. She wept with her head leaning on his shoulder. "Home, home," she begged.

～

LATER SHE WENT INSIDE where Whiteones floated on the couch.

"Tell her come get me," she said.

"Who?" said Gwen.

"Her."

"You mean Joy?"

"No . . . *him.*"

"George?"

"Tell him home!"

"This is your home, sweetheart. This is where you live."

"Faawk!" shrieked Livia.

"Now, now, don't get going," said Gwen.

"Faawk! Faawk!"

Gwen closed her eyes and shook her head and said, "Easy, girl." Then she looked at Livia and said, "Let's finish watching our soap opera, then we'll dance."

"Dance," said Livia, pointing at her feet in their gray slip-on pretty little things.

She stood at the sliding glass door and watched the snow falling on the driveway and over the trees.

She talked to Harold.

Told him he should shovel the walk.

He said he would in a minute.

Harold was a good man. But lazy. All he wanted to do was sit in bars and drink and dance. Harold was a dancer and a banjo player. It's what attracted her to him, his singing and dancing. Clear the floor, Harold is going to dance. Hot stuff baby. He was a handsome fellow. A bit short and thick-waisted but wide shoulders and fast legs and the clearest bluest eyes. Big wrists. Kind hands. Those feet of his like a boogie-woogie blur. Hips shifting, arms flying, legs like drumsticks beating the floor . . . and down in a split, back up and turn and leap and land and can't stop Harold when the music's got him and everyone yelling *Go! Harold go!*

"Jesus, Harold is fun," said Livia. "I'm gonna give him a call and see what he's doin." She touched her hair, patted it. Tugged at her sweatshirt and checked her breasts and thought she could use some tissues in her bra or some folded socks in there for allure.

She remembered that fellow who danced with her and how fresh he was, how he gave her a smooch and squeezed her butt and she got all fired up ready for anything. The man and Harold got into it. Over her! Two men fought with fists for her and Harold knocked the man on his ass. Threw him out the door. That's how she knew Harold was *the one*.

"Harold," she called, "Harooold."

She turned around and saw the couch in an open O in front of the TV and a Whiteone staring and one snoozing and one pacing up and down the hall.

"Where Harold?" asked Livia.

"Harold? Your husband?" said Gwen.

"Greek?" said Livia. "No. Nikos. Ahhh . . . uhmmmm—"
Fading . . . fading.

She tried to hold on to Harold but he wouldn't stay.

"You there?" she whispered. "You there?" She knew where he was. He was at the bar, the one on the lake.

"You let me out. Let me out! I sue you!" she told Gwen.

"Now, now, sweetheart, don't start up."

"I want my son! You call my son!"

"I don't know your son's number," said Gwen.

"Oh," said Livia and she burst into tears. She put her hands to her head and squeezed. "What happen to me? What happen to me?"

Gwen was there with a pill and water. "Take this," she ordered, and Livia took the pill.

She went into her room and started clearing the drawers and the closet. Piling clothes on a bed.

When she had them piled she looked around for her suitcase and found it in the closet.

She packed the suitcase.

Gwen came in and watched. "What are you doing, sweetheart?"

"Where-zit?"

"Where's what?"

Livia made a gesture of slipping a strap over her shoulder.

"Your purse?"

"Yop," said Livia.

"On the chair."

"Oh."

Grabbing her purse she sat down. Searched inside it. Took everything out—her wallet her cards pennies and nickels some keys a police badge. There were old gum wrappers. *Juicy Fruit.* Who was the one who always had bad breath? She kept feeding him gum. Was it George? George Miles, yes, when he got sick. He was a fine man before he got sick. "Booze'll kill yah, George," she told him.

"I loved that man, the love of my life."

"Who?" said Gwen.

Livia waved her off and rooted through the purse some more.

"Where-zit?" she said.

"Where is what?"

"My money! My money!"

"What money?"

"I had thousand dollars. Seventy thousand."

"Your daughter has it."

"Stealed my money! I had thousand thousand. You can't trust your kids! They want me die so they get my money! It's what happened!"

"Sweetheart, please calm down."

"I want to die! I want to die! Nobody wants me, nobody wants me." She wept and thought about her ungrateful children, a clear image of them, son and daughter. They would be sorry they treated her bad.

"God will get them," she said. There was satisfaction in knowing God would get them. "You know, you try your best. You raise them and you do your best and you work like a dog to raise them and they turn on you. They turn on you. Why don't they want me? No one wants me."

"Sweetheart, you're getting yourself upset for nothing. Your children love you. Your daughter sent you here because she loves you, because here she knows you'll be cared for. Your son comes every week, doesn't he? Don't you remember your son reading to you the other day?"

"My son?"

"Well, he's sort of your son."

Livia thought it over. "Wuz his name?"

"George."

"George! George Miles! My God, he slip my mind. You know, I should give that man a call. I think I'll call and see if he wants to go out. A cop, you know." Livia held up the badge that had been in her purse. "His . . . his . . . ummm."

"Police badge," finished Gwen.

"Yop."

"Well, if we're going out with him, we better get our hair done. Eddie is coming today. Do you want him to do your hair, Livia?"

"Yop."

"Can you vacuum the rug, and then it will be time for lunch, and after that Eddie will be here to do your hair. Won't that be fun?"

Gwen pulled the vacuum from the hall closet. Plugged it in. Turned it on. Handed it to Livia. Went to the laundry room to wash clothes.

Livia vacuumed the rug for a few seconds, then the Whiteone

pacing the hall came over and reached for the vacuum and Livia let her have it.

Back in the room the clothes were sprawled over the suitcase and the bed.

She picked up the police badge. Held it to her cheek. Cool and hard. "George . . . George!" she wailed.

Waited.

Listened.

No answer.

She hooked the police badge to her sweatshirt.

She packed the suitcase.

She put on her long white coat and tried to button it but couldn't work the buttons. She let the coat hang open.

Over her shoulder she looped the purse.

When she picked up her suitcase the lid fell open and everything tumbled out.

She dragged the suitcase to the sliding glass door.

Opened the door.

Stepped out.

She heard the tune.

Somewhere, my love, there will be songs to sing . . .

"Our song," she said, cocking her ear.

She hauled the suitcase sledlike over the snow. "Work like a dog all my life," she said.

She opened the gate and stepped along the driveway and headed up the hill.

Snowflakes swatted her face.

Her feet were instantly cold.

She climbed to the stone fence and the white road and turned downhill.

She let go of the suitcase.

White hills went up and down in front of her.
Home?
She pointed a quivering finger.
Somewhere, my love.

I, George

Joy's eyes are swollen from crying and she says she's never cried so much in her whole damn life as she has these past few months. Her lips curl in a wounded grin. I have watched her drinking all afternoon and listened to her talk about how bad she is and how everything that happened is her fault, she is no good and she wishes she would die. She says she has seen my mother's ghost. It won't talk, but it was there and it wasn't happy and it was going to get her.

"For what?" I ask.

"Because I'm worthless," she says. "Your mother was a genius and I'm a fraud, a fucking fraud."

Buck says, "We gotta get outta this town. Soon as I can travel, we're going to California."

The phone rings and I answer it. It is Gwendolyn Welsh. She talks fast, tripping over her words. "Something has happened she's *gone* she got out I don't know how I've got the police looking for her."

"Who's on the phone?" says Joy.

"It's Gwen. Your mother's wandering again."

"Jesus, dear God."

I tell Gwen that I'll come over.

When I turn toward Joy to ask if she wants to go with me she screams at me, "Don't be blaming me for every damn thing that's happened, George!"

"I'm not blaming you, Joy! That's what you've been doing! You've been blaming yourself for everything. You gotta knock it off. You understand what I'm saying? You're mother's missing. We gotta find her."

"Shoulda left her where she was in San Diego," says Buck. "She was safe there."

"Don't you think I know it?" says Joy. "Do you think I don't know anything?"

Painfully Buck rises from the couch. He stands with his hands on his hips, his head hanging. The TV is mute, but images move across it: happy dogs, a commercial for Milk Bone.

Buck says that Joy is reaping what she sowed. She never would listen and so she's paying for it now.

She jumps up and pushes on his chest. "You! You're the reason! You! You did it!"

"Everybody's fault but poor little Joy's."

"Oh sure, let's blame me, Mr. Know-it-all! You know everything, don't you! You're so much smarter than the rest of us. You told George I tried to shoot her. Go on, tell him the truth now."

"Joy tried to shoot her," says Buck. "I stopped it."

"You liar! Don't believe him, George. I wanted . . . all along I wanted to take care of her . . . do the right thing . . . would have if it wasn't for you."

Buck's reply is swift, he tells Joy that it must be nice to have someone to blame for her fucked-up life, have a scapegoat like Buck Root to blame. He tells her she is full of shit. He says she is a fake a phony a *lying cunt*!

Shrieking insanely, Joy leaps at him. He catches her wrists, throws her off-balance and she tumbles to the floor. She lies there beating the rug with her fists. She screams that Buck has ruined her, frozen her heart, stolen her mind, killed her life, robbed her of her soul, her feelings. After all she has done for him, after all she has gone through for him.

"Threw my life away on you," she says, sobbing into her hands. "For a cheatin, murderin bastard. Poor Connie! You've done something to her, I know you have. God help her. God help us all."

"You're crazy," says Buck. "I never murdered nobody." He sits down. His head shakes like an old man with palsy. "You treacherous bitches, all of you."

"Don't you dare call me a bitch!"

"Bitch."

"I hate you! God, how I hate you!"

I pace the floor with the dog. He burrows his head under my arm. I go into the kitchen and put a pot of coffee on and then I lean against the back door, my head on the cool glass as I stare at the glittering snow over the garden, the trees, the houses. The frozen lake gleams in the distance. A skater is there, bent forward, his legs working. He looks like a question mark gliding over the ice.

Buck comes into the kitchen and tells me that he always knew that somehow Livia would come between him and Joy. And he says he took off with Connie because he couldn't take Livia being around, always wedging herself between him and Joy and making them both feel guilty because she was sick and needed them and all they wanted to do was live their own lives, not hers, why should they? It's what she had done, she hadn't stopped to help anybody, but now she wants the world to stop for her. And then he says that the old tart is probably sitting in a bar this minute and getting drunk and trying to seduce some stupid sonofabitch and she knows we are worrying about her and that is just how she likes it, being the center of attention. He calls her a vampire and says she doesn't know what love is and never loved nobody but herself, so screw her!

"Don't go there again!" yells Joy from the living room. "Keep your filthy mouth off my mother!"

"Man, you and that old bitch! She knows how to bust your buns, how to fuck your mind. Well, I say fuck her! What she always tell you? 'You made your bed, now lay in it.' Well, now it's her damn turn. Jesus Christ, I'm tired. My head is buzzin."

His face is lopsided. I can't find his eyeballs within his swollen lids. He is pitiful-looking and I can't help but feel a little sorry for him. Buck might be full of shit, but who isn't? He has reasons enough that make sense to him, given where he came from, given what his life has been. It is something I forget more often than not, that there are sides to every story and that people have their reasons. I stare out the window, at the snow-bound world where the skater whirls. *Livia* is out there somewhere. Not in no bar flirting either, Buck couldn't be more wrong about that. Probably dead by now. A block of ice.

I head for the front door, past Joy sitting on the sofa blubbering with her head in her lap. I put on my jacket, grab the dog and leave.

Joy's voice catches up with me on the snow-packed walk, "George!" she says. "Tell her to come home now and no more nonsense, you hear? Tell her Boo . . . Booboo said so." I glance over my shoulder at her, but keep moving toward the car. "Tell her Booboo's sorry, George, okay?" I get to the car and turn around. She is framed by the doorway, shivering, her face bleached by winter light. I am reminded of the drive to Tender Loving Care when Livia pointed at the child on the billboard, the fragile-eyed waif who made her think of Joy. The caption had asked WONT YOU HELP THIS BABY?

"I'll do that," I say.

Buck appears at the living-room window and starts gesturing. His arms frantically stir, frantically wave me off. I watch his mouth exaggerating the words, like an actor in a silent movie crying out, *No! No! No!*

PART THREE

Fire Monsters in the Milky Brain

Livia Miles

FIRST HER FEET got so frozen she thought she might have to go back but it wasn't long and she hardly felt her feet and it was like walking on wooden blocks. She looked down and yop, there they were but they didn't bother her a bit.

A man sat on a yellow machine digging a hole in a yard. The machine's mouth brought up mud. Made a pile on the snow. She watched the man move his hands on the handles as he made the arm rotate back and forth and go up-down. Another man went to a truck loaded with pipe. He took a piece of white pipe in his arms. Held it up like a pole and watched the iron mouth go down and the mud come up. The roar of the machine was all the sound in the world. She shuffled to the hole.

"Watch out there, lady!" yelled the man.

Livia pulled the police badge off her sweatshirt and threw it in the hole.

"Hey!" said the man.

The operator on the machine stopped working and the engine idled and he said, "What's she doin?"

While they talked it over she moved on.

~

BIRDS ON BRANCHES looked like leftover leaves. Her brain knew what kind of birds they were but she couldn't say at the moment. The birds were lined up looking at her. They were not afraid. When she held her finger out a pretty bird coasted down. Perched on her finger and she said, "You such a pwetty widow sing yes you are. Mama would feed you but she got nahsing."

Several more birds came down and talked to her. They were an impatient bunch, chirping and hopping and insisting on attention. They made her think of children, especially Booboo always wanting to talk, hold hands, always wanting to sleep in the same bed, always wanting there to be no one but her, never walking out the door without saying *I love you* and waiting to hear *I love you too, Booboo*.

Livia waved her arms and shooed the birds from around her head.

She heard Cody's spurs jingling and whistling in the western wind.

She turned and saw him riding into the woods.

"Cody!" she called. "Wait up!"

She hustled after him. Then stopped and wondered why she was breathing so hard.

IT WAS A DEAD-END STREET then woods. She went where the woods were quiet, the snow filtering down through the trees and the arms of the trees making patterns holy. She enjoyed the cathedral feel of it. The weight. The solitude. She felt safe among cocoa-colored birds swimming through slender twigs.

She found a dog caught in a trap. Smooth iron jaws bit into its leg. The dog looked at her with red eyes and growled. It stretched the chain as far away as it could. The dog's leg in the trap was bleeding. The fur and meat were gone and she could see white bone.

She tried to pet the dog. It nipped her hand.

"Ow!" she said. "Shame on you! Don't bite me, E Ching. Bite the bad-bad man." The dog bowed its head in shame. It limped around to show her its predicament. She bent down. The dog growled, showed fangs. She told it, "Bad dog no!" Livia knew dogs and she was not scared. She pulled the mouth of the trap and it shot off the dog's leg and snapped on her fingers.

The dog loped on three legs vanishing into the trees and Livia was by herself with her fingers in the trap. She looked toward the cathedral tops and wondered why God was picking on her. She dragged the trap around, walking back and forth at the end of the chain scraping the snow.

She lay down and closed her eyes and whimpered.

~

THUNDERING HOOVES WOKE HER. Shadows filled the spaces between the trees. Six posse riders rode in and knocked her down. They flicked her with knives. They beat her. Then they started raping her, lining up to take their turns. But she could take it. She wouldn't cry for mercy.

"You can kill me if you want," she told them.

But now they weren't interested in her. They were looking at a dark figure. The figure came into the light and she saw it was Cody with fury in his eyes. He stood facing the men. She could hear the angry cry of the wind.

Then everything exploded. Cody drew his gun and dropped two men before he was shot himself and went over backwards firing, shooting two more as he fell. He rolled in the snow and took another bullet and lay still. A moment passed, then the last two men looked at each other and one said, "The phantom of the Pecos is dead and we kilt him. We'll be famous now."

"Let's take his scalp for proof," said the other. His knife came out. He reached for Cody's long black hair and a bullet got him between the eyes and another tore through the other man's heart.

Cody reloaded, then got to his feet. Blood poured from five

mean wounds. Six dead men lay sprawled in the snow. To Livia he said, "Get up, angel. Let's go."

~

SHE GRIPPED COLD IRON in her free hand and tore her fingers from the trap. The jaws clacked. Her fingers were bruised swollen pulsing. She wondered if the bones were broken.

In the pocket of her coat she found gloves. She paused to put them on.

SHE WENT WALKING on ice, a frozen pond. The ice made cracking noises. Beneath it silver fish shimmied. She stomped her feet and the fish vanished.

~

WHEN SHE GOT TO THE MALL she saw a pet store and went in and played with puppies in a basket. She stayed there a long time taking the puppies out and petting them and talking baby talk kissing them and listening to them whimper. "Poor teeny E Ching," she cooed.

A girl asked her if she wanted to buy one.

"E Ching," she said, holding a puppy up.

"What?" said the girl.

"E Ching."

"For good karma?" said the girl.

At the counter Livia opened her purse and gave the girl a nickel for the dog.

"Fifty-seven dollars and thirty-one cents," said the girl ringing it up.

Livia handed her a dime. The girl looked closely at her. Then she told Livia to wait a minute while she called somebody to check the price. She went to a phone on the wall and punched in a number. She turned her back on Livia and whispered.

The puppy was on the counter. Sniffing. Whimpering. Piddling.

Livia left the puppy there.

Down a vast hallway she heard echoing noises and saw a policeman with another man who was gesturing toward the pet store. A glass door swished in front of her and she went outside.

~

A MUGGER TRIED to take her purse. Livia gripped her bottle of gin in a sack. She swung the gin at the mugger. E Ching attacked the mugger and bit him on the leg. He took out a knife and stabbed E Ching. Livia hit the mugger with the bottle of gin. It smashed to pieces over his head and the mugger fell. Blood poured from his head. He tried to crawl away but couldn't. The police came and picked him up. The police took her and E Ching to the hospital. E Ching died. She cremated him and poured his ashes in the ocean. The article in the paper told how brave she was—MUGGER MEETS HIS MATCH. That article used to be in her purse. She had shown it to hundreds of people.

Pausing a moment she dug in her purse for the article. "Mugger meets his match. Mugger meets his match," she said.

After examining her purse, her eye caught the eye of a familiar-looking man heading toward the mall. He was wearing a parka, his hands in his pockets, his breath steaming.

"When I die pour me in the ocean with E Ching," she told him.

The man looked at Livia like there was something wrong, "Scuse me?" he said.

"What?" said Livia.

"I thought you were talkin to me," said the man.

"I said the ocean. Put me in the ocean."

"You all right, lady?"

She looked him over. "Are you Harold?" she asked.

"No, ma'am."

"You George Miles?"

"I'm Kevin."

"Kevin? I don't know no Kevin." She scurried away from him, worried he might follow.

~

THERE WAS A BUS STOP at the corner.

She sat on the bus-stop bench.

She looked at the whiteness and at the cars going by.

At the people staring through frosty windows.

She pulled her coat tight and hunched forward.

Snow peppered her face and hair.

She slumped to her side on the bench.

Curled her knees to her chest.

She closed her eyes and felt a hand stroking her body, fussing with her clothes.

She heard Cody's spurs jingling and whistling in the western wind.

In a moment she would rise up and go with him.

I, George

A BUS DRIVER RADIOS the police and they pick up Livia at a bus stop and take her back to Tender Loving Care, and that's where I find her in bed with blankets piled on and the heater high.

"I can't believe this happened," says Gwen. "It's the first time anyone ever . . . I think the groundskeeper left the gate open. He'd been shoveling snow. I was in the laundry room, the vacuum running. The noise. I didn't hear the bell. Mr. McLeod, I feel so bad, I can't tell you how awful—"

"Joy wants me to take her home," I say. I am angry but trying not to show it. It isn't Gwen's fault but I'm mad at her anyway. Mad at the whole thing. "She shouldn't have been here in the first place," I say. "Should have been home where she belonged. People dying belong to home."

Ho Tep struggles to get out of my arms, so I put him on the bed with Livia and he nestles next to her leg, his head in her lap, waiting for her to pet him.

~

FOR AN HOUR I sit by her, giving her body time to warm up. Her color improves but she doesn't wake. "She's going west," I say. It was something my father always said about people who were dying, they were going west. I take hold of Livia's hand. The fingertips are cool. Her other hand is swollen purple across the first knuckles of all four fingers. Gwen reaches over my shoulder and pinches the skin on Livia's forearm and the skin sticks together and Gwen says Livia needs fluids, she's dehydrated.

I prop her with pillows and put a cup of water to her lips but she won't drink it. Gwen brings an eyedropper and we get water into Livia that way. I push the pillows to the side and sit with her head in my lap and drip water into her mouth, until finally she has taken in a full glass drop by drop. Gwen opens a can of Nutriment health drink and I eyedropper that into Livia too.

When the can is empty I sit Livia up on the edge of the bed and shout her name, "Livia! Livia!"

With my thumbs I lift her eyelids. The dog whines and paws her leg.

"Mama!" I yell.

At first she has a dead-eyed look, and then her head moves slightly to one side and her crossed eye focuses on me, recognizes me, and she smiles baby-gummed, and her arms reach out, reaching for me, and my heart leaps with gratitude.

"Here I am," I say.

But it is only a few seconds that she's with me and then the light goes out of her eyes again and her arms go limp and try as I might to wake her it is no use. The dog goes to the foot of the bed and curls there watching us.

"She recognized you," says Gwen. "She fixed on you, you see that? She's still in there, George."

"Livia! Livia!" I yell. "Livia! Wake up!"

"Let's walk her," says Gwen.

We try to walk her around but she can't control her legs. She walks tippy-toed spastic and finally we have to sit her back on the bed.

"That tippy-toeing is a sign of stroke," says Gwen. "I've seen it before in stroke victims, that tiptoe prancing."

Gwen thinks she should call the hospice and have them take over. "They're good with the dying," she says.

"I'm taking her home," I say. I yell in Livia's ear, "I'm taking you home, Mama! Home!" She understands the word *home*, and she kicks her legs and shakes her arms and it looks as if she is saying *goody*!

"See that? She knows," I tell Gwen.

I pack her suitcase and put it in the trunk. Then I come back for her. I lift her in my arms and it's like she is filled with helium. She floats in my arms as we go through the house, Gwen opening doors, leading us out the front as the chime plays "Lara's Theme." Gwen opens the car door for me and I lay Livia in the backseat. Ho Tep jumps in the front, eager to go.

Gwen stands on the porch, looking huge and useless. "I'm so very sorry," she keeps saying. "It never happened before. The gate. The bell. I've always heard it before. I don't know what happened."

~

I DRIVE HOME over slippery crunchy roads and park in front of the Lincoln. Ho Tep does an old man's hipsore shuffle over the snow in front of us as I carry Livia to the door. He barks and the door opens to Joy's startled, appalled, terrified face.

After I put Livia in bed I go into the kitchen, where Joy is sitting at the table smoking a cigarette. She has vodka in front of her. Buck has his elbows on the table, his head in his hands. A gamy-sweaty odor permeates the air. It takes me a moment to realize that I am smelling fear.

"She's where she belongs," I say. "With us. I told her I was taking her home and you should have seen how excited she got. She knows what's going on."

Buck is blowing his nose into layers of Kleenex. He blows tentatively, then harder and a clot shoots into the tissues. He looks at the clot. It is bloody. He dabs around his nostrils. "Jesus, no wonder I couldn't breathe," he says. Tenderly he touches his nose and winces. "Do I still look like Victor Mature?" he asks Joy.

She won't answer him. He chuckles and says, "Fuck you too."

"Just shut up, will you?" she says.

Buck's eyes squint at me and he tells me that I shouldn't have brought Livia home. I should have left her to the experts who know how to handle dying old ladies.

Joy starts breathing hard. She coughs wetly.

Buck continues, "I mean, is it the dumbest thing you could think to do, bringing her here and cramming her down our throats? No respect. You've got no respect for our feelings to do a thing like that."

"Who are you?" I say. "I don't know you."

"Listen, George. She could last for days or weeks like that. Are you prepared to give her the care she needs? Are you prepared to dedicate yourself to her for weeks, maybe months? Because knowing her, she's going to last months. That is one tough old tart, George."

"She's dying, Buck, come on—"

"Months like that."

"She's dying, I say!"

"No she's not!" says Joy. "Don't you tell me my mother is dying!"

I walk over to the sink and look out the window. The land looks unfathomable. The air is lavender, the snow is lavender snow. I see the glacial lavender ribbon of Medicine Lake. Through the shadows of evening coming on, tiny black figures move over the ice. "The skaters are there," I say.

"She's the last thing we need," says Buck. "This is the last straw." He downs his drink and slams the glass on the table and says, "Joy's life's been shit because of her! Tell him, Joy."

"Tell him what?"

"Tell him what she's done to you."

Joy takes a sip. She holds the glass to her forehead and rolls it back and forth. "I don't know anymore," she says. "I'm wondering who did what to whom."

Buck looks exasperated, his mouth moving as if words are tangled in his throat trying to get out and get someone. He dabs at his nose and coughs and takes a breath and lets it out—"George, you just don't know what that woman has put Joy through. Unless she tells you about it, you'll never understand. No one will, no one knows how she's torn up inside. Am I right, Joy? Am I?"

He is quiet a second, then he touches her hand, makes her look at him. "What's that you told me about her? Always talking one thing and doing another. *Oh, I love my kids, I'd die for my kids, my kids mean everything to me.* But her actions spoke louder, is that what you told me?"

"What's it matter now?" says Joy.

"What's it matter?"

"Are you talking about your mother or my mother?"

"Both goddamn bitches!"

He closes his eyes, composes himself. "Look here, sweetness, if I've got a hard heart it's because—"

"Don't tell that story about that goddamn hole again. For God's sake, Buck, I'm sick of it!"

He looks daggers at me. "Nobody ever give a shit about me."

"I do," I tell him. "I give a shit about you."

"Bullshit. Everything is bullshit," he says. He blows his nose again, fills fresh tissue with bright red blood. Then he tells me to take Livia back to the home. Says he called Gwen and she said hospice was best now, ease the old girl through to the end.

"They know what to do. Take her back," he commands.

"She's not your mother," I tell him. "You don't give orders for her. Joy, what do you want me to do? You said to bring her home, so I did. Is that what you still want?"

"I can't stand it, I'll go crazy!" Joy cries. She starts sniffing. Her forefinger works back and forth beneath her nose. She looks ugly, her face all blotchy and scrunched and bluish around her mouth.

"I'll take care of her," I say. "You won't have to see her if you don't want. I know what to do."

Joy polishes off her drink and nods at me and says, "All right . . . okay."

I touch her shoulder. "First off, a bath. She loves baths and fresh pajamas. And I'll feed her through the eyedropper. I know how to do it. I'll give her some Nova Life pills. They'll make her feel better."

"Get real," says the weightlifter.

I dig in my pocket and come out with some bills. "How much you want? Here . . . here's a hundred shitten dollars."

"Get real," says the weightlifter.

"Gimmee all the pills this money will buy." I put the money on the table and go to the window again and look for the ice-skaters but it's getting too dark.

"And we'll read Cody Larsen to her, she'll like that," I say. "Ease her out of this world, no fear, no pain, so she'll hardly know when she steps from here to there. Did I tell you she can hear us? She can squeeze your finger if you tell her to. She looked at me once and tried to hug me."

"Cousin George," says Buck. His ruined eyes slide away from me. He brushes the tissues across his chin and leaves a smear of blood. "Aw, cousin, what a mess you got us into. It's all gotta end miserable."

Joy raises her head and says, "Now it's too late for her and me. It's too late to make things right. I never explained about Nikos. I waited too long and now it's too late to get anything straight."

"Let it go," says Buck. "George, you never have respected me, have you?"

"What the hell's that got to do with anything right now?"

"No, you haven't. I'm telling you not to put us through this but you don't care. No respect, that's what I'm saying."

"Oh, will you shut up, Mikey!" I say. "It's got nothing to do with my respecting you. What it's got to do with is Livia dying. You want to beat me up later and teach me respect or whatever, then go ahead. But for right now, let's concentrate on her. One helpless old lady dying. For God's sake, behave yourself!"

He glares at me. "You'll be sorry for this," he says.

~

I PUT HER in the bath and as I'm scrubbing her, the door opens and Joy comes in and kneels beside me, picks up the soap and starts sudsing her hands, building a froth. I stand away and let Joy take over.

After Livia is soaped and rinsed and dried, Joy rubs her all over with lotion and brushes her hair. Then we put the cowboys and Indians flannels on her and carry her to bed. I feed her Nutriment through the eyedropper while Joy sits in a chair and reads aloud from *West of the Pecos*:

Wounded and dying Cody Larsen stumbled through the snow. It was still dark and the snow had a hard crust that broke under his feet, making him sink into soft powder that clung to his pantlegs, wetting them, freezing his ankles and slowing him down, forcing him to take steps like a bird walking through water. He was puffing hard with every step, and his breath blew back in his face and froze there, froze on his unshaven jaw and cheeks and on his eyebrows and lashes, froze in his hair, turning his whole head white, making him resemble a hoary Jack Frost gathering up the cold, carrying it with him, burying the land.

He trudged on in a daze, dreamy and untroubled and feeling no pain from his wounds. Dark gave way to the cold sun rising and the wind whipping the snow into the air, driving at Cody's back, making him crouch like a cow with its tail tucked. He left tracks on the snow, but they were quickly filled in and smoothed over by the wind.

He walked until at last he sat down exhausted in the snow, then drifted over onto his side, his legs tucked, his hands wedged into his armpits. He told himself he would rest a few minutes, then go. The Pecos pueblos weren't far off, just over the hill. He knew the markings around him, the two-breasted mountains side by side beyond the bluffs, the island of spruce permanently bent by the constant wind. It was all familiar to him. White Dove was close. The dwellings. Home. The tribe nestling above Golden Valley Creek trickling toward the Pecos River. Warmth and safety were waiting for him there. All he had to do was push his body a little longer. He could be home by nightfall, but first he would rest and gather strength for the final push. The snow covered him snugly and soon he was a bump of white on the surface, with the snow piling higher and higher and himself as warm and safe as a child in bed. It was very quiet, very calm. No pain. Nothing but the sense that for the first time in his life he was where he was supposed to be and everything was fine.

Joy quits reading. She pats Livia's leg. The leg quivers and Livia makes a contented noise, a kind of kitten mew. Joy's thumb moves over the back of her mother's hand. "Of course he dies right there in the snow and finds Lily Miles waiting for him in the clouds," she tells me. "A maudlin ending for a Western novel. Most of them end in shoot-outs and red sunsets framing the hero. But Mom always loved this ending. She used to quote it by heart."

~

"IS IT OVER YET?" asks the weightlifter when I come out of the room. I shake my head no. "This is what I wanted to save Joy from," he says. "Dying can be real ugly, George. I found my mother after she killed herself. It was a mess. I didn't recognize her. She suffered and it showed. Don't let anybody tell you that pills are the easy way to go, that you just go to sleep and that's that, uhn-uhn. She had vomited all over herself and the bed and her face was ghastly, all contorted with this grimace. Tell you the truth, I think maybe she had changed her mind and wanted to live and stuck her finger down her throat, but it was too late. Too fuckin late. It was like somebody else laying there, not her. I'll never forget it. Joy won't forget this either. She'll take these last hours with her wherever she goes to the end of her days."

I stand at the front window and watch a covey of girls going by, bundled in coats. They have school books in their arms. Buck comes up behind me. We watch in silence and then he says:

"Beautiful girls walk a little slower when you walk by me."

A thin figure in black watchcap and denim jacket lopes by and says something to the girls to which they make X-rated gestures. The boy laughs and hurries on, blowing into his cupped hands.

Buck clears his throat, takes a deep breath and says in a loud voice, "Nuff of this gloomy shit. Hey, George, how can you tell if your wife is dead?"

"How, Buck?"

"The sex is the same but the dishes pile up, heh, heh."

"The dishes pile up."

"Did I ever tell you about the Chinese couple that had a black baby? They named him Sum Ting Wong, heh, heh."

"Sum Ting Wong."

"Don't you get it? Sum Ting Wong. Sum Ting Wong."

~

DURING THE NIGHT Livia's lungs fill with fluid. Her eyelids are half-open, but her tacky eyes see nothing. She is limp. Her skin is hot, feverish, dry. Joy lies on the bed with her, stretching out the length of her, so Livia can feel (if she can feel) the human touch. Joy hugs her all night, breathing deeply in time with her mother, one arm wrapped around her neck and one hand caressing her face, the broomstick arm, the washboard ribs.

In the morning, the sky is clear and sunlight moves tentatively, searchingly into the room and I can hear Joy whispering to her mother, telling her she shouldn't be afraid, it is okay to go. The sunlight touches the old lady's hair, turns it bright orange, almost blond.

A moment later there is a pause, then a gasp, then another pause lasting ten or fifteen seconds, then a long exhalation. And that is it.

I wait to make sure, then I look at the clock on the dresser: the time is eight-eighteen. My knees wobble and I sit down in the chair, breathing hard. My chest seems too small for the air I need. I am close to crying and cannot trust myself to talk. I remember my mother dying much the same way as Livia (the same breathing pattern, the gasp, the long exhalation) in the very same bed, and I think of how it seems that we can't stand it and yet somehow we do. Our hearts don't stop and we don't die with them as we think we will. Our turn is coming, we tell ourselves. Our turn is coming soon enough. Be it forty more years or whatever, it's soon enough—in the frame of time a trifle.

"My hand was on her heart. I . . . I felt it stop," says Joy. She is looking at her hand, studying the palm.

Livia's nose is prominent, it hooks over her face like a tile knife. It is not the nose I'm used to seeing, the softly curved nostrils, the freckled saddle, the tiny upturned ball at the end. Another nose has grown in its place, tight-skinned-rigid and flanked by eyes stamped *canceled*. The oval mouth is wide, screaming in silence. A nightmare picture she would never have wanted anyone to see.

"It's over?" shouts the weightlifter.

"She's gone," I say.

A few seconds pass, then the weightlifter says, "She'll haunt me now. I'm in big trouble now."

In a hiccuping voice Joy prays for forgiveness: "God . . . for-give me . . . God . . . for-give me . . ."

~

FROM THE FUNERAL HOME, two men arrive and carry Livia away—a light load, no fat, all bone and cold skin and quieted organs—in a canvas slot that forms around her body like a hammock.

The funeral home cremates her and puts her ashes in a shiny copper urn. Joy and I talk about having a memorial at The Body Shop, but we go home instead and sit around the table with Buck, having drinks and trying to find things to say about Livia. The guest of honor sits like a gleaming monolith at the table's head.

"She sure liked to dance," says Buck, raising his drink to the urn.

"A feisty old girl," I say. "I liked her. She did it her way."

"That's true," says Joy. "She never looked back, never had regrets. Pushed herself fearlessly and lived life to the limit."

"How about those Westerns?" I say. "You ever see anybody so nuts over paperback Westerns? She told me she was a cowboy in another life."

"Cody Larsen," says Joy.

"Basically, you know, she was good people," says Buck. He is calm now. He smiles a lot, his bruised eyes sadly humorous, his brows curved sympathetically.

"She never deliberately hurt anybody," says Joy. "That's what you can say about her, she was never mean on purpose. She made mistakes, but it wasn't because she was evil, it was because she wanted to live large and she took chances."

"She wanted to live large. That's right. That's what I've wanted to do too," says Buck. "I've took the blows."

"She wanted to die large, too. She used to talk about dying a lot. She saw herself going with dignity, all the family gathered round to hear her last words." Joy looks at me. "We don't get to write our own scenarios, do we? Nothing ever happens the way you want it to or think it should."

"That's true," I say.

"I know it didn't seem like it," says Buck, "but I liked her. I mean really I did. It's just that when her mind went, I couldn't cope. I mean, who can cope with that? I had seen it again and again with my mother, when she'd go off the deep end, then come back, and then get sick again. Back and forth, back and forth, my whole goddamn childhood with her, and I couldn't do it no more."

"We know, Buck. God knows, we know," says Joy wearily.

"Being human is right here." He taps his head. "When that goes, you're no different from a dog or a goat, you're just another animal in the food chain. You understand what I'm saying? And what's death anyway? Death is nothing, and sometimes it's damn sure better than life. What's so bad about being nothing? We all gotta die. All living things die. Buck is a living thing. Buck will die."

Ho Tep comes over and paws my ankle and I pick him up.

"You know," continues Buck, "we've got to get back in shape. We've got things to do." He takes Joy's hand.

"Bucky is destined for something big," she says, her eyes doubtful, her tone ironic.

"Soon as my body heals, I'm back on the weights and the bodybuilder's diet. Beef, beef, beef and two-a-day workouts," he says. "Get rid of this body fat." He pats his belly, then shows us biceps muscle not so big as it was before. "You know, I don't know why it is," he says, "but ever since I was a kid I've felt special, like I was picked to do some special thing. It's a feeling I have in my bones. Surely all that's happened to me hasn't happened for nothing. I'm here to make an impact."

He goes on about his destiny, but I only half hear him. I drink fast, hoping to numb my heart. I see the image of Livia sitting on the edge of the bed, the turned-in eye, like faded slate looking nowhere, then abruptly taking me in, knowing me, reaching for me when I called her Mama.

"You know about E Ching?" says Joy, reaching across and rubbing Ho Tep's ears. "E Ching was stabbed by a guy who tried to mug Mom. She hit the guy with a bottle of gin and knocked him cold. Swear to God, Mom was a pistol." Joy laughs and we all laugh.

"Tough old tart. That's good," says Buck.

"She had E Ching cremated and we all went to the pier and Mom sprinkled the ashes in the ocean. That's what she wanted, she said, her ashes thrown in the ocean with E Ching and my brother Hal. Both went back to mother sea." Joy grabs a tissue and blows her nose, wipes her eyes. She smiles at me as if she is saying, *Ain't I just the biggest baby.*

"Closest thing we've got to an ocean is Lake Superior up north," I tell her. "It's the biggest of the Great Lakes."

We stare at the urn.

"This is how ancestor worship gets started," says Buck. He finishes his drink and lets out a sigh and grins and says, "Hey, what did the Nazi women call their tampons?"

"Twatstikas," says Joy.

"I told you that one before?"

"This is Mom's day," says Joy. "Let's talk about her."

"So who's stopping you?" says Buck.

Joy thinks a second, then she tells a story about Livia one time dating a farmer's son and he took her and Joy and Hal to the farm and showed them around and they came across a pig in a crate—

"And Mom says to this guy, 'Why you got that pig boxed up?' And he tells us that she ate her babies. So Mom says, 'My God, a loony pig.' And she bends down and says to the pig, 'God's truth, I identify with you. I damn near ate my kids a time or two.'" Joy's smile is asking us to laugh.

I chuckle. Buck squints like he's in pain.

"It was sort of funny at the time," says Joy. "The way she said it."

"Rabbits will eat their babies too," I tell her.

"It's unnatural being caged up," says Buck. "That's why animals eat their kids."

Joy shrugs. "Anyway, she was funny that day. She made pig noises and she chased us all over and when she caught us she pretended to eat us, calling us pork chops and nibbling our necks. It was fun. When we were little like that, she was fun lots of times. She made us laugh. My brother put a garden snake on her pillow one time, all curled up like an ashtray. And when she went to bed and saw the snake there on her pillow, she screamed and pretended to faint. She was laying on the floor just faking, but it scared hell out of Hal. He thought he'd killed her." Joy giggles into her hands. "We laughed about that one for days and days, that look on Hal's face."

"She had a good heart," I say. "That was my impression."

"She had a thing about animals. I never saw a dog or a cat that didn't love Mom."

"Animals can tell about people," says Buck.

We all nod like we know it's true.

I put Ho Tep on the floor and go to the window, hoping to see the skaters again, but the lake is empty. Beads of snow, like busy white flies, rise from the garden and vanish.

"Be dark soon," I say.

"I got a joke," says Buck. "What's the difference between oral sex and anal sex?" He waits a moment, grins and says, "Oral sex makes your day, anal sex makes your hole weak." He spreads his arms, wiggles his fingers, coaxing us to laugh. "Get it? Get it? Hole weak: H-o-l-e w-e-a-k."

"You're not funny anymore," Joy says.

He scowls at her. "Neither are you," he says. "And neither was your mother."

Buck Root

THEY GOT HIM in his sleep. There was a command voice asking him if he was Michelangelo Routelli, alias Buck Root, and he felt a light in his eyes and had to shield his eyes with his hand and he said, "Hey?"

"We're the police. We want to talk to you, Mr. Routelli," said the voice.

"I had to let em in, Buck," said George. He was standing at the foot of the bed in his bathrobe, his hair tousled.

In a panic, Buck leaped out of bed and ran for the window and before they could stop him he dived through it, the frame and the glass shattering and going with him as he fell to the snow and rolled and came up running, not noticing how badly he was cut and how he was leaving blood in his own barefoot tracks.

He didn't get far, not even to the corner before they tackled him, three of them, driving him facedown in the snow and ice, the ice cutting his hands as he tried to break his fall. He heard himself snarling and cussing and heard the cops ordering him to stay down, but he wouldn't stay down and so they started beating him with their batons, his head cracking as he charged them and got hold of one and crushed him, ribs popping, while batons continued pounding him furiously.

"My back!" shrieked the one in his arms.

"Break his head, break his goddamn head!" screamed another.

Buck dropped the cop. He turned to run and slammed into a tree and bounced off, a blazing light searing the inside of his head.

~

MAYBE TWO DAYS or two months went by, Buck didn't know, but he could feel when the seizures were coming. They came and they went. He had had enough of them to know the symptoms: a growing dryness in the mouth that went bitter, a change in pressure in the ears, a distant ringing, muscles turning to mush, his left eyebrow would twitch, there would be the sensation of falling.

And then the dream of Connie would come:

HER EYES WON'T STAY CLOSED. He keeps pushing the lids down, but they spring back and she is looking at him. So finally he tapes her eyes shut, running the ring of tape round and round her head, until he has covered her eyes and her nose and her gap-toothed mouth and he kneels over her, listening to his own breath, his heart thundering. He looks at the dark sky and wonders how it has come to this. It seems absurd that he has lived in such a way that now he is a murderer. He thinks about his wife Patsy and he wonders what might have happened if he had stayed with her, and he wishes he had, no matter how restless and troubled he had been when he was with her. Everybody said she was a good woman, a fine human being, and he was crazy to leave her. But something had pinched him. He can't remember exactly what it was, maybe it was her goodness, her fineness, and his own rottenness pinching him like a stiff old shoe.

The weather is getting worse, the rain turning to sleet. An icy wind blows against him and his face cools and his mind gets cold. He straightens her out, ties her ankles together with more tape. Crosses her arms over her stomach and binds her wrists. Her hands are violet. She feels rubbery to the touch. Cool violet rubber.

He puts his hands on his hips and burps beer and salami, has heartburn and nausea and feels like he might heave. One, two, three he counts, then picks her up and slings her over his shoulder and she is surprisingly heavy and awkward. Using a flashlight, he carries her across the snow-dusted field into the dark woods, to the hole he has dug. He is sucking air, his breath smoking. He is sweating beneath his jacket. He feels her belly sinking over his shoulder. He hears one of her ribs cracking. Her bound hands tap against his buttocks as if she is trying to get his attention.

He gropes his way through the trees to the hole. He tells himself that she won't feel a thing. She is beyond pain or worry or heartbreak or diseases or any of the terrible things that happen to people. She will never get old like Livia and go doddering through the world in a daze. In a strange way, he has actually done her a favor, cut her off at the peak of her glory, no time to decay, no more years of fearing old age and death.

He leans forward and flops her off his shoulder and into his arms, a sleeping child, her head far back, her blood-stiffened hair cascading, nearly touching the ground. He lets go and she rolls raglike into the grave. He jumps in and straightens her arms and legs, puts some wet leaves over her face, then he climbs out and stands for a minute with his head bowed, trying to think of something appropriate to say.

"It was an accident," he tells her. "I didn't mean to. I'm not an evil man. You shouldn't have kicked me. Called me a loser like that, got drunk and stupid like that, not when I've got a weapon in my hand. That was pretty stupid, Con." He shakes the flashlight at her, its beam stroking her body. "I'm sorry as can be, I really am. If God is up there somewhere, I hope he takes you in."

He sets the light down, picks up the shovel. He gets busy.

Afterward he goes back to the woodpile, gathers all the bloody kindling in his arms, makes three trips down to the basement and burns the kindling in the furnace. He throws the ax and his jacket in the flames too. Slams the iron gate shut. Listens to the roaring, everything consumed.

~

"So where is she?" said the first detective.

"I told you," said Buck.

"Tell me again."

"C'mon, man, I'm dyin here," said Buck.

"You're dying? Is she dead?"

"My head is killing me."

"Can you give him another one of those pills?" said the detective.

The male nurse put a pill on Buck's tongue and gave him water.

"Ordinary man would have died," said the first detective.

"Ordinary guy would be dead for sure," said the second detective. They both seemed to regard Buck with grudging admiration.

"I'm no ordinary man," he told them.

The soreness in his ribs made it hard to breathe. An iodine smell hung in the air. Gingerly he touched his ribs and winced. Very tender there. His hands were so thickly wrapped that they looked like paws.

"I didn't mean to hurt that cop," he told them.

"Two ribs, a slipped disk," said the first detective.

"Hazards of the job," said the second.

"Course now they've added resisting arrest and assaulting a

police officer," said the first. "Might even get you for attempted murder, we'll see." His voice was nonchalant.

They were nice guys. He didn't mind them too much. He wished he could think of a joke to tell them. He felt like he had a fever. The bandage on his head was too tight. His feet throbbed.

"Hey, guys, I sure am sleepy," he said.

"Not yet," said the first detective. He scooted his chair closer to the bed, touched Buck's arm. "Try to help us out here, Routelli."

"Here's a good one," said Buck. "Which sexual position spawns the ugliest children?"

The detectives looked at each other and shrugged.

"Ask yo mama," Buck answered.

They both smiled and the male nurse laughed.

The detectives questioned him, the same questions over and over and sometimes he got confused and didn't know what he said or what he was saying. They were writing it down and coming at him from this way and that way, but he clung to the basic core of the story: she had run off with a guy in a red Corvette.

~

HE WOKE with moonlight painted over the bars and the window, giving the room an iridescent glow, filling the walls with shadowy crossbars. He found himself wishing he could go back and live his life again, start fresh, knowing how to do it now, knowing not to be so impatient. He had always been too eager for the future to come, always expecting something fabulous to turn up, a Mr. Universe title, a Hollywood contract, publishers with deep pockets wanting his memoirs, interviews on TV, recognition in the streets, maître d's knowing his name, saying, *Right this way, Mr. Root.* And it might have happened, given patience, focus, and the right sort of moves. Those Nova Life pills, what the hell was that? He had lost nothing but money on them. The phone confession thing had paid all right. Maybe given time something more would have happened with that. But the affair with Connie, what in the world was he thinking? Why couldn't he have waited until a safe night, get some of that pussy on the side the way smart married men do, instead of sneaking out to the van and having Joy show up. He had hurt her bad. She didn't deserve it, the way he always hurt her.

And then the move to Chicago and that mess down there, the standup comedy thing that went sour the second time he did it—because he was too drunk to talk, slurring his words and forgetting the punchlines; the Mr. Chicago contest for which he could have been a judge if he had just showed up looking buff, instead of like some boozy bum in unwashed clothes and a three-day beard.

The interview, though, it was good. Got on television.

Perfecting your body is a way of worshipping God:

Called "A Weightlifter's Wisdom" by the guy at the local TV station. The guy had run it quite a few times, with Buck, "the former Mr. Los Angeles," etc. etc. sitting there, his face a little ravaged, maybe, but his eyes sincere, his words thoughtful. And yet even so, nothing really came of it except the stack of video-tapes he and Connie had given away to radio and TV stations. No one had called for him to come and give an interview or a talk or anything.

And then what? Then it was bang! The hell with it! Fuck Chicago! Fuck everybody! And off to Minnesota and that smelly farm, the last place on earth for a man named Buck Root.

One stupid move after another.

He couldn't remember ever being at ease or satisfied with anything. Not ever. A pretty wife, a fine apartment, his red Corvette with turbocharge, the many trophies acknowledging his beauty, bit parts in action films, articles about him in muscle magazines. Never satisfied for more than five minutes: restlessly moving from longing to fulfillment, from fulfillment to longing. Always the sense that there had to be more. When Joy came along offering herself to him, he was already primed for her. She was another perk to add to the full, rich life he demanded. But that was where he had made the wrong turn. Joy Faust and her hero worship of him. Six years later he was a killer in a hospital with wounds all over and a cracked skull and seizures.

He looked at the rise of his body under the sheet. He was shrinking, his muscles wasting. The sheet was trying to become a winding-sheet, his shroud. From behind the door came the sound of a gurney being rushed down the hall. A race against death? He wondered if he had it in him to go on much longer and decided that he was so far down, there was nowhere to go but up.

I'll make a comeback, he promised himself. *I might look through, but I ain't through. I'll get well and start pumping iron and eating right and I'll show all them muthers.*

He saw himself onstage again, trophy in hand, headlines shouting THE COMEBACK KID!

Where there's life there's hope. Stay alive. Get well. Start eating steaks and salads and drinking protein drinks with raw egg and wheat germ. Get on the iron the way I used to. I'm still full of potential, by god. Down but not out. Still got the hammer, still got the guts. Never say never to Buck Root-and-toot.

The door opened. The light came on. He shut his eyes. The two detectives pulled up their chairs. The male nurse padded in.

"Open your eyes, Mr. Routelli. Let's talk about Constance Hawkins some more," said the first detective.

"We'd sure like to find her and close this case," said the second detective. "C'mon, Routelli, we know you're awake."

Joy Faust

IN THE DAYS AFTER HER MOTHER DIED and Buck was taken to the hospital, Joy got more depressed and silent and gloomy. Each time she looked in the mirror, it seemed to her that she had aged another year. Her face sagged badly. Wrinkles spread like spiderwebs from the corners of her eyes. Her lips thinned and got vertical lines. Hanging from her chin and jaw were loosening folds of skin and the beginning of a wattle. Her shoulders drooped, her breasts collapsed as if someone had taken a pin and let the air out.

Now I'm old like her, she told herself.

She was always freezing and she took scalding baths to improve her circulation, staying in the water for hours, renewing the heat when the water cooled, filling the tub with scented bath oils and scrubbing herself with lemon soap. She wandered the house in a brown sweatsuit and with the black-and-yellow afghan draped over her shoulders. Despite the baths she still smelled awful. She had an irritable, fiery colon and morbid armpits and an anal breath.

And she asked herself, "How could I have treated her that way? How could I have been so awful? What's wrong with me? Where's my heart?" And she remembered the revelation she had had the time she left her mother at the home and drove to The Body Shop, the dreadful insight that had come to her after

269

she had hit the deer, how capricious life was, how pain and misery went on endlessly in the midst of ordinary living, the little mundane events juxtaposed with unspeakable horrors and how we turn our minds away from suffering, how we refuse to care too much because caring too much might kill us.

She took to her room, to her bed, curling up there and rarely coming out. George tried to comfort her but she wouldn't be comforted. There was something satisfying in tormenting herself. The image of her dying mother stuck like an icon to the walls of Joy's mind—the wide cancer of a mouth, the glazed eyes. She had seemed scarcely human.

I could have eased her last days, Joy kept reminding herself. *I could have been nicer. I could have had some compassion. But I didn't know she was dying. I never believed she could really die. Not her.*

George came in day after day, bringing her meals and sitting on the edge of the bed talking to her, telling her to do something, quit being so self-destructive. She should take the job offered by Picasso Blue. She should go into St. Paul and talk to the museum curator there, the one who had seen the paintings and wanted to hang a few. She should get up and go make deals with the dealers who had called.

Wobbling in one night, he flopped on the bed and rolled over, spooning her from behind and telling her that living alone for so long had made him cynical about love. He had always believed it wasn't for him. But over the past few months Joy had changed his mind.

"You woke me up," he said. "I don't want to live alone anymore, and I don't want to live at all if I can't have you."

"I smell," she said.

He sniffed her. "You smell good," he said. "You practically live in the tub."

"You're drunk," she said.

"Yup, but that don't make me a liar. You know what I do now that I never did before? I'm such a homely mutt that I've avoided mirrors all my life, but now I primp in front of them, pushing my little bit of hair this way and that, trying to make this side grow over the top to hide my baldness. Putting Grecian Formula on my sideburns. I'm even using some of that face cream of yours and I've got a dental appointment to get my chipped tooth fixed. I'm doing exercises, God forbid, and I'm on a diet. I don't know if you've noticed, but all I'm eating lately is chicken salads. A man my age doesn't do those things unless he's trying to make an impression. I'm going to lift weights and get muscle, so you'll notice me."

She kept quiet as the seconds ticked away, feeling him behind her, his hand stroking her arm. She wanted to feel what he felt. She wanted to be in love with him. But there was a deadness in her that wouldn't allow it.

"I can't right now," she murmured, keeping her eyes on the wall.

He delayed a few seconds, his breath inaudible, then he rolled over and left her, closing the door without a sound. She stayed in the midst of an inflexible despair, wishing she could feel bad about hurting him. But he was one weight too many and she couldn't add him on.

~

ONE NIGHT WHEN GEORGE WAS OUT, Joy got up and poured herself a drink and sat alone in the kitchen staring at her mother's urn on the table. After a couple of hours and a number of drinks, she had an inspiration. She decided that her mother's ashes needed to be let loose. It made sense to Joy, her wandering mother shouldn't be confined in a box. Joy grabbed the urn, stood up and went into the bedroom.

"It's what I'll do," she said. "My last respects."

She made defiant gestures with her fist, daring the powers above to try and stop her. She put on her red outfit, her gold-heart earrings and gold choker, her spike heels and fox jacket. She tucked the urn under her arm and left the apartment and went to Connie's van at the curb. She slid behind the wheel and started the engine. Then she put the urn on the passenger seat and buckled it in.

"All dressed up and places to go," she declared. She buffed the urn lid with her furry sleeve. Made it gleam in the night like a precious stone.

~

"I LIKE MY PUSSY YOUNG," was what the man said.

She winced and looked at the bartender and he gave her a look she wasn't used to seeing. The voices had stopped. A dozen eyes were turned toward her. She retreated outside. She breathed icy air. Tried to clear her head. She could see the outlines of gantry cranes in the distance, their beaks reaching out as if to reel giant fish from the water.

She walked uphill and stopped. Duluth was hilly, lots of up-and-down moraines that made her wish she had brought tennis shoes. She took her high heels off and felt the freezing concrete beneath her feet. At the bottom of the street was the van, its tires cocked against the curb. She had taken a long nap on the mattress and she still felt the glue of sleep in her mouth. She gazed at the dirty snow in the gutter beside her.

Tomorrow she would go when the sun was high and cast her mother to the waters and say a prayer, but right now she was hungry and she needed a drink.

What had he said? *Young pussy*, he had said. She walked uphill and looked around the corner where a neon sign said *Bar Dante*. She looked in the window, saw silhouettes at the bar. She put her shoes on and went inside and ordered vodka on the rocks.

A basketball game was on TV. The Bulls playing the Timberwolves. Score was forty-four to forty-five. The bartender set a napkin and her drink in front of her, then went back to watching the game. There was a black boy in a shiny gold jacket sitting at a table drinking a beer, eyeing her over the rim of his glass. Joy estimated he was maybe sixteen or seventeen years old.

She put her cigarettes on the bar and went to the rest room. It was a narrow box with a rust-coated sink, a broken mirror and a stained toilet with mold growing round the rim. "Good god, I can't sit on that," she said. She pulled down her underpants and hiked her skirt over her waist and squatted inches above the bowl. There was a urine smell in the air that offended her nose and made her think of Tender Loving Care. Afterward she wiped herself with a rough paper towel and flushed the toilet. The water rose dangerously, then whirled down.

The mirror was full of bluish and gold moisture lines. What she could see of her face in the mirror made her sick. No wonder he had said he liked his pussy young. Her eyes had bags beneath them, her mouth turned down like a half-bent horseshoe, her hair looked ratty and brittle. Roots beneath the red looked gray, not blond.

"What a godawful mess," she said. She fumbled in her purse for a brush and some lipstick and tried to fix herself up. "All I asked him was to buy me a drink," she said. "I didn't say a thing about pussy." He had looked at her with such vicious disdain it had scared her.

She had a vial of Binaca and she sprayed it at her armpits and between her breasts. Then she went out to finish her drink. It was halftime. The Bulls were ahead by eight points. The men were bitching about it.

"Every year, every year," said one of them.

"Where's Harmon Killebrew when you need him?" said another.

"Killebrew," said the black kid. "Who's Killebrew?"

"Killer Killebrew to you," said the bartender. "Only the greatest baseball player Minnesota ever had."

"*Base*ball. Who gives a shit about *base*ball?" said the kid. "This is *basketball* season, man."

"You don't know for shit," said the fellow sitting closest to Joy. "You young bucks think you know everything, but you don't know shit. You watch Harmon Killebrew blast one four hundred feet, then you know somethin."

"Uh-huh, Papa Cone," said the kid. "What I know is that baseball is for boring old farts like you. Basketball is a young man's game."

"Smart-mouth punk." His mouth barely moved, his words easing over razor-thin lips.

"Old fart."

"You don't shut up this old fart will kick your ass."

"Anytime, bad motherfucker, anytime you not too lazy to get off that stool."

"Aw, fuck him, Papa Cone," said the bartender. "Neon Leon, whyn't you get out of here and go home? Everything's washed up and set for the night. You can come back tomorrow early and do the floor."

"I'm gone soon's I finish my beer," said the boy.

The men turned their backs on him. They started talking about Harmon Killebrew and what a great player he was and how the recent generation of players were punks and prima donnas. Harmon was a workingman's player. They named other names, but Joy hadn't heard of any of them until she heard Tony Gwynn mentioned.

"Yeah, Gwynn is great," she said.

The men turned to her as if seeing her for the first time. They looked interested in what she had to say, so she made up a lie. She said, "I know Tony Gwynn. You'll never meet a nicer guy."

"He's a hell of a hitter," said one of the men.

Joy nodded. She tried to think of something to say about baseball. She had gone to a game once when the Dodgers were playing the Padres and Gwynn had gone four for four and Buck had said there was nobody nicer in baseball than good ole Tony Gwynn.

"I saw him go four for four," she said.

The bartender said, "You say you know him?"

"Yes."

"Where from?"

They were all waiting to be convinced. She decided they were not very nice-looking men. There was something wrong with them, something not right about their eyes.

"I met him at a party in San Diego when I lived there. We had some drinks and we talked. He's the nicest guy in the world."

"Well, I wish we had him on the Twins," said the man named Papa Cone. The rest of them made noises of agreement.

"What you drinkin?" said Papa Cone.

"Vodka."

"Give the lady another vodka," he said. "My name's Oswald Cone," he told her. "They call me Papa Cone." He was cartwheeling a matchbook in his hands, turning it over and over on the bar. The back of his hand was furry. Hair curled from under the cuff of his denim jacket. His reddish white whiskers and reddish white hair bristled like a stubby brush. He had pitted cheeks. Old acne scars cratered his cheeks and nose.

"I'm Joy Faust," she said. She smiled at him, but he didn't smile back. His eyes were damply luminous as if he had taken them out and oiled them.

"You a druggie?" he said.

"Drugs? No."

"Because drugs are for Turks."

"Un-American," said the bartender.

"Un-Duluthian," said Papa Cone.

They were looking at Joy.

"I never touch them," she said.

Papa Cone looked at his buddies and something passed between them, some sort of agreement.

The bartender set the second drink in front of her, then Papa Cone slid down one stool. He wanted to know more about Tony Gwynn, so she made up some lies and Papa Cone listened.

"Sweet swingin, Tony Gwynn," he kept saying.

The black boy was staring hard at her. She raised her eyebrows at him. He put his forefinger up and wiggled it back and forth.

What's that mean? she wondered.

He got up and started for the door. When he passed by her, he leaned in and whispered, "Wouldn't if I was you, Mama." And then he left.

"What a fresh kid," she said.

"What'd he say?" asked Papa Cone.

"He just hit on me, the little stinker."

A couple of the men snickered.

Papa Cone shot a look at the bartender. "Got no respect for nothin, that fuckin kid. Who's he think he is?"

"He's Neon Leon. He's the man."

"He scores," said one of the men.

"Neon Leon be the man," echoed another.

"I don't like him no fuckin way," said Papa Cone.

By the time she finished her third vodka, she was drunk. She had the bartender put a hot dog in the oven for her and she bought a pack of Fritos.

Papa Cone kept buying her drinks. He told her about Duluth. He had lived in Duluth all his life, he said. He worked down at the docks, unloading freighters. He was a crane operator. He said he could put the hooks in the palm of her hand. "Can't I, Bill?" he said.

"What's that, Papa Cone?"

"Put the hooks in the palm of your hand."

"Papa Cone's the best," said Bill.

"The best," they all agreed.

She ate the hot dog with mustard and relish. She ate it in four famished bites, washing it down with vodka, the ice clicking against her teeth. Papa Cone pulled out a wad of cash and paid for her hot dog and another round of drinks. Joy glanced at the money. She saw a folded fifty on top. She put her foot on the lower rung of Papa Cone's stool. His features became more appealing the drunker she got. She decided he had a nice face after all. Unless he turned sideways. Then his profile was hawkish, his nose curving toward his lips. He had a thin neck and a slack chin and a busy Adam's apple. He was going on about cranes and the hooks and shackles and spotting loads and a crane rodeo he had won.

"They gimmee the trophy," he said. He shifted his body toward her and their knees touched.

~

AT ONE O'CLOCK she went home with him. He led her around the corner to an upstairs apartment. It was a one-bedroom, with a kitchenette. He had his hand up her skirt as soon as the door was closed. He pushed her against the door and grabbed a handful of her ass and kissed her, his nose pressing like a rubber hatchet into her cheek. She stared over his shoulder, taking in the apartment, the sofa and TV, the kitchenette and a window, the black rungs of a fire escape slanting diagonally across the glass. Papa Cone was digging into her with his fingers. His unshaven cheek was scouring her neck. She saw the opened bathroom door revealing a fragment of tub. *I used to dance at The Sands,* she reminded herself.

"I'd sure love a bath," she told Papa Cone.

His face went down and was burrowing into her breasts. She thought maybe he was biting her, but she wasn't sure.

She repeated herself. "I'd sure love a bath, Papa Cone."

"No way," he said. "I want you stinkin." He was on his knees now, his head beneath her skirt. He pushed her leg up and put it over his shoulder. "I want to stick my head up your pussy!" he said.

"You'll smother," she told him. She held his head with both hands, her fingers clutching his hair. Mostly all she felt down there was pressure, vague, distant, happening sort of to her.

~

LATER, while he was sleeping on the couch, she went to the bathroom and drew herself a steaming bath. She rummaged in the medicine cabinet and found a disposable razor. In the bath, she soaped her legs and shaved them. Then she shaved her armpits. Then she held the razor to her wrist and wondered if it would go deep enough. She looked at the plastic handle with its curved head and wondered how she might get the blade out of it. She pressed the razor's edge against the thin, blue veins and made a double slice. A moment later blood seeped into the cuts and ran slowly down her forearm toward her elbow. She pressed on the cuts, squeezed them, but they weren't deep enough and very little blood ran out. The wounds began to sting. She lowered her wrist into the water and watched thin veils of blood dispersing. She thought about breaking the plastic handle and extracting the blade and making a deep gash, but she wasn't sure how to smash the handle open. Maybe there was a hammer somewhere she could use.

After a minute, she got out of the tub and let the water out and thought of her mother's fear of drains. The old lady had lost her sense of proportion, had seen herself as small enough to get flushed down the pipes like a helpless bug. Who could make sense of such a thing? "Not me," she whispered. It made everything about her own sense of reality seem open to question. The mystery of the mind. The mystery of what it thinks it knows.

She watched drops of blood fall into the receding water. Taking a wad of toilet paper, she pressed it against the cuts. When they stopped bleeding, she wrapped a towel around herself and went into the kitchenette and searched for something to drink. She found an unopened bottle of Gordon's vodka. She got a glass from a cupboard and poured herself three fingers full. Added ice from the freezer.

Next to the TV on a shelf was a small golden gantry crane and a picture of a duck-built man with reddish hair and a trophy in his hands. The shining moment of Oswald Papa Cone.

"It don't mean nothin," she said. "I danced at The Sands and that's history now, blown to bits."

Papa Cone lay stretched on the couch, snoring loudly, his nostrils huge. She could have put her pinky in his nostrils and not touched the sides. She searched in his pants and found the fold of cash and put it in her purse. She started dressing. She pulled her panties to her knees, then stopped. The crotch of her panties were stained. She let them drop around her ankles and stepped out of them. With her toe she flung them across the room. She grabbed her skirt and wriggled into it. Buttoned up her blouse. She started to put her fox jacket on but stopped. The fur was filthy. It was stained with mustard and something that looked like a giant dandruff flake. She took Papa Cone's jacket and while she was zipping it, he came off the couch and slugged her. "Thievin bitch," he said. He hit her again and she went down on her knees. He hit her several times more. Hit her very hard.

I, George

I LET THE AD RUN one more day. It says:

JOY WHERE ARE YOU? COME HOME. G.M.

I call Jim Faust in Nevada and he says he knows nothing about her. I try to win his sympathy by telling him all that has happened, how gruesome Livia's death was and how it broke something in Joy.

Jim takes his time answering me. I can feel him thinking on the other end of the line and at last he says, "If she was there holding her mother like you say when she died, then I'm not surprised something broke in her. When our last baby came dead, she insisted on holding it, but she came unglued when it was in her arms, you know, and went into a depression deep as hell. Wouldn't eat, wouldn't get out of bed for weeks. Kept asking me to kill her."

"I never heard that," I say.

"I don't know, I've always felt it was more than just the baby's death. Joy's whole life has just been one fucked-up thing after another happening to her. She ever show you those photos of when she was a kid? She looks like an angel, picture of purity, picture of innocence. And then things happened to her and she was way too young to handle it. Her mother, you know, she should've looked out for her better. You probably know how much Joy worshipped her mother, worshipped the ground she walked on."

"It seemed like she did and she didn't. I never knew what to make of those two."

"You know about Nikos Pape?"

"Her stepfather."

"One of many. But she was mama's girl until that asshole came along. I had hoped I could make up for what he did to her. I was going to be her keeper. But I wasn't strong enough. I'll tell you the truth, though, I didn't think Buck would do any better than me and obviously he didn't."

I tell him how sick the weightlifter is, how he is having terrible seizures.

And Jim Faust says, "Seizures! How can Mr. America have seizures? Ha!" There is anger in his voice, a kind of gloating anger.

I ask him about the baby. "How did the baby actually die? I'm not sure of the story."

"What does it matter?"

"I was just curious."

He hesitates. I hear him clearing his throat. "Stillbirth," he says. "Little thing was born dead. Sometimes that's what happens, it's nobody's fault, just like the miscarriages weren't her fault. I tried to tell her that, I tried and tried, but she won't listen to nothin. She's a hardhead. She has to flog herself for every misstep she ever made. She kept saying, 'I smoke, I drank, it's my fault, I killed our baby.' That's what she said, but it ain't true. She took care of herself just fine, did everything the doctor said to do, but the kid came out dead, and she wouldn't let up on herself, wouldn't let it go."

"Buck said Joy smothered the baby. She fell asleep and smothered it with her breast."

"Say what?"

"Yhah, it's . . . it's what he said, but then he also said it was crib death."

"What was your name? George? George, Buck is full of shit. You must know by now that the man is a pathological liar. I hope you know that, George."

"I think I do."

"He lies even when there's no reason to."

"That's true."

"You bet it is. He needs to figure out why he's such a god-damn liar. Livia was that way too. The two of them swapping lies all the time. Rather tell lies than the truth. Love to drama-tize themselves, you know."

"They've been an experience," I say. "But just the same I really got attached to Joy and I'm worried about her, wish I knew where she was."

"Let me tell you something, George. From what you tell me she thinks she failed her mother, probably thinks she killed her, just like she thought she killed our baby. And so she needs to do something about that. She thinks in her beady little brain that she has to pay. And so that's what she'll do. And if her suffering is long enough and hard enough . . ."

I wait for him to finish, but he doesn't.

"She might have done some bad things, but there's a lot of good in her too," I tell him.

Jim Faust says, "Yeah, there is. Well, look, George, I'll call you if she shows up out here. But I'm married now and have a kid and I hope to God she don't show up. I don't want her around. I don't know how I ever stood her. She was a constant problem, constant agitation. She wanted to be Las Vegas legs, wanted to be a dancer, a hotshot showgirl. Then she wanted to be a housewife and have babies. Then she wanted to go back and finish college and be an art expert. She wanted to be a moviestar too. She wanted, she wanted, she wanted. One of those persons, you know what I mean, that never know really what they want? I'm well out of it. I covet peace now. I wouldn't go through that again for nothing, not for a million dollars!" He takes some deep breaths and his voice grows calm and he says, "So, anyway, what's your number, George?"

Joy Faust

WHEN SHE WOKE, she found herself in a bedroom. She was tied to the bed. The wounds on her face had stiffened and they ached. She could breathe through only one nostril. Her arms and legs were stretched wide, touching the sides of the mattress. Her hands and feet had no feeling. Her stomach was sunken, ribs rigid against her skin.

She listened for Papa Cone but heard only the sounds of traffic outside and the faint noise of a radio or a TV somewhere. She closed her eyes and concentrated on breathing and told herself that she had always known she would end like this.

~

SHE IS STANDING in her mother's house reading a golden inscription painted on a heart-shaped plate—

Mothers
Are
Special

She wanders the house, looking at the posters and plaques hanging on the walls. A narrow poster with a plastic cover tells her to—

*Listen
to Your
Heart*

A wood-framed placard says—

*My life has been touched
Because we have walked
A special walk together*

Then there is the proverb embroidered on a purple silk pillow—

*Her children shall rise up
And call her blessed.*
PROVERBS 31:28

Her mother tells her that God won't give her anything she can't handle. She turns and sees the old lady standing in half light, half shadow. "Where have you been?" Livia says. "Have you heard from your brother? He went off with his surfboard. Said he'd be back at noon."

Joy walks toward her mother to give her the news, to tell her that Hal has drowned. She reaches out ready to comfort her, ready to cry with her. Teary words filling her mouth.

~

"AIN'T GONNA ROLL PAPA CONE no more, not in this life," said Papa Cone. He had his thumbs on her eyelids, pushing them up. Her vision cleared and he came into view and she could see that his face looked impossibly red as if it had been singed by fire. Her lips were gooey and she knew he had been kissing her. The lamp was on beside the bed. Papa Cone was naked, sweat dripping from his body. His breath smelled like oyster shells.

"I swore any bitch ever do that to me again I'd cut her tits off, yhah." Tufts of fur were backlit over his shoulders. He brushed his hand through his hair and she could see a white asterisk scar above his middle knuckle. It looked as if someone had jabbed him with a nail. He took a corner of the sheet and wiped her mouth and wiped her chin.

She swallowed. Her throat felt clogged, there was a sweet-salt taste on her tongue. She tried to say his name but nothing came out. She tried to tell him she was sorry, but only her lips moved. He was standing beside her, his penis drooping, getting smaller and smaller, until it disappeared in a wiry thatch. She raised her head slightly and looked the length of her body. Her nipples were still there, but they were bleeding over the stretched coronas, two mounds of ice cream trickling with cherry sauce.

Blood, she tried to say, but couldn't say it. The blood ran down the valley to her ribs. Her navel was a pool of blood through which the gold earring poked as if panting for air. She could see her blue-black feet, but she couldn't feel them. She looked at Papa Cone.

"Women," he was saying, his lips barely moving, his voice almost inaudible, "how many times you think you can get away with it? I'm fifty-two years old, and you know how many times I've been rolled? Too many. You know, a fella just gets fed up, just says to himself, 'Papa Cone, ain't no use being nice to her, she don't appreciate it, she takes you for a sucker, all of em do. You fall in love, you bring her home, you let her drink your liquor, you offer to marry her and take care of her for the rest of her life, and what does she do? She waits till you're sleepin and steals you blind.' Well, the tables have turned. Papa Cone in charge. He's gonna put his hooks right up your snatch and pull you inside out."

"Water," she whispered.

"Huh?"

She licked her lips.

"Water?" he said.

She nodded.

Papa Cone studied her, his mouth grim. Then he said, "I spose." And he got her a glass of water. He held her head up and she drank the entire glass. When she was finished, she was able to talk. "I'm sorry, Papa Cone," she said.

"Too late," he said.

"If you'll just listen."

"I don't care what your story is. Every bitch has a story. Every bitch bitches about her story. I bet it was a man, right? It's always some man. Men give you all the excuses you need."

She tried to tell him about her mother, about the horrid death and about herself, the treacherous daughter, but he wouldn't listen.

"I hope I haven't made a mistake about you," he said, half to himself. "You didn't give me a whore disease did you?"

She shook her head.

"Better not have," he said. "It's a dangerous world. If you did that to me I'll roast you and eat you! It's a promise."

She shook her head again.

"I wonder," he said. "I know damn well you've been around the block a few times. But you smell all right. I go by the smell. If it don't smell right, I don't mess with it. Yours stinks just fine. Just it better be, that's all I can say." He went out and closed the door.

She lay with the lamp on, her eyes gazing at the stained ceiling. She could hear a horn in the distance. She could hear the TV in the other room. Applause. She looked at her breasts again. There was no blood.

"Did I dream it?" she asked herself. "Is this all a dream?"

She tried to call Papa Cone, but her voice wouldn't rise above a whisper and every effort to speak made her throat burn. Her body burned. Every joint burned. She was thirsty again and she had a bursting bladder, itchy cystitis. It felt like embers were living in her crotch.

~

PAPA CONE DIDN'T COME BACK until dark. He had scrambled eggs on a plate and he tried to feed her, but she couldn't eat. She turned her head away. "I can't swallow," she said.

"That's cuz I choked you," he said. "I lost it, man. When I saw what you were doing, I lost it. I almost killed you. You were this close." He held his finger and thumb an inch apart. "I may still do it yet. I haven't decided. You messed with the wrong boy this time."

"I have to pee so bad," she whispered.

"You better not. You pee this bed, I'll do it then. I'll twist your chicken neck off."

"Please," she said.

He stared at her. "What am I gonna do with you?" he said. He scratched his arms, riffling the hair. He walked up and down at the foot of the bed, glancing at her, his eyes glossy.

A minute passed and then he started untying her. When he had the ropes off, he pulled her to a sitting position, but she couldn't walk, so he picked her up and carried her to the bathroom and set her on the pot. She looked down at her wrist. Thin crusts had formed over the razor cuts. The blood was rushing back into her hands and feet. It was painless at first, but then it felt like needles stabbing. Spurts of urine came out of her. Her bowels were locked.

"You done?" said Papa Cone.

"I promise to be good," she said. "I'll stay with you. Whatever you want, I'll do." She reached for his crotch, brushed the thatch of hair.

He considered her offer. "Maybe we'll work somethin out."

He let her take a bath and then he gave her his robe and let her sit on the couch, finish the plate of cold eggs, chewing and swallowing slowly, washing them down with a glass of iced vodka. In a few minutes the vodka took over and her pains diminished. She and Papa Cone sat together watching TV. It was a show about the Sonora Desert, rattlesnakes were having sex and then going off to hunt.

"Rattlesnakes," said Papa Cone. "Nobody fucks with them. Mean fuckin eyes, ain't they? They never blink."

Papa Cone kept feeding her vodka and talking about nature and how vicious it was, how nothing lived if something else didn't die. She fell asleep listening to him. Vaguely, she felt him turn her onto her stomach and the weight of his body pressing down. Vaguely she felt her body being pounded from behind.

~

A BABY IS TEARING at Joy's nipple and Joy is doing nothing to stop her, feeling the justice of it. And then the baby is nursing nicely and Joy can feel the milk oozing and the soft head pressing against her chin, the hair fluffy, the sweet virgin smell of it in her nostrils, her arms cradling, holding tight, unable to get enough of her, until she bursts into feathers drifting over the bed.

~

WHEN SHE OPENED HER EYES, it was morning again and she was tied up and Papa Cone was gone. On the wall in front of her was a Jesus figure hanging on a cross. She hadn't noticed it before, but now she stared at it carefully, trying to imagine how it must have felt to have nails driven into your palms and feet. She wondered how a person like Papa Cone could have a cross of Jesus on the wall and yet do what he was doing to her. How was that possible?

She prayed to Jesus. She said, "Father, take this cup away."

In and out of consciousness throughout the day, there were moments when she saw herself, a tiny girl, writing another letter:

I put my stuff in my wagon. Now I am ready to go. I go into the jungle. I think all lay down. Wants that furry thing on my head a lion. He will eats me. Want will I do I think I better pack. I will go home to mama. I am home at last. Hi mom where have you been.

your loving daughter me

She thought about the letters she had showed to George and she wondered why she had done that, why she had lied to him like that. There was nothing to be gained by it but his sympathy. She realized that she had wanted him to feel sorry for her and to think of her as a mother missing her daughter, a mother with a broken heart, a victim. She told herself that she was as much a role player as Buck and her own mother had been. *I've been an actress, a faker all my life*, she admitted. And now she was in a place where fakery wouldn't work.

~

ANOTHER NIGHT WENT BY and she was amazed that she was still alive, amazed at how much her body could stand. Papa Cone kept her drunk and tied to the bed most of the time. He had bought some Depends and kept her in them during the day. He would come home and bathe her and spray scent over her and feed her and let her watch TV. When men from the bar started showing up, he would tie her to the bed. That's how they wanted her, open and helpless. Some of the men wore masks.

~

ONE NIGHT she noticed a spot of light on the wall. It took her a while before she realized that someone was watching. She saw other holes, other points of light. She could hear the holes gasping, breathing, chuckling now and then. They were paying to watch her, paying to see her through a peephole. A man entered her and moved in and out and came on the sixth stroke and told her she had the hottest pussy he had ever dipped his wick into and the holes in the wall laughed. She was hot all over, burning up. Her head and joints were killing her, aching like they had never ached before. She moaned and the man said, "That's right, baby, moan. Jesus, you love it, you love it!"

Later on, she told Papa Cone that she wasn't a hot pussy, she was burning with fever. She could feel fluid in her lungs. She coughed and phlegm rattled and there was a sharp pain in her chest.

"I'm drowning," she said.

"The doctor," he said. "I'll bring him."

A man showed up in a suit and tie and looked her over and he said to Papa Cone, "Women are vastly overrated, Oswald. They're not worth half the trouble they put us through. You have to decide what you're going to do with her. She's very sick. You hear her lungs bubbling? You better take her to the hospital."

"It's over then," said Papa Cone.

"Does she know any of us?"

"Just me is all."

"So much trouble," said the man.

"You want one more go at her?" said Papa Cone. "I'll cut her price in half."

The man snorted and he said, "Jesus, Oswald, you really are dumb."

They left the room. She heard the door click. She heard the TV's garbled voice. She waited for Papa Cone to take her to the bathroom and feed her and let her watch TV, or at least cover her up with a blanket, but he didn't come.

I, George

BUCK HAS BEEN VERY LITTLE TROUBLE since I got a bail bonds-
man and bailed him out and brought him home from the hospital. As long as he takes his medication, his seizures are mild and
he goes whole days sometimes without having one. He has no
desire to lift weights, nor could he if he wanted to. He's still got
a lot of healing to do. The weights are in the basement gathering
dust, waiting for when he's ready.

He came home with a different attitude. He shuffles around
the apartment, trying to help out, does the vacuuming and dries
the dishes. He tells me over and over that he wants to make a
significant contribution to life.

What he tries first is to learn to paint. I let him use my
mother's painting tools and he goes at it. He makes whirls on
the canvas, slashes and clumps and delicate drops and he tells
me he is an intuitive artist, a Jackson Pollock type.

When I see the completed paintings, I decide to be honest
and I tell him that art isn't his thing.

And he says, "Just playing. Having fun." He smiles but his
face is gray with grief as if his veins are drying up. "The world
isn't ready for my peculiar vision," he says. He puts his elbows on
his knees. Slowly his head drifts down through legs wide apart.

Then he takes to writing on a yellow pad, using a pencil,
which he sharpens every few minutes with a potato peeler. He

says his true passion is to be a novelist. He writes and writes for days and fills the pad, then he reads some of it to me and it is all about a weightlifter who saves the president of the United States from an assassination attempt. Buck calls the weightlifter Buck Bound and makes him a member of a secret government agency. Every few pages Bound is in bed with a gorgeous woman, who is a counteragent trying to kill him. Buck Bound always kills his enemies by snapping their necks.

He tells me to be perfectly honest with him, what do I really think? I say with regret that it all sounds pornographic and that his characters are too predictable.

Buck says, "Yeah, it's shit. I shouldn't be writing commercial formula crap like this. I'm better than this. I'm going to write my biography. Write what you know, that's what they say. I have my bio in me clamoring to get out."

"That's good," I tell him.

"What is the greatest autobiography you've ever read, George?"

"The greatest? Maybe Mark Twain's, I guess."

"Mine will make Twain's seem a pale imitation. I've led a fascinating life, George. No brag, just fact. It's made me a fascinating figure."

"If you say so, Buck."

"Hey, I do say so. You want to know the title? It's *The Extraordinary Life of a Bodybuilder*. Is that a great title or what? It will sell like fruitcakes, I guaran-tee it."

He doesn't write his biography. But he tells it to me, talking for hours one night about all that has happened to him and all he has done in his forty-four years. That's when I learn he is a plagiarist, that none of the poems I've read are exclusively his own work, a word or a phrase here and there but that's all. He says he had talent once, but it got away from him, he doesn't quite know how. And he finally tells me about Connie, explaining how she maddened him when he was splitting wood and somehow the ax found its way into her head. He says I can turn him in and be a witness if I want to. He won't hold it against me, he says.

But I don't want to. I can't see the point in it right now and I dread having to be involved, having to say anything against my cousin, who has suffered quite a bit for what he's done. And besides, when the snows melt the cops will be all over that farm searching for a sunken grave and they'll find it and that will be the end of Buck.

Joy Faust

THE NEXT DAY it was quiet again in the room. A light snow fell outside, flakes bumping the window. She was hot and she was cold and she shook all over and she coughed. Every time she took a deep breath to cough, a pain would pierce her heart and burn her chest. She tried to concentrate on shallow breathing, little puffs of air passing back and forth through her mouth. She had no spit to swallow. She dozed and she woke and she wondered where she was and she dozed again.

She heard glass breaking and in a moment she heard footsteps and the bedroom door opening. In walked a black kid wearing a gold jacket. It was the same boy she had seen in Bar Dante, the one who had tried to warn her. He stopped when he saw her, his eyes fixing on her like she was some curious specimen.

He started opening the drawers where Papa Cone's underwear was kept. He went through the drawers, throwing pants and sweaters and boxer briefs on the floor. He found a watch and a ring and a sock with some change in it. He looked at Joy.

"Where is it?" he said.

"What?" she answered hoarsely.

"His stash. He's made a mint off you, every motherfucker knows it." The kid stepped close to her and poked his finger in her ribs. "He said you were dead."

THE ALTAR OF THE BODY

"I'm not dead."

"You look like you ought to be." He stared at her, his eyes going over her breasts, then fixing on her pubic area. She thought he might climb on her for a freebie. She watched the backs of his fingers brush over her bush. "Keeps you naked and tied up all day long?" he asked.

She nodded. "Usually he puts a diaper on me."

The kid made a face. "Some sick motherfuckers in this sick fucking world," he said. His head tilted sideways as he contemplated her. Then he took out a knife and flicked it open. Joy closed her eyes.

"Thank you," she said. She lifted her chin, her neck, toward him.

"What you thinkin, Mama?" he said. "Neon Leon ain't no murderer of helpless whores." She felt a tug at her arm and then the strain was relieved and her arm fell to the side like a dead twig. Then the rope was cut holding the other arm, then her ankles were freed.

"You better haul ass," said Neon Leon. He turned away. He disappeared.

"Where?" she whispered. She looked at her wine-dark feet and felt the needles coming. She told herself that she was in a bed in Duluth and the boy with the knife was real and she was free.

Inch by inch she moved to the edge of the bed and forced herself to sit up. When she tried to stand, she fell on the floor and had to lie there for a minute breathing and coughing. She crawled to the clothes the boy had strewn around and she picked out a shirt and some pants and put them on. She tied the pants around her waist with a piece of the rope that had bound her hands. She went to the closet and felt with her fingers in back, where she had heard Papa Cone lifting a board. She found the loose board, flipped it over and pulled the shoebox out. In it were four little piles of cash wrapped in rubberbands.

She put the box under her arm and rose to her feet, felt faint and teetered against the wall. She groped her way into the living room and saw the smashed window and the fire escape behind it. She took a bottle of sherry from the cupboard and went into the bedroom and poured the bottle over the mattress. She lit a book of matches and threw it on the bed. Seconds later the blankets burst into flames. She found her purse and slipped the strap over her shoulder.

She went out the window and scooted on her butt step by step down the fire escape, until she got to the ladder at the bottom. She grabbed hold of the ladder and tried to climb down, but her hand slipped and she fell. The box hit the ground and broke open. She lay on her back gasping.

Neon Leon was there, squatting over her.

"I figured you knew," he said. "Ole Neon Leon, he ain't a slow wit." He gathered the bundles of money strewn around and tucked them into the pockets of his jacket. Then he grabbed her under the arms and helped her up.

"The blue van," she said, pointing toward the street.

He supported her to the van, which was at the end of the alley and half a block over. There was a parking ticket on the windshield.

She felt in her purse, trying to find the keys. He took the purse away from her, got the keys, then opened the side door and helped her in. She sprawled on the mattress, the very mattress on which, light-years away, she had caught Connie and Buck together. The jealousy and anger she had felt at the time seemed absurd to her now.

A moment later she heard the motor turning over and over, the starter grinding, and finally the motor caught and roared and she felt the van moving, turning, speeding up. She closed her eyes and concentrated on shallow breathing. A tickle in her throat kept making her cough. She heard the radio playing hard rock, the noise mixing with sirens getting closer and closer and passing the van.

"Fire trucks!" said Neon Leon.

The van dipped, jostling her. She gripped the back of the seat and tried to pull herself up on her knees.

"Take me home," she said.

"Where's home," he said, turning the radio down.

"Where?" she said.

"Where's home? I said."

She didn't know.

The van had turned onto a highway and was moving faster. She looked out a window and saw treetops and dark clouds. She wondered if Neon Leon was going to dump her and take the van.

"So where's home?" she heard him say.

"South," she said.

"What?"

"South. South."

"South it is," he said. "I'll take you to the Gulf and drive you into the sea, Mama."

She could hear the tires keeping time. She thought of Buck and wondered if he was all right. And George, what about him?

"Hey, Mama, what's this?" said Neon Leon. He was tapping the urn in the seat beside him. "What you got in this thing?"

"My mother," said Joy. "Her ashes."

"Her ashes!" Neon Leon glanced at her, his eyes aghast. "What you doin with dead-woman ashes, lady?"

"I wanted to turn her loose in Lake Superior. I wanted to free her. My mama."

There was a long pause in which she could hear him breathing hard through his nose. She could see his fingers tapping the steering wheel. And then she felt the van slowing down and turning left. It speeded up again. She saw a sign that said High-way 13. A few minutes later, the van pulled over and stopped.

"Well then, let's let her go," said Neon Leon.

He helped her out of the van and steadied her as she took the urn and walked with a heavy wind at her back to the edge of the lake. Powerful gray waves curled and crashed on the shore.

"The wind will carry her," said Neon Leon. "It'll blow her way out there."

He let go of Joy and stood off to the side. She hugged the urn and felt the wind tugging at her hair and clothing. She looked at the water. "It's almost an ocean," she said.

"Go on," said Neon Leon, "turn your mama loose, let the water have her."

She opened the urn. Inside was a parchment bag filled with ashes. Joy pulled the bag out and tore the top off and whirled it back and forth over her head. The ashes flew in the wind and vanished. Minute pieces of bone fell among the smooth, wet stones at her feet. When the bag was empty she folded it and put it back in the urn. Her heart was beating slower, slower. "There," she said. "There now." She closed her eyes and sunk down on the shore, drooped to her side, longing for sleep. She felt Neon Leon trying to lift her, but she couldn't help him. She was puddling in all directions. It was a comfortable slide, no pain, no fear. A sweet peace . . . oblivion.

I, George

IN THE EVENINGS, Buck and I have dinner and watch TV, him on the couch, me in the big chair, watching the screen between my feet, smoking my pipe, Ho Tep dozing in my lap. Every other minute I think of Joy and try to guess what's become of her. My inclination is that she's gone to California, back to what she knows in L.A. or San Diego. Or maybe she's in Las Vegas. Or maybe she's dead.

One night Buck tells me that he's lost everything he ever cared about. He says he doesn't know how it happened. He says that he had a plan and he thought he knew how to make the future just what he wanted it to be, but somehow-someway nothing turned out.

And he says, "I think I could have been a fine man, a decent fellow, if I had just gotten a couple breaks. I mean, think if I had won Mr. Universe or if I had gotten that part in Stallone's movie. What if that had come through? Man, I don't like the way the world works. I don't like how so much depends on luck or who you know or who you blow. Think of all the talent out there that never gets noticed, George. Think of that. Life is luck, George. A smidgen of talent and a whole shit-pot full of luck. I've always had the talent, but no goddamn luck."

"If it weren't for bad luck I'd have no luck at all," I tell him.

"Me too, cousin. Me too." He smiles at me and briefly he is

Mikey again. "You're a good man," he says and he chuckles and he adds, "Or maybe just stupid. Sometimes goodness is stupidity in disguise."

"In my case, that's probably true," I say.

"Nah, I'm just kidding," says Buck.

He pulls me into a hug and I notice that he smells stale and his vertebrae are pushing like arthritic knuckles against my palms. His collarbone beneath my chin is as rigid as the back of a knife.

~

ONE DAY Buck doesn't take his medicine and he has a severe seizure and is out for an hour, but I don't call for an ambulance because he has made me promise not to. He's told me that he wants nature to take its course.

When he wakes up he says, "Thought I died."

"Not yet," I tell him.

I start giving him his medicine myself. He makes faces, but he takes the pills and he says, "Thank you, Mommy." I think he needs me to do this, to care enough to give him the pills.

The rest of the days are all the same, the TV plays his favorite soaps and game shows while he lies on his side on the couch, head resting on his arm as he watches and snoozes and wakes to watch some more.

~

THE PHONE RINGS on a Wednesday and a voice asks to speak to George and when I say, "Speaking," the voice says, "I got your name from Joy's purse. You know Joy Faust, man?"

"Joy? Where is she?"

"In the hospital. You wanna know where? She's in Rochester. Saint Mary's Hospital. She be dead tomorrow. You wanna see her you best get your ass in gear, man."

The phone clicks, but I still shout, "What do you mean?"

Buck looks up from the couch. "Joy?" he says.

"In Rochester, in the hospital."

"Hey?"

"Said she'll be dead by tomorrow."

Buck closes his eyes and shakes his head. "Nah, baby, no way. The Joy Fausts of this world never die young." He stands up. He is breathing hard and his eyes roll back and he goes down.

I jump for him, but it's too late. He collapses on the rug, his muscles twitching. There is nothing to do but wait him out. I put a pillow under his head and a blanket over him and put the radio on the classical music station to soothe his brain.

Later when he wakes I say, "I best go alone to Rochester, Buck. I don't think you can handle it. I'll find out what's what." I help him back to the couch and put his medicine on the coffee table and make him promise to take his pills every four hours.

"Go," he says, "just go."

~

IT TAKES TWO HOURS to drive to Rochester, but Saint Mary's Hospital is on the city map and easy to find. When I get to Joy's room I see her breathing through a bubble mask. I hear air hissing. Above her stands a chrome tree with a bag of clear liquid hanging from it. The liquid trickles down a tube into a needle stuck in the back of her hand. Her arm is tied to a padded board. There is a silent machine reading her vitals in digital code.

I sit on the edge of the bed and stroke her hair, expecting any second to be her last. A nurse comes in and asks me if I'm a relative, and when I say I'm just a friend, she says, "That boy took off like a shot. He dumped her and split."

"Who was he?"

She shrugs. "I have no idea. Do you know if she has insurance?"

"No, ma'am. But give her what she needs. I'll cover it. I don't care what it costs."

The nurse goes away. Comes back with a form, which I fill out, promising to pay for Joy's treatment. "I'll turn this in," says the nurse.

"Joy gonna make it?" I ask.

"She's holding her own."

"Is it pneumonia?"

The nurse tells me that Joy has pneumonia, but antibiotics are working on it. Her problem mostly is her heart. "She has inflammation of the pericardium. There is fluid between the inner and outer layers of it, which is compressing the heart. We'll just have to see," says the nurse. "She's holding her own so far. She seems to have a strong will to live."

I think about what Buck said, the Joy Fausts of this world don't die young, and I tell the nurse that Joy is tough, she'll make it.

When the nurse leaves I grab a chair and sit beside the bed, listening to air hissing and the tread of feet up and down the hall. "Livia, can you hear me?" I say. And then I realize what name I used and I say, "Joy, it's George McLeod. Squeeze my hand if you can hear me. Squeeze my hand." I take her hand, but it stays limp. I rub her knuckles with my thumb and try to think of things to say. I tell her that she has to fight, she has to stay alive, there are people who care, people who love her and want her well. I go on and on, mumbling what it seems a sick person needs to hear.

Later, I call home and tell Buck what is what and tell him I will stay till it's over.

~

Around two the next morning Joy dies and the nurses come running. I retreat to a corner of the room and try to stay small, while a doctor works, pushing on her chest, giving her a shot with a long needle in the heart, then zapping her with electric paddles. It is a tense three or four minutes, the doctor saying, "Clear!" and the machine buzzing and Joy's body jumping. It takes three jolts to get her going again.

"She's back," says one of the nurses. A green line is lunging on a black screen. "Ninety over forty," says the nurse.

"Good girl," says the doctor. He puts a stethoscope on Joy's chest and listens a long time and then he says, "Let's draw that fluid and give her heart some room to work."

She is taken away. I stay in the corner, wishing I hadn't come, wishing I was drunk at The Body Shop, watching the girls, or maybe just home with my pipe, my TV, Ho Tep on my lap and Buck on the couch. I think about sneaking off and going back to Medicine Lake. I don't want to witness her death. Too much death around. Livia, Connie, and now Joy.

"Always comes in threes," I tell myself.

~

THE NEXT MORNING I wake up worn-out, my bones aching, but my courage has returned and I feel ashamed that I even thought about running off and leaving Joy to die alone. I am still in the chair. Joy is in bed. Light from the window lays a band across her face and I can see fine hairs growing on her chin and upper lip. I watch the rhythm of her chest rising, falling. Her throat rattles each time she inhales. My eyelids burn and I want to stretch out next to her and go to sleep. I think of her lying next to Livia dying on the bed, hugging the old lady to the end. I will do the same for her if it comes to that.

"I need some coffee. I'll be right back," I tell her, patting her hand.

Down the hall an orderly tells me how to get to the cafeteria. After coffee and a toasted bagel with cream cheese, I clean up in the men's room, wash my face, brush my teeth with my finger, slick my hair back a bit. Then I go outside and walk around the streets and smoke my pipe and feel the sun on my dome. Rochester is a nice city, old buildings and new ones, old houses off the main streets, tilted sidewalks, deep gutters, lots of trees.

A woman in a jogging outfit runs by, her breath foggy. I turn to watch her and realize that a bouncing bottom doesn't do what it used to for me, not so pleasant as it was before, and I tell myself that I am getting old. Or maybe it's just my mood. Maybe if Joy recovers and comes home and the trees blossom, the garden grows, then bouncing bottoms will be worth watching again.

Joy Faust

SHE WAS ALL ELBOWS and knees knobby and she had too much cheekbone and her skin was so thin and white it made her veins look like roadmaps, but she was home and she said to herself, "She's dead, I'm alive." She imagined her mother in a clean, well-lighted place: there were gold-leaved trees and a blue river and she was doing a jig for Jesus and that was the image to cling to whenever the other image, the gasping skull on the pillow, slipped into Joy's mind.

She looked around the room. Nothing had changed, the same blond chest of drawers and the mirror, the same framed photo of melancholy Sissy and the silver comb-and-brush set and the clock next to the photo, the yellow wallpaper with its blue-feather swirls and the same *Nude Descending* on the wall.

Buck shuffled in, his slippers whispering. There was more gray than black in his hair and his face was so gaunt she hardly recognized him. His moonish eyes and ruined nose made his cheeks and chin look small.

She could hear the click of nails and then the dog was standing on hindlegs, his front paws touching the bed. He was looking at her. "C'mere," she said, hoisting him up. He moved his head beneath her hand.

"You're the last link," she said. She felt her heart moving sluggishly as if each beat might be its last. "I've been awful sick," she said.

"Me too," said Buck. He flopped heavily into the chair and stared at the floor.

George entered with a tray. "You hungry?" he asked. He put the tray down and propped up her pillows, then put the tray in her lap. He sat on the side of the bed and fed her. The dog sniffed at the food but kept a distance. It was oatmeal and toast and orange juice. The spoon came toward her.

"Mother George," she said.

"Open up," he said.

After two bites of oatmeal she was pushing his hand away.

"You're skin and bones," he told her. "You've got to eat."

"I've been thinking," she said.

He put the spoon down and wiped her lips with a napkin. They stared at each other and she felt an impulse to say that she had been thinking of him and how much she loved him and how grateful she was that he had stuck by her, but instead she said, "George, you remember those letters from my daughter?"

"Sure."

She cleared her throat and looked him in the eye. "My daughter didn't write them. I don't have a daughter, George. Those letters were written by me to my mother when I was little. I found them when I put her in the home in San Diego. I was going through her stuff and there they were, all my silly letters tied with a ribbon. I never knew she saved them. I couldn't even remember writing them at first, but then I remembered. And that's when I broke down and got really depressed about putting her away."

George said, "Those were good letters. If you had been my daughter, I'd have saved them too."

"Well, now you know what a liar I am." Her voice cracked and she had to cough.

"Joy, I—"

"Don't talk, George. I've got more to tell you." Then she told what happened in Duluth. She talked about running short of money and trying to roll Papa Cone and how he beat her and tied her to the bed and how he sold her and how she wasn't really sure that it all happened the way she was telling it because at the time it felt like she was hallucinating. As she talked she noted that both George and Buck had bowed their heads, each man keeping a palm on his forehead.

"Then Neon Leon came and cut me loose and took me to Lake Superior, so I could finish what I had gone there to do. After I let her go, I collapsed. That kid saved my worthless ass. The next thing I knew was when I woke up and there you were, George."

George touched her arm. His mouth worked, but he didn't speak.

"I feel like I did it to you," said Buck, his voice so soft she barely caught what he was saying.

"I did it to myself," she replied. "But as long as we're being honest I might as well tell you that if you'd just kept your pecker in your pants none of this might have happened."

"That's right," said Buck, giving her a baggy-eyed look.

"Mikey Routelli."

"It's me."

"Right," she agreed. She felt her chin trembling. "Buck's always been a manipulator," she said.

"That's true," said Buck. "My fault."

"Oh, quit your whining," said Joy. "Truth is, you damn near manipulated me to death. I thought I was bad because I made you leave your wife and I left Jim. But I'm not bad, I'm just stupid."

"I'm the one who's bad," said Buck.

She shook her head. "You're just you," she told him. "Every-one is just who they are, they can't help it."

"Close your eyes now," said George. "You're all tuckered."

"I'm tuckered," she said, chuckling. "What a word, *tuckered*. Like I'm compacting."

She scooted down and pulled the comforter tight and held the dog close, feeling his warmth. His fur smelled of pine tree.

"You sleep," said George, rising, patting her leg.

"Don't touch me," she said. "You men."

~

LATER THAT NIGHT, she opened her eyes and saw a thin violet light hovering over her and she thought it might be Sissy's ghost, but it was only moonblush. She got out of bed and went into the bathroom and sat on the pot waiting for the poisons to pass.

When she had finished she went to the other bedroom, where Buck was sleeping. His mouth was open, sucking and puffing. She turned the lamp on and studied him. His eroded face made her think of a baked apple. The hole where his ear stud used to be had shriveled into a minuscule pocket.

"You got old," she whispered.

Buck's lips smacked and he stirred, then he was looking at her. Six years of him unfurled in her mind: man-mountain Buck onstage, a trophy held triumphantly over his head; Buck in the weightroom spotting her as she did bench presses, his sweat raining over her breasts; Buck beneath her in the Lincoln, her pelvis rotating both of them to orgasm; Buck in The Body Shop, a flashy entertainer showing his muscles; Buck selling Nova Life; Buck singing "Lil of the Golden West"; Buck writing love poems to her; Buck naked, dancing his joy of being alive; Buck in every minute of every hour since the moment she first saw him.

"God, I loved you *so much*," she said. She put her hand on the headboard to steady herself.

"I don't want to die with you hating me," he said.

"I don't hate you, Buck," she said. "I never could. Not for long. When you hurt me, I hated you, but I don't hate you now."

He shifted his body and patted the sheet. She eased into bed. The sheet was warm, dampish. They lay side by side and she could feel the heat radiating from him. He took her hand. "I always loved you best," he said.

~

ANOTHER WEEK WENT BY and the wheezing went away, but she was still running a mild fever and had to stay on antibiotics. She spent most of the day on the couch with Buck, the two of them sprawled with their feet on the coffee table, watching TV and nodding off now and then, sometimes waking with their heads together.

One gloomy afternoon he was sitting at the window, watching people go by and making jokes about this or that one. His jokes were making her laugh again. They were both laughing at him saying, "She's got eyes like a trout," when suddenly he had a seizure and fell off the chair. The way he threw his arms out and rolled and kicked the chair into the wall made Joy giggle, but it was not really a sight to be laughed at. She put her hand over her mouth. He stayed still for a few seconds, then rolled onto his back.

"There I go again," he said.

"You don't stop doing that, you'll make yourself sick," she told him.

"That's what happens. It hits me like a hammer and I go out and there's nothing I can do about it, not a goddamn thing. I mean, after all I was Mr. . . . Mr. . . . was it Minnesota? Mr. Minnesota?" His voice rose in panic. "What's wrong with me?" he asked. "Why can't I remember who I was?" He was touching his head with his fingertips, touching it gingerly here and there as if every spot was sore.

And then he told her he remembered being Mr. California, yes that was the title he was trying to think of. Not Minnesota, but California.

"But that's not—"

"It took me a while but I got it. It's like a spell comes over me, then it goes and I'm myself again, until the next one comes. What bothers me is that maybe my memory won't come back one day. That's the trouble, you see, that's what bothers me most." He smiled at her, his mouth crooked, his teeth dull, his skin pee yellow in the cold noon light. "Would you miss me, Joy, if that happened?"

"I'd miss you," she said. She took a tissue and blew her nose. Wiped her eyes with the back of her hand. *God,* she told herself, *I'm so sick of crying.*

He yawned. They stayed quiet, listening to the tenant in the apartment above flushing the toilet. Then flushing it again.

"How did I come to this?" he said. "Look at me, look at my body. It looks like . . ." His brows furrowed as he tried to come up with the words.

"Mashed potatoes?" she offered.

"Yeah, mashed potatoes," he said. "Lumpy mashed potatoes."

He got slowly up and crawled to the couch, flopping next to her. "I gotta go to court next week for injuring that cop. I guess his back is really bad. I'm born to hurt people it seems."

"What will happen?"

"I don't know. Probably I'll do some time. They're still looking for Con, you know, still trying to get that on me."

"I don't want to talk about it."

"Me neither," he said.

"What can I do for you?" said Joy. "Am I any use to you?"

He shrugged.

"Hey, I really wish I knew what to do."

"Hay's for horses. All I know is I don't want this. You know what I'm saying?" He tapped his head. "Mental case. Crip-dip. I want Buck Root at his best, or not at all." His raw, plum-wet eyes bored into her and she felt her throat tighten again. *So sick of tears,* she reminded herself.

He put his hand in his lap and scratched himself, then his hand started moving around as if feeling for signs of life. He gave her a look. His eyebrow arched. "It's funny how this thing still works . . . It's like those bulls who mount cows at the slaughterhouse. They can smell the blood, they know they're gonna die, but they want one more piece of ass."

"They can't help it," she said. She reached inside his robe and noted his penis felt the same, though nothing else about him did. He didn't even smell quite right. Milk gone sour.

He watched her hand massage him. "My cock hasn't lost its cunning," he said. "If I don't have a seizure, we can . . . use it . . . if you think you want."

"For old time's sake?" she said.

They went to the bedroom and she lay on the bed and opened her robe and he shed his robe and there wasn't any energy expended on foreplay except he spit on his finger and wet her for a second. She watched his face as he moved over her, into her. His face was that of a man utterly exhausted.

After a few thrusts he asked her if she could come.

"I don't think so," she said.

He went on another minute, then stopped and lay panting. His skin felt repulsively moist.

"We did have fun, didn't we?" he said. "Vegas, L.A., Chicago, New York, the nightlife—shit we had fun." His voice trailed off, then he said, "I wanted more. I wanted to be James Dean and Elvis rolled into one and Mr. America too. The hardest thing for me was to accept my limits. The second hardest was to admit to myself that I've run out of options. I'm out of options, sweetness."

"I know."

"All out."

He slipped onto his side, a hand cupping her breast, thumb moving over the nipple. "Your mother didn't understand that little truth about herself and look what happened to her."

"You don't want it that way."

"Amen." His mouth was touching her ear, tickling it. "Reach over the side, under the bed, and pull that box out, will you, sweetness?"

She found the box and set it on her stomach.

"You want it?" she said.

"No," he said. "You."

She took the cover off, dropped it on the floor, reached inside the box, unwrapped the dish towel and held the chrome gun in her hand. They admired it together.

"Big," she said.

He raised his hand, not to shield himself, but to place the muzzle in his mouth. He wrapped his lips around the barrel.

It was all very *otherworldly*.

She told herself he would go quick and clean and not have to endure what lay ahead, the force that had kept her mother going, the thing in us that lives beyond reason. She was sweating with fever and a little shaky. She wondered if she were hallucinating and if everything that seemed to be happening was only another dream.

"*Fweet*ness," he said.

"Sweetness," she answered.

He forced the hammer back with his thumb.

When the gun went off blood burst out the back of his head. His eyelids drooped lazily but did not close. She saw some of his teeth on the pillow. A gray haze surrounded her. The smell of gunpowder prickled her nose. Behind him she could see an abstract design slipping down the wall. She tried to pick up the gun and put the muzzle in her mouth, but the recoil had hurt her wrist and thumb and she couldn't grip the handle. She switched to her left hand, but was clumsy with it, and by the time she got the hammer back and her lips around the barrel, George was bursting through the door and bellowing. The barrel was off angle in her mouth when she pulled the trigger and felt her head kick back and a numbness seize her instantly.

She heard George screaming, "No! No! No!"

Something warm bathed her jaw. Something copious gathered in the well of her throat. She wanted to reach out and touch Buck beside her, wrap her hand in his, but nothing would move. She had a sensation of being underwater. She watched George's mouth above her, moving fishlike as if trying to regurgitate a hook. His face wavered, became indistinct, then went away. She saw vague lights floating somewhere, fluttering, becoming dimmer and dimmer. She swam toward what seemed a fading beacon, a tantalizing hope.

I, George

I CLOSE THE LITTLE BOOK and lean back in my chair and feel satisfied that I have done the right thing. I turn the slim volume over and stare at it and tell myself that the title, *The Root of Youth,* is inspired. One of my mother's drawings is reproduced below the title, an inkblot woman rising like an abstract tree, feet unseen in the snowy earth, arms reaching like branches, hands curving like leaves. At the bottom of the page it says: *Love Poems by Buck Root.* They are all the poems that were in the nightstand. I have rewritten them a little, adding some words here and there and deleting others, but essentially the poems are Buck's, the ones he pilfered from other poets and rewrote for Joy.

Months have gone by, wounds have healed, health has returned and I have adjusted, but it hasn't been easy and I have often thought about how my cousin came back into my life, bringing Joy and Livia and a crazy year. He had entered my world with an aura of indestructibility and it was impossible to think of him gone so instantly and forever and that eons would roll and there would never be another exactly like him taking up space. The past kept swelling up to meet me in the form of a boy, Michelangelo Buonarotti Routelli, timid and shy, who, twenty-nine years later, came back as a man who seemed larger than life, but was not so large after all. His ashes flew gray and dusty over the waters of Medicine Lake. Settled on the waves. Sank out of sight just as any ashes would.

After the trauma finally passed, I was a little surprised at how much I missed him, his pure physical presence, his rumbling voice trying to flim-flam everyone, give them something— youth, a Hercules body, Nova Life, his imitation of Hank Williams, his jokes, his way of living in the moment no holds barred. It seems such a man as Buck Root should have been famous and rich in a world like ours, but all summed up I would have to say that nothing much happened except the chase itself and I'm not even sure about that. I mean, was Buck really chasing life so hard, or was he running from it? His past, I mean. Was he chasing or being chased?

It wasn't until August that I took the poems (thirty-three in all) to a vanity publisher and got them printed and bound. Fifty paperback copies sit in piles on the coffee table. I'm not sure what to do with fifty copies. I'll probably give them away to anybody who will take one. Women might want them. I might go to the mall and hand the books out to women passing by, the ones who look careworn and receptive, the ones who look like they need romance in their life. It seems like a good enough plan, and it makes me happy to think about it, handing the poems out and the women going home and reading them, getting sentimental and weepy. Maybe they will dream of lovers writing verses. Maybe they will dream of Buck Root.

Other things have happened over the course of the year. My mother's paintings are hanging in the Minnesota Museum of Art in St. Paul and in galleries from New York to Chicago to San Francisco and L.A. Quite an accomplishment for an obscure old lady who died fifteen years ago. It's a small irony to see how she has the very thing that Buck had wanted: fame as an artist. But she hadn't known she wanted it; she hadn't craved it the way he did. She had stayed home and worked hard and a posthumous recognition had eventually followed. Not that Buck hadn't worked hard, sure he did, but in the end the body won't hold up as a work of art.

~

I GO TO THE WINDOW and look at the stump. I finally replaced the pipe that ran from the building to the street. Rented a backhoe and dug the drain up and put down new pipe. When the pipe and the fittings were done, I sprayed a caustic around them called Rootkill, guaranteed to dissolve encroaching roots for ten years. The spruce is four cords of firewood now, and I hollowed out the stump, filled it with mulch and flowers. There is a scar on the earth where I laid the pipe. The dirt is dark and rounded on top like a grave, but it will sink over time and flatten out and get concave and have to be filled in again and the grass will grow over it. I went through the apartments testing the toilets and they flushed fast, and I felt the pride every man feels when he does a good job.

~

I LOOK AT MY WATCH and see it is time to exercise. I turn from the window and go down to the basement. Ho Tep follows me, moving with his hipsore shuffle, taking the steps cautiously sideways, until he gets to the last one, where he sits with his tongue out and his chest wheezing.

The disks and the long bar squat in the middle of the floor.

I do some jumping jacks and some shadowboxing and some stretching, then pump some light weights, and then when my muscles are warm and ready I put all three hundred pounds of iron on the bar and try to deadlift it. But can't.

"What a guy," I say, grinning at my weakness.

A rectangle of light comes through the basement window, polishing the floor. And then the light fades behind a cloud and

I stare at the darkened panes. Shy thunder rumbles in the distance. The cloud goes away and the sun shoots through and I see Joy's eyes fastened to the weightlifter parading his wares in the yard.

"This is for her," I say.

Taking hold of the bar, I roll the disks away from the furnace, toward the window.

"This is serious," I tell the dog.

The dog pants, *Uh-huh, uh-huh*.

"Use your legs," I command myself. Then I count to three and heave and the bar goes up a few inches, before I let go and the weights crash down.

"Jesus, who could lift so much?" I say, rubbing the small of my back, groaning and stretching. My cousin could, that's who.

~

I GO UPSTAIRS and grab a book of the poems and go outside with it. Ho Tep comes with me and starts searching through the flower bed next to the porch. While I rest on the steps, I promise myself to go to the basement and lift three hundred pounds until I can stand up straight, knees locked. I light my pipe and smell fresh cedar. Smoke vanishes in the rain-scented breeze. Golden-eyed daisies flutter around the dog.

I hear the Lincoln coming. Slow as vodka logic it comes, the champagne and chrome flicking past cars at the curb, before it pulls in behind the Impala. The engine runs a few seconds, valve lifter ticking, before she shuts it off. The car looks like a massive jewel, gleaming, twinkling, the tinted windows darkly lustrous.

She gets out and waves.

"Can't get over it," I say, pointing at the car.

"It's like brand-new, George," she says. "I can't ever thank you enough. Did you tell Joe Cuff how happy I was? Did you thank him for me?" She takes a hanky from her purse and wipes at something on the hood. Buffs the spot.

"We're going over there tonight. You can tell him yourself."

As she comes up the walk in her green pants and pale green sleeveless blouse, I note with satisfaction that her body is no longer bony California. She has changed it for a soft rounded Minnesota look. She is getting a tummy too, a small pooch in her abdomen that looks mature and knowing and sexy. Time and care have worked on her and you would never know that she is a woman who has literally come back twice from the dead. You might not catch the marks of what she did to herself, unless the wind catches her hair just right, blowing it back, exposing the left side of her jaw, the misplaced dimple where the bullet tore through.

Her heels click like dainty hooves as she walks from under the trees, into the patchy sun. Ho Tep leaves the flower bed, stands panting, his tail wagging, glad to see she has made it home. She bends to pet him and, glancing toward the sky, toward the approaching clouds, she says, "Think it'll rain, George?"

"A little more rain would be fine," I say. "We could stand it."

She sits beside me and takes *The Root of Youth* from my hands and looks it over and tells me it is nice and that Buck would have liked it a lot. "He wanted so badly to have a significant soul," she adds wistfully.

I ask her how her day went and she says she sold another painting, number forty-four: *Woman Womb-Ballooned*. "It's going all the way to Germany," she says. "A Hans Bellmer fan came in this morning and bought it just like that"—she clicks her fingers—"as soon as he saw it. I showed him some of the others and he said he would be getting in touch with me. We had a nice talk. A sweet old man with a white goatee and mustache. Very smart too. Very knowledgeable about art. You want to know what he said about Sissy's work? He said it is full of erotic variations influenced by Bellmer. *And* he said they are *not* variations of exploited women grieving, or symbols of feminism, as some critics have said. He insisted that that was nonsense."

"Is that how you see them, 'erotic variations'?" I ask.

Joy shrugs. "Who knows? Maybe it's all of that and more. I like it that there are so many different opinions. It's what makes her so fascinating, I think. All the different takes on what she was doing. No one critic will ever get it all. She was multilayered, George."

"Everybody I know is multilayered," I say.

Ho Tep, god of happiness, is back amid the daisies, a lacy yellow-and-black-winged butterfly fluttering near his nose. I put my arm around Joy and run my cheek over the side of her head, the soft hair, the scent of floral shampoo. "If you hadn't come along, Mom would still be in the closet. I wish she could see what's happened. I wish she knew."

Joy takes my hand, kisses it, says, "She knows, honey, she knows."

Leaning her head on my shoulder, she opens the book, leafs through it. My fingers move over her ribs, relishing her fullness. At her waist I stop and pinch an inch of delicate fat. It makes me think of how well my garden is growing and the bounty it will give.

"Would you read me this one, George?" she says. "I think I like it best of all."

She hands me the book and I read to her:

> *My honey love, by God I swear*
> *Your eyes outshine the fire more clear*
> *No silken girl has thighs like thine*
> *No doe was ever Buck'd so fine.*
> *Your hand is white and red your lip*

Your dainty body I will sip.
Let's down to sleep ourselves then lay
And hug in dark and kiss and play.
Let's cling together like bark to stay,
Though leaves will wither and roots decay,
And all our beauty will fade away.

Acknowledgments

My heartfelt gratitude for the unwavering support I have received from Alicia Brooks, whose tireless reading and editing saved *The Altar of the Body* from many a listless line. For all the pep talks and confidence-building observations she made, I am eternally grateful. My love and thanks to my personal cheerleading trio: Tom Kennedy, Ricki Muller, Barry Brent. A more encouraging, generous and constant friendship I have never known. My thanks to Sally Wofford-Girand, whose instant enthusiasm and faith in *Altar* was exactly what the author needed at exactly the right time. For patience and support above and beyond the call of duty, my thanks to Nancy and Dean Brenna, Sheila Theis, Kevin, Christine, Brendan and Caitlin Neilan. And special blessings to Michele Jones for allowing me to drive her crazy that pine-scented summer in Prescott, when I was writing yet another draft in her comfy basement. I love you all.

Author's Acknowledgment of Sources

Many a Lecherous Lay is from *The Canterbury Tales,* Geoffrey Chaucer's "Retraction," 1399: "Wherefore I beseech you meekly . . . that you forgive me . . . [for] many a song and many a lecherous lay."

Do Not Go Gentle is from Dylan Thomas's poem "Do Not Go Gentle into That Goodnight," *Collected Poems,* 1952.

Fire Monsters in the Milky Brain is from *Collected Poems of Wallace Stevens,* 1954.

"Just a Country Girl," lyrics and music by Janine Sherry and Arella Hanvold, 1999.

"Song of Myself," *Leaves of Grass,* Walt Whitman, 1855.

"Mother's Bad Luck Child," Muddy Waters, 1973.

"Giddy Hair," lyrics and music by V. J. Chouinard, 1990.

"The only way to resist temptation is to give in to it" is from *Lady Windermere's Fan,* Oscar Wilde, 1892.

"Lil of the Golden West" is sung to the melody of "Your Cheatin' Heart," Hank Williams, 1954

"Lil of the Golden West" lyrics by Paula Hokkanen and Stan Brenna.

The sentence, "You are an artist of the beautiful" is from a short story by Nathaniel Hawthorne entitled "The Artist of the Beautiful."

"Tangled Mind," lyrics and music by Fred and Eddie Gulbrenson, 1957.

"Boogie Chillun," "Boom Boom Boom Boom," "I'm in the Mood," from "Boogie Chillun," John Lee Hooker, 1993.

"Silver Dollar Lady," lyrics and music by Doc Lindgren.

"Where there is . . . underwear" is from "Howl" by Alan Ginsberg.

"God may reduce you on Judgment Day" is from the "Elegy to Louis MacNeice," by W. H. Auden, 1945, qtd. in *Auden,* by Richard Davenport-Hines

"Lara's Theme," composed by Maurice Jarre for the David Lean film *Dr. Zhivago,* 1965, was chosen by George and Livia Miles as "our song" and sung so often by Livia that even in her dementia she never forgot the lyrics, *Somewhere, my love . . .*

About the Author

Duff Brenna is the author of three novels: *The Book of Mamie,* which won the prestigious Associated Writing Programs Award; *The Holy Book of the Beard;* and *Too Cool,* a *New York Times* Notable Book. He is the recipient of an NEA grant, *Milwaukee Magazine*'s Fiction Award, and a Pushcart Prize nomination for the first chapter of this novel. *The Altar of the Body* also won the California State University, San Marcos, President's Award for "recognition as a valuable addition to courses in literature." A Minnesota native and onetime Wisconsin dairy farmer, Duff Brenna teaches literature at California State University in San Marcos. He lives in Poway, California.

Lots of hip smacky
foul language

sly silly
Foulmouthed
cautionary
Fairy tale.